As It Lies

Robert Wesley Clement

ISBN
978-1-962868-70-9 (Paperback)
978-1-962868-71-6 (eBook)
978-1-962868-69-3 (Hardcover)

DEDICATION

I feel very fortunate to be part of a family that models hard work, a positive attitude, and displays a terrific sense of humor. Our mother, Capitola, was our guiding light. She saw to it that the fifteen children - eight boys and seven girls 'acted as good as we looked,' on a daily basis.

This book is dedicated to all my brothers and sisters. You have all helped your brother, Bobby, in so many ways over the years. Thank you: Marie, Richard, Russell, Loretta, Laura, George, William, Phyllis, Patricia, Daniel, Nora, David, Kathleen and Zane.

Table of Contents

PART THREE

Acknowledgement

There are many people who have added to this effort. I would like to single out a few.

Thank you Jack O' Shea for igniting a spark and kick starting the fire.

Thank you Tom Keegan, publisher, at Old Kings Road Press in Flagler Beach for believing I have a story worth telling.

Thank you Patty Reid, friend and highly respected English teacher at Carrabec High School; your careful reading and constructive criticism make this a much better book.

A special thank you to my children and their families for believing in me. son Khristian, daughter Shellee, husband Tim and sons Nick and Joe

The beautiful lady I get to wake up with every morning, my wife Carey, you are my best friend. We have many beaches to walk.

viii

Introduction

Dreams not pursued
Remain as half-filled balloons;
They lack shape
They will never soar.

R. Wesley Clement

CHAPTER

One

"Chicken salad sandwich with sweet pickles on the side and a diet coke. No chips please; don't tempt me. Oh, and put that on whole wheat. Thanks."

The same food, the same little eatery, the same seat by the window. Michael was even beginning to recognize other regulars. He looked out the window, sipped on a glass of water and laid out his napkin and silverware. He took in the silent motion of life that appeared just beyond the glass. A sudden thought; (This was how his own life was unfolding-Michael the silent observer. No highs, no lows, no emotion invested. No noise in his world.) Michael was snapped back to the real world when Jack O'Shea appeared on this silent screen, walking right past the cameraman.

(My God! Jack O'Shea! I've got to catch him.)

Michael jumped up just as his chicken salad sandwich arrived, at nose level and he turned directly into it, literally. After all the apologies and clean up, not to mention a bloody nose, Michael made his way out of the diner to the stares and murmurs of his fellow diners. Jack O'Shea was nowhere to be seen. (What would Jack O'Shea be doing in Orlando? The PGA Tour was well North by now.)

Michael kept track of Jack's career through the newspapers, but hadn't seen him for several years. They had played college golf together and roomed together on the road. Jack played at number one while Michael always struggled to make the traveling team.

Jack had spent several years after college on the various mini tours and just two years ago he had qualified for the big time. He'd made the cut often enough to keep his card and last month had finished in tenth place. Michael had tried to reach him after that tournament, but Jack was somewhere on the road.

(Well, might as well check and see what's shaking at work,) thought Michael. He entered a large building with an official looking sign out front. He made his way to his office, which was a cubicle among a dozen others.

"Good morning, Michael," reached his ears from several directions as he found his very own cubby complete with nameplate-Sergeant Michael Grason, Detective. He was early and didn't go on duty until three pm so he spent some time going over several investigations he was involved in. Fellow detectives drifted in and out harassing one another. Michael had a good sense of humor and enjoyed the sick jokes that kept the atmosphere light in what is a very serious line of work.

He had continued to play golf, an outlet that allowed him to get away from a 24/7 profession. Golf meant a lot to Michael and he did his best thinking playing nine holes at seven am, after pulling a double shift.

Right now, he was trying to think why Jack O'Shea would be in Orlando? He tried the one number that he had that was supposed to get through to Jack eventually, but it just made a funny noise.

Michael knew, when he left college, that golf above the recreational level was not in the cards so he had joined the State

Police. Three years of handing out traffic tickets, manning roadblocks, weighing and measuring trucks, and performing truck inspections had left him looking for something different.

The same could be said for his personal life. Michael didn't drink which closed a lot of doors in the social arena. He was fun loving and social, but the women he met all seemed to have an agenda, one that didn't take long to figure out. In fact, it was Michael's innate ability to read people that had gotten him to rethink his law enforcement career and apply for a police officer's position in Orlando. His college education and prior police experience had moved him rapidly into a role Michael was born for, Detective. Lots of the guys bitched about the hours, but Michael truly loved the work and with his personal life nonexistent, he was always either at work or on the golf course thinking about work.

The next twelve hours flew by as man's inhumanity to man claimed center stage. Michael's current caseload included a loan sharking operation that was taking advantage of a group of people who worked for day wages.

Most people, even those who work for minimum wage, have a steady job, and receive some benefits. They get a paycheck at the end of the week, have a basic structure to their life, and can at least plan and hope for something better.

Day workers however, exist to fill a void in industries that have peaks and valleys in their employment needs. Oddly, it's a phenomenon that in the best of circumstances might actually work. Michael didn't get to meet any of those success stories. His clients had a track record that usually involved drugs or alcohol or both. Despair was a constant.

The usual scenario included an early morning van or truck ride to a construction site or agricultural business. A long day's work, a day's wages and a ride back to some obscure drop off point. The challenge for these workers was to make it back to that pick up point day after day.

Loan sharks don't operate in back alleys or try to remain anonymous in the new millennium. Neon signs and bold advertisements, actually seeming to celebrate failure, are used to attract clients. Bankruptcy-that's no problem. Bad credit? Come on in! Need a loan? Five minutes is all it takes- all perfectly legal. (Hell, I can't get a loan in five days,) thought Michael. Instant money for those who are the most ill equipped to pay it back. The typical scenario for a day worker, bringing home his money day after day and beginning to believe it's going to last, would go like this. (I'm clean and sober, got me a woman and kids, even paying the rent. Maybe we can get a little of that American dream after all. Need a TV or stereo or both, let's just borrow a little money, be a lot easier if we had a car, drive right to work.) With their credit history, instant loan is the only game in town. Borrow $1,000.00. Pay back $200.00 a month for 24 months. The whole concept boggles the mind, the rational mind that is. ($Two Hundred divided by 30, that's only $6.60 a day, couple packs of cigarettes. Maybe I'll quit smoking, that will pay off the loan. Works for me. Where do I sign?)

Michael notices the guy is still smoking. He had a fight with his old lady, kids got sick, he started drinking or drugging again. Whatever the reason, he didn't make it back to that obscure pick up point, job ended. A million reasons, one result, loan default. Guys find themselves desperate and the bills got to be paid.

(Can't we work this out?) Working this out takes many forms, none of them part of the American dream. Threats, strong arm tactics and, in some cases, larceny in the night becomes the solution.

This is where Michael enters the picture. The loan shark hires informally of course, the guy to perform illegal acts. He forgives a portion of the loan while getting the value of the misdeed. Stealing jewelry, selling drugs, carjacking, strong arming a fellow defaulter. The guy eventually gets caught and the story unfolds. (What a tangled web we weave,) thought Michael as he rubbed his eyes.

He'd been watching the ABC Loan Office for the past nine hours but nothing was shaking. This guy is smart. Maybe heard on the street one of his clients got busted. Whatever the reason, the owner had been quietly going about his business since five pm. (Even the hours of operation should be illegal,) Michael mused. (I mean come on. Who borrows money at two in the morning if they aren't desperate?)

Michael yawned, stretched and touched his nose, immediately bringing Jack back to mind. Still no returned call. Well, Michael had the next two days off. He'd just work a little harder to find Jack.

Michael actually slept in when he arrived home. The sun had begun to turn its back on the day by the time Michael rose and entered his spare room. Free weights, dumbbells, and a pull up bar helped him to maintain a strong, well built body. He called the room his chamber of torture but actually enjoyed the raised heartbeat and exertion that made him feel alive. The two miles that he jogged three times a week and the eighteen holes of golf that he walked four times in seven days added endurance, kept his mind clear, and his senses sharp.

During Michael's jog, he tried to think of whom else he could call to help him make contact with Jack. Jack's parents were divorced and, as far as Michael knew, were not even in the picture. Jack hated them both, had since grammar school, or so he'd told Michael. Michael mentally created a list of possibilities. Best chance seemed to be Ron, a fellow golf team member who was working as a club pro further upstate.

After fifty push-ups and a long hot shower, Michael put on a bathing suit. He made himself a BLT sandwich and an ice tea and walked out onto his small balcony. Balancing a portable phone, the sandwich, and the tea, he managed to open the screen door with his knee and make it to his favorite spot. He looked out over the neighborhood and could hear the sounds of lawn mowers, each telling a different story as they tidied up a patch of green. Between bites, Michael dialed The River Course and after three rings a male voice answered. Ron was out giving a lesson, but Michael was assured he'd get the message, the voice agreed he'd convey how important it was that Ron call back.

"He should be done in thirty-five to forty minutes," the voice said.

Michael hung up, finished his sandwich and decided that this might be a good time to vacuum and straighten up the place a little. Michael was not a slob, but things can get a little messy when you live alone.

The voice had done his job apparently, for just forty minutes later Michael heard his phone, above the sucking sound of the Oreck. As the vacuum shut down, Michael was thinking about bowling balls all over the world being sucked up at this very moment. He chuckled to himself as he picked up the phone. "Hello there Ron, nice to hear your voice, how's the golfing business?"

"Michael, I'll tell you, I've got a position here that is above par," quipped Ron. "In fact, it's a lot closer to a birdie most days. It's good to hear from you too, buddy."

"That's wonderful Ron, and how does the family like coastal Florida?"

"Well, my son would like to live at Disney World. He can't understand why I don't work for a course near Mickey Mouse, where he could run up and down Main Street USA everyday."

"What is he now eight years old?"

"Actually, Nick is nine and a half but who's counting. Beth loves it up here though and is trying to convince me to have one more child. She's been hired as the social director for the entire private community and organizes everything from dance classes to volleyball and tennis. She also does the hiring for the restaurant. So I would say we have settled in. What's up Michael? Are you calling for a free lesson?"

"Ha, ha, that was cold Ron but I am struggling with the driver. Any suggestions?"

"Yuh, lighten your grip. You always tried to murder your driver by choking it to death. If you choked anything else that hard, you'd be arrested for it." They both laughed.

"By the way, how do you like being a detective? You had just been promoted the last time we talked."

"You know Ron, I've watched you give lessons, and even back in college when you practiced, it was obvious you love what you do. That's how I feel about being a detective. I relate it to my own golf experiences. When I had success at golf I was patient, reading the conditions and trusting my instincts. I didn't try to birdie every hole. I just put myself in position so at the end of the day I was happy with the effort. I find I do a better job of repeating that formula as a detective than I did as a golfer." "Sounds right. I'm pleased for you Michael. You need to get up here and play the course. It's beautiful. I will take a look at your swing for you. I miss all the guys; we had a lot of fun," said Ron.

"Me too," said Michael. "Actually that was one of the reasons I called. I need to contact Jack and can't seem to reach him." "I saw him earlier in the spring when the tour was in Florida. We had a couple of beers early in the week and Jack went on to make about forty thousand dollars for his efforts."

"Yeah, I follow his results in the paper and I'm proud of him," said Michael. "That top ten finish should keep his card for him for at least another year. Anyway I was trying to contact him. Did you hear he might be down this way?"

"No, the tour has moved North for the warmer months so I suspect he's in the Carolinas about now."

"That's funny, I swear I saw him on International Drive in Orlando last week and he gave me a bloody nose."

"What?"

"It's a long story, but I did see him, I just couldn't catch up to him."

"OK, you can tell me about the nose when I see you but I'm lost about why he'd be in Orlando."

"So how can I contact him Ron? Any ideas?"

"Actually I do. He's rooming with a guy I met a while back who's now on the tour. His name's Tim Fischetto. He's a little younger than Jack and I think Jack took him under his wing. We've kept in contact, got his cell number right here."

"Thanks. I appreciate it."

"By the way what was the other reason you called?" "What? Oh, oh, I was calling about maybe when you have time, a free lesson," laughed Michael.

"Any time. And if you come across any free tickets to Main Street USA let me know. My son would love that. Let me know what's shaking with Jack, say hello to him for me. Tell him to call me."

"I certainly will and I promise to get up there real soon. I should have some vacation time coming. Michael hung up and immediately grabbed his clubs. He planned to gently squeeze his driver and do some thinking before he called the cell number.

Hot, sweaty and tired of thinking, Michael got back to his apartment around seven-thirty pm. The driver however did seem to respond to a gentler touch. He'd have to thank Ron when he talked to him again. (Yeah, we do need to get together. Ron's a good guy,) Michael thought. He cleaned his clubs and put them back in the trunk. After 50 more push-ups and a long cooling shower, Michael decided to call the number. Quit thinking about it, just do it. Michael dialed and on the third ring, a lady's voice answered.

"Hello, is Tim Fischetto there?"

"I don't know. Who's calling?" The lady asked.

"My name is Michael Grason. Tim doesn't know me, but a mutual friend Ron Allen, told me to call."

"And what is this about, this call?"

"Excuse me, I don't mean to be rude, but this is a private matter. Is Tim there?"

"He's in the shower. We're getting ready to go out for the evening. Besides, Tim is my boyfriend and I screen all of his calls these days."

(Oh great, well let me try a different tack.) "Uh, do you know Jack O'Shea?"

"Yes I do. Actually, he introduced me to Tim."

"Do you know where I can find him or how I can reach him?"

"He was living here but when I moved in, he left. I haven't seen him since."

(Smart man,) thought Michael. "I really need to speak to Tim if I can. It concerns locating Jack."

"Well, all right, but make it quick. We've got a date."

(Poor Tim, he's going to need a lot of showers to wash this girl out of his hair.) After what seemed minutes, Tim came on the line.

"Hello, this is Tim."

"Hi, Tim, I'm a friend of Ron Allen the pro at The River Course. He thought you might be able to help me out." "Go ahead," said Tim.

"I'm an old friend and teammate of Jack O'Shea's and I'm trying to track him down. Any idea how I can reach him?" "Funny you should call and ask. I'm trying to reach him myself. He didn't show up for the tournament last week. I haven't seen him since he moved out when Ellen moved in."

Michael decided not to pursue that comment. "Did he seem upset?"

"Only for me, he thought I was getting into a situation that would end in a double bogey. He said he'd be surprised if she survived the cut."

Tim couldn't see Michael nodding his head in agreement with Jack's witty assessment.

"Is Jack in some kind of trouble, you think?" asked Tim. "Nah, Jack can take care of himself but if you hear from him or see him, please have him call me, ok?"

"Sure thing Michael and if you hear from him before I do, have him call me."

"I will do that," said Michael, wondering if Jack would get to speak to Tim if he did call.

(That answers one question, thought Michael after hanging up. Jack wasn't at the tournament so he could have indeed seen Jack in Orlando. I'm not completely crazy!)

∾

It was Saturday night. Tim at least had plans. Michael, on the other hand, sat listening to a Billy Joel song that attempted to create a family out of lonely bar patrons. As he sang along he wondered if being with someone like Ellen was better than being alone. Looking out the window Michael saw his Volvo S40 shining in the amber light, appearing as lonely as he was feeling. (We might just as well be lonely together. I believe we'll just cruise the strip and check out the sights and sounds of a Saturday night in Orlando,) he said to himself.

After changing into a pair of chino shorts and a tank top, Michael grabbed his keys, started whistling "Piano Man," and took the stairs one at a time. Moving his body seemed to lighten his mood and by the time the red tail lights multiplied tenfold in traffic, Michael was actually looking forward to whatever.

He hadn't eaten since early this afternoon. His stomach growled and it was time to try out a new recipe. He liked all kinds of food and dabbled at being a cook; his specialty was anything grilled. Most of his ideas came from re-creating, and slightly changing, menu items he tried at the different chain restaurants. (Tonight I think I'll see what's new and exciting at Applebee's; I'll be eating good in the hood,) he chuckled to himself.

Michael parked his Volvo and looked back as he locked the vehicle with his key fob. His baby winked back at him that everything was cool.

The hostess told him it would be a twenty minute wait to eat so Michael slipped the vibrator in his pocket and sat down at the bar. He ordered a ginger ale. The sports channel was on and he quickly noted that when the complete listing of tournament participants for the week's PGA venue was announced, Jack O'Shea's name did not appear.

Michael sat swirling his drink straw in the ice thinking back to how he and Jack had come to live together as golf team members.

That first team practice found the coach pairing the strongest players with the not so proven talent, creating a nine hole match. The losing teams would be cooking the spaghetti and serving the winners. It was all in good fun but still it brought out the competitive juices and that was in part the coach's intent.

Jack drew Michael as his partner and immediately set up a game plan. The rules dictated that the players alternate shots and through this format begin to support each other as teammates in a sport that is usually played as an individual. That was also the coach's intent. Before practice began the coach talked about the Ryder Cup and how the best players from the United States, guys who competed with one another week after week, had to come together to represent America against Europe, every other year. The coach and captain of a Ryder Cup team employed all kinds of strategies to promote camaraderie during the matches. Michael remembered one line specifically that his coach used to bring their team together. He said, "When your college career is over and your lives move in different directions, the importance of having someone there when you need to make a clutch putt or a decision or are in any other tight spot, will take on even greater meaning. My goal is to create a team of young men who will be there for one another from this day forward."

(I wonder if Jack's in a tight spot? I wonder if he'll call me if he needs help?)

The vibrator went off, signaling that his table was ready. Michael came back to the present and was escorted to his table. He looked around for the first time. People were laughing and chatting and the tables were filled with two or more people. He noted most of the singles were eating and drinking at the bar. (Why is that?) thought Michael as he subtly surveyed the crowd. (Do people feel more approachable if they sit at the bar together, alone? Do you stand out in a crowd, as a party of one at a table? What is it about the number one? Why is the number considered an odd number?) Michael continued to play number games in his head.

The waitress finally got his attention. "Nodding off a wee bit are we sir? A little early for that on a Saturday night isn't it?"

Michael's first response was to the lilting Irish tenor of her voice. He couldn't help but smile and when Michael smiled he lit up the room, well a table at least. When the waitress smiled back, Michael's light was a mere spark in comparison.

"I was engaged in solitary thinking, Miss. My job is to enter Applebee's throughout the nation and by appearing preoccupied, bring out the true personality of Applebee's soldiers.

"Do I still have a job then or should I turn in my uniform immediately?"

"You, soldier, have passed muster and can expect a promotion or at least more sour cream with your next potato. Should you choose, in fact, to order a potato in the foreseeable future."

The beautiful young woman standing slightly above him laughed out loud. Meg, her name plate stated, gave him a menu and listed the daily specials. Michael asked for a refill of his ginger ale. As Meg left his table to place the drink order Michael could still hear her Irish accent soothing his mind. Michael ordered his meal piecemeal, (the better to see you my dear.) He asked Meg to repeat each of the choices, (the better to hear you my dear.) By the time he'd finished a dessert he didn't normally order, he had made a decision. When Meg brought his check and told him it had been her pleasure to serve him this evening, Michael suddenly asked Meg if she would join him for a meal in the near future. Perhaps, she might help him evaluate another foot soldier. (The better to eat with you and get to know you my dear.)

Meg laughed. She seemed surprised but pleased. "Do you always ask your waitress for a date? That's a novel approach sir. Have you added in my tip already, or are you waiting for an answer?"

It was Michael's turn to laugh out loud.

As he slipped behind the wheel for a ride down the strip, Michael couldn't believe he'd actually made a date so spontaneously. There was something about Meg that had set him so at ease that it had seemed the natural thing to do.

He selected a CD for the ride. Soon Neil Diamond was singing and Michael pushed the selector to a song that fit the occasion. "Sweet Caroline," began and Michael found himself singing along substituting the words-Sweet Meg of mine. Traffic was heavy this time of evening but his baby seemed to be moving in a lane of its own.

It was still early but Michael didn't feel like cruising. (Maybe I'll call in and check out the ABC location for a little while.)

The lieutenant said it was a very busy Saturday night. He thanked Michael for caring enough to put in some extra time. He'd clock in three hours for Michael and talk to him Tuesday morning.

Michael swung through the Dunkin Donut drive-through and was soon sipping a hazelnut decaf as he watched a lighted entrance from the shadows. Parked in a line of cars, playing music softly, Michael let his mind wander.

He was watching the store and thinking about Jack, but Meg's voice and smile kept drowning everything else out and clouding his vision.

He very nearly missed the sudden movement inside the loan store. Michael had to shake his head several times to focus on what was going down. Did he see a man's hands go quickly into the air and suddenly go back to his side? Michael couldn't see anyone but the owner, but something didn't seem right. Could Michael have missed someone entering while he was daydreaming, or in this case night dreaming? Sudden stress adrenaline rushes always made Michael a little giddy and his sense of humor took over even when there was nothing funny going on. Michael could see fear in the face of the owner but still hadn't seen anyone else appear. He called in his concern and asked for backup. Michael was not a cowboy and his ego didn't get in the way of using extreme caution when time allowed.

The two units arrived without lights or sirens. Michael appreciated the approach his lieutenant used regarding sights and sounds. He quickly moved to fill them in and develop a game plan.

The decision was made that Michael, who was in street clothes, would enter the building as a customer. Two uniforms would cover the rear while another would be ready to rush the front at a signal from Michael.

Michael entered the building whistling and humming a tune, feigning slight inebriation he moved to the counter.

The owner, shaky and ghost-white, muttered a greeting and asked how he could assist Michael. Michael said he was a little short and needed to pay his rent by Monday or be evicted. He said he worked a day wages job but wouldn't have any problem with a hundred a week payback for the next ten weeks. As he was filling out the paperwork, Michael took in the scene and surmised that below the counter lurked a dangerous individual. Though Michael didn't much care for the business the owner was involved in he figured he probably didn't deserve to die. He tried to make eye contact so he could flip out his badge from his wallet as he showed identification for the loan. The moment the owner connected the dots Michael signaled for backup with a wave. In that same instant he hauled the owner over the counter in one quick burst of movement.

Suddenly, shots rang out from beneath the counter and Michael dove for cover, smothering the owner as he readied his own weapon. A policeman burst through the door just as the shooter ran toward the back. Shouting filled the back room.

When Michael got there, a small Asian man was on the ground being cuffed.

When the smoke cleared no one had been hit. The owner was vomiting in a corner. Michael told the officers to take the shooter to headquarters and ask for his lieutenant.

"Let the lieutenant know I want to be part of the interrogation. I'll be there within the hour. Oh, yeah, and tell him to put a few extra hours on the clock. Looks like I'll be around for the night." Michael left the owner to be interviewed by other detectives. He couldn't stomach spending any more time with him. He had watched this guy operate for the past month. He suspected that the young man being led away in handcuffs was as much a victim as the loan shark. (Who knows, maybe he was stealing to pay back a loan himself.) Michael just shook his head.

The interrogation revealed, (surprise, surprise) another hopeless helpless individual addicted to drugs and their effects, both physical and emotional.

(Well,) thought Michael, (nobody died and maybe this twenty three year old can get rehab in prison. He'd certainly have the time if not the opportunity.)

When Michael arrived home at about three am, the first light he noticed was the red blinking one on his phone. He turned on the overhead light and pushed the message button. Meg's voice brought a smile to Michael's lips. Her Irish voice, filled with mischief and wit, told Michael that indeed a Sunday brunch would fit into her busy schedule. She gave an address and finished with an admonition not to be taking her to a place that has fruit as part of its name. Michael laughed out loud.

Another voice, this one a feigned Irish brogue, spoke as if they had conversed only recently. "Hello Michael me boy, heard you were looking for me. Seems everyone wants to reach me after my recent success. I called Tim to check on his mental health. He's in the clutches of a woman on a mission I fear. Anyway I am in fact in Orlando. Call me tomorrow night at nine pm. The number is 813-362-1212. By the way, I'm glad you called. A click signaled the end of the message.

Michael played both messages again. One promised to be memorable, the other was just as mysterious as seeing Jack in the first place. Sleep didn't come easy as Michael tossed and turned. His mind was on overload. Mysteries, Meg, and muggings were all competing with Michael's need for rest.

Up at eight am, Michael decided to forgo any overt physical exercise. He would simply walk 9 holes to clear his mind. As he teed off number one, a 435-yard par 4, dominated by sand bunkers along the right side, Michael was reminded of that first nine hole match he and Jack had teamed up for.

They had parred the first four holes; Jack bailing them out with a chip or putt or sand save. They were using a match play format, winning, losing or tying each hole. The winning team, the one that won the most holes. When they reached the eighth hole,the match was dead even. Michael sliced his drive on the eighth into a sand bunker on the right about 200 yards out leaving 215 yards to the pin. Their opponents were straight down the middle with 160 yards left to the flagstick.

Jack had a five wood in his hand as he walked into the bunker. Michael apologized when he saw the fix he'd put Jack in. There was an eight foot embankment about fifteen feet in front of the ball. When Jack selected a five wood and walked into the bunker Michael questioned him about being able to hit a wood up over that lip. Maybe he should hit a five iron, get it within 60 yards, and hope they could get it up and down in two. Jack, who celebrated his Irish heritage whenever he could by talking as if he'd just got off the boat, looked at Michael and said, among other things: "It's little harm I'll be doing to that wee bit o' grass there. Tis this white object I'll be striking as if it were about to bite me in the arse." With that, he squared his shoulders, voiced a philosophical statement and took one last look at his destination. He executed a flawless swing that indeed moved that white object to the fringe of the green 200 yards away. Jack didn't celebrate, he merely asked for a rake and, whistling <u>Danny Boy</u>, tidied things up a bit. Then the two moved toward the green.

Michael became a believer in Jack O'Shea that day in the bunker and his belief never faltered. Jack had all the golf skills necessary to become a tour player. They went on to a spaghetti supper that they neither had to prepare nor serve, their friendship solidified in pasta.

ఞ౼౩

Michael walked nine holes and hit every shot but he couldn't tell you how he played. The sudden noises and movement in his life, Meg and Jack dominated his thoughts, made him a little dizzy even. The irony of Jack and Meg both being Irish wasn't lost on him either.

When he got back to his apartment he did his push-ups and shaved and showered. His heart beat with anticipation as he called the number written on an Applebee's napkin.

Meg answered on the first ring with a spontaneous, "And tis a pleasure to hear from you on a morning such as this, Michael." "How did you know it was me?" asked Michael.

"Who else would it be but an Applebee's inspector, checking on how we soldiers survive when we're not on duty."

Michael laughed and could visualize those dancing eyes on the other end of the line.

"Truth be told, no one but me mum has my number, and any conversations we have on the phone mostly start with a ringing on the other end."

Michael decided he'd leave that statement alone, maybe for another time.

"Well, it is me Meg and I thought maybe I'd ask if you've ever been to Disney World."

"No, I haven't Michael and would you care to ask me if I'd like to go?"

"That would have been my next line, yes," laughed Michael. "You'd use a mouse, a duck and magic to sweep a girl off her feet now would you, Michael?"

Michael belly-laughed; suddenly, they were both laughing into each other's ears. The plans firmed up and Michael's heart continued an upbeat tempo long after hanging up.

The sun promised it would provide Michael with a warm afternoon. Spring in Orlando can be sticky but a breeze was acting in concert with the sun to begin Michael's date in near perfect weather. Meg was sitting on the outside steps reading a novel when he drove up. Dressed in khaki shorts and a light green top, Meg rose and stretched. Michael noticed how athletic and fit she looked. He smiled, (seems like more than the weather is near perfect.) When they were in traffic, Michael asked Meg to tell him how she managed to be working in an Applebee's in America. Meg spoke to Michael like she had known him all her life. She was twenty-six years old and had been in the states for just over a year. She'd been a private secretary in Ireland. Meg had played soccer at the high school level and had first seen the U.S. as part of a touring team when she was nineteen. One of the American girls she'd met had continued to correspond with her, and eventually Meg decided to come to America herself. This much, Michael learned of Meg during the twenty-minute ride to Disney.

Michael got a large ticket discount when he showed his badge. Management was always glad to have a little more security around, post 911. Like two teenagers, they walked hand in hand along Main Street USA. They watched the excitement at the castle and toured Mickey and Minnie's house. "I'd kill for a house like Mickey's," said Meg.

"Then I'd have to arrest you," laughed Michael, "and live here by myself - me and Minnie."

"Did you know Mickey was Irish?" asked Meg suddenly. "Can't say I've heard that one," said Michael watching her eyes sparkle, "but I've got a feeling I'm going to."

As they sat on a bench oblivious to the crowd streaming by, Meg began a story of her people. "Seems that when the potato famine struck the Emerald Isle, a couple of hundred years ago, the land lay fallow and people's pantries became increasingly empty.

You've no doubt read of how the poor people left the country by the thousands, seeking passage in all manner of vessels. Me Great Nana told me of her people and what a terrible time they had raising passage money. Many were bonded for years to a party in the states who paid their fare, securing a servant for next to nothing. Nana's great great uncle Malachy was just a bit of a boy when he entered the ship's belly for a trip to the USA. Resourceful Malachy was, for he not only survived the adventure as he called it but actually thrived. He roamed the lower levels of the ship at will, making friends with all he met. Anyway, one day crawling around, he spotted the cutest little mouse busily chewing on something obviously edible. Malachy watched and watched. Finally, the mouse scurried through a hole. Malachy put his eye to that hole and he saw light there. He looked through and lo and behold it was the ship's pantry. It wasn't long before Malachy and the mouse were both eating well and Malachy was feeding his relatives as well. On the last day aboard he trapped the little mouse and took him ashore. Little Mick is what he named him. The story of that little mouse and how he helped keep our family fed on that ship has been part of our family lore for many years." Meg grinned.

"When Mickey Mouse got discovered and became famous, it was no surprise to the Casey clan. The word is sure to get out, but even if it doesn't, the Irish believe Mickey started his journey to success in Ireland."

Michael, who had listened to the story as a child being read to, was left with the image of Mickey Mouse leading a St. Paddy's Day parade and he chuckled to himself.

The day continued to be blue skies and Michael, who had been to Disney World half a dozen times with friends, experienced the real magic of the kingdom for the first time. They didn't go on a single adult ride, contenting themselves with cups and saucers, merry-go-rounds, and re-creations of the stories and characters from early childhood.

It was eight pm and darkness was falling when Michael realized his own fairy tale had to end. Jack had told him to call at nine pm and he needed to do that. He wasn't sure what was going on but he needed to make this call. Something wasn't right about the whole scene. The detective in Michael needed to solve this mystery.

When Michael left Meg at her door, the embrace and kiss were as natural and magical as the day had been. Seeing each other again was not an option but a given. Michael said he'd stop in for a salad for lunch tomorrow and let Meg know his schedule for the week.

Meg seemed as comfortable with the pace as Michael. She ended the evening with the request to hear Michael's life story next time and if there were any mice or other creatures in his family history she especially wanted to hear about them.

❧

Michael didn't need his radio on for the drive to his apartment; there was music in the air. When he arrived and parked what might just be relegated to the second love of his life, he looked back as the headlights winked that everything was still cool. Again, a flashing light greeted Michael as he entered his apartment. He snapped on a lamp and moved toward the phone. "You have one new message, message one," the automated voice announced. It was Ron telling Michael he'd heard from Jack and Jack wanted Ron to call him back tonight at ten pm.

"I'll call you after I talk to him." Ron said, "By the way, he left a cell number."

Even before the message ended, Michael was picking up the number he had and comparing it, (Yup, same number. What is going on?) thought Michael. (Was Jack planning a golf team reunion or what?) It was nine-eighteen pm. Michael grabbed his portable phone and walking to the balcony, dialed the number. After several rings Jack answered in his Irish brogue, "And its nights like this, waiting for the phone to ring, that tests a man's patience. You're nineteen minutes late, lad."

(Well, Jack still had his sense of humor,) thought Michael. (Jack who was late for every practice or social engagement Michael could remember.) "Sorry Jack, I must have been out of my mind keeping you waiting like that. Anyway, top of the evening to yuh! Oh, and by the way, where in hell are you and why in hell are you there?"

Jack chuckled, "Good to hear your voice, Michael. I can sense an edge of concern in your blasphemy."

"Ok," chuckled Michael, "so where are you and can you share with me what's going on?"

"Would it surprise you to learn I'm in a fix, Michael? A real jam it is I'm afraid."

"How can I help?" asked Michael, endless possibilities swirling through his mind.

"I don't know if you can but I'm hoping you can help me muddle through some possible solutions at least."

"Are you in physical danger? Is someone after you for something?"

"I can't talk about it over the phone. I need to see you in person, somewhere soon."

"Ok." said Michael, "Where and when?"

"I've called Ron too. He's supposed to call me later tonight. Tim, the guy you called but haven't met yet is a great young fellow. I'd like to meet with all of you. If Ron agrees, I'll meet

you at the River Course for a round of golf on Wednesday morning at seven am, before the course opens for the day. We'll get out,enjoy some golf and I'll tell you what's going on. Then we'll establish a game plan just like the old days I hope. I'll have Ron call you with the details if he agrees. See you soon." The phone clicked and Michael was left feeling even more confused than before.

That night Michael's mind alternated between extremes. The pure joy he was feeling about Meg and the possibilities of a relationship that might eventually go somewhere. It had been a very long time since Michael had felt like this; in fact, he didn't think he'd ever felt quite like this. When he thought of Meg, it was like he felt after a great workout, a lightness of body and spirit that running usually gave him. The other extreme was the confusion and fear, yes fear, that someone he'd been close to and still cared deeply about was in trouble, danger even. (Why couldn't Jack tell him about his situation on the phone? How is Ron involved? The young guy Tim, where does he fit? On top of all this, Michael's work wasn't usually something he could just leave for a few days without notice. He'd have to convince the lieutenant of the urgency for some time off. Wednesday, what was the logic of waiting three days to meet? What the hell was going on?) Michael's mind fairly screamed at the mental pushups it was being asked to perform. When he awoke, his sheets looked like they had attended a toga party.

After Jack hung up, he felt better. For three weeks he'd been wrestling with how to deal with this situation and even though he didn't have a plan yet, just talking to Michael and Ron had helped. Those road trips, back when they were part of the golf team, seemed like the best time of his life. Jack couldn't wait to play a round of golf with Michael and Ron and let Tim hear some of the exaggerated stories of how they spent their little bit of free time. It would be good to laugh again. (I could write a book about those days, and the last fifteen years for that matter,) thought Jack.

In fact, Jack had kept a meticulous log. It had started out as a way to learn from past mistakes. It documented everything and anything to do with golf.

At age thirteen, Jack lost a junior tournament because he didn't prepare for bad weather. The last nine holes were played in a downpour. Jack had no extra golf gloves, no umbrella, not even a dry towel. He vowed he'd never enter a tournament unprepared again. From that day on, when Jack got up in the morning he'd record temperature, weather patterns, what he had for breakfast and lunch. That information was minute compared to the writing that documented his golf efforts. Date, time of day, how many holes played, course conditions and who he played with in practice were all recorded every day. Then the log got serious-ball flight, distance, club selection and result, how many putts, driving range time, any new ideas about his swing and those results. Jack recorded every match he'd ever played, the result, how he felt after winning or losing, what he did well and what he needed to work on.

What started out as a way for Jack to keep organized for golf, evolved into his own personal confidant. Jack took his log with him virtually everywhere he went. He even named it Dannyboy. His schoolmates, and even his teammates ribbed him about it, mostly good-naturedly.

One incident however, ended any ribbing that wasn't good-natured. The classic school bully teased everyone and Jack let a lot slide because he didn't feel singled out. One day however, it got personal when the bully knocked Jack's journal onto the floor. Jack picked it up and set it back on his desk, letting things slide. This happened several times during the class. His classmates watched Jack continue to pick up the journal, give it a light pat, and using his feigned Irish brogue whisper to his journal, "It'll all soon be over; now won't it Dannyboy."

Perhaps, Jack meant the class would soon be over and the bully would be on his way. Or maybe Jack meant something else entirely. What was meant became irrelevant shortly after class ended, when the bully knocked Dannyboy out of Jack's hands. Who knows, things still might have ended there, if the bully hadn't chosen to pick up the journal and begin to leaf through it. Laughing loudly, he began to recite weather and temperature. Just as he finished the words cool and cloudy, a storm moved in, packing a powerful punch. It was a brief storm, yet it managed to land the bully in a prone position, bloody his nose, and turn daylight into darkness, complete with stars.

Jack carried a lot of anger, usually, quiet anger. He wrote to his journal Dannyboy to vent the frustration of his parent's divorce when he was nine. His father left, taking his younger brother Sean to live in another state. Jack became the man in a house that was no longer a home. Jack had been devastated; his whole world was turned upside down. He became the invisible boy, a watcher, faithfully recording the unfairness of life.

Jack lived with his mother, a bitter vindictive woman, who had fought without gloves using Jack and his younger brother, Sean, as pawns in a bloody court battle.

Sean was only six when the breakup occurred so it was left to Jack to try to explain to his little brother what was going on. Jack would hear Sean crying in the night in the bed next to him. Jack would join him, hold him, and tell him Irish fairy tales, making many of them up as he went. It was during this time that Jack took on an exaggerated Irish accent. This voice and his later journal writings would play a large role in defining Jack the golfer and Jack the Man.

His father had meant everything to Jack. Mr. O'Shea was a large man, whose gentle way with his children started early in the morning. He would include the boys by adding an Irish story to whatever was in the newspaper that day.

Jack, laying there in the night, silently cried to himself after Sean was fast asleep. He had to smile between tears though, as he remembered sitting at the kitchen table looking at the back of his father's newspaper; waiting for his father to peek around the edge and to begin a story. Some days, he'd hear an obituary of a famous Irish person, one Jack would do well to emulate. Other stories would be about an Irish policeman or fireman coming to the rescue of a child. Jack would silently eat his breakfast listening to the story, always read in an Irish brogue expecting to be quizzed as he always was. It was a magical time for Jack.

Mrs. O'Shea always seemed to be busy in some other part of the house during these stories. If by chance she found herself in the kitchen, she would always order Mr. O'Shea, the only name she had for him, not to fill the boys' heads with such nonsense and urge Jack to finish his breakfast.

Jack's father would wink across the table and go back to his newspaper for a bit. He never contradicted his wife, but when she was out of the room, he would give a deep sigh and in his best Irish voice say, "Jack, the good Lord gave us these gentle creatures to protect, you know. Left to their own devices, I fear laughter and a sense of humor would join Dinosaurs and the Studebaker in a museum. So Jack, always leave 'em laughing. Tis a medicine that might not cure all the world's ills, but it's better than the alternative we're faced with daily." He did not elaborate; there was no need.

CHAPTER
Four

Mr. O'Shea had served with the Army Corps of Engineers in Vietnam. His job was building landing strips and barracks for the enlisted men. He felt like he'd served his country well. While he was not part of any hostilities, he believed the leaders of his country and felt the war was a righteous cause. When he came home facing indifference, both from his wife and his country, he stopped watching the news on television and avoided offering an opinion on the subject.

Mr. O'Shea was a big strong man weighing well over 220 pounds. He loved to dance and sing and tell Irish stories; many were invented on the spot. He was a social drinker. His own father had helped keep Guinness Ale in the green for the relatively short time he spent on earth.

Mr. O'Shea had never seen the Emerald Isle. His grandfather had though, and Mr. O'Shea loved hearing of this fabled land where leprechauns, fairies, and the good people of Ireland avoided the nonsense of the rest of the world. Never knowing his own father, he lived with his Grandfather and Grandmother for the first seventeen years of his life.

An avid reader, but not really interested in school, Mr. O'Shea joined the army on his eighteenth birthday intent on seeing the world. Clever with his hands, his wit, and his sheer size, he stood out at work. He was sent to a fort in Kentucky after basic training in New Jersey.

One evening, Mr. O'Shea was entertaining his buddies with a story of how his grandfather had arrived in America (hidden on a freighter). He stood to demonstrate the swan dive executed by his grandfather upon being discovered as the ship was being unloaded. Standing on a chair with his hands out in front of him, his buddies laughing and cheering him on, Mr. O'Shea left the chair and landed in a Kentucky coal mine, (so to speak). The exact second he took flight, a Robin flew by. Robin Walters was her name and she was there with a friend who was dating a fellow soldier.

Mr. O'Shea, after untangling himself, feigned the Irish brogue he'd learned through listening to all those stories at his grandfather's knee. "Well 'tis with an angel I've landed. My own grandfather landed in a muddy bit of water and had to swim for his life; while I believe, I've just found the love of mine."

Robin Walters didn't know whether she was hurt, mad, or what this huge man was saying, so she just sat there. Two strong hands lifted her to her feet and before she could protest Mr. O' Shea had placed her gently in the middle of the dance floor. Mr. O'Shea, a strong believer in fate and being an Irishman who was a true romantic, waltzed his way into a quick relationship and even quicker marriage.

When Mr. O'Shea shipped out to Vietnam, his Wee bird - as he called Robin, had an egg in the nest. The marriage was a mismatch from the beginning with Wee bird pecking away at a man who believed in fairy tales.

When he returned to a wife he hardly knew, he quickly learned not to argue. A strong Catholic background had been part of his upbringing and while he did not attend church as a man, he remembered well the many ways he might enter hell.

Mr. O'Shea went to work for a small construction company in Massachusetts when he was discharged from the army. He'd learned a lot about moving earth and how best to utilize equipment to meet deadlines. Within a year he was promoted to foreman, liked, and respected by his crew.

Wee bird, on the other hand, hated the North. Her strong southern accent turned heads in the grocery store where she protested the way people pushed and pulled to get to a box of Tide or to be next in line at the checkout. Wee bird, had landed in a world that kept her feathers ruffled most of the time.

Mr. O'Shea was beginning to make good money and wanted to begin going dancing again. The boys were growing. Jack, the oldest, seemed enthralled with the stories Mr. O'Shea made up while reading the newspaper.

The morning was the only time he had with the boys and he tried to instill in them, through his stories, their heritage. They were too young to understand about heritage, but Mr. O'Shea told stories that made Jack laugh and think. Mr. O'Shea had read a good deal of Irish history mostly through fiction writers who could make the history come alive. The Irish history that Mr. O'Shea enjoyed the most was written by Leon Uris. Between what he read and the stories his grandfather had shared, Mr. O'Shea felt he had a good grasp of his ancestral home. Whether a newspaper article or a fairy tale at some point during a story Jack would be quizzed. Sean, who was too young to stay interested, would wander off to watch cartoons.

Mr. O'Shea, always looking for ways to keep the Irish on the front page, told Jack about the real birthplace of golf. He bought Jack a set of plastic golf clubs and balls. On the rare occasion Mr. O'Shea got home early Jack would show his father his ability to hit a ball in the backyard. Mr. O'Shea loved his sons and vowed to be part of their lives unlike his own Dad.

Robin continued to peck away at Mr. O'Shea. He was never home. He spent too much time with the boys when he was home. She wanted a job! She had too much to do! When were they going to get their own house? She wanted to go home to Kentucky! She didn't like Jack's friends, didn't like the music, the weather, the heat, the cold! Mr. O'Shea refused to argue. He'd nod his head; yes, Wee bird; no, Wee bird.

The boys were growing. Mr. O'Shea kept them happy and that kept him happy. Sean inherited Jack's plastic clubs which had been replaced time after time, as Jack loved to practice. Mr. O'Shea, not a golfer himself, had his first opportunity to be part of a golf course when the construction company he worked for was hired as a subcontractor. A new course was to be built on the outskirts of Worcester, Massachusetts. Mr. O'Shea moved a lot of earth and directed a crew of men following an architect's plan to create a beautiful links course whose design replicated the open rolling nature of courses in Ireland and Scotland. Mr. O'Shea, who loved history, read all he could about the design and origin of these courses.

He told the boys, "Golf, it seems, was not an original Irish idea. After all, weren't the Irish too busy digging in the dirt, scraping together a meager existence, or burying a loved one? Striking a round object and putting anything else in a hole was left to the Scots. Ireland had their course though, built when the cursed James took the throne of England. The Irish applauded the effort as a good use of the English and Scott's time. Anytime they were striking a ball was a time when the Irish were not being bothered" he chuckled.

"The O'Shea's, according to folklore, have fairy blood running through their veins, and in difficult times can conjure up a bit of magic."

This childlike approach to problem solving held the O'Shea marriage together and the little leprechauns, named Jack and Sean, provided the laughter and magic that sustained their father. Only a man with fairy blood could turn a story of golf into an Irish folk tale. Mr. O'Shea sat the boys down one Sunday afternoon on one of the new green mounds of earth. Looking over the ebb and flow of the terrain, he told the boys this story:

"The Irish have a sense of humor and wit that has been sharpened over the centuries by the grinding wheel of oppression. The game of golf itself is a perfect example. As I told you, we Irish had our own golf course. During the day we allowed this new course to be played by the English and the Scottish." The boys sat smiling up at this gentle giant.

"What challenge is that?" your ancestor, John O'Shea would ask.

"John O'Shea was a giant of a man, who lived four hundred years ago. His blood runs through your veins, boys. John, who was a builder of that first course, knew the shape and roll of every hole. After observing the English and Scott's play the game, he devised a way for the Irish to learn the sport. He managed to acquire a single club from the place and several of the little white leather balls. He invited some of his cronies to

join him and at night with the moon and stars providing the only light, the men learned to play the course like a fiddle.

Word eventually leaked out.

The English pondered a proper response and determined that this was a perfect opportunity to show how inferior the Irish were. They invited John O'Shea to play a round against their club champion. John showed up with the one club he would use to accept the challenge. The laughter of the English and Scottish onlookers watching him approach the first tee fairly shook the earth.

Without even playing, John could claim a victory of sorts for the English intent on embarrassing the Irish had declared a holiday. The locals smiled as they laid down their shovels and made their way to the match.

Word of Irish humiliation would be spread throughout the isle; that was the English plan.

The match turned out to be a close one however, and was all square going to the final hole. The English were grumbling but they too found themselves caught up in the excitement. If their man could win in the end, they could still claim victory. The final hole boys, was shaped very much like this one with a huge pot bunker just to the left of a green with a lot of break to it.

John O'Shea knew every break on that green. His moonlight rounds had spotlighted the sandy surface revealing each shadow that told its own story.

The Englishman reached the green with two mighty shots. John, using a shorter club, was ready to putt in three.

The club champion seemed confident as he putted what came to be known as the 'shot heard round the world'. The break took the ball first toward the hole; then, as if a fairy was standing in the way, it turned to the left and stopped, leaving a three foot putt to the cup.

John O'Shea stood over his ball and began to whistle softly. It was so quiet that his whistle seemed deafening. He was whistling to conjure up a bit of magic.

He launched his ball lightly in the air and carried on the wings of a fairy, it passed all those breaks. The ball struck twice, first the ground, then the center of the hole. The Irish clicked their heels in glee and, truth be told lads, that began the Irish dance some call clogging. But, there's still a putt to be made, isn't there? The Englishman, obviously shaken by this turn of events, tried to gather himself for the tying putt. A mere three feet, a yard, thirty-six inches-boys, it became that day the longest putt in golf. The Englishman looked at the millions of grains of sand and tufts of grass standing between the ball and the hole and he knew his fate. He plumbed the putt, walked around it, and asked for advice. Even his countrymen grew impatient with him and began muttering, 'On with it!'

Finally, the Englishman settled over the ball with the cheeks of his arse tightly squeezed and his hands choking the life out of his putter. He pushed that ball another three feet beyond the hole and missed the putt coming back.

Hardly a soul witnessed that final miss, for the Irish had left dancing their way to the pubs, while the English simply disappeared into thin air.

The English never forgave the Irish that sound trouncing, and animosity between the Presbyterians and the Irish Catholics continues to this day.

Mr. O'Shea looked at the boys and said, "So use that gift you've been given boys, the ability to bring laughter and the imagination it takes to turn defeat into victory."

As the project took shape and Mr. O'Shea's understanding of golf grew, he realized golf could be an opportunity for his sons. Sundays in the O'Shea home had always been disjointed. A Catholic man who did not attend church, Mr. O'Shea nonetheless could not bring himself to join the Baptist church, which found a true believer in Wee Bird. Both boys attended Parochial school. That was the one and only battle Mr. O'Shea had fought and had won. He had insisted only to honor his grandparents. Parochial school taught enough religion, Mr. O'Shea believed, and so on Sundays he packed up the boys and took them out to this beautiful piece of God's green earth. He called the course, "The Isle of the Leprechauns." It was there that Jack hit his first real golf ball. A magical moment it was when the ball lifted, as if it were on fairy wings, and settled in the dust of the freshly turned earth

Over the next six months the boys watched the course rise and fall and become the color that they would forever call leprechaun green. Sean was six and Jack was nine. As the course became a reality and Mr. O'Shea's work was completed, it seemed the fate of the O'Shea family had been shaped as well; Mr. O'Shea's role there was finished too.

While Mr. O'Shea was busy chasing leprechauns and fairies with the boys, Robin O'Shea had found a good Baptist man who would listen to her complaints, long after Sunday worship had finished.

Mr. O'Shea would never hear about Albert Brooks. Albert installed, tested, and repaired large photographic machines for the Eastman Kodak Company. Traveling from one region of the country to the next, he was alone on the road for six months at a time.

Robin was certain she would be traveling to his next assignment, for didn't he promise that if she would comfort him, something good would surely develop.

When Wee bird told Mr. O'Shea of her wanting out of this Godless, loveless marriage, he heard it as simply another item on the laundry list of endless complaints. It was only when he received the walking papers, as he called them, and the locked door when he returned from work, that he finally heard the complaint he could no longer turn a deaf ear to.

If only Mr. O'Shea could believe the message he'd given his sons and turn defeat into victory in this situation. Imagine that if you can. Me neither.

Jack's father practiced using his wit right through divorce court, and the only gloves that came off were Jack's mothers. The judge himself had no sense of humor. Mr. O'Shea found it impossible to convey to the court the special bond he shared with Jack. Sean wanted to stay with his mother and Jack wanted to go with his father. Jack's father tried to rationalize why this couldn't happen. When he came to pick up the few possessions he was allowed, Jack was in the back yard swinging his club for all it was worth.

Sean, one of those few possessions, was in his room packing. Mr. O'Shea joined Jack in the backyard to say good-bye. They sat on the swing set and cried silently while Mr. O'Shea, Jack even called him that, told one last story.

"The Irish are masters at saying good-bye." said Mr. O'Shea. He began by telling Jack about the Emerald Isle. God had deemed it the jewel of the world, a place where music and laughter became a language all of itself. Where the colors of the seasons were gently washed by the hand of the almighty. The gentle folk called themselves Irish, the shamrock was their lucky charm. Indeed life was good.

"If only it could have remained a secret," said Mr. O'Shea. Again a deep sigh and he continued.

"It seems the word of good fortune of these Irish folk reached across the water to others, who were not gentle and had no laughter or sense of humor. Many wars took place and thousands of Irish died, were driven out of their land, or changed forever by their conquerors. Many were simply driven to drink and exaggeration. The Irish began to doubt themselves and God, watching from above, refused to interfere. Famine and pestilence were allowed to take root, the conquerors finding that Ireland was not a jewel at all." He paused and looked Jack straight in the eye.

"We are like Ireland Jack; they are trying to destroy our family. We mustn't let that happen. Use the two things I have left to give. Keep your sense of humor and imagine us back together someday, Jack. See the humor in the newspaper or your classes and the people you have to deal with. Use your imagination to overcome any obstacle in your way. You'll have the last laugh son that I promise you. It's God's gift and all that we've been left with."

A hug, a handshake and a large hole in his heart was what Jack carried back into that house.

Jack's father left for another state soon after and it would be years before Jack would understand the pain that was his father's. His own pain screamed desertion and he turned that anger into the game of golf that would later challenge both his sense of humor and his imagination.

CHAPTER

Five

After his morning ritual of push-ups which he did in the bathroom waiting for his shower to heat up, Michael dressed and woke his Volvo with a gentle tap on his key fob.

"Good Morning, darling. You're looking special on a Monday morning. What's that perfume you're wearing or is that the scent of a woman?" The thought of the movie by the same name brought a smile to his face. Looking in the mirror he saw a young Al Pacino looking back at him, glad he had his vision. Couldn't imagine not driving his baby or seeing Meg again for that matter. New visions and voices but all part of the same movie playing in his head and his heart.

The first thing Michael did Monday morning was to go see the lieutenant. It wasn't a workday for him but he hoped he could get in to see his boss. He entered the open area housing the detective's cubicles and was surprised to see a flurry of activity at this time of day. He was greeted by smiles and a round of applause from the three detectives who gathered around him. Before he could ask what was going on, his lieutenant came into the room.

"Come with me," he said and walked into his office. He gestured to Michael to sit down. Michael had a quizzical look on his face and a question formed on his lips.

The lieutenant spoke, "I just called your apartment, you must be psychic; that was good police work Saturday night, Michael." "Well," Michael began, but again the lieutenant spoke.

"That was really good police work Saturday night."

"You already said that," managed Michael before the lieutenant continued.

"Yup, what starts out as just doing your job, maybe putting in a little extra time, putting a little extra shine on your shoes so to speak can bring bountiful rewards."

"What are you talking about?" asked Michael. "Don't tell me that Asian kid worked for Osama Bin Laden or something."

The lieutenant laughed, "No, you won't be shaking hands with the President this week I'm afraid but the captain wants to see you." With that, the lieutenant rose and led the way down the hall to Captain Benjamin J. Harrison's office.

A direct descendent to the past President, the captain had filled his office with artifacts and his walls were covered with framed pictures of his famous ancestor. This morning however, he shared his office with the police commissioner and the mayor. (What's going on?) thought Michael.

Michael was introduced and hands were shaken all around. The police photographer busied himself snapping pictures. Michael looked around the room and he was struck with a thought that maybe a hundred years from now his own great-great grandson would have today's pictures on a wall somewhere. Why framed pictures of Michael might be on a wall was still a question that he hoped would soon be answered.

After what seemed like two rolls of film, the photographer left and it was up to the lieutenant to lay out the story that would later reach print and the networks.

Once the young Asian had told his story, and while it was a sad one indeed, it didn't immediately solve the case Michael had been working on. Michael had not wanted to interview the owner of the ABC Loan Company because:

A. He couldn't stomach the guy.
B. He might not be as understanding as the situation warranted.
C. Part of Michael wouldn't have minded one of those stray bullets ending up in the kneecap of the victim.

It was as simple as A. B. C. really, which wouldn't have been the best way to comfort the guy Michael had thought at the time. The lieutenant began a story that Michael couldn't have dreamed would unfold. It seemed that Mr. Smith, the victim of the ABC armed robbery attempt, had never been held up before. Mr. Smith, whose business had reaped a wonderful return on his investments had never been shot at before. Mr. Smith, it seemed, suddenly saw how his life might end rather badly if he continued this profession.

Over the past two days Mr. Smith decided, for his family's sake of course, to turn into a law-abiding citizen. He had given the detectives a list of activities and individuals he was involved with that stretched the length of the East Coast.

Mr. Smith was to become a star witness who would help unravel a snakelike network of illegal money laundering and drug shipments, and he had named names of men who ran the operation.

"We have Mr. Smith and his family safely hidden away, and the Feds are already trying to worm their way into this." the lieutenant added.

"For now Michael, your effort, diligence and the way you organized the rescue of Mr. Smith is about to become page one news. You are a hero, Michael." The men in the room applauded and Michael, red-faced, simply stood there too numb to speak. Later that morning, Michael finally got the lieutenant alone and told him of his need for some time off. (All the stars must be lining up,) thought Michael as the lieutenant not only agreed, but told Michael to use the department credit card for gas and food since he'd still officially be doing undercover work as he traveled.

Michael smiled, "And I suppose I have to check in with you too, sir."

"Once a week just like clockwork. You have three weeks coming to you; enjoy yourself; you've earned it. Maybe a little promotion will be waiting for you when you get back."

☞☜

Michael called Meg at her job to ask her to dinner. When she got on the line, Michael offered only the barest of details but managed to convey the urgency of seeing her tonight. "I'll tell you about it over dinner. Pick you up at seven PM."

Meg hardly got a word in except, "Dinner should be enlightening."

It was twelve-thirty PM. Michael grabbed a salad at Wendy's and headed home to pack. While he cleaned the perishables out of the fridge, a local radio station playing soft hits of the past and present kept a tune on his lips. When the news came on, the weekend robbery attempt was mentioned but said nothing of Mr. Smith turning states' evidence.

(That's good. The longer that stays out of the media the better,) thought Michael. I can see the headlines now-'Mr. Smith goes to Washington,' he chuckled.

Ron called and confirmed the golf date for Wednesday seeming as confused as Michael about what Jack was up to.

They chatted for a few minutes about the new course and the best way to get there.

Michael told Ron he'd take him and his family to Disney World when this whole mystery was solved. "And, Ron, I've met this girl. I'm hoping she'll come with me. Can you arrange a room or motel in the area for me?" Michael asked.

"Hell, we're living in a four-bedroom house on the canal, hot tub, big boat. It's part of my deal with the company."

"If you're sure you've got enough room, I'll pick up something to barbecue, so tell Beth she can take a break from that household chore at least."

"She'll be glad to turn over her apron. Tell me more about this girl. As I recall you never met a woman at college, or on the road for that matter, who raised more than lukewarm interest. You actually sounded excited when you mentioned this girl. What's her name?"

"Meg, an Irish girl, and I don't know if I can talk her into coming with me or not but she is special. I hope you'll get to meet her."

"Why don't we plan to meet for dinner tomorrow night? You've got my cell number so call me when you get to Daytona. When you get to I-95, you've got about thirty-five minutes to my place. We will go to Sonny's Barbecue in Palm Coast, a friend of mine owns it. He'll treat us special," said Ron.

"Thanks, Ron. It will be good to get back together. Hope we can help Jack." "Me too," said Ron.

Michael hung up the phone and called his landlord. He told him he'd be gone at least a week and asked him to take in his paper and mail. Michael didn't really have anyone else to call so he started packing. Beyond shaving gear and a couple of golf shirts, Michael planned to live in shorts and tee shirts. He pulled out a bathing suit, golf socks, a light wind breaker, and a sweatshirt. (Evenings could get cool along the coast,) he thought. Michael kept his golf clubs in his trunk at all times. He couldn't think of anything else - a cooler maybe for some drinks. Michael took the stairs two at a time and headed toward the two women in his life.

CHAPTER

Six

When Michael reached Meg's door he heard talking from within. Meg's voice sounded exasperated so Michael waited. The only words Michael could make out were a loud, "Well, good-bye then!" The words followed by the sound of a receiver being replaced with authority. Michael counted to five and knocked.

A muffled, "Be there in a second," was followed by a full minute before the chain was removed and Meg opened the door. She had been crying. Michael's first instinct was to take her in his arms but he thought better of it and pretended not to notice. He followed Meg to the kitchen table and sat down, neither of them speaking. The scene was like a play being acted out on stage.

Michael looked around the studio apartment taking in the bed and single overstuffed chair. The bed folded to become a sofa but probably didn't very often. He looked at several trophies and team pictures sharing counter space with a can opener and microwave. (Small but neat, thought Michael. No hidden agenda here. As Popeye would say, "I am what I am.") The apartment seemed to reinforce Michael's first impression of Meg.

After what seemed like an hour but was closer to a couple of minutes, Meg spoke, "Thank you Michael, for letting me get to where I needed to be." Meg had been silently sitting on the kitchen floor with her legs crossed and eyes closed.

"Thank you Meg, for letting me be where I need to be," responded Michael. Those were the only words spoken as they held each other and both understood perfectly.

While Meg excused herself to fix her eyes, Michael studied the trophy and pictures more closely. Twenty well-conditioned young athletes peered back at Michael as he searched for Meg. He found her in the back row, looking satisfied. The trophy in the hands of three teammates said it all.

The small personal trophy on Meg's counter was from the same European tournament Meg's team, called "The Shamrock", had won. All twelve teams were listed and The Shamrock was at the top with the number 1 beside it. The trophy had Meg's name as a player on its base.

When Meg emerged from the bathroom, her eyes were fixed. The twinkle had returned and she grabbed Michael and did several dance steps toward the door.

Michael drove to the mall where they sat in the food court oblivious to the people around them.

Meg took Michael's hand, "Tell me about yourself."

"Well, there's really not a lot to tell." Michael leaned back and thought for a moment

"I grew up in Vermont in a small town that has managed to stay off the beaten path. Skiing and tourists, as well as cheese and maple syrup, keep the state in business." Michael paused.

"I have a sister who lives in Utah, up in Park City. She's a thirty-seven-year old ski bum who manages condos when she's not on the slopes." Michael smiled as he thought of his sister living her life to the fullest.

"Both of my parents have passed away. Mom from cancer and Dad from a broken heart, I suspect, within a year of each other. Mom lingered and suffered terribly for a full year so her death was a blessing. Dad's death was sudden and hit me hard but, I think to him it was a blessing." Michael paused once more. "As a kid I remember skiing, skiing, and more skiing. Dad managed a small resort above our town and he got to live his dream. He met Mom while he was on leave from the Air Force. Mom was from Utah; they met in Colorado on the ski slopes. From that first day, they seldom made a ski run without one another.

Both my sister and I got our first view of the outside world from a knapsack that Dad fashioned into a kid carrier for his back. We flew down the mountain long before we could walk." Michael stretched and continued.

"I hated school, hated being indoors, but Dad and Mom both practiced and taught self-discipline so I never missed a day.

We grew up eating Cream of Wheat with a dab of Vermont's finest maple syrup, bananas, and walnuts on top. That was breakfast always, and lots of times, supper. Mom and Dad exercised on a daily basis and going out for a walk usually involved scaling a ridge or it might turn into a light jog. Eating right, drinking moderately, reading and stretching the mind and body was the family religion." Michael sighed.

"I remember Dad saying when Mom died that he was glad he hadn't spent years in church. If God felt it necessary to take one as good as your mother, he obviously was not paying attention to man's personal business." Michael looked at the moon peeping through the glass roof, as if prompting what he would say next. "God for our family was the blue sky and the brightest stars in the universe on the coldest winter nights. That same Moon you see up there guided us home on many evenings.

You know, with that wood fire providing warmth and security and Dad and Mom always there for us, I had no doubt Dad was right. So no church for us." Michael flexed his shoulders.

"I played soccer to get in shape to ski and I skied for my first sixteen winters on earth. Dad ran the resort, as I said, but in the summer he was the keeper of the greens at a nearby golf course. He started out as a kid mowing grass and doing other little odd jobs. He was such a good worker that he became invaluable to the owners. He eventually took over caring for the course itself. I played around with the game and since I began very young, I got pretty darn good. We didn't have a golf team in high school so I always figured I'd get a ski scholarship. Then during my junior year, I blew out my right knee and serious skiing was over for me. That summer I was recuperating. I couldn't run, and soccer was out of the question for my senior year. I had to do a lot of walking, and since a golf course had the only flat ground in the state, I began hitting the ball every day all day long. I bet I walked thirty-six holes every day and fifty-four some days. My leg healed and golf became my passion." Michael took a breath. "I went to college here in Florida, cause that's where golf is, at least on the East Coast. I walked onto the college golf team and managed to stay on it for all four years. I even made the traveling team which brings me to the question I want you to say yes to." "Well, Michael, that's quite a story you tell, even without any creatures. I'm truly sorry about your Mom and Dad." She squeezed his hand. "So, what's the question? If it concerns golf, I'm afraid, beyond Tiger Woods or Padraig Harrington I know next to nothing."

"I don't have any animals in my story, but I do have a friend who can do magical things with a golf ball. He's an Irishman too. He was my closest friend in college. He may be in deep trouble and I've taken some time off beginning tomorrow to see if I can help. I have to go to the East Coast and I want you to go with me."

Meg looked directly at Michael, gave him a fixed stare and said, "Will I be having my own room then, or is this a bold attempt to take advantage of a poor working Irish girl in a foreign land?" They both laughed. Meg asked Michael how he had gotten time off on such short notice. Michael explained the stakeout and the result down playing the danger he'd been in.

"Anyway, I had some time coming to me so here we are." Do you think you can get off work for a few days?

Meg said she was getting less than twenty hours a week so saying good-bye to the neighborhood wouldn't be a tragedy. "Come help us pack now Michael, I'll brew you up some special tea."

☞•☜

When they got back to Meg's, over a cup of tea, Michael asked Meg if she was ready to tell him why she had to fix her eyes earlier. Meg closed those eyes, sighed deeply, and began.

"You know, Michael, you're so lucky to have had a loving family. Even though they're gone now you're blessed with memories that made you smile as you were telling me about your youth." It was Meg's turn to look back.

"I was born in a part of Dublin that wasn't green and shiny. I too remember the sky, but it was from the fourth floor of a building that nearly touched an identical twin, no matter which window you looked out of. So I looked up at the sky too, mostly soot-filled, sometimes brighter, but never the religious experience your family felt.

We had our religion though. Parochial school with the sisters who had promised the Pope they wouldn't smile nor teach without a stick in hand." She sighed digging further into her memory. "I remember being made to feel guilty for where I lived, how I lived, even that I lived. Once a week God would forgive me." She coughed lightly.

"Actually, I did find solace in the rosary. As I numbly chanted the required prescription for salvation, my mind would soar and maybe I did see that blue sky and those same stars." Meg stood up and walked to her window. She turned her head back toward Michael.

"Maybe, I even saw you on that ski slope of yours. Anyway, I did believe. I believed God had placed a spark of life within me and it was up to me, and me alone, to keep that spark alive." Meg's spark was clearly alive.

"I don't remember a father. I had quite a parade of uncles traipsing those stairs though. Me Mum was close to those uncles too for many spent the night. My father must have had a huge family." She chuckled at her own naivete. "I was so young I didn't know from nothing. I remember asking some of those uncles if they remembered my father. They would just laugh and say, "Oh yes, he was a swell fellow." Meg didn't display any bitterness in her voice.

"Thinking back, I don't know if my Mother ever saw the sky. For all I remember is her looking down. Never meet your eyes, but your ears, lord she could meet your ears. Never a conversation in our house, it was orders I received. Mostly regarding the flat. Sweep this, wash that, dust this, and polish that. Everything sparkled in my little world except the people."

Michael took Meg's hand and conveyed his own strength without a word.

"You hated school, you say? I loved school. Even the sisters couldn't kill me spark, and it was through books and physical activities that I fanned that spark to a flame." Meg's eyes glistened with the memory of her determination.

"Why was I crying when you arrived, Michael? Must have been tears of joy don't you think, when your Mum reveals she's to be married, once again? Over the years lots of those uncles came to be stepfathers. None of them stayed too long, but me Mum always managed to wring a bit of alimony from them. Nothing was given freely in my house, especially affection." Meg moved to her team picture.

"This will be the tenth gentleman to carry a picture of me in his wallet and claim a bit of the success I had with soccer." Meg laughed without mirth.

"I'm famous, you know! In that little piece of slum. I'm that bright star children are urged to emulate. The sisters use my success to motivate the girls as if they had anything to do with it." Meg took Michael's hand again.

"Me Mum, when I called her to tell her about a wonderful man I had met, continued the family tradition of giving orders. I'm to attend her day of bliss, she says, and come back to be her maid of honor. A big to-do this time with the church involved," Meg laughed.

"She must have caught a big one this time for the church to be involved. I'm thinking they are a little tired of wasting wine and biscuits on that one. Somebody pulled some strings if the bells will be tolling and a priest able to keep a straight face. There will have to be more than one sister standing behind his skirts with a stick to make that happen." She sighed, "I love me Mum Michael, and that's why I cried. If only she could realize she's got to learn to love herself before she can love someone else." She shook her head.

"None of those nine stepfathers ever stood a chance. I put a lock on my door after one of those uncles thought he'd cry on my shoulder. I'm not going home, Michael. There is no home there, and until I said it on the phone I guess I still thought it possible. So I cried, not for me Mum but for me. America is my new home."

She brightened, "And it looks like I'm about to explore it a bit."

Michael grabbed Meg's other hand and pulled her to him. "We don't leave until tomorrow so let's go dancing and I can hold you in my arms without you thinking I'm taking advantage of a poor working Irish girl."

❧

Monday had been a day that filled Michael's head, first the lieutenant, then Meg saying yes to the trip, and now Meg in his arms holding on for dear life. He couldn't even imagine what the next few days might bring.

Michael could have spent the night at Meg's, but he felt she was too vulnerable and needy right now, and he'd be taking advantage of that. When he made love to Meg and he had no doubt he would, he wanted it to be after a day of laughter and blue skies and an evening of bright stars and with a little luck maybe even the moon. That was to be the world he wanted to introduce Meg to - a world of possibilities.

CHAPTER
Seven

It was a beautiful morning in Florida. As Michael ran along the sidewalks he gazed at front and back lawns of the single family homes in this residential area. The well manicured grounds and flowering shrubbery spoke of people proud of what they had and working hard to keep an attractive neighborhood. Parked along the streets were lawn maintenance trucks and in the distance he could hear a garbage truck emptying the week's evidence of a prepackaged existence. Michael's own approach to the environment was simply to pick up what he'd put down, plus one. He carried a plastic bag tucked into his waistband and was forever stopping to clean any litter that came into view. He would shake his head finding it impossible to believe people just open a car window and dump stuff.

When he entered the driveway of his apartment building his landlord George was picking up his morning paper. "I'll take that, George. I'm not gone yet. By the way, thanks again for picking up my mail too."

George, a man in his mid-sixties, looked at Michael holding the bag of garbage and laughingly said, "What, you don't make enough garbage yourself; you have to bring it home with you?"

Michael smiled, "George, I'm just keeping the neighborhood looking good so you can keep charging those exorbitant rental fees. Don't want property values falling now do we?" Both men laughed.

George owned three apartment buildings with four tenants in each. He had retired ten years ago from a career as a firefighter in Michigan. George looked like he could still put out a fire if he had to. The repairs and maintenance of the three apartment houses kept him in shape.

This morning he was mowing lawns and trimming shrubbery. "Come over here Michael; I want to show you something. You're a good observer. You have to be to be a cop. Tell me what you think about this shrub."

Michael looked at a gnarly bush that looked as if its appendages were victims of severe arthritis.

"See those stubs; they're a miracle. This is a crepe myrtle, Michael. Every year I cut this down to a single stump or maybe leave a few of those little stubs. If I left it alone, it would become a tree; there is no room for that. Anyway, from that stump all these little shoots pop out and before you know it they're branches and they begin to flower." George looked at Michael like a teacher giving a lesson.

"Amazing isn't it? It's a miracle I tell you, and it's God's work. Since I've retired and have the time to really look around, I see a lot of God's work. I don't even read these any more." George handed Michael the newspaper. "That's man's work just like that bag of garbage you've got there. That's man's work. Give me a tree or a bush anytime." With that, George walked off muttering to himself.

Michael stood there looking at his folded paper in one hand and the bag of garbage in the other and could find no argument with George what-so-ever.

Michael checked in with Meg to hear how her boss reacted to her asking for some time off.

"Well, it was a lot like listening to me Mum it was. Him hollering and declaring me morally bankrupt I believe he said. Him being manager and all, he had to use the big words, and God forbid I even attempt employment at an Applebee's." She continued in mock horror, "I fear I've had an apple branded on me forehead so I'll be packing a stocking cap if you don't mind." Michael laughed, "Well we will avoid that particular chain at least until you grow a beard and mustache."

Meg laughed, "Did you get to run this morning?"

Michael having told her of his daily regimen answered, "Yes, and did you use that balloon of yours?"

Meg, a little more cautious about running the streets, used an air-filled rubber ball to do squats, push-ups, and all manner of exercise to keep trim. "I spent an hour rolling around the world. I would guess we'll be ready for whatever comes our way." said Meg.

"You run them ragged and I'll bounce up and down and spin them dizzy."

Michael roared, "I'll see you in about two hours, Meg." After hanging up, Michael did his push-ups, jumped in the shower, then still wrapped in a towel opened a box of cereal. Between bites he opened the newspaper that was still lying on the table. What kind of mischief had man's work created in the last twenty-four hours?

The large headlines dealt with war and pestilence. The smaller headlines exposed the latest woes of the shuttle program. Further down was the President's new tax cut proposal. Michael slowly turned the pages and noted there seemed to be no good news today. In the local news, murder and highway mayhem, but still no story on Mr. Smith. Michael opened the sports page. Even there, everything above the high school competition, tended toward suspensions, investigations and trash talk.

(Maybe George was right,) thought Michael. (This is man's work.) He didn't even open the classified section. Unless you were looking for something specific, it was just mind-boggling. Michael made one last check of what he'd need. His clothes were packed along with his running shoes. His favorite CDs, flashlight, and notepad were already in the car. Michael grabbed his gun and put it on top of his duffel bag. He looked around once, turned up the air conditioning to 82, and snapped off the light.

Meg was sitting on her steps looking like a kid ready to go to camp when Michael arrived. Soon they were working their way to I-4, the East-West highway that would bring them to Daytona Beach.

Walt Disney had created his Magic Kingdom but there was nothing magic about what followed. Central Florida had moved from an agricultural economy to a major urban region where competing theme parks and shopping centers grew faster than crops. I-4 was constantly expanding lanes, exits, and diverting traffic from point A to point B in its attempt to handle urban sprawl.

Meg and Michael bantered about everything under the sun. They observed drivers, frustrated with their place in bumper to bumper traffic, risk their lives to move ahead 2 or 3 cars. Meg turned on the radio and found a country station. (That answers that,) Michael thought, but he had to ask, " What's an Irish girl like yourself doing listening to country music?"

"Well, as a girl we watched reruns of Gunsmoke and Bonanza, so there's a lot of us Irish who grew up learning about your famed cowboys and Indians. Willie Nelson actually came to Ireland for a concert. You being a golfer, Michael, would appreciate that he played the old courses and I believe wrote a song. He sang it at the concert, big headlines, about his golf and his description of Ireland." She settled back in her seat.

"So I like Willie, Waylon, Patsy Cline, and the old songs. The new stuff I don't like much."

"Have you heard Neil Diamond," asked Michael, "or Billy Joel?" "I guess I've heard of them but never really listened to them," said Meg.

Michael dropped in a Billy Joel Greatest Hits CD. Just as Billy started the musical intro to "Piano Man" Michael's phone rang and fumbling the key pad, he answered it on the fourth ring. "Glad I caught you, Michael. I was hoping that damn message service wasn't going to kick in."

"Ron, is that you?"

"Sorry, Michael, yeah it's me. I guess I'm a little shook up." "What's happening?" asked Michael, his mind beginning to churn.

"I had a message from Jack and it really got me concerned. First of all, he didn't call me at the course where I could have talked to him. He just left a message at the house. He knows I'm at the course on Tuesday. Why wouldn't he call me there?" Ron was starting to repeat himself and Michael could tell he was upset. So like a good detective, he didn't butt in; he just let Ron ramble on a bit.

Finally Ron paused long enough for Michael to ask, "What did he leave for a message? Ron, try to remember as close as possible the exact words Jack used."

"Hell, I'll never forget what he said. I played that thing over at least six times. He said, I can't make it for the round but get Michael and Tim to your course. I'll call around eight am. tomorrow morning." Ron paused before delivering the last line. "Tell Michael that it'll all be over soon Dannyboy. He'll know what I mean." Ron sounded bewildered, "Those exact words. I wrote them down. What does it mean, Michael, and who is Dannyboy?" asked Ron.

"I need to think about this," said Michael. "We're about twenty miles from Daytona. Give me the directions; we should be there in an hour or so."

Ron told him how to get to A1A and the small ocean front community, Flagler Beach. Ron lived several streets back from the ocean in a house owned by the private golf course community. When Michael hung up the phone, Meg could sense this was not the time to probe. Just as Michael had let her gather herself last evening, Meg was silently saying, "Right back at yuh."

When they reached the interchange for I-95, Michael stopped at a Quik Mart. He gassed up the Volvo and returned with two bottles of Arizona Ice Tea. He handed Meg a bottle, their eyes met, and she could see that Michael was ready to talk.

"Tell me about Jack O'Shea and how you two became so close," said Meg.

Michael told Meg the story of that first golf practice, the road trips, and what Jack had told him of his early years. He spoke of how generous Jack was and how he cared about his friends. "After getting that message from Ron - those words - 'It'll all be over soon Dannyboy.'

There's a hidden message to me in those words. Over the years I roomed with him, whenever Jack uttered those words, violence, or trouble at least, followed. Jack's in danger or at least serious trouble."

Meg, her green eyes open to every word, smiled then and said, "Then we'll have to help him, Michael. You run them ragged and I'll bounce up and down on them."

That brought a smile back to Michael's face, and he knew he'd made the right decision in asking Meg to come along. They exited in Ormond Beach and began the ride North along the coastal highway A1A. The Ocean was on their right and soon the beautiful homes along its beach gave way to the Ocean itself. What a scenic piece of road. A squadron of pelicans flew in a perfect inverted V formation along the shoreline keeping up with the Volvo. Meg said she felt like they too were flying, part of the squadron, the last bird on the left. The road was very straight and they rode in awe of both the birds and of the beauty of the Atlantic Ocean. The sun's slanted rays reflected off the Atlantic Ocean and blue sky spit white bits of cotton into the air where they hung as if on a string.

(Well, there is some of the beauty I promised I'd show Meg,) thought Michael.

Meg must have had a similar thought, for her hand gently found Michael's and they both sensed this was to be a memorable trip for many reasons.

By five-thirty pm. they had reached the center of Flagler Beach where tourists walked along a wooden sidewalk while locals fished along the beach and from the pier. "We'll have to come back to this place," said Michael. Meg nodded her head in complete agreement.

CHAPTER

Eight

The sign on the left read 4th Street. Ron, watching for Michael, was out the door and waving even before he pulled into the driveway. Michael opened his window and kiddingly asked where the bag drop was. The two men gave each other a big hug and pat on the back as Michael exited the vehicle.

When Meg joined them, Michael said, "Ron this is Meg, my new friend."

"Hello Meg," said Ron, "welcome to our home."

"Nice to meet you Ron; what a lovely area. The ride up A1A was breathtaking."

Ron helped carry the bags into the house as he answered Meg, "Come on in and meet Beth. If you get the time, she will show you some other beautiful spots up this way."

Beth was quick to capture Meg after introductions. She hugged Michael then began a walk through, beginning with the guest bedroom where they deposited the luggage.

Ron ushered Michael to the lanai after putting the bags down. An icy pitcher of lemonade and four glasses sat on a raised table under an umbrella tilted to offer shade from the late afternoon sun.

Ron remembered that Michael didn't drink so decided to wait till dinner for his own whiskey and ginger with a twist of lime. "So, what's going on with Jack? Did you find anything out?" asked Ron.

"I'm as baffled as you Ron. I just know he needs us. Jack prides himself on taking care of his business so this must be serious."

"What do we do?" asked Ron.

"Not much we can do till Jack makes contact. By the way, when is Tim coming?" asked Michael.

"Should be here anytime. I told him we were going out to dinner at seven pm. He's bringing a friend too. Maybe he's got some insight, he sees Jack a lot more than we do." said Ron.

"Let's hope so. Otherwise, we just get to worry all night," said Michael.

The girls still had not come out to join them.

"I guess the ladies are hitting it off. I knew Beth would like Meg and vice versa. By the way, where's Nick?"

"He's spending a couple of days with one of his friends. I told him to pop in tomorrow so you could say hi. He's really into his friends now so Beth and I watch and guide from a distance. He seems to have it together and has earned our trust. It's kind of scary being a parent. The rules of the road so to speak, are straight as hell, but the street signs aren't as clearly defined. Every sin known to man carries the message that being cool is where it's at; drugs, alcohol, body piercing, sharing body fluids. You name it."

"Yeah, I know," said Michael. "When I was with the state police we got to mop up after a lot of those street signs collided. Now as a detective I still clean up, only it's mostly adults making the same mistakes." Michael was thinking, (I hope Jack hasn't run into one of life's stop signs,) as Ron continued.

"I've introduced Nick to golf. Lately he's been inviting some of his friends along. I'm hoping the idea of teaching his friends helps his self confidence. Been taking Nick and a couple of his friends out in carts, letting them drive, use the driving range, and play a couple of holes."

"Sounds like a great idea to me," said Michael.

"What sounds like a great idea?" asked Beth as she and Meg stepped onto the lanai.

"Oh, Michael and I were discussing the perils of parenthood," said Ron. "I was telling him about taking Nick and his friends golfing."

As Meg poured herself and Beth a glass of lemonade, Beth added her take on being a kid in the new millennium. "It's a completely different world than when I was that age. Of course, I was a girl you understand and had two brothers to keep an eye on me. But the biggest difference I see is the number of distractions for a kid today. How do they know who they want to be when every cereal box, commercial, video game, every department store, rap group, and athlete screams - 'Be like me!' Kids are never alone with their thoughts any more. A cell phone stuck in one ear and an i pod in the other. How do you convince them that reading a book can bring the same excitement?" Beth paused and took a sip of lemonade. No one spoke; it was obvious she had not finished.

"I will say those Harry Potter books have done a wonderful job of re-creating some of the fantasy we grew up with. I've read them along with Nick and it's given us a common ground for communication - good vs. evil, risk management, trust, and friendship. We've talked about everything except sex. I'll leave that to the father," she laughed. "Besides, I think he already knows more than we do about that at least as much." Beth finished with a big sigh. "He's growing up so fast."

"Still it must be a wonderful experience." said Meg who had been listening completely engaged with the idea of someday being part of a family that was a family.

"Yeah, it is," said Ron, reaching over and touching Beth on the arm. Their eyes locked for just a moment.

Michael cleared his throat and checked his watch, "We really ought to get cleaned up a little and get ready for dinner. It's six-thirty now."

As Beth and Meg cleared the glasses and stepped into the family room, the doorbell rang.

"That will be Tim. I'll get it." said Ron.

Michael heard talking at the front door, and when a woman's voice reached his ears, he smiled to himself as he glanced at Meg and Beth at the sink. (This ought to be quite an evening and next couple of days for these two.)

Meg caught his smile and looked at him quizzically. Michael just shook his head and said, "Oh, just thinking to myself."

Ron ushered Tim and Ellen into the family room where introductions were made. Beth took them into the other guest room as Michael and Meg went to their room to change.

Everyone eventually reassembled in the family room. Ron said that they could all go in the van. Tim had a beer going

and Ellen was drinking wine. "Hell, bring them with you. I'm driving," said Ron.

"I'll drive home," said Beth, "so you guys can relax and enjoy yourselves."

Michael and Meg got into the third seat. Ellen and Beth were in front of them; Ron and Tim sat up front.

Ron announced that dinner was on him and both Tim and Michael argued, but Ron insisted. "Look, one of the members owns this place, we swap lessons for food. Good deal for both of us so be quiet and enjoy the ride."

"Tomorrow night I want to do dinner," said Michael, "and we won't have to go anywhere. All I need is use of your grill and Beth's spice rack."

It was then that Ellen began to emerge. "Oh, you cook, Mike? Ron's eyes widened. Nobody called Michael, Mike. "That's women's work isn't it?" Giggling, she nodded to Beth and Meg for agreement.

Before Beth or Meg could respond, if they in fact had intended to, Michael had a comeback. "Oh, do you cook for Tim?" he asked, fairly certain of the answer.

As Ellen digested this, Tim announced, "Are you kidding? Oh, yeah, you've heard of painting by numbers? Ellen cooks by numbers. It's amazing the meals she can create, if she has a phone book."

Everyone laughed except Ellen. Michael watched the dart go right through the bulls eye, without throwing it himself. The look Ellen gave to both him and Tim indicated the battle had been joined.

Michael thought he was going to like Tim, for he obviously has a sense of humor. While Ellen had indicated in that earlier phone call that she handled all of Tim's business, Michael now doubted that.

Ron's friend, the owner of the restaurant, was there with his wife to greet them and usher them to a back table. After introductions and good natured bantering the six were left to order drinks and study the menu. Everyone ordered a drink, a beer, or wine except Michael who ordered iced tea.

Ellen saw her next opening and threw out a jab, "Iced tea, Mike, that ought to put hair on your chest."

Michael thought briefly of what Jack always said about letting things slide and simply smiled.

Beth, sensing conflict, tried to move things along by asking Meg how she and Michael had met. Meg explained about being Michael's waitress and how well they had connected immediately. "How sweet," said Ellen, obviously feeling the wine she had consumed earlier on the way to Ron and Beth's place. She had just now polished off a glass and ordered another one. "How sweet," she said again. "Actually, that's how Tim and I met. Only I was waiting on Jack at the time."

Tim tried to hush Ellen but she continued.

"We were back at Jack's place after a party. I was waiting on Jack as I said. Only poor old Jack, he couldn't finish what he ordered." she snickered

"Then he got angry and told me to get out. Tim was rooming with Jack and he heard me crying. He rescued poor little me. Didn't you Tim?" She reached to cover Tim's hand.

"That damn Jack, he's a waste of time." She smiled and looked at Meg. "So I guess we're both waitresses of a sort. Aren't we, Meg?"

Everyone became deathly quiet but Meg broke the silence with her Irish wit.

"Well Ellen, I would say you are right in a way. Only difference I see is I remove my apron when my shift is over and you remove your uniform when yours begins."

Everyone roared except Ellen. Michael was becoming more and more impressed with this beautiful lady.

(She can obviously kick ass on and off the soccer field,) he thought to himself.

The food arrived and a truce seemed declared for now. Ellen ate in stony silence, angry enough to polish off the ribs, bone and all.

Michael asked Tim about his golf background and how he had met Jack.

"I'm from California by way of Maine," said Tim. "I was born in Maine. My Dad was a long haul trucker. He used to travel to Pennsylvania and back. He'd spend most of the week on the road and be home on weekends. My Mom worked in the school food service program." The table was silent wanting to hear about this young man.

"Anyway, Dad got stranded in Pennsylvania one winter, and it didn't look like anything would be moving East for awhile so he took a load west. He landed in Bakersfield and spent a week waiting for a return load. He looked around and found a little town he liked. He took a job at a local transport company and called Mom. He told her to pack up my brother and me and sell whatever she could. We didn't own our house so that wasn't much of a process. He told Mom he hated snow and now that he had seen a place without it in January, he wasn't coming back." Tim chuckled remembering how angry he'd been.

"I was just Nick's age, nine years old, and my brother was eleven. We both thought the world would come to an end. We cried for the two weeks that it took Mom to get things settled. We blamed Dad for all of this, and we made a pact that as soon as my brother Scott was fifteen, we'd steal a car and come back to Maine. We even cut ourselves and sealed the pact in blood." He smiled.

"Anyway, we got used to California and made new friends. Dad was home evenings for the first time and got to watch us play school sports. He took up golf and started asking me to tag along to caddy for him. Dad is kind of a loner so I guess I was company for him. Every once in a while he'd let me hit a ball but I didn't think it was much. I liked to look for balls in the woods though and Dad would sell them to the members for me. I didn't know he was keeping a little back each time. One day when we went to play he took me inside and there was a new set of clubs for me. I said thanks Dad but he just said, "you paid for em; now let's see if you can hit em." Tim took a sip of his whiskey.

"We played together as equals from that day on. Dad never told me how to hold a club or which one to use. When I got to high school, I was the only freshman to make the varsity golf team. Coach said I had the most natural swing he had ever seen. He asked who taught me? After thinking for a minute, it became obvious; my Dad had. When I told my Dad that night what I'd said to the coach, he just looked at me and walked away.

Mom told me later that he said he couldn't say anything or he'd have started bawling. I became the state champ in my junior year. Dad never missed a match. I realized years later, Dad didn't move to California just for himself. Mom told me that he had checked out schools and sports opportunities. He had to quit school as a kid and there was no way his boys were going to miss out. My older brother kind of rebelled and never took advantage of what was being offered. He went into the service and is making it his career." Another sip. "Dad and Mom stay in touch. I went to college out there on a scholarship and spent two years after that trying to get on tour, scraping a living working in pro shops. That's when I met Ron." The two reached over the table and high-fived one another. "I finally got my card and began playing in some second tier tournaments, traveling and living in a VW mini-van."

Ellen excused herself to the ladies room.

"Probably a good time to tell you how I met Jack. It was on the driving range at one of those tournaments. I found myself next to this guy who hit one beautiful shot after another. He talked to himself and kept writing things down in a journal. He'd change clubs and hit a dozen balls, as I said, talking to himself the whole time. Then he'd stop, write some stuff down, pick up a different club. He repeated this formula with every club in his bag. Later, I saw him on the putting green. He whistled while he putted and took notes there too." He raised his glass as if to toast the missing Jack.

"Anyway, that was Jack O'Shea as I'm sure you've figured out by now. I didn't really get to know him until we were paired together on the first day of a second tier tournament. There weren't many big names, but with a top prize of $150,000, there was plenty of competition. Jack shot a 69 that day and I shot a 73. Jack was within one shot of the lead." Another raised glass and a sip.

"That night we had a few drinks in the bar and when the evening ended, I headed for my van. Jack didn't want the evening to end and a table of 'lovelies', as Jack called them, seemed to have similar thoughts. I ended up staying at Jack's place with five of us in three beds. I had to scramble to get to my early tee time, but Jack didn't tee off until 11:30 am. When I left the room, he was sound asleep with a girl tucked in beside him. Remind me to tell you a fairy tale I made up about him." Tim paused, smiled, and continued.

"I shot myself out of the tournament with a 77. Jack not only made the cut but also got his first top ten finish. He asked me to room with him after that, saying I must be like a lucky shamrock or four leaf clover or something."

Ron raised his glass this time. "Here's to the man we all know and love."

Michael could understand why Jack, who kept so much inside, would enjoy having this young, open, good humored guy around. Meg said, "I can't wait to meet this Irishman. He sounds like a puzzle to me."

"He's been great to me, too." said Ron. "He's sent hats, gloves, and balls autographed by different players for me to display in the shop. A couple tour players even stopped in when they were in St. Augustine. Jack told them about the course and they played eighteen holes with a member and myself. Jack's a great friend and he never forgets a kindness."

Ellen, who by now was more than slightly intoxicated, had rejoined them and had heard enough. "Jack, schmack, wack, I'm sick of hearing about Jack. Tim's twice the guy Jack is and he's going somewhere too. Tim is going to be a great golfer. Aren't you honey? And I'm going to help, keep you happy, and all that stuff."

This seemed like a good time to call it an evening. Ron suggested they go back and get in the hot tub. Beth and Meg went to the ladies room and Ron went to bring the van around. Michael was sitting at the end of the table counting out the tip when Ellen spoke up.

"Why didn't you tell them your roommate's little secret?" Michael's eyes locked with Tim's.

Tim turned to Ellen and said, "I think I made a big mistake bringing you with me. These are Jack's friends and, I hope, mine too. You are embarrassing yourself and me. In the morning you take the car to Jacksonville, leave it there, and fly back to wherever."

"But, but, what about us and all our plans?"

"All your plans you mean! I want you out of here. You take the room. I'll stay on the couch."

Ellen began to blubber and made a return trip to the ladies room.

"I'll explain later," said Tim, "I guess with all that's happening, maybe it's important. I don't know. I didn't want to say anything." "I have no idea what you are going to tell me but how is Ellen involved?" asked Michael.

"Who does Jack confide in, Michael? That's right, his journal. Ellen got into it one night while Jack was out. That's more than half the reason I've let her stick around so she wouldn't try to get back at Jack by starting vicious rumors. Anyway, I'll tell you what I know after the women are tucked in for the night."

They rode home with the headlights of oncoming cars illuminating each passenger briefly. Thoughts like those flashes of illumination ran through Michael's head, (What was Jack's secret? What was Ellen alluding to earlier? What would Jack have in his journal that was not for publication?) The smell of sweet Meg beside him brought a happy thought, (Boy I'm glad she's with me. And Ellen, what makes a person like her tick? What was the secret Tim would be telling? Ron and Beth were oblivious to all this.) Michael shook his head to clear away any more thoughts and closed his eyes. He squeezed Meg's hand.

Ellen went straight to her room, well not straight, but she got there after a fashion. She spent a long time in the bathroom and when she emerged, looked as though she wouldn't be sleeping on a full stomach.

Everyone else got in their swimsuits and showered briefly before entering the hot tub. The hot tub was Ron's baby. He used it almost nightly to unwind after a day at work.

Beth put together a tray of veggies and dip, brought out plastic glasses, water and iced tea. They sat in the bubbling steam gabbing about the area, the weather, kids, movies, and, of course, Golf.

Tim asked Michael what he did for a living. Michael told Tim he was a detective with the Orlando police department. He told Tim about being in college with Jack and of their friendship. The girls climbed out after twenty minutes and excused themselves. They were going to get ready for bed.

"We'll join you shortly," said Ron. "We've got to plan for tomorrow. See you in a bit." He kissed Beth lightly and she was gone.

Meg grinned, kissed Michael on the cheek, and delivered her version of a line from the movie, The Terminator, "You'll be back!" She went inside.

The three guys laughed and then laughed again when Michael said, "I think she's right."

"Here I am, stuck with Ellen, and she won't be back," said an exasperated Tim. They all laughed again.

When the house was quiet Michael looked at Tim and said, "Okay Tim, what's this all about?"

Ron, who was in the dark about all this asked, "What's what all about?"

"Be patient Ron; you're about to find out. Tim?"

"All right, this is all I know. One night, back when Ellen was trying to become Jack's girl before I became his roommate, Ellen got into his journal. She found out some stuff about Jack that no one was supposed to know." "What was it?" asked an anxious Ron.

Michael knew this was the time to just let Tim talk so he repeated, "Just be patient Ron."

"Well, it's kind of mysterious really. From what Ellen told me, it was a series of entries written to some guy named Dannyboy. Each entry indicated Jack was either paying out or receiving thousands of dollars.

"How did Jack explain it to you?" asked Michael.

"He just said that it was his way of keeping count." said Tim. "Keeping count of what?" asked Ron in a raised voice. "This is weird."

"Why did Jack think that Ellen's knowledge of the entries posed a threat?" asked Michael.

"She was putting a gay spin on it. You know what that could do to Jack on tour," said Tim.

"Well, who in the hell is Danny Boy?" asked Ron.

"Damned if I know," said Tim, "Jack wouldn't tell me anything more than that. He didn't even tell me to try to keep Ellen quiet. He just told me to clear the air and let me know he wasn't gay." Michael yawned, "Well, I'm going to bed. We're just going to have to wait to hear from Jack to clear up this mystery. Besides, I need to get out of this hot tub before I lose all of my strength. After all, I am going in to meet the Terminator. Hopefully, I'll be back!" They all laughed.

❧

Soon the house was dark and the mystery that was Jack remained just that.

When Michael entered the guest room, a small table lamp cast his giant shadow on the opposite wall. He removed his trunks and reached for his pants to get his underwear.

There arose a deep Irish voice from the darkened bed, "You won't be needin' those."

Michael found himself chuckling as he reached to turn off the lamp. The enlarged silhouette of Michael followed his every move.

"You won't be needing to turn off the moon," said the deep Irish voice.

Michael chuckled again. He turned toward the voice and said, "Okay, what am I going to do next or not do, Oh Great Irish Spirit?"

"You will enter my chamber at your own peril. The risk is great, the journey long and arduous, but if you survive the night you will live forever."

Michael sat on the edge of the bed, looked over at Meg, and whispered, "Am I worthy - Oh Mighty Spirit? For I am but a mere human and you are so God-like."

The covers opened and a softer voice whispered back, "Those are the magic words; you are indeed worthy."

The shadows on the wall would silently play out a story of two love-starved creatures wrapped in sheeting finding one another again and again. This love story would continue uninterrupted. The moon and stars followed the action peeking in the window. Slowly, the theater brightened with the gray light of dawn. The creatures quieted and were as one.

Michael was the first to stir. His senses were always heightened when he was in a different setting which had helped him on more than one occasion in his work. Right now it was his sense of smell that was taking over. Someone was brewing coffee. The clock on the nightstand said five-thirty am. When Michael reached over to turn off the lamp, no voice sounded to stop him. Darkness once more filled the room. He took one last look at the mound of blankets that contained Meg, smiled to himself, and slipped quietly from the room.

Beth was alone in the kitchen stirring up a batter for pancakes. Michael poured himself a cup of coffee and sat down at a table in the nook. The radio was quietly playing a golden oldie. Michael had known Beth since she began dating Ron in college. He'd always thought Ron had made a great decision in hooking up with Beth.

"Well did you guys solve the world's problems last night?" asked Beth.

"Not really but we got our army formed at least. We just need to hear from General O'Shea." quipped Michael.

Beth laughed. "Meg sounds like she could lead a pretty good charge too if she was needed. I already like her. Me, I'll cook for the troops. Seriously though, Ron told me that it's obvious Jack is in trouble."

"He's supposed to contact Ron this morning so we'll just have to wait it out."

"Who could this Dannyboy be and why would Jack be paying him?"

Michael shrugged and excused himself. He wasn't going to get a run in this morning, but at least a walk outside would help. He needed to think. A detective's instinct had led him to keep the identity of Dannyboy a secret. He certainly didn't suspect Tim or Ron but keeping his knowledge of the journal to himself made sense for the time being.

He was watching a pair of lizards darting around the cement columns on the front of the house when Meg covered his eyes from behind. "Fine lawman you are," Meg whispered, "I could have grabbed your gun and tied you up, just like on TV." Michael turned to meet those eyes and the wide smile, "Good morning, Miss Meg. You're looking radiant on what promises to be a beautiful day here in sunny Florida. Let's take a walk."

They held hands and walked down the street crossing the main road to the beach. Climbing the steps of the wooden landing, the beach and ocean beyond dazzled their eyes as the sun was just now taking control for the next twelve hours or so. The tide was out and the lovers walked along the sand stopping to examine seashells and starfish washed ashore.

Meg had said very little but Michael needed a sounding board. "Jack is supposed to call Ron this morning while we are playing golf. I'm hoping he will end this mystery. I'd love to spend some time on this little beach and explore this beautiful area. "I'm thinking all this with Jack is going to get worse, Michael. You said yourself Jack doesn't like to need people.

Please, be careful. I've a feeling the Jack you've described must be desperate about something."

"Well, I have found out money is involved at some level but I haven't figured out if Jack is receiving or paying out," said Michael.

"If he's living in the shadows it would seem someone is looking to receive rather than deliver."

"That would be a logical conclusion; I agree. According to Tim, Jack has been documenting some money accounts in his journal."

"As you said, hopefully Jack can clear all of this up. We'd better get back. Beth would probably like to serve those pancakes hot," said Meg.

Nothing about last night's intimacy was mentioned. Both understood perfectly.

Tim and Ron were having coffee on the lanai. Ellen, taking Tim's car, had left in a huff indicating at the top of her voice that he hadn't heard the last of this.

Meg helped serve the pancakes. The murmurs of approval for Beth's cooking becoming the focus of conversation.

CHAPTER

Nine

By seven-thirty the guys were headed for the course. The River Course was located between the Atlantic Ocean and the Intracoastal Waterway. This part of the Florida coastline was one of the last to be developed. The wilderness still appears just off the roadway and while pockets of development are apparent, Old Florida can still be experienced. Fingers of the Intracoastal meander along through marshes where egrets and pelicans play. Alligators sun themselves along muddy shores framed by underbrush as thick and impenetrable as a Brillo pad. The River Course was carved out of this wilderness.

The River Course got its name from its design. The eighteen holes flow through and around marshes and small ponds. Long wooden bridges separate holes offering a panoramic view of hundreds of acres of undisturbed marsh and wetlands. The silence of one hundred year old oaks draped in moss-like shrouds bear witness to a well executed approach shot that lands softly on a green carpet near their feet. The designers and builders amplified this natural experience by planting marsh grass along the edge of each hole. White sand bunkers, some a hundred yards long, offer the eyes if not a golf ball a reprieve from the expanse of green. Ponds and creeks provide a challenge to the golfer while serving as a playground to endless wildlife. Ron proudly showed Michael and Tim the clubhouse and pro shop. When the threesome drove to the first tee, the empty seat beside Michael reminded him that today's game of golf would be the last thing on his mind.

The first three holes found Ron and Tim trying to play serious golf as they had set a bet match play style. Tim was up one when they reached the fourth hole.

Michael had been eyeing his watch and it was now nine am. a full hour later than the time Jack had said he'd call.

Hole No. 4 is a long par four that is sand bunkered down the right side. It's the only hole that can be seen from the road coming into the course. The ideal tee-shot stays well left of those bunkers which effectively quash any chance of being on in two. Tim, hitting first, put the ball dead center in the fairway 270 yards out. Ron rode the left side and stayed there with a great angle to the green. Michael with his mind wandering pushed his drive into the treacherous right bunker 250 yards away.

As the two carts moved down the paved path, Ron yelled, "Don't get hurt in the dirt; see you on the green, Michael." He and Tim stayed on the cart path while Michael took a right turn Clyde toward the long sand bunker.

Michael found his ball, selected a club, and was just about to swing when he heard a noise. Before he could locate the noise it became a voice.

"Square your shoulders now and just turn the body. Don't dip that right shoulder or you'll surely dig a grave deep enough for us both." Lying on his stomach peering over the outer edge of the bunker was Jack O'Shea.

Michael was about to shout or yell but Jack put his finger to his lips.

"The fewer people who know where I am the better, Michael." "Can we talk, Jack? I need to know what's going on." "I'm staying at a motel on A1A down in Flagler Beach. I've been lying here a full half hour waiting for you to appear. After your round today, make an excuse to go to Flagler. I'm at the Topaz Motel, South of the only traffic light. Room 121 - I'll be waiting. And Michael, loosen your grip; you'll cause a hernia squeezing that tight."

Then he was gone. An alligator couldn't have disappeared into a muddy pond any slicker. Michael squinted at the roadway just beyond the sand trap and caught a glimpse of an automobile heading away from the course. He was so confused he forgot the instructions Jack had imparted and created what could have become a mass grave. After digging another shallow burial spot, he finally exited the long bunker and chipped onto the green. "Where you been?" asked Ron. "We thought maybe the golf god got yuh out there."

"Well, he did, kinda." answered a dazed Michael. Dazed was how Michael finished the round. Tim and Ron were so involved in their match that they had completely forgotten about the call that hadn't come.

They were sitting in the clubhouse having a beer when Ron finally realized that his phone hadn't rung.

All of a sudden he jumped up as if struck and exclaimed, "Oh my God, Jack didn't call!" Michael played along and expressed as much concern as his two friends.

"We better head back. The ladies will be calling if we don't beat them home from their shopping trip," said Ron.

The gals arrived home at nearly the same time as the guys. Meg made an Irish salad, with bits of bacon, lightly fried potatoes cut up, and cooled baby peas. A dressing of balsamic vinegar, mustard, and mayonnaise added the bite needed "to open the mind", as Meg expressed to all.

Michael patted his stomach. " Maybe Ellen was right; cooking is woman's work. I don't think I can follow that act." Everyone laughed.

"However, I will try. Speaking of tonight's meal I need to pick up a few things. Anyone need anything?"

"Want me to go with you, Michael?" asked Meg.

"No, that's okay. I'd kind'a like to be alone to think about Jack anyway. Where's the nearest supermarket Beth?" During lunch, they had told Meg and Beth about not getting a call from Jack so Michael's excuse to be alone seemed valid to all.

Michael started up the Volvo and spoke to it for the first time in several days. "Thanks for your patience," he said, as he patted the steering wheel. "I may need your help in a little bit so be ready girl." The Volvo responded to Michael's soothing voice and sped toward town. He decided to drive around Flagler just to place things in his mind.

Flagler Beach had small businesses across A1A from the Atlantic. The actual downtown area near the pier boasted several restaurants serving locals and tourists alike. The Flagler Beach pier which Michael and Meg had seen coming in was packed with people. Michael passed Route 100 which led to the Interstate to Palm Coast and Bunnell beyond. Music, which sounded as if it were live, was coming from the rooftop of a place called Finnegans. Michael smiled as he thought about taking Meg in to see if they served a good Irish ale.

He turned around a mile or so past the motel where Jack was staying and when it came back into view parked along the side of the road a hundred yards from the entrance. Some people were crossing to the beach while others were parking beachside, angle parked. (A busy little community,) thought Michael, a good place to remain anonymous.

Michael noted that unit 121 was an end unit. He made his way there while seeming to blend into the background. He knocked, instinctively stepping away from the door taking a look over his shoulder. The door opened slightly, Michael turned just as it closed, a chain lock could be heard. The door opened wider and Michael heard Jack bid him come in. Jack moved to the edge of the bed.

Michael grabbed the only chair in the room and straddled it directly in front of Jack. "Okay Jack, what the hell is going on?"

PART TWO

Jack was the best golfer in his high school and later in college. His understanding of the mechanical side of golf was as good as anyone on tour. Jack's problem was he had trouble feeling; his game as well as his personal life lacked the ability to trust. Jack had always found it difficult to form relationships. It had taken him four years of college golf to become close to his golf mates, Michael and Ron. Even with them he had not shared any of his inner turmoil.

When college ended Ron and Michael moved on. Jack turned further inward. He'd stayed in touch, but barely, and his journal Dannyboy became his only confidant.

No one but Dannyboy would know the depths of despair he'd experienced in college.

The first year away from his friends found Jack reaching out to reconnect with his father. He actually moved in but found no Irish stories being shared. His father had married twice since leaving Jack. Sean, Jack's younger brother, was an alcoholic who prided himself on being the local tough guy.

Jack's first full day in his father's drab apartment set the tone for what their relationship had become. Jack got up early and made coffee. He had shopped for food the day before and felt good about preparing breakfast for Mr. O'Shea. He brought in the morning paper and was reading it when his father came to the table.

"Good morning Mr. O'Shea, and how would you be liking your eggs and toast," said Jack in his feigned Irish brogue.

Mr. O'Shea looked up from the table and for just the briefest moment Jack thought he saw that old flicker of good humor enter his father's eyes. When Mr. O'Shea answered, the flicker and the dream Jack had about coming home failed to ignite.

"Don't call me Mr. O'Shea. You're a grown man. Call me Jack. I'm just Jack."

Young Jack felt in that instant the truth in the old adage - "you can't go home". It would take young Jack six months of waiting on his father, who no longer worked, to realize this. He would lose his own sense of humor and any O'Shea magic he might possess if he gave up on his own dream of playing on tour. One Sided conversations, cleaning and washing, buying food using coupons provided by the state convinced Jack that Mr. O'Shea had lost his courage, his pride, and any feeling he had ever had for his son. Jack took it as a challenge to get Mr. O'Shea back. He would try to work two dreams at once.

❧

When he asked his brother Sean what had happened to their father, Sean invited Jack to hit a pub and he'd tell him the story as he knew it.

Sean ordered two pints of ale and began by toasting his older brother. "To my brother Jack, may your past success bring future rewards in the color of Irish green." He paused, "green bucks that is." he chuckled. "I'm looking forward to you attempting to tear me away from all the success I'm having."

The two brothers clinked glasses. "Anyway about Dad, I remember when the break up came and you stayed with Mom and I went with Dad. I was looking out that window when you and dad were saying good-bye. I went out in the living room to ask Mom where something was, I saw her watching out the window too. She must have really hated dad, for I swear, she had a smile on her face. It was like Mom had to get in the last word. It was plain even then as little as I was that Dad wanted you." Sean looked straight at his brother. "Mom didn't want you. She knew you and Dad had a special bond so she just wrecked life for both of us."

Jack could hear the bitterness in Sean's voice.

"Dad treated me alright I guess, but we never kidded around. He spent a good measure of time trying to reinvent himself. I never had a baby-sitter Jack. Dad said since you had to be the man of the house for Mom that I might as well get used to being in charge here. I came home to an empty house everyday. My job was to clean and cook and do whatever else Dad left for orders. He'd come sauntering in whenever, sometimes sporting a new hair-do or a mustache or beard." Sean took a drink.

"I bet he tried twenty different jobs, never sticking to one for more than six months. He'd go to the clubs he'd joined, all kinds of Orders of this or that. He'd show me his cards. He was always proud of those clubs. I was the parent. He was the kid."

Sean took a long drink.

"He'd bring women home late at night never so I'd meet them but I'd hear them. Dad laughed with them. He'd tell them Irish stories and make stuff up like he used to do with you. He'd have them ladies doing whatever he wanted done in no time. I'd lay in bed wondering when we'd ever get to laugh together. I came home everyday like a good boy hoping Dad would notice how nice the place looked and what a good cook I'd become but he didn't." Sean ordered another beer.

"Then one day out of the blue he tells me he's getting married and wants me to stand up with him like we're good pals all of a sudden. Tells me maybe we can be a real family. I haven't even met the woman and he's talking like it's gonna be the Partridge Family. It's not like I had a say in it brother but in fact I'm thinking, maybe this broad can cook and clean and I can check out what being a kid would be like." Sean laughed out loud. He drained his glass.

"Remember, I'm 10 years old. You know if Dad had been mean to me, or was a drunk who hit me, I could have had a real good excuse to hate him but it wasn't like that." Sean ordered up another round and without Jack interrupting, he continued. "So the wedding day arrives and the happy couple are getting married in one of those clubs Dad's a member of. We get to the place, Dad puts his card in the slot thing and damn, I think I'm on a safari or something. Animal heads hanging off every wall. We go into this little room off to the side and five minutes later I got me a real Mom. Dad forgot to introduce us so it's left to the justice of the peace to let me know my new Mom's name, Mrs. Loretta O'Shea. All I ever knew her as was Mrs. O'Shea." Sean shook his head.

"Funny how you and Mom always called Dad, Mr. O'Shea. Now suddenly I had me my very own Mrs. O'Shea." Having been ignored on that last beer order, Sean whistled loudly through his teeth and motioned the waitress to bring those damn beers. Sean continued once more.

"She was nice to me though and she could cook too. Dad even started relaxing a little bit. I told him I wanted to try out for the middle school play and he said that was good. We need some good Irish actors in this country. "Show 'em you've got a good sense of humor," he said, "and you'll have 'em eating out of your hand." The waitress approached; Sean ignored her and continued.

"Well, I tried out for that play Jack and I did have them cheering for me, everyone except Dad. Seems he had club business to attend to. Mrs. O'Shea came through and I could tell she was proud of me." Sean studied his amber liquid.

"She was a little woman, thin and really quite pale most of the time. She never let on that she was sick and followed Dad wherever he wanted to go. When she finally collapsed she didn't last a month." The beer, now gone by half, prompted a question. "Is the glass half full or half empty; that is the question? Before Jack could answer Sean polished it off and gushed, It's neither brother. It's empty just like my life with Mr. O'Shea." Sean didn't miss a beat and spouted the next line.

"Dad didn't grieve, at least I never saw him, but I could tell he missed her. I became invisible in Dad's eyes. He hit the clubs even heavier if that's possible. And for the first time, he started coming home drunk." Another wave of his hand had the waitress scurrying.

"Three months later there was another Mrs. O'Shea. I didn't stand up with Dad for this one. Hell, I don't think they were standing either. Near as I can figure two drunks collided and before they could figure out how to separate, they were joined together."

Jack couldn't help laughing at Sean's biting wit.

Sean chuckled too, shook his long blond curls, and had more to say. "Dad stopped changing jobs though. He gave unemployment his full attention. The two of them spent their time in bed either hanging onto their heads or each other." Another beer arrived for Sean. Jack's third beer stood untouched.

"I just went my own way. Didn't seem to matter if anybody cleaned the house or cooked. I started hanging out with kids my age and older. I know you want to know about Dad Jack, but please understand, this is about me too." Sean was about to let Jack know who his little brother had become.

Sean told of his anger and the enjoyment he felt when hitting someone in the face. "Know what Jack? I laugh when I hit 'em! I guess I've got Dad's sense of humor after all."

Jack listened and knew that his ability to write about his feelings had probably saved a lot of faces, for he carried that same anger.

When Sean ordered a fourth beer, Jack pointed to the full one setting there and waved off any for himself. He didn't try to stop Sean but he'd had enough.

Sean seemed fine though and after a hardy swallow said "Brother Jack I haven't gotten to the good part yet. As I said, Dad and the latest Mrs. O'Shea just laid around the house half the time in their bed clothes smelling sour all day. I kept up my room, the kitchen, and the bathroom. God only knows what the rest of the house was becoming. Seemed like the only time either of them left the house was to get something to drink, or some god awful smelling fish; pickled herring I think it was. The whole house reeked of it." Sean shook his head.

"Then I met a girl at school, Jack. She had been in my first play. I started talking to her and before you know it I was hanging out at her house after school doing homework together. It was the best time I can remember. I was respectful. We fooled around you know but no serious stuff. My grades were getting better anyway. I guess you could say we were a couple. Things were better." He took a drink his blond curls taking wing as his head tipped back.

Suddenly, it sounded like the Mr. O'Shea of old had taken over Sean's body. "So wouldn't it be time for an Irish God to step in and see to it that my misery wouldn't be long interrupted,"

Sean laughed. "That would be Mr. O'Shea's way of saying that it was about this time I got into trouble at school."

Sean studied his glass. "This new kid showed up at school and, I don't know, maybe he needed to get noticed. Anyway, we were all in the cafeteria, I was sitting with Crystal, eating, flirting and all that. I had a reputation in the neighborhood of being good with my fists. But I never had a problem in school. Suddenly Crystal gets hit with a French fry. I look around and this kid says, 'Sorry that was meant for you.' If he hadn't hit Crystal, I might have let it go. Crystal even said, "Don't do anything Sean, you will get in trouble." The whole cafeteria was watching. So I tried to let my O'Shea wit end it," Sean chuckled and took a drink, remembering.

"If you can't throw any better than that, maybe we ought to change the name to Sissy fries and you can throw underhand," I thought it was a great line. Everyone started laughing, everyone except the new kid. He turned red and came right at me. I don't even remember hitting him. They say I broke a food tray over his head too." Sean shrugged, "So much for the Irish wit."

"Dad got called, came in drunk, tried to use his sense of humor on them. Nobody was laughing and I got sent home for ten days. Crystal couldn't have me over anymore so my grades dropped below sea level. Not "C" level Jack, sea level, down with the whale shit," Sean took a long pause and an even longer drink. "Nobody pressed charges, but I had to agree to see a school counselor for my anger." Jack started to respond but Sean wasn't quite finished.

"That was just middle school, Jack. Wait till you hear how Dad and I went to high school together." Sean took a long drink and sighed.

"Well brother, we're bonding anyway and I appreciate your being here. Stay tuned for the next episode."

When Jack left the bar Sean was still drinking. This was obviously what Sean did quite often. Jack went back to his father's place and went to bed.

Coming back to find his father was only part of Jack's plan. The next morning found him seeking out a place to put the second part of his plan in action. He didn't know anyone in the area but he knew how to find a golf course. With Dannyboy sitting on the seat beside him he drove out to the private course and introduced himself to the head pro.

After a few minutes of conversation and a demonstration of his golf skills, Jack had secured driving range and playing privileges. In exchange, Jack was to conduct a series of junior golf clinics twice a week. Summer in Pennsylvania can be busy for kids and hot. Jack realized if he wanted more than just a couple of kids for his lessons, evenings would probably work best. He went to the range and began hitting different clubs stopping to record all pertinent information. Standing there all by himself Jack recognized what a solitary shadow his life cast. Would there ever be anyone to talk to, except Dannyboy? (Maybe Sean,) thought Jack, (he was the younger brother he had shared a bed with way back when, maybe they could bond. It seemed Sean at least was reaching out. He'd try. He really would.)

Nobody really knew Jack O'Shea, even Michael and Ron, whom he considered his close friends. Behind that Irish wit and facade that Jack created, was a man desperate for some answers, answers to a lot of things. His Mom and Dad splitting up; what was that really about? Why he and his father had to be separated? Could Sean be saved? And Mr. O'Shea, had he found him too late? Standing there hitting long lazy drives that seemed to ride the wind, Jack understood the centerpiece of his questions concerned Jack himself. Why couldn't he form

personal relationships that would allow someone to enter his life and share his dreams.

Jack stayed at the range for four hours oblivious to the comings and goings of people around him. When he finished he was drenched with sweat. He wiped down as best he could and drove home to shower.

That night Jack went to Sean's apartment and they had dinner together. Sean was right. He was indeed a good cook and his house was clean and neat. Jack told him he really enjoyed the meal and praised his housekeeping.

Sean looked at his brother with a little lump in his throat and said, "Thanks, I needed that, about a dozen years ago." They hugged and both men moved to the sink to wash and dry the dishes as well as their eyes.

Jack suggested they stay at home and just talk. He'd like to learn more about Sean and his father.

"You are a good storyteller yourself, Sean. Though I don't believe you have created a hero that we Irishman according to legend, are supposed to emulate." Jack's Irish brogue brought a smile to Sean's face.

"I'll go to the store and get a six pack; be right back." said Sean. "Put on some music if you like. Maybe I can find something good to say in chapter two."

When Sean closed the door, Jack looked around the apartment. Maybe it was normal for a young man to have no pictures or posters on the wall but Jack didn't think so. It seemed Sean really didn't have any heroes. The kitchen, a light shade of brown, contained a small wooden table and two mismatched chairs, a stove and refrigerator, no calendar, and no clock. The living room was just as sparse-chocolate brown walls that revealed nothing. A faded sofa and a directors chair completed the seating arrangements. Jack wandered into Sean's bedroom-a bed and single dresser, no lamp, just the overhead light. Sean had a stack of blue jeans piled neatly in a corner. Jack discovered the only personal look into his brother's life the apartment held when he found Sean's music collection. An old Dan Fogleberg album sat atop a record player that was probably picked up at a lawn sale. Sean apparently listened to music when he was in bed. Sean's musical tastes were from the seventies and eighties it seemed; Early Billy Joel and the Eagles.

Maybe that was the music Sean remembered from a happier time, thought Jack. Sean's apartment seemed to reflect a young man not ready to carry any more baggage than what he was enduring now. His approach to life reflected in an apartment that screamed for color and life.

Jack laid on the bed and closed his eyes as Fogleberg's, <u>Leader of the Band</u> played. He wondered how much of his father ran through his and Sean's blood. He dozed off.

Sean returned with a large bag of peanut M&Ms and a twelve pack of beer. When Jack looked at the beer, Sean just shrugged, "Lot cheaper this way, man. What I don't drink now, I'll have for later."

Jack wondered what later meant as he opened them both a beer and sat down on the sofa to hear more of The O'Shea story, Father and Son.

"Here's to a happy ending," said Sean.

They touched cans. Sean took a long drink giving Jack an even longer look. He continued with his story as if twenty-four hours hadn't passed.

"I told you my grades were below sea level and I had to see the school shrink because of my anger. I actually came to enjoy talking with her but that came later. At first she just pissed me off. She was the first woman I remember being able to swear around without getting into more trouble. It was like she was daring me to shock her." Sean took a drink; again just as if twenty-four hours hadn't passed.

"That first session was a hoot. I was testing her and she was trying to figure out if I was testing her. I was still pretty shy around girls. This lady was maybe thirty and good looking. I was impressed. When she asked me why I hit the kid so many times and so hard, I said the first thing that popped into my head. "I just pretended he was my father."

'Have you ever hit your father?' she asked.

"Have you ever seen my father?" I said. "Of course, I've never hit my father. I love him, and besides, he's huge."

'Why do you think you said that then, pretending the other boy was your father?'

"Just something to say, I guess. Look, I don't know. I already did my ten days; can't I just go back to class?"

'Of course you can Sean, but I want to see you again tomorrow during your math class. You're going to be here to do summer school for that class anyway.'

"That was news to me. She was full of surprises. I had ten or eleven weeks of school left so every day I went to see Mrs. LeBlanc. She knew a lot more about me going in than I could imagine. First thing she does is give me a little bag of peanut M&Ms." Sean held up the bag before putting several in his mouth. He offered Jack the bag. He took a long drink washing down the sweetness and began again.

"How did you know I like chocolate?" I asked her.

'All young people like chocolate. Am I right?'

"So while I'm popping M&Ms and thinking I'm getting away with something, she's continuing to build a relationship. About the third week into our little talks, she starts asking me about my mother. I told her my mother was none of her f-ing business. My mother didn't hit that kid, I did so leave my mother out of this." More little colorful candy disappeared.

"She smiled and agreed I was probably right. Then she said if I could tell her my mother's phone number, she'd let me go back to class and I wouldn't have to come back to see her again." "You're just trying to trick me." I said.

'No trick, just give me her phone number and we are done.'

"You just want to tell her I'm in trouble."

'No, in fact I'll just ask my secretary to verify the number is your mother's. I won't even make contact. That's a promise. So, what's her number Sean?'

❧❧

Sean emptied a can and squashed it with one powerful squeeze.

Jack could feel the anger, and then Sean's features softened.

"I stuttered, stammered and stalled and then I started to cry. After that I was putty in her hands. I learned more in those eleven weeks about myself and the world and what a frigging mess people make of their lives. Probably the biggest thing I learned was that it's not easy to fix a kid." Sean opened his second beer and took a swallow.

"I mean after all those sessions, I did a bunch in high school too. Look at me. I drink too much. I don't trust anyone. I have no friends. Guys are afraid of me and pretend they don't know me. That in a nutshell, Jack, is a summation of school days to the present. Ain't I fun? Know what? I still don't know Mom's phone number. Sorry I couldn't create an Irish hero, brother.

You're the only one I know."

Sean pulled the metal tab on a third beer and said, "I love that sound," took another long drink and his eyes watered. "Are you going to stick around Jack, to save us that need saving?"

Embarrassed at his question and his show of emotion, Sean added, "I still like that chocolate too." He shoved a handful of peanut M&Ms into his mouth. "Especially with beer."

Jack knew Sean was uncomfortable letting his emotional guard down and it had happened twice this evening. "Always use the humor," Mr. O'Shea had said.

(Who's laughing now?) thought Jack, certainly no one in this family.

Eleven

Jack used his Irish wit to convince the head Pro he should get his lunches free since they didn't serve dinner in the small restaurant. "It wouldn't look good to have me fainting dead away from hunger now would it. Those children might think this golf business is hard work and they would scatter to the winds."

The Pro had laughed and called ahead to clear the way for a daily sandwich and cup of soup.

The first evening clinic arrived and twelve kids, ages seven to ten, stood looking at Jack O'Shea like he was the latest video game.

Jack found in that first hour that he was a natural born teacher. He made the children laugh by hitting golf balls from his knees. He played a game tossing a golf ball from youngster to youngster. If the ball was dropped, as he knew it would be, the child had to shout out their name three times. At that first clinic he taught them not a golf stance but an athletic stance. He taught them to form a strong base and tested their balance by playing tug of war. Jack had purchased some inexpensive

Frisbees, charged to the club of course, and using their new stance the kids threw frisbees with their left hand.

When the clinic was over he brought the kids together and sent each one home with a Frisbee. Their assignment was to set up two sticks about ten yards apart and a hundred feet away and practice throwing the Frisbee for distance and control. Jack explained to the parents what he wanted the children to do and asked for their help. When some of the parents looked at him as if he were crazy, he asked them to trust him and to come watch some of the next session.

One of the parents was a beautiful, tall, tanned lady with jet black hair. She listened as Jack explained. He was simply bowled over by her presence. When she left the range with her daughter, Jack feared he was about to make the same mistake he'd made many times before.

∾∾

Jack hadn't had any counseling like Sean did growing up. He wrote down his thoughts and actions. Sometimes those thoughts and actions had led to writing a confession to himself.

Jack didn't date in high school, but college threw him into a social scene that was prime time 24-7. A good looking athlete, he had no problem getting a date or making friends. He went through the motions of pretending to be interested in some of the girls he met. Sometimes he even dated the same girl more than once.

Sitting on the steps outside his dorm on a clear day, Jack realized he seemed to be attracted to older women. He was a freshman in college watching upperclassmen walking by. Some were couples walking hand in hand on their way to class or the library, laughing and kidding around, the older college girls throwing their hair back. Jack found himself watching only these more mature women with a guy on their arm. They looked so happy and secure.

Jack was finding it difficult to get past the awkward first stages with young women his age. He was not without emotion or needs, but nothing had clicked and he found he preferred to just watch from the sidelines as he had in high school.

Many of the freshmen guys in the dorm strutted around in the showers boasting of how they had scored big last night. An equal number of the college ladies were celebrating their own victories, sporting fraternity pins and college rings. Jack was confused. By the spring of his first year, many of the guys, who in the fall and winter had been bragging of their sexual powers, now seemed powerless. They now marched in lock-step, pinned to a girl's sweater. Back in the dorm, all he had ever heard was the scoring part. How did these relationships happen? Jack wasn't close enough to any of them to ask. In the dorm they didn't talk about how happy they were or how wonderful they felt about this new love in their life. In fact, Jack noticed the more serious a relationship, the more moody the guy.

The college seniors seemed to have it together. These guys had an eye on the prize. They would be graduating in a few weeks and many would leave for that first professional job with their college sweetheart there to support them.

Jack envied them. How did they get past all that he was seeing in his own friends?

Jack, sitting there, realized he couldn't play the game under the same rules. He wanted to enter a relationship that had already passed the awkward stage. He wanted what these college seniors had. Figuring this out about himself, and admitting it to himself, should have been the first part of solving the problem.

Maybe it would have been, with counseling, but his journal Dannyboy offered no opinion.

Over the next three years, many of Jack's affairs remained only in his mind. No harm was done except the enormous amount of guilt he felt for coveting a wife or fiancée.

Every once in a while, Jack would act on his feelings and no good would come of it. Jack's affairs started out innocently enough. Jack would see an older woman and a guy together at a function, athletic event, at the beach, or even the mall. They looked so happy. Man, I'd like a relationship like that, he'd think. Many times he would follow them at a distance and when time would allow, write to Dannyboy about it on the spot. His handwriting would change; it was like a stranger was recording his lustful thoughts.

He'd follow their car to see if they were living together or just dating. He'd look for wedding rings and record what they bought for food, a sure sign of marriage. At one level Jack knew this was wrong and felt guilt and shame. The excitement of being the unknown observer, the watcher sharing in their relationship, taking a little piece of happiness for himself seemed harmless at first. Most of the time it was.

One day walking into the college library, Jack saw an older student he'd been watching. She was alone. He went up to the stacks, found a book, and managed to make it to her table.

He was about to speak up when the woman said, "I've seen you before."

"You have?" said a flustered Jack.

"Yes, I mentioned it to Larry. I told him we were being stalked. We even made a joke about it." Jack didn't know what to say.

Suddenly the girl smiled and said, "So, are you the neighborhood stalker?"

"I, I, I, I don't think so," stammered Jack.

"Just kidding," the girl responded, "but seriously, who are you?"

Jack quickly recovered, smiled his famous Irish smile and said, "I'm Jack O'Shea."

They talked and that first conversation led to others always without Larry. Her name was Rachel; she was twenty-eight years old. She was taking classes and working part time at the mall. She and Larry had been dating for a year and a half. He worked full time in real estate and was trying to become a broker. As time went on the relationship became physical and it was obvious she was falling in love with Jack. Six months into their secret rendezvous, Rachel expressed her feelings for Jack. She explained she'd have to break it off with Larry soon. She couldn't stand deceiving him like this.

Jack had reached a hurdle he couldn't seem to get over. He laid there in Rachel's arms knowing he could not deceive her either. As long as no love had been declared, Jack kidded himself, they were simply two people enjoying one another. Jack closed his eyes, remembering his mother giving Mr. O'Shea his walking papers. When he opened his eyes, Jack told Rachel in as kind a way as possible that he didn't want a permanent relationship. Rachel was livid.

"How can you say that? We just spent the last six months together. You seemed happy. What am I, suddenly too old for you." She stood up. "You said you liked my maturity. How can you just lay there and pretend? I've shared my body and soul with you, Jack O'Shea. Oh, I hate you." Rachel stormed out of Jack's life.

She laid a guilt trip on Jack that should have shattered him. Little did she know he was, in fact, much harder on himself as Dannyboy bore witness. He learned later on that Rachel did, in fact, break up with Larry and they were both still miserable about it. Jack had destroyed them both.

After one of these affairs, Jack would vow never again and he would mean it, really mean it. His handwriting during these times was altered as if someone else committed these sins and he was left to pay for them.

Golf and his teammates were the only normal part of Jack's life. He found that if he met a girl at a party, or after a match on an away trip, he could sweep her off her feet using his Irish wit. Jack really enjoyed that part of meeting women. The problem Jack had was when he got them to the bedroom. He found he was unable to perform sexually in these situations and would be both embarrassed and angry with himself.

Jack was never mean to the girl he was with, he'd just make a joke out of it and blame it on the church. He'd say he was raised such a strict Catholic that when he was about to perform he'd imagine a long line of nuns standing on both sides of the church aisle. They all held a stick in one hand and a Bible in the other, shouting he'd have to get by them, by God. Jack could talk when he needed to but it was always surface talk. Inside he needed help. He shied further and further away from creating his own relationships but became increasingly attentive to those of other people.

By the time Jack had finished college and found his way to his father's home, he had caused the breakup of half a dozen couples. Those shattered lives were not something that he was proud of. Those relationships had, however, been the only successful sexual encounters Jack had experienced.

(Here I am,) thought Jack, (living with a father who needs help desperately and a brother who is looking to me for a way out. What am I doing? Why am I thinking about married women, a mother besides. Oh, Dannyboy.)

Jack continued to live at home and every morning would fix breakfast and lay out the paper for Mr. O'Shea. Some mornings Mr. O'Shea would appear, muttering to himself. Many times, even after a morning weight workout and a trip to the practice tee, Jack would return to find the food untouched. Jack established what could be called a daily routine. Up by six, go for a run, or lift the dumbbells he'd brought with him from college, then make coffee and shower while it was brewing. Breakfast usually consisted of a bowl of cereal, a piece of toast and half a banana. Jack used Mr. O'Shea's food stamps now that he did all of the shopping. Having to shop with food stamps troubled Jack, but he used the negative feeling it caused in him to re-establish his career goals. He would eventually provide for his father and his brother that he promised himself. Jack would get to the driving range early most days and after two or three hours he'd break for lunch. Most afternoons would find him spending three or four hours chipping, putting, and writing in his journal. Then home he'd go, for it was time to fix supper for his Dad.

The evenings that Jack wasn't doing a golf clinic, he'd usually connect with Sean and they'd talk or listen to music. Jack's presence had been good for Sean in several respects. Sean wasn't hitting the bars as often and it seemed to Jack that he was drinking less.

Jack had been home for about six weeks when his mother called. He didn't know that his mother had any idea where he was; he just knew that the call was not to exchange pleasantries.

Mr. O'Shea had fielded the call and written a caustic message that ended with a phone number. Reading the shaky writing, Jack could see that Mr. O'Shea still possessed the Irish wit deep inside, and he sensed an everlasting bitterness.

"Your Mother called or so she said.

First I've heard that voice since she left my bed.

There's precious little she had to say.

Wanted to talk to you, anyway. 817-643-2971."

Jack decided since it didn't sound like an emergency to let her wait a bit.

That evening Jack had a clinic. The kids were making rapid improvement. Jack had invited the parents to come and walk 3 holes with their child. He broke the large group up into competitors according to their progress. Two kids, followed by parent or parents, would tee off on hole one and play holes one through three. Two more would play holes four through six and so forth.

Armed with only a five-iron and a putter, they would play three holes and come in for lemonade and a chance to evaluate their round. The parents were as excited as the kids, the first opportunity to see their child play. Jack explained to the parents that they were there simply to watch, not to coach. They could keep the score card if they wished. The kids were expected to carry their own clubs and to walk with the other players. Parents were to walk behind.

All parents showed up except one. Greg, who had arrived on his bicycle, kept his head down while Jack explained the plan. Greg's head dropped even lower when the pairings were announced; he was going to have to play with a girl.

Jack sent the groups off and waited until the others dispersed before saying, "I'll be walking behind you, Greg."

Greg immediately picked up his head and gave Jack a big smile. "Thank you, Mr. Jack," he said. Jack experienced that good feeling a teacher gets when they realize they've reached a pupil. Sometimes fate has a way of dealing cards that offer a number of ways to play the hand, such as the hand Jack found himself wanting to hold on the way to the fourth tee. You see the little girl, Whitney was her name, was the daughter of the tall black haired lady Jack had already fantasized over. Jack reintroduced himself to Mrs. Houston. "Call me Carey," she said.

As the children ran ahead, Greg was already forgetting his disappointment of playing golf with a girl. Jack was forgetting his own promise.

Walking along in the coolness that was arriving as the sun moved closer to the end of its workday, Carey told Jack a little about herself. She had a husband, Wallace. They both loved golf and Carey it seemed, was an accomplished player. Wallace, who owned his own small plumbing and heating company didn't get out as often, so Carey actually defeated him nearly every time they played.

Jack found this out on the first two holes. She wanted her daughter to have the opportunity to do more with the game if she showed an interest.

"I must say Jack, I've been intrigued by your coaching methods. Did you learn them from a former coach?"

"Not really, it's just my own method of trying to keep the game simple. Over the years I've recorded my own practice sessions and in revisiting them for these clinics, I've formed my own methods of teaching to visualize and feel. Hopefully, I can teach a simple approach to the game." Jack went on to explain that every player brings his own mental approach to golf. "Many of today's best golfers have a sports psychologist." The children were putting and the two stopped talking. When both children made their two foot putt, Jack and Carey applauded. The children moved to the next tee. Jack continued.

"I can't teach the mental side. What I am attempting to offer is to virtually eliminate the physical mistakes. Someday hopefully, I can write an instruction manual that will change the way people are introduced to the sport."

When everyone arrived back at the driving range, the kids agreed they all had a great time, and the parents were enthusiastic about the results of the lessons.

Jack left that evening feeling really good about a lot of things and he kidded himself-(It's all about the golf.)

Jack got home at eight-thirty, opened a beer, recorded a few notes in his journal and with a sigh, grabbed the phone. "Hello Mother," he began, when he heard her voice asking who was calling.

"Jack, Jack is that you? I hardly recognize your voice!" "Yes, yes, Mother it's one of your boys," not responding to the guilt trip being sent across the wire.

Jack had learned a long time ago to just listen, nod his head where appropriate, and say "yes Mother" to most of their one sided conversations.

As Jack's Mother droned on about how lonely she was, how she missed her son and was he ever coming home, Jack thought back to when he was a kid and part of a whole family. He remembered his father nodding his head and saying, yes Wee bird, no Wee bird. He had to smile.

(Why did you divorce Dad?) he wondered, but still hadn't asked after all this time. (What part are you playing in my personal life?) He really wanted an answer to that.

"It's hot as hell here! The air conditioner isn't working correctly and I can't get anyone to work on it." On and on, she continued saying nothing.

Jack threw in an occasional, "Yes Mother. No Mother. That's terrible Mother," and continued to think about the past.

He remembered it was always he and his Dad at the breakfast table. Sean sometimes there but usually he was watching cartoons and slurping Fruit Loops. Where was his Mother?

She always seemed to have something else to do. (Where were you, Mom?) Jack wanted to scream.

"Yes, Mother."

"What are you doing there anyway?" she finally asked after getting through her laundry list of crises.

For the first time that he could remember, Jack had an opening and he finally threw some guilt back.

"I'm here to visit Sean. You do remember Sean. Don't you, Mom? Maybe you'd like his phone number. He doesn't seem to have yours." And for the first time that Jack could remember, his Mother seemed to have nothing to say.

"Sean is a wonderful young man, Mother, but he's got some problems and I'm going to try to help him. He seems to have some anger issues Mom. I can't imagine what he's got to be angry about, can you? And Dad is a broken man, Mom. He needs my help too. So, what I'm doing here is trying to figure out who we O'Sheas are Mom and in the process trying to straighten out my life too. But Mom, if it's really important for me to come home to motivate the air conditioner guy, I'll just drop everything and rush right there."

The sarcasm in Jack's voice made him sound like a different person. Lately it seemed Dannyboy was giving back a little emotional control to Jack and he was just learning to manage it. Jack's Mother remained speechless. As Jack ended the conversation, he gave her Sean's number and told her a call to Sean would be a clear signal that she was willing to be part of the healing process for one very screwed up group of people. Jack hung up and noticed his Dad standing in the hallway with tears in his eyes.

"Maybe I should start calling you Mr. O'Shea," his father said. The emotional freeze in both Sean and his father seemed to be melting, at least all the tears he'd witnessed in the past month, would indicate that possibility.

Over the next several days Jack found himself thinking about the future. He would have to make a break with his present living arrangements if he were going to pursue his golf career. He had precious little money and he really couldn't get a regular job because it would take too much time away from his practice sessions. On the other hand, he seemed to be making progress With Mr. O'Shea and brother Sean.

He decided he needed to talk to someone about the whole situation. He wrote to Dannyboy and laid everything out for himself. All options were explored and he set a deadline of September to get on with his own life. Once the children's golf clinics were over, Jack would head to California and start the process of getting his tour card. After getting settled, he'd ask Sean to join him, teach him to caddie, and they would live together. Jack's father was a different matter. Jack would try to coax him to get some help with his drinking and see if a sober Mr. O'Shea could still function. Once everything was written down and thought through, Jack felt much better.

Thursday evening the kids arrived once again for their clinic. After a demonstration on the range, they moved to the sand trap. Jack asked the kids if they enjoyed the beach and they all responded "yes," in unison.

"What do you like about being at the beach?" he asked.

A series of answers filled the air.

Jack heard the answer he was waiting for and exclaimed, "That's it, playing in the sand! I want you to enjoy being in sand traps. Every time you hit your ball into a trap, pretend you are having fun at the beach and just relax." Jack asked the kids to circle the bunker but to leave a gap where the ball would exit. He placed a ball in the sand, then explained:

"Most of the sand shots you'll play will not travel very far." He told them that the proper technique for getting out of a trap was as simple as an underhanded toss. Jack demonstrated by scooping lightly through the sand with his right hand picking up the ball and gently tossing it onto the green. He repeated this several times.

"Remember that first night we met and we were tossing the ball back and forth to one another? Tonight we will do something similar, only now you will be tossing the ball onto the green." One child at a time entered the sand trap. Once their results showed that they understood the concept Jack reentered the bunker with a sand wedge.

"Do you all like money?" Jack asked.

"Yes!", the kids shouted.

"Watch this. I'm going to uncover a dollar bill." Jack had placed a dollar bill just under the sand, a quarter inch or so. A golf tee marked the spot. He placed a ball on top of the hidden dollar. He then swung his sand wedge in the same manner as he had used his right hand. He brushed the sand with his club face, exposing the dollar bill. At the same time the ball rose in a lazy arc, landing gently on the green. The children gasped and murmured approval.

"Remember the fun at the beach every time you enter a trap and always try to find the money. Jack had each child try to find the money. Soon, each had a dollar in their pocket that they were to post on their bedroom wall. Jack hoped this simple demonstration would always stay in their minds.

When the parents came to pick up their children, they waved their dollar bills and Jack had to let them show their parents what they had learned.

Carey and Whitney stayed behind as the other parents moved toward their vehicles.

"That was incredible." said Carey, "If there is one part of my game I struggle with, it's my bunker play. Would you mind going over it for me and letting me give it a try?"

Jack repeated the instructions and Carey entered the bunker. Whitney giggled, quietly watching from the edge behind her Mom. Jack placed a dollar bill and a ball in the trap and Carey tried to visualize the concept. The first time she swung it was too deep an arc and the ball moved forward but did not leave the bunker.

"Remember you are at the beach," said Jack, "and you are playfully tossing sand underhanded. Find the money."

This time Carey swung smooth and light. The ball landed on the green, gently rolling toward the flagstick.

Whitney clapped and shouted, "Good for you, Mom. Keep practicing and you'll be as good as me."

All three laughed. Jack gave Carey a hand out of the bunker and they headed to the parking lot.

"Would you be able to give me a complete lesson sometime?" asked Carey. "I like the way you make everything so simple. Of course, I would pay you for your time."

"Well, sure, I guess I could," said a flustered Jack.

"What about Daddy? He needs a lesson, too." said Whitney. "I'd be glad to Mrs. Houston. Just let me know when." "I will check with Wallace, and please call me Carey.

Jack left the course and went to Sean's apartment. Sean reheated his special spaghetti sauce for Jack. The two brothers sat at the kitchen table, sipped cheap wine, and just talked.

Jack told Sean of his plan to leave in September. He also invited him to come to the course to begin to learn the role of a caddie. Sean was as excited as Jack had ever seen him. He promptly proposed a toast then slowly put down his glass of wine.

"What's wrong?" asked Jack.

"Nothing's wrong," said Sean, "but if you're going to give me this opportunity, I'm damn sure going to attempt it sober." "We're going to have a great time Sean. I know I can make the tour, having you with me will just make it sweeter."

When Jack went home that night at least one part of his plan had come together. How to tell Mr. O'Shea, knowing his vulnerability, was going to be very difficult.

Jack lay in bed in the dark, his thoughts turning to Mrs. Houston. Surely he could control this situation and strictly limit their relationship to golf. Besides, she was probably happily married and little Whitney was a sweetheart. (Wouldn't want to cause any problems for the Houston family.) No siree, Jack.

Twelve

By the beginning of August Jack was down to his last four golf clinics. He would hold a little tournament for the kids the last two weeks they met. Mrs. Houston hadn't been to the last several clinics and Whitney had arrived with the parents of one of the other girls. Jack pretended to himself that he didn't miss seeing her but on this night when she showed up his heart began racing. The clinic was again successful. This week Jack had the kids hitting cardboard boxes with an old club he had provided. The idea was to drive hard through the impact zone. Jack demonstrated, and the box, packed with old newspaper and covered with duct tape, absorbed the blow and moved forward several feet. He explained that the critical part of the swing is at impact and follow through.

After half an hour of hitting the box, the students moved to the driving range. Jack again emphasized the point of impact and the students hit balls. For fifteen minutes he watched the students show they could drive through the ball. Jack asked the kids to gather in front of the outdoor tables at the clubhouse. "I am very proud of you. Now I am going to end your summer vacation early. The kids groaned.

Jack laughed. "I am going to be your teacher for a bit. I would like you to write about what you have learned." Each golfer was given a piece of paper and asked to write about their golfing lessons. Jack had written down a topic sentence for each of the weeks they had met. He wanted the concepts they had been taught further planted in their minds. He also wanted to know what the kids had learned, as much for himself, as for them. Introducing them to the idea of keeping notes might prove as valuable as the lessons they were getting. They might not stick with golf, but if they learned to record events in their life to refer to and to learn from them, it could prove useful. (Dannyboy might just be chuckling to himself,) thought Jack.

Jack asked the parents of the younger kids to help them record their ideas. As they handed in their papers, Jack reminded them of next week's tournament and told them they had helped him learn a lot as well.

Mrs. Houston and her daughter Whitney were the last to hand in the assignment. Jack tried not to read anything into what appeared to be planned but found his heart racing nonetheless.

Carey said she was really pleased with Whitney's progress. "Well, she's a bright, athletic little girl. I hope she sticks with it. She could be very good."

Small talk continued. Whitney asked if she could hit some balls.

"Sure," said Jack "if it's alright with your Mom." Whitney wandered over to the driving range.

"I haven't seen you here for the past several weeks."

"No, my husband has been doing a job out of the city and I wanted to be home when he gets in. He's finished with that job now so he gets home a lot earlier."

"What about the golf lessons for you two? I'm leaving in a few weeks so we'd better set a time soon."

"My husband is really busy. I'm afraid it'll just be me if that's alright."

Jack was able to nod his head and manage a - "Sure that's fine."

Whitney was going to be at camp with her grandparents for several days next week. They settled on Monday at nine am. As Jack drove home, he was still trying to convince himself that it was all about the golf. He didn't write Dannyboy of his plans. Somehow seeing the plan in writing would have forced him to be honest with himself.

The rest of the week flew by and when Monday morning dawned bright and sunny, Jack found himself in a light mood. He was at the course early, hitting through every club in his bag. He had a change of clothes to put on after showering in the men's locker room.

At promptly nine am., Carey Houston approached Jack who was sitting in a golf cart with his clubs on the back.

"Good morning," said Jack. Kidding he added, "Houston we have lift off; we are in control."

Carey Houston looked radiant in a sleeveless pale yellow top with a small familiar swoosh on the shoulder. Dark blue shorts with a bright yellow belt and matching visor would turn heads on and off any course. When she smiled, Jack forgot what she was wearing, and maybe most importantly, forgot that it was all about the golf.

They drove to the parking lot in Jack's golf cart where he retrieved her clubs from the trunk of an SUV and loaded them onto the cart. They stopped to get bottles of water and moved to the first hole.

Small talk dominated the conversation until Carey was ready to tee off.

"I want to watch you play the first couple of holes," said Jack. "I would like to see what your natural swing looks like using different clubs. Then we'll stop to evaluate your impressions and compare them to mine, ok?"

"Sounds right to me," answered Carey. "I prefer not to talk when I play, just really focus. So I'm not ignoring you, I'm just in a zone."

Jack was in a zone of his own as he watched Carey send a drive two hundred yards down the right side of the fairway. Jack's zone had nothing to do with Carey's smooth graceful swing or the follow through and good balance she showed after each shot. Jack was imagining Carey at his side on a drive of a different sort along a country road. The wind was blowing her jet black hair in a hundred different patterns, each framing a gorgeous long thin face with full lips and a nose created to complete a perfect silhouette.

The golfer in Jack unconsciously took note of what Carey was doing with each shot, but the conscious Jack could only see those long well-muscled legs and perfect butt when Carey tightened her lower body to execute a shot.

By the third hole Jack had seen enough, too much really. His heart was racing. His imagination was running wild and his promise long forgotten.

Jack was in trouble. No words had been spoken but Jack was sure he had found the perfect match. This time it was different he assured himself. He'd always been the pursuer. This time everything had just happened naturally.

When they pulled the cart to the side of the fourth tee, Carey Houston turned to face Jack and said, "So what do you think?

Can you help me get better?"

Jack had to shake his head several times, a trick he'd learned from his college buddy Michael, to bring himself back to reality. When he looked blankly at Carey, she repeated the question. Jack's golf knowledge took over. He talked about shortening her back swing about half a foot. What his golfing mind had recorded was a slight fluctuation in the downswing into the ball. Mrs. Houston was getting her back swing well beyond parallel making it impossible for her to drop into the same slot repeatedly. The result was a beautiful drive and iron shot about sixty percent of the time. During the other forty percent, the club face was making contact with the ball at a slightly different angle away from the sweet spot at the middle of the club face. On those occasions the ball would be topped, pushed, pulled, or popped up.

At the end of eighteen holes, a forty percent failure rate translated to fifteen possible mis-hits with varying results. The teacher in Jack took over and explained to Carey, that with one minor change in her swing she could realistically shave five strokes off her eighty-four average round score. Jack had also noted that she was slightly out of square on her set up.

"First things first let's get you square to the ball. He told her to stand over the ball with her toes and shoulders parallel to her target line. Jack took a club and laid it down directly in front of Carey's toes and asked her to step back and join him behind the barrel of the club. Carey was at least six degrees off to the right of her target line. Jack showed her how to sight in a line by standing over the ball with her feet together to establish a parallel position and then to slide her right foot

back. To check for square Jack had her hold a club across her thighs and take another look at her feet and target line. Carey received instant feedback from this drill and Jack knew he'd established the trust he'd need to make the big change shortening her long swing. She played three more holes and her setup became very natural. She actually gained a little distance and that got her excited.

"If I don't learn anything else today Jack, the lesson has been worth it."

Jack, still in his teacher mode using his Irish brogue said, "A lesson half learned is money half earned. I'll be expecting full payment before the sun sets on this walk in the woods." Carey Houston looked Jack full in the face and returned the volley. "Well, Mr. Jack, I'm enjoying this particular walk in the woods and the sun shows no sign of setting just yet so let's have at it."

Jack laughed and knew he'd met his match and what a match it would be he thought. At that moment, Jack thought anything was possible.

He suggested that they break for lunch back at the club. He needed to pick up several props for the next part of the lesson anyway. They grabbed a sandwich at the little restaurant and returned to the golf cart which Jack promptly moved to the shade of a large maple tree. Between bites of his tuna on rye and sips of bottled water, Jack laid out the next part of the lesson.

"What I'm going to ask of you Carey, is do you really want to take your game to the next level? It's going to require you to be willing to accept the possibility of higher scores for a while. If you say yes, I would suggest that you not compete for a month or so, just practice. If you do compete, you may lose some matches to people you have beaten in the past. Can you accept that?" "I… I think so but how do I know it's going to work?" "Well, let's try a little experiment and then I'll tell you about a real risk taker."

Jack got off the cart and placed a leaf on the grass in front of him. He took a five iron and began a short backswing then pulled the club under the leaf. Jack repeated this swing again and again-the leaf rising and falling as the club face kept it dancing. "The concept that I want you to understand Mrs. Houston, I mean Carey, is to get the club face to hit the leaf, or ball, the same way every time. The further that I take back the club, the less chance I'm going to repeat it consistently. I want to shorten your backswing by six inches. It's going to feel awkward but if you decide to do this and are willing to work at it, you will be the envy of every woman at your club and beyond."

"I like the sound of that, but poor Wallace probably won't play with me. I already beat him rather badly I'm afraid."

"Well, you'll have to find other ways to make him feel special. I'm just the teacher."

Carey Houston smiled, "Guess I can practice that too. Wallace is a go-getter and he's taking on a new line of hi-tech furnaces for the business. He's gone to Kansas City, Missouri for a week of special training. Wallace says this new furnace is going to change the way we heat and cool our homes and he wants to be on the front burner, no pun intended," she laughed. "Where did you say your daughter Whitney was? Jack's mind was racing.

"She's spending the week at camp with her grandparents. That's right, she won't be at your clinic this week."

Jack had all he could do to keep his mind on the lesson as the possibilities of a week with Carey had his imagination running rampant.

Shaking his head to get refocused, Jack told Carey about the beginning success Tiger Woods experienced on the PGA tour. He had just won a major, The Masters, by eight or ten strokes. He celebrated by completely taking his swing apart and putting it back together, losing some consistency, and possibly some tournaments in the process.

"Why would someone as successful as Tiger Woods do that?" asked Carey.

"Tiger, and probably only Tiger knew his clubs were not making the consistent contact with the ball that he wanted. Tiger understands that he probably has the strongest mental toughness the game has ever seen. Knowing that made it even more important for him to reevaluate the mechanics of his swing. Remember when my clinics began that I told you the mental side of the game rests with the individual. The mechanics of the game I feel comfortable tinkering with. Anyway, Tiger is engaged in an ongoing project to create the flawless swing. So really Carey, there is no risk. It's a guaranteed success story if you want it badly enough."

"Ok, you sold me. I'm in your hands. Where do we begin?" said Carey.

"Actually, we need to get you in front of a full length mirror, several mirrors at once if we can manage it." said Jack. "By the way, I don't need a full length mirror to tell you what a beautiful woman you are."

"Why thank you for that kind sir" Carey gave a little curtsy and they both laughed.

Jack sent Carey to the ladies locker room to borrow a mirror while he borrowed one from the pro shop and another from the men's locker room. They took the mirrors to the range where Jack propped them up with bag stands.

"I want you to be able to watch your swing. If I had a video recorder I would break it down in slow motion but I think this will work. We are not really trying to change any mechanics, just shorten your backswing.

Jack had Carey stand facing the flags on the driving range. He adjusted the mirrors slightly so that she could watch her back swing without changing her posture. One mirror allowed her to watch her backswing and another her follow through. (That third mirror probably wasn't necessary, but seeing four Carey Houston's at one time is not a bad thing,) mused Jack. He watched Carey get comfortable with the idea of seeing herself swing a club.

After several swings, Jack told Carey to stop her back swing when she reached the very end of her take away. It was clear that she was beyond parallel and in fact, she said she could see her club head perched just below her left eye.

"The problem," said Jack, "is bringing that club back into the proper swing path on your return to the ball. You do a remarkable job of getting it right as often as you do. Let's try something that will give you immediate physical feedback and shorten your swing in the process. On your take away, let's tuck your left arm a little closer to your chest. Feel the muscle part of your left arm rub lightly across the material of your shirt, and on the down swing your right arm will reverse the process. Try this a couple of times, back and forward, back and forward, back and forward. Can you feel the material?" Carey said she could. "Again, back and forward, back and forward. That's good. Now this time, stop at the end of your backswing. There, can you see your club head now with your left eye?" "No, I can't." said Carey.

"Try it a few more times. Can you feel your triceps brushing your shirt?"

"Yes, I can."

"Ok, now let's hit a few seven iron shots. The target is the flagstick one hundred and fifty yards out. Hit ten shots and then we'll talk. Remember, establish your target line using the new set up we worked on and then feel your body lightly keeping contact. Let's see what happens."

When Carey just let the swing happen, the ball was on line and her distance was good.

"Don't think about anything except the physical feedback," said Jack and soon the swing took on a life of its own. "Very good, you're a quick learner. Let's move to the five iron. As the clubs get longer, the margin of error is greater, so it's important that you believe in your swing. Remember to brush your shirt with your upper arms. Good. Great!"

Carey was excited. Jack was too.

"Ok, here's the first big test. Grab your driver and aim at the blue flag stick on your right two hundred and fifty yards out. We're looking for direction right now, a consistent shot pattern. Take ten shots. Let's try for eight out of ten online, that would be a fifty percent improvement."

Carey took to the new swing and indeed reached the goal of eight out of ten shots in her first effort. "That's incredible! I don't think I lost any distance either!"

"If you practice you'll actually gain about fifteen yards," said Jack. "Your timing will be better. Timing, and solid contact translates into more opportunities to be on the green in regulation, putting for birdies and tap-in pars. You can shave five strokes off your score by making these two changes." Jack started whistling.

"When you master this part of your game, I'll show you how to put music into your putting," said Jack. "Music into my putting, are you kidding?"

"Not really," said Jack, "but that's for another day. Let's take this new swing out onto the back nine and see what harm we've done."

Jack watched as Carey went through the new setup and swing. At first she seemed tentative and after a poor execution would look back at Jack with an exasperated expression.

Jack encouraged, "Trust your body and the feedback system we've developed." Jack the teacher gave a lecture. "If we would

take our driving range swings, when it didn't mean being out of bounds, in a bunker, or in the rough and use that swing on the course, we'd all be better players. The minute that it means something the average golfer tenses and his swing changes." Jack assured Carey they would not be scoring the back nine, "So just relax and let the swing do its thing."

By the fifteenth hole Carey was striking the ball better, she looked back at Jack, only this time with a look of satisfaction. Jack nodded his head in agreement.

On the last hole Jack said, "Ok, let's play a one hole match. This is a par five. I'll give you one stroke. The loser buys the winner a beer. You game?" "What if we tie?" asked Carey.

"We Irish believe that all ties should be settled with a wrestling match," kidded Jack. "So unless you're willing to muddy that beautiful outfit, I suggest you go for the win."

Carey laughed out loud, "You Irish seem to be a dangerous group. Should I be fearing for my safety, Mr. Jack?"

"Fear not Lassie, the sight of a beautiful woman most often finds we Irishmen in the mud, wrestling with ourselves." Again Carey laughed, "You hit first Jack, since I seem to have an advantage in both distance and gender on this hole."

Jack chuckled, set himself, and hit a beautiful hook shot that started out on the right, and landed on the left side of the fairway leaving him with a two hundred and twenty-five yard second shot.

They rode to the ladies tee as Carey remarked on the beautiful drive Jack had just executed.

"How do you do that?" she asked.

"There are things even I can't explain," answered Jack.

Carey hit a drive straight down the middle of the fairway. Jack exclaimed how compact her swing looked.

The eighteenth hole was a four hundred ninety yard par five that dog legged slightly to the right. The only trouble spot was a small pond, just to the right of the green itself.

Jack hit his second shot landing the ball on the fringe approximately thirty-five feet from the pin.

Carey Houston applauded. She had one hundred ninety yards to the pin, and she knew she'd have to really bust a three wood to get close. As she set herself, Jack was tempted to say something to relax her but he thought better of it. He could see she was a competitor; she would want no consideration while the bet was on. She squared herself, took a deep breath, and hit a magnificent shot that trickled onto the edge of the green about fifteen feet from the pin. Jack found himself clapping and Carey was so excited that she gave him a big hug.

"That's the best fairway wood I've hit in years!" That ball jumped off my club! I can't believe it!"

Jack reluctantly let Carey out of his arms. He simply said, "It's the power of love." No follow up was added.

Jack had a slightly uphill rather long putt. As he walked around the green checking distance and line, he thought, (Should I try to make this putt or two putt for a tie? Would Carey really go for a beer? Would she be upset if she had to buy the beer?) Jack set himself over his putt. It all became clear. He began whistling, and calmly ran his ball into the center of the cup. Carey shook her head in amazement, "Looks like you don't want to wrestle, Mr. Jack." Jack smiled.

Carey did her own assessment of line, distance, and break. She stood over her putt, then backed away for one more look. She reset herself, took a deep breath, and put her ball right on top of Jack's.

Jack began a hearty laugh, a belly laugh, that seemed to echo off the trees. Carey chuckled, then she too became giddy and soon both had tears running down their cheeks.

Maybe it was the stress release Jack had needed for so long, someone to laugh with. Whatever it was, it took on a life of its own for just the briefest of moments and it was infectious. When they finally quelled all but the occasional giggle, they wiped away their tears. The ride back to the club house was reflective, for each was carrying away a different memory of the afternoon.

"Well, what do we do about the beer?"

Jack removed their clubs from the cart. "Unless you want to see me all covered with mud, tearing at my ears and eyes, let me suggest that we put the beers on hold and place another bet." suggested Jack.

"What's the bet? Do I have a fifty-fifty chance? Is this a double or nothing, Mr. Jack?"

"I'll wager if I ask you to dinner you'll say no," said Jack, "and yes, you do have a fifty-fifty chance. It's either yes or nothing, I suppose."

Carey Houston took a long look at Jack O'Shea, the teacher, the golfer, the handsome young man. She had thoroughly enjoyed the day. She said yes to the bet if Jack would let her cook the dinner. Jack agreed and when the SUV left the parking lot, he was left to wonder if maybe this time, there really could be a happy ending.

Jack drove home to shower and change and even the dismal surroundings of his father's home could not dampen his spirits. Mr. O'Shea was quietly watching TV and managed a weak wave of his hand as Jack entered humming to himself.

He asked Mr. O'Shea if he'd like him to prepare a meal. The ice had apparently not all melted from Mr. O'Shea's emotional state, for he didn't answer, he merely shrugged his shoulders. "Supper will be ready if you want it. All you need to do is turn on the burner." Jack made a quick spaghetti sauce and cooked the pasta. His Dad could eat it hot or reheat it later.

Jack stopped by Sean's apartment but he hadn't arrived home. He wrote a note and since it was still too early to go to Carey's house, he put on a record and closed his eyes for a minute. The next sound Jack heard was Sean coming up the stairs and noisily opening the door.

"Hey Jack, what are you doing here? Did I wake you? You look startled. Wanna beer?" Sean washed his hands in the kitchen sink. His job at a local garage left him feeling his hands were always dirty.

None of Sean's questions seemed to require an answer. Jack had been in such a deep sleep that two hours had passed like a flash. He checked his watch and jumped to his feet. This time it was Sean who was startled. Jack mumbled something about being late for a very important date and tore down the stairs. It was only after Sean closed the door and found Jack's note that he realized Jack indeed had a date.

"I guess I will have to eat alone tonight. On second thought, maybe I'll go see what the old man is having for supper." Sean nodded his head, living alone had him talking aloud. "Jack with a date, this O'Shea family may make it yet."

Jack followed the directions Carey had given him. The golf course loomed on the left and he noted that the closer he got to the course, the better fed the houses appeared. They certainly were larger. The lawns and flowers too were more expansive and the pools appeared to be a part of the design rather than an afterthought.

Carey's home overlooked the ninth green, far enough from automobile and cart traffic to offer a silent postcard of life as it could be. A small pond surrounded by flowers served as a boundary to what had to be at least a two-acre lawn.

Pulling into the drive, he noted the house was well back from the street. The lives of the Houston family could be shared with or shielded from the rest of the world on their own terms. Jack exited his vehicle and looked at the Houston home. He was stunned by the simplicity of design that allowed the house to fit the property and not dominate it. Built on one floor, the home allowed the mixture of maples, oaks and softwoods to frame its white Cape Cod style. The front of the house cleverly hid a twelve foot drop in elevation, which allowed for a daylight basement with a screened porch on the back. That basement housed a game room complete with bar, fireplace, comfortable sofas and chairs, and a large screened TV. Several daybeds and rocking chairs on the screened porch offered a view of the ninth hole that brought the entire scene into focus. Clearly, this was where the family spent their leisure time.

Carey answered the door, shook Jack's hand, and took him on a tour of the house. Every room in the home reflected her personal touch.

"How long have you lived here?" asked Jack when they were comfortably seated in the rockers drinking a beer that settled nothing.

Jack had brought a six pack of individual brands since he didn't know Carey's preference.

"We've lived here for about a year. Wally and I used to look at this property from the ninth green and imagine what it would be like to turn the picture around and look at the golf course from these woods. That was eight years ago when the business was just getting started. We'd come out here to play on Saturday evenings." Carey smiled. "We didn't belong to the club back then but after five pm on weekends the locals could enter a lottery to be part of Saturday evening foursomes." She sighed as she remembered the lean years.

"The plumbing and heating business sounds kind of bluecollar, but it's amazing what four years of seventy hour weeks can accomplish. Wally and I worked the business alone for the first two years. In the third year we hired two part timers, then two full timers. We bought three vans, did some creative advertising, and suddenly it was blue skies." Carey picked up a picture of daughter Whitney, and holding it on her lap, continued. "Whitney spent the first three years of her life playing with pvc pipe and being hugged and kissed by at least a thousand men in blue shirts. I finally got time off for good behavior but Wally can't seem to get enough of it. He could work just part time now that we've got great people, but he just can't let go of it." Jack remained the listener, content just to be here.

"Anyway, one evening we were playing golf out here and Wally said, 'What would our house look like from here if we owned that land?' I thought he was kidding, but obviously he was not. He is a smart businessman. He knows all the building contractors and he found out who owned the property. There were thirty-five homes to be built in this cul-de-sac, all five acre lots. This was the best piece of property. Wally contracted all of the plumbing and heating for those homes." She chuckled. "He plumbed and heated all of those homes himself for the cost of materials. He received this five-acre lot with two hundred feet of golf course frontage in return. It took him a full year. He was out of the house before daylight. He would work for several hours at one of these homes, then go to the business. After a full day there, he'd go back to those homes being built and continue working till nine in the evening. Whitney and I barely saw him that year. It was like he had challenged himself to run a marathon or something. Wally worked every night except Saturday. Saturday nights we'd grab Whitney and our clubs and play golf until we'd get to the ninth hole. Wally always stopped there, as if drawing strength from those woods." Carey paused. "Quite a story isn't it Mr. Jack." Jack took a sip of his beer and nodded.

"About six months into that year we arrived at the ninth hole, looked at our property, and could see this ridge for the first time. That's when Wally told me to start designing a home that could sit here on that ridge. I started bawling like a baby. Whitney couldn't understand why I was crying. She thought that I was upset that someone had cut some of our trees. She started crying too and pretty soon we were all baying at the moon that had risen over what we named Wailing Ridge. That got us all laughing." She laughed, recalling Wally naming it that night, while the tears were flowing.

"How did you happen to choose a cape style? That style dominates coastal Massachusetts."

"Is that where you were raised?" asked Carey.

"Yes, for a time anyway but not on the coast however. Anyway, how did you come to design a cape home?"

"I've always been intrigued by the ocean. In pictures the homes standing above the shoreline looking out over the endless water seem to radiate strength. A port in the storm of life, I suppose." Carey became reflective.

"When I stood on this ridge, I actually placed a step ladder there. I climbed to where I thought I'd be standing when looking out over this sea of green. I knew then and there that I wanted a cape. I designed it with the idea that from the golf course our house would look like a port in a storm."

"Why didn't you point it out this morning from the ninth green?" asked Jack.

"I wasn't sure how it would be received. I didn't want to leave an impression that I was bragging about my home, or money, or anything else. Besides, I didn't expect to have you here. It was that damn bet." laughed Carey.

"It's a beautiful home and I love your taste in decorating-simple but very effective."

"Thank you, actually I'm doing some decorating work for several of the contractors. It's given me a lot of confidence. She looked directly at Jack as if seeing him for the first time. "How old are you Jack, if you don't mind my asking?" "I'm twenty-four going on fifty. Why do you ask?"

"You have old eyes. Oh, I don't mean that in a bad way." said Carey tapping Jack's arm. "They say the eyes are the gateway to a person's soul. So I guess I mean that you look like you have a very old soul."

Jack smiled and in his exaggerated Irish brogue answered, "I was there when Ireland glistened as an emerald across the sea."

Jack related the history of Ireland as he had heard it from Mr. O'Shea. He finished with his own brief history told in as humorous a way as possible. Jack cleared his throat when he finished and asked Carey if she'd like another beer.

Carey sat there with a sad smile on her face. She tried several times to speak but seemed unable to decide where to start. Finally she rose and said, "I'll get you a beer, Mr. Jack. If you ever give up that game of golf, you should become a storyteller. Your way with words is an incredible gift, and should you write them down, you'd surely have a best seller."

Jack said nothing. He'd never intended to lay his life story out like that; only Dannyboy had ever let Jack bare his soul. Carey returned with two different brands of beer and asked Jack which he'd like. Jack looked at the Killians and the Heineken. "I'll have the Heineken. I think I've spent enough time in Ireland for one evening." Jack chuckled, still uncomfortable with himself. Carey asked Jack why he had brought six different kinds of beer.

"To tell you the truth, I wasn't sure which kind you'd like. At first I was going to get domestic beer, but then the Irish in me took over. The Irish see a story in everything, beer included." Jack looked exasperated. "There I go again with the Irish, but I can't help remembering those last words my father told me. That all I was left with was a sense of humor and a creative mind." Jack stood. "Recently, I've come to realize that I was left with more than that. I don't have a recognizable family, at least not by most standards, but I do have a beginning, roots if you will, that stretch across the sea to the Emerald Isle. He sighed and took a drink. "So, Jack O'Shea is an Irishman first, and proud of it, just like Mr. O'Shea was way back when."

Jack raised his beer and toasted the Irish wherever they may be tonight, whatever their lot in life. "May their dreams survive; mine have." finished Jack.

"Do you have dreams?" asked Jack, a blinding light suddenly filling his mind.

"Yes, I guess I do though I'm not sure I have any right to them when I look around at all I have. I have a wonderful family. My daughter is an absolute angel, and Wallace has given so much of himself to provide us with this lifestyle. I'm not sure my dreams should even be voiced."

"Dreams are like half-filled balloons," said Jack, the light in his head beginning to show the way. "Try squashing them with rational thought and they just raise a bump somewhere else. Besides, a half-filled balloon won't rise or ever take the shape intended."

"You really should be a writer, Jack. Your use of imagery is magical."

"Don't change the subject, Carey Houston. Close your eyes and dream."

Carey Houston did just that. "My dream has to do with golf. I'd love to feel some of the excitement of a final round and have some ownership in the outcome. It's too late for me personally. I guess that's one reason I hope my daughter grows to love this sport as much as I do. I'd love to be able to watch her compete, set goals, and live dreams that might see her there on that last eighteen holes with a chance to win. I'd like to have a piece of that feeling." She opened her eyes. " I guess that's the shape of my balloon, Mr. Jack."

"Do you love your husband?" asked Jack, as he suddenly sat bolt upright with a wild look in those timeless eyes Carey had commented on.

"Well… well… of course, I do. Wallace is a wonderful husband. Why are you asking me that question, Jack?"

"Because I've had an epiphany."

"I thought it was a Heineken." laughed Carey, "Seriously, you had a what?"

"You know, a breakthrough. It's like the clouds just parted and I can see the future."

"Are you about to tell me another story Jack? You still haven't answered my question."

"The future I see has everything to do with both you and your husband."

"Ok, enlighten me, Mr. Jack, but remember I don't have your ability to see the future so go slowly and lay it out in simple terms."

"Alright, here goes. It may sound complicated at first, but hear it through to the end and please don't interrupt, no matter how much you'd like to. If I stop, I may not be able to understand this myself. Dannyboy might but not me."

Carey started to open her mouth to ask who Dannyboy was, but Jack put his finger to her lips.

"When I came here tonight, I was hoping you didn't love your husband. I was hoping we'd have a torrid love affair that might last and no one would be hurt. I've hurt a lot of people over the years. I'll tell you about that some other time." Jack looked around the room. "I've never actually spent time in a woman's home until tonight. All these things you have are here because you and your husband worked together to get them. They are more than possessions; they are your common bond." Jack got up and looked out into the darkness. "The view from this house is a shared view. I suddenly realized how selfish I am, and how shallow my needs have become. When you shared your dream about helping your daughter find the limelight, your own satisfaction coming through her success, you completed my thought. I suddenly saw both of our balloons rising over this very ridge. I want you to love your husband, and I want him to trust that love because I want to become part of this family." With that said, Jack took a long deep breath of air and an even longer pull on his beer.

Carey, thinking Jack had finished, started to reply, having no idea what she was going to say.

Jack stopped her once more, with his finger to his own lips, he continued. "What I mean by family is your business family.

I want you and Wallace to invest in me, in my future, and in your dream. I'm going to make it on the PGA Tour, Carey, of that I have no doubt. I'd like you and Wallace to be my business managers. You'd get to come watch some of the tournaments, meet some of the players, and be part of the whole scene. What do I get out of it? It's expensive to get my tour card. I have to start out on mini tours that don't pay much, and I have to eat and have a place to stay. When I make it on the Tour, you'll be paid back with a percentage of my winnings. You and Wallace can check out what the going rate of return is. I trust you. I know this can work for all of us. I'll even throw in free golf lessons for your family. It's all I have to offer except my word."

Carey sat back. She studied this young man with the eyes of time, closed her own eyes, and when she had it right, she began. "Jack O'Shea, I should be outraged that you came here to seduce me but instead I'm flattered. If I didn't love Wallace like I do, maybe I'd even be interested." Jack started to speak, this time Carey put her finger to his lips. " I've watched the gentle way you have with children. You are a good man. It's obvious you understand the game of golf, Mr. Jack; it seems it's in the game of life you have some growing up to do. Perhaps that has begun tonight. I guess if I can add value to a piece of real estate, I ought to be able to help you choose a little more wisely in different areas of your life." Another shush allowed her to finish. "As far as my dreams go, let's take one step at a time. If Wallace and I can agree on this and I can't guarantee he'll see the promise in you that I do, maybe we'll add air to my own balloon, a little at a time."

The two remaining beers, one from Mexico and the other from the great state of Missouri, were put on ice for another time.

Looking back once more at the house on Wailing Ridge, Jack stood with his car door open. Carey Houston was right on. This home would serve as a port in any storm. This home had a solid foundation. He felt he'd arrived at a safe harbor in his own personal life too.

He sat at his father's kitchen table telling Dannyboy about the evening. He could feel a lightness in his writing that had been missing. There was no rosary wrapped around the pencil, trying to wring every ounce of guilt out of each word he recorded.

Jack slept the sleep of the dead, and it was nearly noon when he heard Mr. O'Shea banging around in the kitchen. He stumbled out into the midday light and was surprised to see Sean fixing lunch, not his father.

"What are you doing here?" asked Jack.

"I came over for supper with Pop last night," answered Sean. "After tasting your spaghetti sauce, Pop said maybe I could come in from time to time and check to see if you was trying to poison him."

Jack laughed, a little offended, but glad to see his brother in the house. "Sean, the Irish always have a plan to bring families back together. My plan worked; effective don't you think? "

Sean laughed, "You sure have Pop's story telling skills. Any other nationality would call it the ability to throw bull shit, but we Irish celebrate it as a sign of a highly developed mind. "True that," said Jack, "and if last night's true story bears fruit, we'll have a lot to celebrate."

Sean looked to Jack to explain but Mr. O'Shea joined them just then. Lunch was a tuna sandwich and pickled beets, warmed with a little beer for seasoning. There was laughter during that lunch and Mr. O'Shea even managed a grin or two as he listened to his two very different sons spar.

❧

September arrived and Jack acted on the commitment he'd made to himself. It was time to move on toward his goal. Things had tidied up a bit at home. Sean was spending more time with Mr. O'Shea and he too now seemed to be drinking less. On the Saturday that Jack decided to leave, Carey Houston and her husband Wallace planned a little going away party. Jack's father and Sean were invited as well as the boys and girls from the golf clinic.

The O'Shea's traveled together in Jack's Mustang and, upon entering the Houston driveway, were surprised to see a large banner hanging over the main entrance. A white banner with emerald green shamrocks at both ends read - Mr. Jack, The World Will Know Your Last Name When You Come Back.

Jack's eyes watered a bit while Sean and Mr. O'Shea swelled with pride for a brother and son who had come to rescue them. All the children gathered around Mr. Jack, as he was known to them, and while most of them did not know Jack was trying to make it as a professional golfer, they loved him as a teacher.

When the children went off to play some games, the adults settled on the screen porch to a catered buffet luncheon. Once the twelve adults had moved through the buffet line and were settled at tables on the porch, Carey closed the glass doors and tapped her lemonade glass to get everyone's attention.

"For those of us who have recently come to know Mr. Jack, this is both a celebration, and a day to sadly say so long for now. Mr. Jack, our children learned so much from you. That final mini-tournament you arranged allowed us to see that golf, when explained correctly and simply, is more than just a game. Our children learned honesty, patience, the excitement of competition, and the fun at the end of the match. The little tags you wrote out with a personal message, a reminder of how they had succeeded during those weeks, will always be on their golf bags as they continue to play." Everyone applauded.

"Finally Mr. Jack, Wallace and I can't thank you enough for helping us realize that we both needed to dream again. So, Wallace has a check for five thousand dollars that will enter your checking account on Monday. We are committed to sponsoring you for two years. You'll receive a similar check every two months. We believe in you and when you succeed, you'll make us all famous," Carey laughed to cover her tears.

Mr. O'Shea was blubbering, Sean excused himself to go to the men's room, and everyone else cheered and clapped. Jack was speechless. After what seemed like an eternity of silence, Sean returned and cleared his throat.

"I have something to say to Jack also. I was going to wait, but maybe it's better said here. Brother, you've done so much for both Pop and me. I think we can make it; I really do. Pop and I have decided to get some help with our drinking. They say you have to publicly declare you have a problem before you can solve it. So, thanks brother for not judging us, for just loving and listening to us."

Mr. O'Shea sat looking at both Sean and Jack with tears in his eyes and pride in his heart.

Jack heard all of the praise but found no words springing to his lips. Mrs. Houston had coffee and dessert brought in and the tension of the moment was broken. Children were gathered up and the celebration ended with handshakes and hugs all around. The drive back to Mr. O'Shea's place was a quiet one. Each reflecting and lost in his own thoughts. Jack planned to leave early the next morning so his final evening was spent helping Sean and Mr. O'Shea finalize their plans for the near future. Jack didn't know that they had already decided Sean would move back into Mr. O'Shea's home to save money and to act as support for each other.

That night Mr. O'Shea spoke as a father for the first time since Jack had arrived. "Since we are bearing our souls today, I might as well put my own Irish twist on what's happening here. Since you've come home Jack, I've had to look at myself in the mirror for the first time in a long time. Sean, I'm sorry I never gave you what you needed in a father."

Sean looked down, his eyes blinking.

Mr. O'Shea continued. "Your mother was able to get her anger out at the time of our divorce. I've carried mine all these years and have lost my imagination and sense of humor in the process." Voicing his pain was difficult for Mr. O'Shea but he swallowed, cleared his throat, and spoke again.

"Jack, when you first came back home I hadn't come to grips with how much I'd lost, but watching you cook and clean made me realize that Sean had done all these things for me for years, and how little I had given back." He faltered, his eyes glistening, but plodded ahead.

"I'm fifty-seven years old and promise you both tonight that the real Mr. O'Shea will reappear. Sean and I will make it just fine Jack. When you are ready for Sean to join you, he'll be ready. I'm going out tomorrow to see if anyone needs the skills of an Irish builder. I've been tearing things down for too long. Who knows? Maybe there's a new golf course to be built somewhere. Maybe a wee bit of magic can be wrung out of these hands yet." He rose and gathered both of his sons in his arms.

Jack told Dannyboy all the good news before going to bed. Dannyboy seemed to turn his own pages as Jack's message danced across what had been a wasteland of white. Tonight, Jack was finishing what had turned out to be one of the few happy chapters of his life.

CHAPTER
Thirteen

Determined to find his way to California, and his way as a man, Jack left the very next morning. Dannyboy, riding shotgun, was a good listener. Jack had told him of the route they would take.

Outside Scranton, Pennsylvania Jack reached Route 81, a major Interstate highway that runs North to South. Jack, ever the history buff, found the numbering system for the interstate highway structure user friendly. Odd numbers for the highways meant the road moved North to South as did Route 81. Jack found his Western route in mid-Pennsylvania where he picked up his first even numbered roadway, I-80, a straight shot to Chicago, where his trip would really begin.

Mr. O'Shea had told him that if he really wanted to see America as he crossed the states he should pick up Route 66, if he could find it. Jack did some reading and discovered that Route 66 had been for many Americans the way to a new life, much as crossing the Atlantic had been for the Irish. Route 66 started out as a way to link various existing road systems into a national route. Starting in Oklahoma and moving West, the route eventually was expanded East to Illinois and West to Los Angeles, California. The celebrated roadway took on greater importance in the 1930s as the great depression and the failure of crops in vast parts of the country sent millions of people scurrying West.

By the 1960s the excitement and trepidation of changing people's way of life gave way to a population just wanting to get somewhere as fast as possible. The Interstate system was launched throughout the nation and much of Route 66 fell in disrepair. Route 66 though at one time had linked eight states. There was a history to that roadway that Jack intended to explore. During the two weeks he had given himself to finish the trip, Jack would visit as many sights as possible.

His plan, carefully laid out in neat lines, was kept safe by his traveling companion. He intended to sleep in rest areas a

couple of nights at a time, then rent a room, clean up, wash his clothes, and get a good night's sleep. He planned to repeat this process from Pennsylvania to Los Angeles. Driving along, the radio tuned to a light rock station, Jack was whistling a happy tune. Jack thought of his father and Sean often, both seemingly making positive changes, their lives too traveling a different route. He smiled; it had been quite a summer. He was in good spirits as he stood in a rest area, watching a young couple hug as they exited their vehicle. Sighing, he thought this was an area of his life that didn't seem to be getting much attention. Yet, he felt good about the personal breakthrough he had achieved. Hopefully, the trip West would fill this void in his life that seemed to have widened in stark contrast to family matters.

Seeing the skyline of Chicago miles ahead, and watching the buildings become larger and larger, Jack remembered a line from an English class: " Hog butcher for the world". Jack would never forget that powerful line. He smiled at the memory of his English class where all the boys protested a unit on poetry.

Poetry was for girls and sissies, they had insisted. His teacher, Mrs. McManus knew what she was doing though and handed out a copy of Carl Sandburg's, "Chicago." When she read it to the class with the emotion that the author intended, she had the entire class hooked. By the time the unit was completed, Jack and most of the other boys had a new found respect for the ability to convey a message in a few words. Jack introduced the poem and author to Dannyboy, who carried this new way of conveying ideas within his pages for months.

A light covering of fog that would soon burn off brought Jack's favorite Sandburg poem to mind. He recited it aloud, remembering his teacher had told him she viewed Jack's demeanor in a similar manner.

"Fog" by Carl Sandburg, Jack had recited to his class.

> 'The fog comes
> on little cat feet.
> It sits looking
> over harbor and city
> on silent haunches
> and then moves silently on.'

(What an amazing country America is,) thought Jack later, as he toured Lincoln's Springfield, Illinois home where an entire block was preserved as it had looked nearly one hundred and fifty years ago.

Back in his hotel room, Jack learned more about our sixteenth President than he'd ever picked up in school. The free brochures and small pamphlet he had purchased held new meaning after walking back through time. Jack wrote to Dannyboy as if writing a letter to a friend. He described the tall clapboard houses and the wooden sidewalk. He wrote of the tremendous inner strength and courage he felt Lincoln displayed when faced with a nation he so aptly described as 'a house divided.' He wrote of his own family just beginning to heal and remembered his father telling him that last evening, in his own unique way, about his failed marriage.

"Jack, me boy, it takes more than fingers and toes and four legs in a bed to keep a marriage from entering the red."

He smiled at the memory. (What if Lincoln had written those words to describe our nation's plight? Maybe a little humor might have softened the hotheads who would send brother against brother.)

Jack slept well that night. So far, Route 66 was providing the stimulus he needed to find his own place in the world.

He left the next morning and traveling southwest, made it to St. Louis, Missouri late that afternoon. The Gateway to the West Jack wrote, looking at his atlas. He couldn't begin to imagine the spirit it must have taken for those early pioneers to begin a trip across the western half of America in a wagon, with barely a path to follow.

Jack was having his own problems trying to stay on Route 66. Much of the road was renamed so he followed a southwestern route and hoped for the best. He wound through small town after small town on his way. He entered the area around the Mark Twain National Forest and thought of the stories of Huck Finn he'd read as a child. Remembering how his father described his own favorite authors, Jack thought, (Now that man could spin a yarn. I wonder if there was any Irish in Mr. Twain's background,) He chuckled to himself.

He didn't spend much time in the small towns he passed through, maybe a bite to eat, gas up, and grab any free brochures available. Jack intended to document his trip and to later, build a scrapbook using the notes he'd written to Dannyboy and the brochures as a framework for his memories.

Crossing the tip of Kansas for only thirteen miles or so, Jack finally reached Oklahoma, the original beginning of Route 66. He found the Route intact for most of the trip through the state. He did get lost several times in Oklahoma City but eventually found his way to the Texas panhandle. Over the next several days he discovered The Do Drop Inn Restaurant and Service Station dating from 1936, a museum of Route 66 nostalgia, and a restored Route 66 gas station which was supposedly the first. He passed a leaning water tower, then The Cadillac Ranch both offering a uniqueness to the adventure. Jack was glad he'd listened to Mr. O'Shea and had taken the scenic route. He drove straight across New Mexico not intending to spend any of the few days he had left sight-seeing.

In Arizona though, he changed his mind when the views stopped him in his tracks. He visited the Petrified Forest and took a side-trip to the Painted Desert. Being from the Northeast, Jack couldn't believe the vastness of this part of the country. The colors reminded him that God certainly knew how to soften even the harshest terrain. He could be at peace out here, as easily as the painted forests he remembered from his youth. He thought back to his autumns in New England when

leaf-peepers arrived by the busloads to view the changing of the seasons.

Jack's memory of that season was not filled with reds and yellows, oranges and tans. He remembered only shades of gray. For what followed the stripping of the leaves, were a string of holidays that found young Jack sitting alone in a small house. Jack's Mother wasn't interested in helping Jack make a Halloween costume and didn't let him join the other boys "Trick or Treating."

Thanksgiving followed with the same attitude from Mrs. O'Shea.

Just as she had been in another part of the house back when Jack sat listening to his father's stories, she continued to be too busy to be a mother to her son. Food and shelter were provided as if they were part of a local utility. Dannyboy had a vivid memory and not a single sleight went unrecorded.

When Jack passed through Winslow, Arizona, he tried without success to remember all the lyrics to the song that mentioned the city. All he could remember was: "Winslow, Arizona, with seven women on my mind, take it easy." He laughed to himself, (How could any man with seven women on his mind be singing about taking it easy?) Jack, just a thought ago, had only one woman on his mind and thinking about his mother had been anything but easy.

"Just let me get to California," said Jack aloud.

After exploring a ghost town and crossing a good deal of desert, Jack entered Needles, California and thought, (Well, that about sums it up. I'm in Needles, California trying to find a haystack.) Jack laughed at the way his mind played word games. He continued to follow Route 66 until it gave up its identity once again. He was going to have to find his own route from here on. Maybe, it was right that the only clear path left for Jack to follow was the one he would forge himself. He seemed to be finding symbolism at every turn.

Jack called Mr. O'Shea and Sean answered. "Wondered when you'd be letting us know you were still alive, brother."

"How are you Irishmen doing? Haven't killed each other yet, obviously."

"Dad's still looking for work but he's optimistic and he's not drinking a drop. I found a library card on the table last night and when I looked in his room, I saw a book of Irish folklore and stories on his nightstand. You know how he used to read when we were little. Looks like he's going to be telling me some stories in the near future." Sean laughed.

"How are you doing Sean, with everything, you know what I mean."

"I'm ok. It's different though. I'm not going out to the pubs and I guess I didn't realize how many hours I'd have to fill to replace that.

"I'm proud of you, Sean. I'm in California and after I talk with you, I'm going to call a college teammate who lives up on the Monterey peninsula. We weren't real close, but we were part of the same golf team so hopefully he'll give me the time of day. Won't be long I'll have you out here caddying for me. Maybe you could use Dad's library card and do a little research on what that might mean for you. There is a lot to prepare for. I want you to know what you are getting into." Check it out on the internet. "That sounds like a good idea brother. It will fill up some time too."

"I'll try to call at least once a week. At the library, look at a map of California you can travel along with me over the next week. I'm headed for the coast, and then North to the Monterey peninsula. I'm not sure where this guy lives now, but I know he was from Carmel. I have his parents' phone number. I'll call you next week. Tell Mr. O'Shea I love him. By the way, has Mother called you yet?"

"Let's just say I don't know her number yet and leave it at that." There was bitterness in Sean's voice.

(I'll have to call Mother,) thought Jack as he hung up. (I was hoping she'd come around. Oh well, I'll just let her know I'm alive. She shouldn't be needing her air conditioning much longer, anyway.) Jack chuckled.

He dialed his mother's number and after hearing the gong of coins dropping, he heard his mother's voice, which was not unlike the sterile sound of those coins. "Who's calling?" was her opening line.

Not hello or any other form of recognition, although Jack felt he'd spoken clearly when he had said, "Hello, Mom." How many sons did she have anyway?

(Let's get to it,) thought Jack in the half second it had taken him to consider his response. "It's me, Jack, your wandering boy. Thought I should check in."

"Well, you took your sweet old time doing it. I've been worried sick. Where are you anyway?"

"I'm in the land of the movie stars where the streets are paved with gold and the next knock you hear might be opportunity." Jack answered in his Irish brogue so hated by his mother.

"Stop that voice! You know it bothers me. You're in California I gather that, but where?"

"I'm heading toward the coast and up toward Carmel. I have a college buddy there. How are you doing?"

His mother began her newest laundry list of complaints but Jack cut her off. "I've only got a minute. Just wanted you to know I'm ok. I'll call next week after I'm settled in Carmel."

Jack's mother began to protest but he simply hung up. Next, he made a call to Khris Erricson's home and his mother answered. After introducing himself, Jack asked about Khris. He was indeed still living at home and working at a golf course on the peninsula, Spy Glass. Perhaps Jack had heard of it. Jack told Mrs. Erricson he was on his way there and would arrive in a couple of days, if all went well. "Please tell Khris I would appreciate it if he'd look around for an opening at one of the area courses."

Jack hung up feeling really good about how things seemed to be coming together. He stayed in a small motel that night and caught up on some conversations he needed to have with Dannyboy. Falling asleep in Dannyboy's lap, he dreamed of making it on tour with Sean as his caddy and his father watching proudly from the gallery.

The next morning he did some push-ups, stretched, and took a long shower as he prepared for the last leg of his journey. One that would end after what had become a twenty-four hundred mile history lesson. (Would Mr. O'Shea ever regain enough of himself to quiz Jack about what he had learned?) Jack wondered. The past two weeks had been the longest time that Jack could remember he hadn't practiced, or played golf. As he put his duffel bag in the trunk, he took a long look at his clubs laying there, patted them gently and said aloud, "You're my ticket to Ireland fellas. Where the grass is always green and there's music in the air or so Mr. O'Shea used to say. Let's be on our way then." Jack found the coast of California and began driving north on Route 1. If Route 66 had given him a clearer picture of Middle America, Route 1 along the Pacific Coast would give him a taste for how the other half lives. Beautiful homes, perched dangerously atop cliffs had him saying, "Oh my God!" audibly over and over.

The beaches were endless. He had never seen such expanses of water and sand. People dotted the warm sand of autumn in California appearing as plentiful and colorful as the leaves on the lawns of New England. Jack thought back to the colors he'd witnessed in the desert and just shook his head. He was reminded of Bette Middler's song, From A Distance, when the blues, greens and whites, engulfed his field of vision. (God indeed was the artist in all this,) thought Jack as he looked over the blue Pacific. The white crashing surf, the sun a golden spotlight for this show that would go on for eternity. He stopped his car several times along the cliffs where he just had to tell Dannyboy of a latest discovery. (Dannyboy has been getting a geography lesson of late,) thought Jack, (broadening the boy's horizons, I am.) He chuckled and moved back into traffic.

Jack arrived in Carmel late in the afternoon and was surprised by the smallness of this beautiful beach community. The city, tucked cozily into a forest as if protecting itself from any storm that might arise, managed to have a front row seat for an ever changing show provided by the Pacific Ocean.

On this late afternoon, people were gathering to watch the magnificent sunset where all colors imaginable merged just above the horizon. Jack parked his car and joined the crowd spread out along a walkway overlooking the ocean below. Much like the world's largest amphitheater, the walkway provided a view that had another, "Oh my God," escaping Jack's lips.

Wandering the boardwalk smelling the salt air and allowed entry to today's final spectacle, his sense of sight and smell became satiated. Jack's stomach suddenly growled and he realized he hadn't eaten since early morning. After ordering a veggie omelet, he found a payphone and called Khris Erricson. Khris had just gotten home. He gave Jack directions and asked, "Have you eaten yet?" "Just ordering as we speak," said Jack.

"Cancel the order and get over here. We'll have a beer and you can eat with us. Mom told me to tell you that," laughed Khris, as his mother shushed him in the background.

"Ok thanks. I'll be right there." He hung up, canceled his order and gave the waitress three bucks for her trouble.

He pulled into the drive at 8 Erricson Lane and one more, "Oh, my God," slipped out as he gazed at a twelve room home that provided obvious comfort to Khris. No wonder he hadn't left home, who would, thought Jack.

Jack walked toward the front entrance. You certainly couldn't just call it a front door. He glanced up and saw a curtain slowly close. He rang the doorbell and Khris was there before the chimes ended.

"Hey, man, great to see you. You look beat. Let me show you to your room where you can shower and then we'll have

that beer." Khris turned. "Mom, this is Jack O'Shea, the best golfer I've ever played golf with on a team or anywhere else."

Mrs. Erricson was standing just off to the side, and Jack liked her even before she spoke. She had a welcoming smile on her face and he could tell Khris had filled her in on what he remembered of Jack O'Shea.

"I'm so pleased to meet the famous Irishman from the East. Khris has been telling us about your golf exploits for the past three years."

"Thank you, I'm pleased to meet you too and thank you for letting me into such a beautiful home."

"You are most welcome. As Khris said, take a nice long shower then we'll have a beer to celebrate your arrival in our little town." Jack nodded and started up the stairs then realized he'd forgotten to bring in his duffel bag.

"Oh, don't worry about that. We're pretty much the same size, I'll pull something together for you." said Khris. "We live in shorts and tee shirts out here, anyway."

"Oh Khris, your father called. It's yes, you are on for tomorrow morning. He'll be home within the hour so save him a beer he said."

"Ok Mom. I'll get Jack squared away and I'll help you in the kitchen." Khris showed Jack a spare bedroom that would be a master suite in any other home. The bathroom was at the end of the room with a full tub, shower, and double sink.

"I'll put some clothes on your bed. See you when you get down."

With that Jack was left to look around and raise his head to the ceiling, which was a full ten feet from the floor. (What a place,) he thought, removing his clothes walking to the shower. A variety of soaps, body wash, and shampoos were sitting in a small hanging tray to the right of the shower. A disposable razor and shaving cream sat on a little shelf with a lighted mirror in the oversized shower stall.

Jack shaved humming a tune and then took a long hot shower. A pair of chino shorts, a maroon tee shirt, and new underwear still in the package were waiting for him on the bed. On the floor was a new pair of ankle socks tucked inside boat shoes. Jack headed down the stairs but paused when he heard a door close off the hallway above.

Mrs. Erricson and Khris, were in the kitchen which Jack found by following the sound of laughter. The room gleamed of stainless steel and a wooden beam framed the cooking area.

A bar made from a solid slab of redwood and surrounded by polished steel stools gave a twenty-first century appearance to what had once been a two hundred year old tree.

A huge fireplace dominated the back wall while stuffed chairs, normally seen in a sitting room, provided fireside seating. To the left, sliding glass doors opened to a large porch that overlooked the Pacific Ocean. It was obvious that this family spent most of their time; reading, eating and probably dozing in these two rooms. He was briefly reminded of the daylight basement at the Houston home. He could feel the love here too.

Jack approached the bar as Khris and his mother continued to banter. When Khris saw Jack, he immediately grabbed a beer from the refrigerator and opened it.

At this point, Mrs. Erricson took charge. She handed Jack the beer, grabbed her own half finished one, and guided him by the elbow to one of the overstuffed chairs. A small flame was dancing in the fireplace; Jack sunk into the butternut leather. He thought, (Yup, I bet a lot of dozing goes on here.)

Shannon was her name. When she said, I'm Shannon, a special light entered her eyes and Jack knew he had found a friend.

"Did you drive all the way here, Jack, from where was it you said, Pennsylvania? Oh, you must be exhausted."

Jack thought of his own mother going on and on with her monologues that concerned only herself. Here was someone fairly bursting to hear from him and concerned about his weariness. Mrs. Erricson caught herself and apologized for rattling on. Khris joined them and Jack spoke for the first time since coming into the kitchen.

"You have a beautiful home and, I can already tell, a wonderful family. This room is awesome. Thank you again for making me feel so welcome, Mrs. Erricson."

"Please call me Shannon. Tell us a little about your trip, any adventures along the way."

"Shannon it is then." Jack closed his eyes briefly and began, "I just finished a drive across the middle and western part of this country. My father told me about old Route 66 and I followed it for the past two weeks. I've learned more about this country than I'd ever imagined. So I guess, the entire two weeks was really an adventure for me."

"Why didn't you fly out here?" asked Khris, obviously not a history buff.

"It would have been quicker, that's for sure, but on the road I saw some beautiful scenery I'll never forget, and probably never see again. Something to tell my kids about, someday." "When we were playing golf in Florida, I even hated to fly home. It took so long. I can't imagine driving," said Khris.

"Well, anyway, I'm here," said Jack.

"It's obvious you are Irish," said Shannon. "Have you ever been there? You know, to Ireland?"

"No such luck. My grandfather swam here from Ireland though." Jack chuckled. "Not really, but it makes a great story. He did come from Ireland. I'll tell you about it if you'd like to hear it."

Shannon was about to say yes when Khris' father walked through the door. After introductions, Khris refreshed everyone's beer and his father set tomorrow's agenda. He told the boys, as he called them, they were playing golf in the morning. Jack and Khris against Mr. Erricson and a playing partner at Pebble Beach. "I had to call in a favor but we're teeing off at ten am."

Carrying their beers, locally brewed ale from a brewery that Mr. Erricson was part owner of, they moved out onto the porch. Jack excused himself to use the restroom and when he returned, the kitchen counter was being covered with a variety of salads, fruits, meats, chicken, fish, cheeses and breads.

"Fill a plate and bring it out onto the porch that's where we usually eat," said Shannon.

When Jack stepped onto the porch with his plate in one hand and a beer in the other, he nearly dropped both. One hundred feet below and less than a quarter mile away, the ocean had turned a deep purple as the moon was beginning its slow trip up the stairs to bed. Just as Jack had hesitated and stalled on his way to bed back when he had a family, the moon would hang on for a long time tonight before a light cloud cover summoned sleep.

"I can see why you'd eat out here. I guess, I wonder why you don't sleep out here as well," laughed Jack.

A regular old picnic table sat in the middle of the fifteen foot wide porch flanked both left and right by a team of rocking chairs. Shannon sat in one of the chairs with her meal on her lap slowly rocking to the rhythm of the waves breaking below.

Khris and his father sat across from one another at the table, ribbing each other good naturedly. Jack joined Shannon in an adjoining rocker.

As he caught the rhythm of movement, he asked the question he'd been dying to, "Are you Irish?"

Shannon looked at Jack and uttered an old proverb, "If you're lucky enough to be Irish, you're lucky enough." She winked and Jack knew he was not alone.

The evening passed quickly. Jack, realizing he was indeed exhausted, climbed the stairs to bed long before the moon gave in. Stretched out full length in the king-sized bed, Jack surrendered himself.

❧❧

Shannon was humming an Old Irish tune <u>Cockles and Mussels</u>, when Jack skipped down the stairs.

Jack recognized the tune and gave Shannon a big smile. The smell of coffee, bacon, and toast combined to attack his nose and make his stomach scream-I give up-feed me. "That's an Old Irish tune, I'd recognize it if struck deaf and dumb." Jack said in his best Irish accent.

"I haven't heard an Irish accent since my own grandfather died," said Shannon brightly.

"Well, and where would the rest of the men of the house be? They haven't gone and left without me, have they?" Jack stayed in brogue.

"No, they're out on the back lawn, chipping, putting, and probably setting bets, if I know those two." Jack headed toward the door and Shannon followed.

"You should know that Mr. Erricson, Paul, takes his golf very seriously and hates to lose. He respects the game, however, and will celebrate the man with the greatest skills. So I guess you'll be in a quandary today, won't you? Liked or respected. Kick his arse, Jack O'Shea," said in a light Irish lilt.

Jack laughed out loud. He joined the other men on the lawn and found the bet already set - use of the Porsche, and Mr. Erricson's credit card for the weekend if they won. Two days of hard labor at the brewery, cleaning bottles and any other menial jobs the boss could think of, without pay if they lost.

Khris, who was obviously spoiled, explained to Jack just how humiliating it would be and hard work too, if they lost. "I think we can beat them though, so not to worry." He had the utmost faith in Jack's golfing abilities.

Jack observed the interaction between father and son. He could see the love, yet not quite mutual respect, they showed one another.

Mr. Erricson was a self-made millionaire. He had paid his dues, peddling insurance door to door before climbing the corporate ladder, finally branching out on his own, and taking his clients with him.

He hadn't been home much when Khris was growing up, and he tended to provide more material rewards than necessary. He had let Khris go to college in Florida when what he believed to be the greatest courses in the world were within a few miles of their home.

Khris seemed to think that money grew on trees. Even his job as assistant pro at SpyGlass was not a position he had competed for. He did a good job at handling the duties of the shop, but there was no future in it unless he got his professional PGA license. So far he'd shown no inclination to do anything more than work his days and play his nights.

Jack knew none of this for sure, yet sensed all of it. One of the reasons he hadn't gotten real close to Khris in college had been his party at all costs attitude. He was very talented and could probably have given Jack a run for his money at the number one position if he'd cared enough. When he heard the bet, he looked at Mr. Erricson and read him like a book. This match was a lot more serious than Khris realized. Mr. Erricson was playing for his son's future.

After an excellent breakfast, Jack put his clubs in the trunk of the family SUV and took a seat in the back. It was a thirty minute drive to what might be the most famous golf course in the world. He closed his eyes and wondered what role he'd be expected to play in this little drama.

Fifteen

Pebble Beach Golf Course, the crown jewel of golf on the West Coast, is one of many beautiful courses that fringe the Monterey Peninsula. Jack didn't ask but thought it cost nearly three hundred dollars to play a round of golf here, and people still had to be put on a waiting list. He would try to memorize everything about the day to tell Dannyboy. From the parking lot to the first tee they were treated like royalty.

While warming up, the rules for the contest were finalized. They would play bestball on each hole and it would be match play. Two tying scores on a hole would halve the hole. The team winning the most holes at the end of eighteen would win the match.

After re-explaining the rules, Mr. Erricson threw in a wrinkle. Each player could use one mulligan any time during the match except on a green. That one extra shot added an element of suspense that could provide a pivotal turn in the match at any point along the way.

Khris started to protest but Jack took him aside and said, "This could help us as easily as it could help them. Besides, your father is paying for all of this; let's just enjoy the opportunity. Think about driving that Porsche."

Khris nodded his head and smiled, already making tight turns along the coastal highway.

The four golfers shook hands and headed for the first tee. The first hole, a four hundred seventy-six yard par four, was halved when three of the four players managed to make par. The match stayed even until the ninth, a breathtaking hole with a green perched out over the Ocean's edge seeming to hang on for dear life. The fourth most difficult hole on the course, this four hundred sixty-four yard par four would challenge the world's best golfers and has. Mr. Erricson hit his drive out of bounds and took his mulligan. He was safely down the middle with his second drive. Khris and Jack both hit decent drives. Scott, Mr. Erricson's partner, was straight down the middle.

Scott pulled his second shot into a green-side bunker. Jack hit his second shot a little fat, a four iron that stopped about twenty yards in front of the green. Khris landed a beautiful five wood shot on the right edge of the green. Mr. Erricson hit a three wood that bounced in front of the green and came to rest twelve feet from the pin. Everyone applauded. Jack mused, (this match is going to go the distance.)

Jack's third shot was within eight feet. Scott hit his shot from the bunker fat, and his ball lay thirty feet away. Putting first, he missed and tapped in for a bogey. Mr. Erricson drained his putt for a rare birdie three. When Jack's chip slipped by to the right, it was up to Khris to make an 18 footer to tie the hole. It didn't happen.

The match seesawed over the next seven holes with all the mulligans being used except Jack's. Standing on the tee at seventeen which was a long par three, Jack and Khris were still down one. A beautiful hole, the seventeenth, plays like two different holes, depending on the wind and pin location. Khris hit a five iron that would normally carry the hundred seventy-six yards, comfortably. However, the wind off the Pacific Ocean today held the ball in its grasp and dropped it well short. Jack asked Khris if he had hit it pure and Khris said that he thought he had. Jack selected a four iron and it was headed safely for the left bunker but struck a rake and darted dead left into the waves. Jack still had his mulligan. (Well, it's now or never,) he thought. Staying with a four iron, he hit it square, landing it toward the back pin location settling ten feet from the flagstick.

Mr. Erricson and Scott hit three irons and both landed in the right bunker twenty-five yards from the flagstick.

After the other players pitched on, Jack humming to himself, drained his putt for a birdie to tie the match.

Mr. Erricson was visibly upset. His team three up only four holes ago was now dead even. Khris couldn't help fanning the flame.

"You old guys running out of steam or what?" he kidded.

Mr. Erricson glared at his son and walked away.

The eighteenth at Pebble Beach is a perfect finishing hole, a par five with a minor dogleg, the ocean on the left daring the golfer to take a risk. The risk taker can cut off a good deal of distance by starting his drive out over the water and letting the ball fade slightly right.

Jack was hot. He had birdied the last two holes and looked like he intended to continue. His drive soared out over the blue water, took a lazy right turn, and landed safely in the middle of the fairway. Khris too, hit a beautiful drive with his ball landing not a yard away from Jack's.

Fueled by inner anger, Mr. Erricson hit his drive. Sometimes anger helps and this was one of those times. When his ball finally came to rest, he was a full thirty yards beyond Khris and Jack and in an ideal position to be on in two. Scott, trying too hard, left one for the sharks. His second ball found the fairway and he was lying three.

Scott's fourth shot landed about forty yards short of the green. Jack and Khris, sitting in the cart chatting away, discussed their next shot. Jack hit a tremendous three wood that rolled onto the green twenty-five feet from the hole. Khris pushed his ball to the right, finding the rough fifteen yards from the green. Mr. Erricson, obviously an accomplished player, struck a three wood. The ball jumped off his club, soared like a hawk looking for its next meal, took one bounce, and rolled to the middle of the green.

Jack clapped his hands. "That was a fantastic shot, Mr. Erricson, I'm impressed."

Khris agreed, "Nice shot, Dad."

Jack and Khris rode silently to the eighteenth green. Then Khris said, "I guess it's up to you, Jack. I'm out of it."

"You're not out of it Khris, a little pitch shot, one putt and you've got a birdie, maybe a halve."

"Dad is going to drain his putt. I just know it."

"Well, then don't chip for the putt; chip for the hole. You can do it."

Mr. Erricson's partner chipped on first, and was left with a long putt for a bogey. He picked up his ball and went over to help his partner read the crucial putt.

Khris's chip just missed the hole and he tapped in for a birdie, normally an exciting event.

Jack was next to putt. He watched Mr. Erricson lining up his putt knowing he would drain his nine-footer. Khris, helping Jack look at his line, suggested the ball was going to break at least a foot.

Jack staring straight at the flagstick from behind his ball thought, (This match isn't really about me. Khris already has a birdie; let's leave this match to the father and son.) Jack knew if Mr. Erricson made his putt the next few days were going to be all about Khris seeing the world a little differently. (Who am I to be settling family problems for anyone else?) thought Jack, and he stopped humming.

Jack stroked the ball a good three feet past the pin, "Right break, just a little too much speed," said Jack shaking his head.

Mr. Erricson took a deep breath and drained the putt for the first eagle he'd ever recorded on that hole. He looked up without celebrating, met both men's eyes, and announced: "Good match men."

They all shook hands, parked their carts, and walked into the club house for a beer. Nothing about the bet was mentioned, not even on the ride home. Mr. Erricson seemed lost in thought. When they arrived, Mrs. Erricson asked how the match went. Khris just mumbled and went up to take a shower. Recreating the drama of the final hole, Jack gave Shannon a quick rundown of the close match. They were sitting in the kitchen on barstools, having a beer when Mr. Erricson joined them.

"Khris up taking a shower?" he asked.

"Yes," said Shannon. "He didn't seem overly happy with the match."

"This will be the first time he's ever had to get his hands dirty, and he needs to see what it's like."

"Would you like me to take a walk or something?" asked Jack. "So you two can talk?"

"No, actually I'm glad you are here Jack. I'd like you to consider staying with us while you're in the area. I'd like you to help Khris figure out who he wants to be. He's a great young man, but he has no direction, no goals. Khris said you're out here trying to get your tour card; maybe we can help each other. I'll help you get on at one of the courses up here and make sure you have plenty of time to practice. Would you take Khris under your wing and help him make a decision about his golf future?

He needs to commit to the work necessary, or give it up, and join me in one of my businesses."

"I'm not really sure what I can do," said Jack.

"I think he'll listen to you Jack. Just be honest with him. I know he respects you and your game. His mother and I don't want to lose another child."

Shannon started to protest but Mr. Erricson held up his hand. "Look, if Jack decides he can live here and help Khris, then he has a right to know who we all are." Khris came bounding down the stairs.

"Think about it Jack after you two work in the brewery for a couple of days. If you are interested, we'll finish our talk."

The next couple of days were a blur for the two college golf mates. Up and out the door by six am, Mr. Erricson delivered them to the brewery on a Sunday morning with the advice, "Just do whatever they tell you to do."

They scrubbed out vats, swept the warehouse, stacked and counted bottles. Later they carried and inventoried bags of malt and grain, and helped deliver bottles and kegs to bars and restaurants. The brewery was attempting to get their product into package stores and large supermarkets. During what should have been lunch, one of Mr. Erricson's partners sequestered both guys and explained the micro-brewing business to them. It seemed ales were the rage country-wide, and this micro-brewery was poised to take off regionally, and possibly nation-wide within the next year. Jack was intrigued by what he learned. Khris said he just couldn't wait to have the two days end.

Monday night, Mr. Erricson planned a barbecue to welcome the working stiffs back to the world. When Jack and Khris came out onto the porch, a cold microbrew was waiting for them.

"Well, what do you think of our little company?" asked Mr. Erricson, opening two bottles of ale.

"I'm glad that's over, Dad. We worked like slaves. Didn't we, Jack?"

"They do work hard. How do you keep guys on the job?" asked Jack.

"Pretty simple really. I pay a fair wage and give them some incentive to stay. You see it costs a good deal to keep training new people. It pays to make a good choice about who you hire and then you keep them."

"What's the incentive?" asked Khris, "You'd have to get me pretty excited about something to have me do most of those jobs."

Mr. Erricson chuckled, "This little company is growing and may even go public at some point. We give the workers stock options that aren't worth much yet but will be. Every week along with their check they get a share of stock. When we set up the company, we created one hundred thousand shares valued at ten dollars a share. The three partners kept seventy-five thousand shares so we have twenty-five thousand shares to give to the men." Mr. Erricson paused to let the numbers sink in.

"We have ten men working right now. We three partners rotate our time running the business. We don't take a salary. Our plan allows us four years to grow the business. When that time comes, we will adjust the value of the company and each man will be able to cash in his stock or leave it with the company to grow. If a worker wants to cash in his stock early, he gets the original ten dollars a share, no more, no less. We believe that at the end of four years, those shares could be worth ten, or fifteen times what they are today, so it's an incentive that holds some real financial promise for the men."

Jack nodded his head, the logic and promise of a future payday, sinking in.

"If we are successful and do go public, which, I believe, will happen, those ten men could become millionaires. We're just starting our second year and plowing all profits back into the company."

"That's exciting, Mr. Erricson. The beer's good too," said Jack, taking a good long swallow.

"Actually, you can thank Mrs. Erricson for that. When I first met her, her father always had some homemade ale in the fridge. We drank a lot of it in those days but really never thought much about it. When the micro-breweries started popping up, I remembered that homebrew and we found her Grandfather's recipe." He held a bottle up to the light. "You're drinking our best selling ale, McNabb's Malt, named after Shannon's ancestors." At that moment Shannon stepped onto the porch. Just behind her walked a tall thin young woman, the spitting image of her mother. All discussion of McNabb's Malt ceased; in fact, everyone grew very quiet. Jack couldn't help but stare at this beautiful but obviously troubled girl.

Shannon took the girl's arm and walked her to one of the rockers. The girl sat and began to rock, not seeming to notice anyone on the porch. Khris seemed agitated. Jack could tell by his body language.

Shannon spoke first, "Your dad and I have invited Jack to stay with us while he's out here Khris; your dad also suggested we let Jack know who we all are. At first I was a little concerned." She looked directly at Jack, "but I'm not anymore. Jack, this is Molly." Shannon put her hand lightly on her daughter's shoulder. "We've been trying to protect her from the outside world, and I wasn't sure it was necessary for you to know all of our problems. In the short time you have been here though, all of us feel we have found a friend that we can count on. You do have a right to know who is living in this house if you decide to stay." Molly continued to rock, oblivious to the discussion.

"Look Mom, I love Molly too, but she doesn't seem to be getting any better here. I think she may need more constant professional help."

"If you think more pills or sitting in a locked room are the answer, I think you are dead wrong," said Shannon.

Jack sat as quietly as Molly, taking all of this in, not knowing what to say. He hadn't realized this family had any problems. They seemed nearly perfect to an outsider. (I guess no one gets away without some pain in their life, certainly Molly hadn't and the family was obviously hurting too,) thought Jack "So, here we are," said Shannon in a brogue of her own, "take us or leave us. Molly's our beautiful daughter. She spent a year in a coma and presently lives in a world of her own." Jack stood up. "Mrs. Erricson, my own family is a disaster. My brother and father are recovering alcoholics, at least they were the last time I talked to them, and my mother has nothing to do with either of them. She won't even call my brother. If ever there was a guy who knew less about what holds a family together, it's me. I'd be honored to stay here, and I'd like to do my share of helping out in whatever way you feel comfortable." He looked at the reed thin young woman rocking to her own beat. "What happened to Molly if you don't mind my asking?"

"Molly is, was, a very good athlete. She excelled at every sport imaginable in high school. When it came time for college, she could have gone anywhere in the country, but she chose to stay right here and pursue her passion-diving. She continued to take classes locally but she knew, and we knew, she'd carve out a career of some sort-underwater."

Mr. Erricson took over. "We tried to reason with her. She kept going deeper and deeper with her instructor taking what he considered acceptable risks." He shook his head. "On a dive exploring some coral, she got wedged in a small area, and though she was able to break free, she panicked and used up too much oxygen. She was without air for nearly two minutes.

She ended up in a coma, as Mrs. Erricson said, and we don't really know the extent of the damage." He brightened. "Since awakening, she has learned to walk and dress herself again but she doesn't talk or even attempt to. The doctors don't really have any idea what to expect. All we know is, we love her, and want her here with us. That may sound selfish but no one has been able to convince us that experimental drugs or any kind of therapy is better than having her home. So we sit here evenings, waiting, hoping for a miracle that will bring our Molly back from the deep." Mr. Erricson had tears in his eyes, Mrs. Erricson massaged his shoulders and tenderly hugged his back.

"Khris has been on a guilt trip since the accident because he was the one who introduced Molly to the sport," said Shannon. Khris, not commenting, excused himself and exited the porch; the room grew quiet.

Jack looked at Molly who continued to rock gently. He walked over and sat down in an adjoining rocker. "Well, Miss Molly, since we're to live in the same house, I ought to tell you a bit about myself." Jack O'Shea in that moment became his father the storyteller.

He began a long one sided conversation in a soft Irish brogue that was at times whimsical and humorous. Jack, the storyteller, opened up his knowledge of the Irish world to Molly Erricson much as he did in his writings to Dannyboy.

Long after Mr. and Mrs. Erricson had retired, two rocking chairs continued to move in cadence to the surf below. Jack was up early the next morning knocking on Khris's door, "Let's get up lazy bones. There's work to be done."

That first morning it took Jack sitting on the edge of Khris's bed, singing one song after another, dodging pillows, to get him to rise. They walked down the path that framed the beach and began a slow jog.

"Are you becoming my personal trainer or what?" asked Khris after getting his second wind.

"Something like that. We'll help each other get into tip-top shape."

"What am I getting in shape for? All I do is sit behind a computer, checking in golfers. I don't need to be in shape for that."

"Well, help me get in shape then. It's no fun to work out alone. You can be my personal trainer and help me get my tour card," laughed Jack.

"I wish I had your skills Jack. Maybe I'd try it too."

"You have the skills, Khris. What you don't have is ambition." The men ran in silence for another half mile as the sun began its slow assent.

"Do you like your job, Khris?"

"Not really, it's pretty boring. I have to do something though, and it beats working at the brewery that's for sure."

"What if I promise that in six months that if you do everything

I ask, you won't be bored with your job or your life?"

"That's a long time Jack."

"Ok, let's make it simple. Do what I ask a day at a time. You can quit tomorrow but not today. How's that?" "That I can handle." agreed Khris.

"Let's pick up the pace for the last mile. Then you can show me around the area after breakfast."

The men entered the drive, walking around back to cool down, laughing and high-fiving each other. Jack glanced up and saw Molly looking out the window, staring toward the Ocean. (I wonder if she really sees herself trapped under there,) thought Jack, (I wonder if she even heard me last night.)

After a long shower and breakfast, Jack and Khris rode to the golf course where Khris worked. Jack was impressed with the beautiful course and asked for an application.

The head pro introduced himself, "Mr. Erricson said you'd be coming in this morning. After you fill out that application I'd like to see you in my office."

Khris went to work behind the counter and Jack was ushered into a small office. After completing the paperwork, Jack knocked on the head pro's office door and was invited in. The

pro scanned Jack's application, focusing on awards and experience.

"Very impressive golf accomplishments in college Jack. I see you conducted clinics over the summer. If you work for us, what would you like to be doing?"

"I'm willing to do anything but if you're asking for my preference, it is giving lessons, conducting clinics, or both."

"That's a good answer. Mr. Erricson is on our board of directors, and he has asked us to assist you in helping his son make a commitment to the game of golf or something else. I have to agree with him. I'm not comfortable talking about someone, but it would be to Khris's advantage to commit to something. His work here is not all it could be." He cleared his throat. "Your job will be exactly what you wanted. Conduct clinics or give lessons with Khris as your assistant. I'm not sure how he'll accept it, but it will be up to you to see that he does. Our hope is that through giving lessons and clinics, he'll begin to see how difficult this game is for the average person and how hard it is to teach. We hope he'll see how fortunate he is to have the skills he's currently wasting. We are looking for you to teach our clients and Khris as well." He became very businesslike. "Beginning tomorrow, your hours will be ten am to four pm, six days a week. We'll pay you $10.00 an hour as well as a fifty percent commission on lessons and clinics you conduct. You may have full golf privileges. You'll be plenty busy, seems everyone is taking up the sport, now that Tiger's on the scene."

"Thank you, Mr. Hendricks. I'll do a good job for you. I hope I can convince Khris."

"Use the money angle if you have to; he'll be doubling what he makes now."

"I'll talk to him tonight. Mind if I look the place over? Khris is my ride so I'll be around for the next six hours or so." "Go right ahead. Check out the practice facility; hit some balls. I'll send your application to the main office with my approval to put you on the payroll beginning tomorrow."

Jack told Khris he was hired and would see him later. "Don't forget me when you leave. I'll be at the practice range." Jack got a golf cart, rode the course, and took notes of distances, blind spots, and landing areas. He made sure he stayed out of the way of players and got to the back nine before morning players made the turn. There were several ocean holes, and he took time to gaze at the sailboats and tankers that dotted the blue water.

He thought of Molly trapped under all that water and couldn't imagine what she'd gone through. Ever the deep reflective thinker, Jack wondered where his present situation would take him. As a power boat pulling a skier entered his field of vision, Jack felt like he too was being pulled by some unseen power plowing through waves, but in what direction? His mind was brought back to dry land by a shout from Khris approaching on a golf cart.

"I got the afternoon off; that's not like Hendricks. He just smiled when I asked him how come. He told me to take care of my buddy, Jack. Have a late lunch put on his tab. What the hell did you do, Jack?"

"To be honest with you, I made him a business proposal he couldn't refuse," lied Jack. While he had actually given a great deal of thought to creating golf clinics for children using the techniques of the past summer, it was only in this moment they crystallized for him. He explained to Khris how the clinics would work. He'd teach Khris his methods and together they'd make a lot of money. Perhaps, they could create a company in the process. They wouldn't have to work too hard after their initial effort and down the road they might train other teachers and branch out.

"We'll franchise ourselves and sell shares to our workers just like your dad did."

"Wouldn't that blow his mind. He thinks I'm rotting away here in this nowhere job."

"Well, he's right Khris but we can turn your knowledge of the members and their families into our first clinic. During the day at least for now, we'll give lessons and regular clinics.

After hours, we'll create our own business and make a profit for the course and for ourselves."

"I like it Jack. Thanks for thinking of me."

Jack just smiled as the ski boat made another pass. (Hold on; here we go,) he thought.

When they got home that afternoon, Jack took Khris to his room and dragged out his journal. By now Dannyboy had become a series of journals. The first was carefully marked with the letter D, for Dannyboy. As each journal was completed the next letter in Dannyboy would appear on the cover. Jack had created a table of contents with the year, month and his physical location at the time. The latest journal was N-2 and he was nearly half way through the pages.

He opened it and found his notes about the clinics he had created. The two men talked about what they should teach, how to keep it fun, and what teaching aids to employ. After two hours of picking each others' brains, they went down to dinner. Khris could hardly contain himself as he explained his promotion. He didn't mention the after hours clinics, but the Erricson's couldn't get over his sense of excitement. The entire meal was spent laughing and enjoying the moment.

Later, Mrs. Erricson brought Molly down to sit on the porch and rock. Jack thought what a shame that this beautiful, twenty one year old couldn't capture some of the life and energy that this family shared.

Khris excused himself, "I'm off to bed. It's been a long day and we've got a workout in the morning, right Jack?"

"That's right Khris. We sure do."

After Khris left the room, Jack asked the Erricson's if they minded him sitting with Molly.

"Of course not, if it's not a burden to you."

"Do you have any Irish folklore or stories in your library?" asked Jack. "If you do, I'd like to read to Molly about her ancestors. My Dad always told me stories. They gave me the ability to think on the spot and be creative. Maybe, I'll think of a way to help Molly or maybe the leprechauns and fairies will work some magic themselves."

Mrs. Erricson brought in books of Irish mysteries, folklore, and several Irish songbooks.

"Thank you, Jack, for everything," said Shannon and she kissed him on the forehead. "I had no idea who would be showing up when you arrived. It's clear we have an Irish fairy watching over this family. As I said earlier, if you're Irish you're lucky enough. I'm not sure I really believed that till just now." With that exit line she said goodnight and Jack was left silently rocking in tandem with Molly. He spent a few minutes looking over the books and gaining a basic premise of a number of stories. He was thumbing through a song book and suddenly smiled, recalling Shannon humming the Song, <u>Cockles and Mussels</u>.

❧

Just as Mr. O'Shea had created his own stories, Jack conjured up an original tale weaving myth, legend, the O'Shea wit, the magic of fairies and leprechauns, and a very loving mother's Irish song. A tale told in Jack's light Irish brogue. "If I told you a true story, would you believe me, Molly?" He paused for effect. "I thought not. Then I'll tell you a magical story filled with possibilities. A story of a girl who shares your first name, Molly Malone. A girl who single-handedly saved the Irish people from a terrible famine many years ago." Jack closed his eyes.

"This Molly was a girl of the sea, much as yourself. As a wee child she lived along the rocky shores of the Emerald Isle. You have Irish blood warming your bones, you know. Perhaps you're even related. Anyway, Molly Malone played along and among the rocks and seaweed, always with a tune on her lips, creating imaginary friends. One day as she was jumping from rock to rock she slipped and struck her head. When she awoke she was in a cavern carved from the world above by the power of the pounding surf. There was a twilight glow of reflected light that gave shape to this underwater world. Molly was frightened at first but was soothed by the rhythmic sound of waves breaking above. When her eyes adjusted to the dim light and her heart stopped pounding, she began to explore.

She found a piece of driftwood and began to poke around what must have been bits and pieces of ships that had gone down off the shores of Ireland.

She found tatters of sailcloth and used it to keep warm. Molly became hungry but found nothing in the cavern to sustain her. She created a little area that would collect drops of fresh water that dripped along the back walls so she would have something to drink. Later, having found nothing edible, she dove into the water at the edge of the cavern. Molly surfaced with a handful of cockles and mussels, many thousands more awaiting her next dive. Molly lived and played in this undersea world for nearly ten years. She was content to sing to herself and to talk to the imaginary friends she had kept alive in her mind. Though she missed her family, she would likely have stayed a creature of the sea if not for a strange dream.

In the dream she was told that her people needed her desperately and that she and she alone could save her beloved Ireland. She found herself asking what she could do, a mere girl, to save her people. It would all be clear in the morning, she was assured. After a night of fitful sleep, Molly arose feeling she'd been part of a long conversation. She wandered back into the furthest reaches of the cavern where a large bit of rock had broken away sometime in the night. There, hidden by the heartless sea, covered with sail cloth and pieces of wood, were gems of every size and description. Some power Molly did not fully understand had provided Molly the means to help her people. Molly made plans. She pieced together a cloak, and fashioned pockets on the inside. After a day of discovery and hard work, once more she slept. The rest of the plan was revealed to her as she tossed and turned, waves of understanding washing into her head. The next morning Molly rose and placed the gems safely in her cloak. She was guided to the surface by an unseen hand.

When she emerged into the world above, she quickly made a hiding place for her gems and scampered up over the rocks she had played on all those years ago. She entered the town wrapped in sail cloth looking like a sea goddess. Carrying cockles and mussels in her pockets and fish in her arms wrapped in seaweed, she was greeted by a mostly deserted street. The few people she met looked like they hadn't eaten in weeks. Molly gladly gave them what she had, as she made her way toward her home. It was deserted; her parents were no longer there. The few people she asked had no idea where they had gone, but they begged her to help them find food. They explained there had been a terrible famine these past two years and people were literally starving to death. Molly knew immediately what she had to do. She walked back to the shore and dove into the ocean back to her little world. She fashioned a basket of boards and sailcloth and gathered cockles and mussels by the hundreds. Molly had taken a wheelbarrow back to the shore where she filled it. Upon re-entering the town, she began singing the song she had learned so many years ago, a song that suddenly took on new words and meaning. The poor starving people came out of their houses to beg this strange lady of the sea for a bit of food. Molly began singing: "Alive, alive oh, alive, alive oh, cockles and mussels, alive, alive, oh." She handed out the shellfish, but wasn't clear how and to whom she should distribute the gems hidden in her cloak. After several trips she understood her power. She had learned to read the eyes. When she met someone who would share with their neighbors, she somehow sensed it through their eyes, and would slip a gemstone into one of the mussels. Molly traveled the land for weeks, returning to her cavern only to retrieve more food and precious gems. She became known throughout the land as Molly Malone, a sea goddess, who took the shape of a lowly fishmonger to save Ireland from famine."

"There's more to this Molly Malone than you've heard tonight, but let's let her sleep shall we." Jack then began to sing the song of Molly Malone in a soft gentle voice.

Molly Erricson remained voiceless, but Jack knew that she had heard him, for tears were flowing down her cheeks.

They sat for another ten minutes or so, and Jack took Molly's hand and led her to her room. Alone in his own room, Jack lay awake for hours wondering if Molly Erricson would ever emerge from her own undersea world. He realized he had fallen asleep at some point, when he heard Khris, knocking, not so softly on his door.

"Rise and shine Jack. I've been thinking about stuff all night and I'll tell you about it on our run."

Jack shook himself awake, trying to get oriented to his surroundings. He moved like a robot, stiffly pulling on his running shorts and nearly falling over as he put on each sock while Khris continued to sputter. Jack thought, (I fear I've created a monster.) The street lights were still on and the morning paper landed with a thump just as the two men emerged onto the driveway.

"Let's walk a bit," said Jack, still feeling like he was on stilts. They walked toward the ocean. Suddenly a sea breeze hit them head on. Jack felt like he'd walked into a cool shower. He breathed deeply. Now, he was awake. They ran and talked; Jack mostly listened. Khris was enthusiastic and excited-two ingredients needed for success in any venture.

That first work day was one of planning, of how best to advertise, and where to gather the materials needed. Jack found that Khris had some of the same management skills as his dad, and both men seemed pleased when they left Mr. Hendricks' office after briefing him on the day's progress. The days passed quickly. Jack and Khris put the plan into action and the results were immediate and successful.

Evenings were spent with the Erricson family and after about a month, Jack approached Shannon with an idea.

"I'd like to take Molly down to the beach."

"I don't know Jack. The few times we've taken Molly out in the car since coming home from the hospital, she's become frightened, and seems to withdraw further from our world."

"I know it's a risk Shannon, but these past nights that I've read, and told stories to her, it seems she hears me best, when I mention the sea."

"Are you sure?."

"I'm not sure of anything. At first I would walk with her around the grounds and everyday edge a little closer to the ocean. I may be wrong but I'll take it slow. I feel like she trusts me."

Mr. Erricson entered the porch and Shannon related Jack's proposal. "Jack, you've worked miracles with my son. I've never seen him so eager to get moving in the morning. He's not partying like he was either; he seems a man on a mission. I questioned him and he hinted about some grand plan in the works but wouldn't reveal any particulars. Whatever it is has made him a new man." Mr. Erricson sat down across from Jack.

"That being said, we're obviously concerned about Molly, and I know you are too. Let's work with Molly very slowly. She is just now beginning to rejoin the family. It has taken six months to get her to join us on the porch. I am not complaining mind you. The doctors held out little hope she would ever function on her own. It's been the hard work Shannon has done, as well as Molly's fighting spirit, that have her joining us on the porch. So let's go slowly, please.

"I will Paul and if I see any signs of her withdrawing, we'll stop immediately."

That night thinking about Molly, Jack decided to call his Father, again Sean answered. Everything seemed to be going well for Mr. O'Shea, as he'd found work doing maintenance at one of his social clubs. Sean was attending a local actors' workshop and had a small part in a local play.

"Who says no good comes from drinking," kidded Sean. "I met a fellow actor on one of those ten steps to becoming a tea drinker. He looks like he's tumbled down those steps a few times, but he has a great sense of humor, and man can he act. Anyway he invited me to try out for a part and I got it."

"Congratulations, should I be looking for your name in the marquee lights," quipped Jack.

"I wish. It is fun though and it takes care of my evenings so yeah, things are good here. How is the view from the hill." "I can see the ocean shimmering in the moonlight but I can't see the future," laughed Jack. "How is Mr. O'Shea doing, really?"

"He's in bed already. This work business tires him out but he seems happy. We are still going to AA once a week. It's kind of funny in a weird way but Dad and I don't think we are alcoholics in the traditional sense. We decided after listening to all the other people speak at these meetings that we O'Shea's are cut from a different cloth."

"What do you mean?" asked Jack.

"Well all the stories we've heard dealt with problems people were having in their lives- a lost job, bad relationship, abuse, you name it. We figured out we started drinking for an entirely reason. We drank for what was out of our lives, not what was in it. It took looking at other peoples lives to finally realize we drank to cover up our loss of family." Sean sounded like he was giving a speech.

"Remember, Dad didn't drink except socially for years. I think, when the second Mrs. O'Shea died, Pop finally realized all that was missing sons included. That is when he started drinking to get drunk. Now that you are back in our lives and we're actually planning a future, neither of us really care to drink all that much." "That is a hell of a story Sean, sounds like you two are finally communicating. Speaking of communication, have you heard from Mom?"

"Nope, we have written her out of the script, brother. She will not be coming to a theater near you soon," Sean chuckled. "Dad and I really are ok. Jack, so get on with your golfing business. Call when you can but don't worry about us. I'll say hello to Mr. O'Shea for you."

After Jack said good-bye, he held the receiver and smiled. Sean had the wit and humor of the O'Shea's running through his blood. Jack thought back to that morning so many years ago. Mr. O'Shea had insisted that a sense of humor, keen wit, and a creative mind was all the boys would need. If you added in Mrs. Erricson's homily, about being lucky enough if you were Irish, it seemed to be working for the family O'Shea too, finally. Late fall turned to what Californians observed as token winter. Jack and Khris fine tuned their lessons and clinics. Feedback from the members of the club had been positive.

Meanwhile, Jack continued to work at his own game. He found revisiting the past with Dannyboy to develop the strategies they were using in his clinics helpful to his game as well. Jack set a March deadline for himself to begin competing on a mini-tour. Jack and Khris formalized plans for the company they would form with Mr. Erricson as an enthusiastic investor. Khris would run the day to day operation and oversee the scheduling and advertising. Jack would provide technical advice and help create the training aids that would support the clinic's unique approach to teaching golf.

"For now Khris, don't quit your day job," kidded Jack.

Life was good; Jack couldn't think of a time he'd been happier. Still he realized he was reaching a critical time in his life. He had overcome so many obstacles and seemed to have quieted his inner demons as well. Dannyboy revealed Jack's thoughts about many things over the years, and now revisiting some of those early entries allowed him to crystallize what he was feeling. Jack had written about his time with the Houston family the past spring. How the need to destroy existing relationships seemed to end when he became part of a functioning family. Had it been about power? The ability to watch from a distance, find what might be a lasting relationship, then destroy it when it demanded what he could not give. Or could his own lack of family have created a jealousy of the closeness his victims shared?

One thing Jack knew for sure, the physical release he'd found in those relationships had left him feeling guilty and small. As he closed the pages, he thought of this new family he was so heavily invested in. Molly was continuing to show improvement. The outdoor walks, baby steps really, yet they had moved her ever closer to the ocean's edge. The nightly stories continued and it was clear to all that a bond had formed between Jack and Molly. Jack couldn't describe his feelings for Molly, but sitting there in the quiet of the evening, knowing she seemed to hang onto every word made him feel good. His stories varied with Jack trying to re-instill feelings of hope, laughter, love, and any other emotions he could create in his characters.

Tonight as he rocked, listening to the night sounds, he silently struggled with how to say good-bye. How would he say good-bye to this family he'd grown to love, and Molly, how could he say good-bye to Molly?

In his bedroom later, Jack found it difficult to sleep. His mind was listing and crossing out different scenarios. His thoughts jumped from saying good-bye, to finalizing plans for tomorrow's adventure. When the early morning knock on his door startled him, he realized at some point he had closed his eyes. The knock this morning was not Khris. After a long shower, Jack dressed and wandered down to the smells of coffee and some kind of pastry. As he sat across the table from Molly, he was still not sure how best to conduct today's big test.

Today, Jack was going to take Molly to the beach. It was a chilly morning on the peninsula. Shannon fussed over Molly's sweater and Jacket, trying to hide her nervousness. The pastries Jack had smelled were blueberry pancakes, cooked by Mr. Erricson, who appeared just as nervous as Shannon about this idea. A lot of nervous energy was being spent, and Molly too, sensed that somehow this day was going to be different. She allowed her Mother to help her with her sweater but insisted on buttoning her own jacket.

Jack remained in the background nursing his third cup of coffee hoping he was right about all this. The walks outdoors had put the color back in Molly's cheeks and she was getting stronger and more alert all the time. Her eyes had come alive; indeed, they had become her voice. Jack had learned to read those emerald green eyes just as his heroine Molly Malone had been given the gift. This morning they showed not panic but something Jack had not seen before.

On the porch at night, Jack had set the stage for today through his stories of Molly Malone. Today, they would walk the beach looking for the cavern Molly Malone had entered. With a light green scarf framing her beautiful face, they were finally up and out the door. Jack took Molly's hand, a strong hand, this morning a gripping hand. As they reached the end of the street and turned left for the first time, the ocean lay before them shrouded in mystery. They walked along the circular boardwalk edging closer to the water's edge and the mystery was revealed. The ocean this morning was calm, flat, and wrinkle free-an expanse of blue fabric designed to soothe a troubled mind. The winter morning sun at nine AM cast more light than warmth. It lit the walkway from behind, inviting them down the steps to the beach. Sound followed light and they heard the gentle lapping of waves washing the shoreline. Jack watched Molly's eyes grow wider and wider. Was it fear Jack saw? They did not go near the water, content to feel the sand crunch beneath their feet. Jack, in the end, had no script for how the morning would go, and it was just as well for what happened, Jack could only liken to his own relationship to Dannyboy.

Molly suddenly kicked off a shoe, walked several steps and kicked off the other. She continued to hold Jack's hand but was no longer following passively, but was rather leading Jack toward the gentle sound. Incredibly as they reached the waters edge, Molly's mouth opened and shut wordlessly.

Jack, not having the time nor opportunity, found his sneakers filling with water. Molly continued to move along the shore; Jack trudging at her side.

She reached down and touched the water, bringing it to her nose to smell. She touched it to her lips and tongue.

Jack was the one holding on for dear life as Molly began to walk faster and faster.

As suddenly as it began, Molly slowed. As though realizing she could become intoxicated, she seemed content to take a little sip, savoring the experience and committing it to memory. She turned from the water and clasping Jack's hand

with renewed strength, trudged slowly back. The look of triumph on her face and in her eyes gave Jack his first glimpse of the girl Molly Erricson used to be.

Jack was struck by how close the look on Molly's face reminded him of the Molly Malone he had created in his mind. From that day on, Molly unfolded like a beautiful flower. Her face softened and her senses heightened. Shannon took her daughter on long walks. Molly began to stop and smell the flowers or watch a bird perched on a limb. She was becoming more and more the Molly of old, and the house was a buzz of excitement.

The evenings were full of Shannon telling of the day's discovery. Molly would sit listening, the look on her face showing she knew her family was as delighted as she, about her progress. Molly would not go to the ocean with anyone but Jack. Shannon tried several different times but Molly would turn away.

Jack continued to walk with Molly whenever he could. Molly now took the lead on their walks and she would always head for the deep blue sea. Jack would sing the song of Molly Malone as they moved hand in hand along the beach, water lapping their feet. Faster and faster she moved, but always clutching Jack's hand. Splashing one another, Jack laughed aloud, while Molly's eyes filled with merriment.

They seemed like two lovers, creating a silent memory they would refer to every time they saw a sunlit beach.

Jack knew he had to leave soon. He wasn't sure what his feelings for Molly were becoming, but whatever they were, he had nothing presently to offer. Writing to Dannyboy, Jack expressed guilt feelings of a new sort. He wrote: It seems ironic that while I feel cured of the need to break up relationships, I am nevertheless having to end another. I am doing this for Molly and her parents sake he scribbled, but his writing did not fool his faithful companion. Jack's handwriting changed as he penned the words of his leaving. Truth be told and some day hopefully it would be, Jack had fallen in love. In Jack's mind the two Molly's had combined to become the woman of Jack's dreams.

"My sponsor is clamoring for me to get off my duff and get on with making a living, don't you know. Mrs. Houston says she fears this coastal living may turn me into a surfer and she's fairly certain there's little money in that." The family laughed and Jack continued. "Seriously though, I do need to start playing on the mini-tour and try to get my tour card. So I will be leaving at the end of the week."

"We are all going to miss you, Jack, for a hundred reasons," said Shannon. "You have helped each of us recognize what we mean to each other and we consider you part of the family." "I feel the same way about all of you; it has been wonderful and I hope I am welcome to come back when I can." Jack struggled to find his next words.

"Before she joins us, you need to know I am finding it hard to say good-bye to Molly, but I am hoping one last story will have her taking you down to the beach."

"She has made a remarkable comeback these past few months, Jack, and we will be forever grateful."

"I want that progress to continue and if Molly is really listening tonight, I believe the water will continue to be her therapy. Those little risks she's been taking are the key to any major breakthrough for her, and hopefully our savior Molly Malone will provide the motivation."

"What are you thinking, Jack? Any insight you have might help me, to help Molly," finished Shannon?

"I am no doctor, but I believe Molly's brain is receiving mixed signals when she sees the ocean. One part remembers the joy experienced as she explored beneath the waves while another part suffers from the shock of being abruptly shut down." As if that was not enough for the Erricsons to absorb, Jack had one more piece of departing news to share. He really struggled with these words.

"You need to know that I've fallen in love with Molly. With your permission, I will continue to be part of her life. I am praying the day will come when she returns to us and I can tell her how I feel."

The room was silent, each lost in his own thoughts. Shannon was the first to rise. She moved behind Jack's chair and put her hand on his shoulder. Mr. Erricson shook Jack's hand and told him nothing would please him more than to have Jack as a second son. Khris seconded the idea with a manly hug and went to get everyone a beer to toast the idea.

Later, as Molly and Jack sat alone listening to the crickets chirp, and the rockers creaking like a ship tied to anchor, Jack took Molly back to their ancestral home.

"Molly, did I tell you about Molly Malone finding her family after all that time? I didn't... hmm..., well, I meant to. Anyway she did and this is how it happened."

"Molly wandered through those streets that were so filled with filth, wreaking of disease, and despair. The only sign of life were the cries behind closed doors. Molly began her song. So full of hope was her voice that people opened those doors and windows and watched this young girl slowly wind her way. Picture it if you can." Jack closed his eyes, as the story tumbled off his lips. "Did I speak of the enchanting singing voice Molly was blessed with? No, well I should have." Jack hummed a few bars of the fishmonger's song. "Word spread quickly, don't you know, about this peasant girl wrapped in sailcloth, giving fish and mussels to all she met. Remember, Molly had gems hidden in the shells and the bellies of some of those fish. Molly could read the eyes she could. When she met the gaze of one that she knew would share their good fortune, she would hand them a fish or a mussel with a gemstone.

"Be sure to check the belly of this one," she'd say, "for I lost a valuable in one of these fish, and if it turns up in yours, bless you and keep you." Jack paused. "But I was speaking of Molly's singing voice a moment ago, wasn't I."

"As you recall, she sang what became a fish monger's song as she moved from town to town. To all that heard it, it became a National Anthem of sorts. A rallying cry for people to cling to life for they were indeed still alive-alive, oh. Molly carried a message of her own in the words to that song. You see Molly was born in a time when so many infant babies never reached an age where a song could reach their lips. Molly herself had lost two brothers before she entered this world of poverty. The first sounds Molly Malone ever heard was her mother praising this little bit of life she held in her arms. Alive, Alive, oh- she would sing softly to her baby daughter, praying through song, that Molly would survive the night. Molly now trudged those streets with that same song on her lips, praying that somewhere her own family had survived, and she might reclaim them. Molly's efforts raised the spirit of an entire nation, and one day her own personal quest was answered. On a late afternoon, nearly one hundred miles away from where she had started her journey, Molly neared a village. She was nearing the shore, preparing to dive for mussels, when the collective sounds of a flock of birds drew her attention. Moving over the boulders and rocks, Molly sat down; the birds darted closer and closer to her. They seemed intent on getting her full attention. The birds were singing in unison as if they had rehearsed for this performance. Molly closed her eyes, and let her mind drift, she slowly recognized the tune. It was the same song she had been singing all this time. The flock of birds rising and falling as one continued to sing, first moving away, and then swooping ever closer to Molly, as if beckoning her to follow along. Finally,

Molly did just that in song as well as movement. Molly fairly skipped across the rocks and soon reached a gnarly thicket. Above the rocks, the sounds of the ocean below were but a memory. After a short time, following the sounds of the birds, Molly entered a meadow where wild roses seemed to frame a pathway. Molly walked along this path nearly overwhelmed by the sweet smells. Turning a corner Molly raised her eyes when a weathered cottage appeared, battered and leaning, but obviously lived in. Molly's heart was pounding and the birds suddenly stilled. She could faintly hear someone singing. When she neared the single step leading up to the porch, the sun reached into the shadows of that porch to bid the day farewell. Molly climbed the step and the sound of a rocking chair squeaking on rough planks, reached her ears. That sound became lost in the voice of Molly's Mother as she sat rocking and singing the words Molly had searched so long to hear-'Alive, Alive, oh.' Molly folded her Mother in her arms, and the two continued to rock as the years of loss disappeared with the end of day's light. Molly would be told that her father had died several years earlier, but on his deathbed had asked his wife not to give up hope of finding their child. Rocking at night, night after night, the two shared stories of the years they had missed, laughing and crying at different turns. They walked the rugged coastline, sang songs, and tended the small garden in the back. Molly had enjoyed the undersea world, but when she found her Mother, she began to reclaim herself."

This time there were no tears on Molly Erricson's face as Jack finished his story. This time Molly took Jack's hand and squeezed, nodding her head, knowing what she must do.

CHAPTER

Sixteen

Jack drove away one early morning in March. As he looked back at the house that had become a home, the curtains in Molly's room were pulled back. Molly stood waving a candle, sending the clear message that she would be here waiting for Jack's safe return. Jack was struck by the irony of what Carey Houston had envisioned for her own home, a port in the storm of life.

❧❧

The months that followed proved Jack would eventually make it to the big show, as the PGA tour was often called by the young men trying to gain their tour card. The list of people Jack was supposed to stay in touch with was growing longer and longer, and he smiled as he dialed up one warm memory after another. He tried to check in every other week with Sean or his Dad. At least once a month he would call Mr. and Mrs. Houston, his sponsors, to keep them updated on his progress.

Every week though, without fail no matter how busy, he called the Erricson's. Jack would start with Khris if he was home and check on the progress of their clinics. It seemed they were really taking off and when Jack got back there, Khris wanted to look at establishing a timeline for franchising their product. Mrs. Erricson couldn't wait to tell Jack about Molly's latest trip to the beach. "Molly fairly dragged me the length of the peninsula and she couldn't take her eyes off the birds. Every time we found an area that could be climbed, she was off scampering across the rocks like she was looking for something. What kind of a story did you tell her anyway?"

Jack laughed, "When I get back there, I'll introduce you to the girl your daughter might have been, in a different life. Sounds like she's making progress though."

"I believe she is a little better each day. She certainly has her strength back. I don't know if she will ever take the plunge into those waves again though, certainly not without you being there."

"Let me talk to her if I could. I have so much to tell her about myself and what I am doing while I am away." Jack told Molly the story of how his father got him interested in golf and his plastic clubs, everything. Inserting humor and a little Irish magic, Jack shared who he was and how the game of golf had landed him on her doorstep. "I love what I do Molly and I know you understand, but as soon as I can, I'll be back to tell you one last Molly Malone story. I know you thought that story was done, but there is at least one chapter I neglected to tell you about." Mrs. Erricson got back on the phone and told Jack how Molly's eyes would light up whenever he talked to her.

"I believe you have captured her heart Jack and it is wonderful to see her so excited to be alive."

"I can't wait to get back. Say hello to Mr. Erricson for me. Good-bye, Shannon."

Jack was playing good golf on the mini-tour and had finished nearly all of the tournaments in the top five. Since early April he had traveled the southwest in a van, trading in his beloved Mustang for a little more comfort. Lying stretched out on the air mattress, with a battery powered lamp providing light, Jack thumbed through one of the many journals that held the story of his life.

Jack had but two goals in mind-to make it to the big show, and to make Molly whole again. No one outside the Erricson family would be told of his feelings for Molly until the first goal was reached. The rain continued to beat on the roof of the van rhythmically, a different tune than the downpour of yesterday. Everyone in this parched area was probably singing a happy tune except Jack. The pages revealed he had much to be thankful for and the reflection offered by Dannyboy, took his mind off his golf game. In the past two years he had found his Father and his brother, and together they had created a family of sorts. Sean had become close, and Jack saw so much of himself in the angry young man. (It's strange how each of us deals with anger in our own way, thought Jack. Sean had turned to fighting and alcohol, while Jack had been busy creating relationships that were not real, but damaging nonetheless.) Jack's writings revealed that both men appeared to have resolved their personal issues and were moving forward.

Molly Erricson appeared in his latest writing and his handwriting revealed a new lightness that was unlike anything he had seen previously. His golf game had never been better as the statistics before his eyes revealed. Yes indeed, there was much to be thankful for. (Now the real work must begin, said Jack to himself and to Dannyboy. It's nearly time to be inviting Sean to share in the dream and be my caddie. I am tired of traveling alone and a promise is a promise.) The rain seemed to be letting up and Jack moved to the driver's seat intent on finding something to eat and place a call to his brother.

"So you will come out then, Sean?"

"Yeah, why not? I love this theater stuff, but it's not like I am getting paid or anything," said Sean. "Besides, if it doesn't work out, maybe I will try to get into the movies. You do plan to be based in California at some point, right?"

"It's always good to have a fall back plan Sean, but I'm quite certain the crowds you will be entertaining will be focused on a little white ball," quipped Jack. "Speaking of entertaining, is the father of this clan doing anything but working? How will he feel about your leaving? Will he be okay?"

"He's not drinking, even socially, and he is taking on more and more responsibility at the club. They call him a maintenance engineer now, or so he tells me, and he is studying for a boiler license."

Sean raised his voice in feigned Irish excitement, "Oh, and did I mention in passing, there's a new shine to his hair, a real glow don't you know."

Jack laughed, "So he's broken out the old Brylcream tube has he, I still remember that smell to this day. Have you met her?" "No and he hasn't said anything, but he's singing the old songs and his feet are moving in little dance steps from time to time so I get the feeling Mr. O'Shea won't be lonely at all."

"That's great Sean. Tell him to follow the papers because soon he won't have to make up any Irish stories to get out the word about the O'Shea brothers." "What's your timeline look like?"

"I am hoping by next spring to be playing in a PGA event, but we have a lot of work to do so get on out here and we'll get there together."

"Is there time to have a little fun then or are we talking all work and no play?" said Sean, still in voice.

"There will be a whole new way of thinking and reacting for you to learn at first, about the game and about your brother, but you won't have to become a priest or anything."

"I am ready to go; just give me the word,"

"I will be sending you a bank check so make your reservations, and let me know when you will arrive. I am trying to find an apartment that we can use as a home base."

"I will plan to be out there within two weeks so happy house hunting, brother. Can't wait. I miss you."

Jack hung up and looked out the window of the road side diner, the sun making its first appearance in two days. (Looks like the sun is going to shine on this little bit of business,) thought Jack. I believe I just might go hit some balls.

Back in his van after an hour on the range and a quick shower in the club locker room, Jack settled down in the passenger seat with the local paper. Straight to the classified ads, Jack made it a point to skip the news and sports section.

Remembering how his own father had resorted to inventing stories to find any good news, Jack was a little cynical about the state of the union. The classified section led Jack through employment opportunities listed alphabetically. Services offered ranged from your home, to your body, to meeting someone who wanted your body. Jack found he could buy all kinds of used furniture, if he was in the market to furnish this apartment, that he still had not located. It seemed to Jack every thing in the world was for sale, or rent, outgrown, or thrown out; a tale behind every transaction.

Jack found a two bedroom apartment that was close to the course he had been practicing at. Two weeks later Sean joined him.

CHAPTER
Seventeen

Jack hugged his brother and helped him put the two large suitcases in the back of the van.

"How do you like the van, brother? That Mustang was a collectible you know. Did you get anything for it at all?" "I'm afraid the dealer didn't have a flair for antiques. At first he said he'd give me salvage value but his heart went out to this poor struggling golfer and, of course, practically gave me the van or so he said," laughed Jack.

The two brothers talked and kidded their way to the O'Shea Hilton as Jack had dubbed it.

Sean, carrying the heavier of the two suitcases, stopped at the top of the first flight of stairs and breathlessly managed, "You told me we had the penthouse but you neglected to tell me there was no elevator."

Jack laughed, "All a part of the training needed to carry my golf bag for four days in a row; don't you see. Consider those flights as step one in your new fitness regimen."

"So, I am to believe these two flights are merely one step." He breathed deeply, "I hope I can convince my heart of that, dear brother. I think those 10 steps Dad and I are to climb to sobriety might be less a challenge," joked Sean.

Jack sat down on the couch and Sean sprawled across the overstuffed chair. They stared at one another wordlessly; then both jumped up to high five one another and began laughing realizing that this was a plan that could work.

The days ran into one another with Jack teaching Sean how to read the subtle breaks in the greens and the protocol to follow from the tee off to putting the flagstick back. Sean was an eager student, and he kept Jack relaxed with the same wit and sense of humor that ran through all the O'Shea blood.

Golf etiquette, how to measure distances, check wind direction and speed, were agenda items on the rigorous schedule the men set. They ran together, lifted weights, and shared cooking duties. In the evening Jack introduced Sean to cribbage and Sean taught Jack how to play poker.

"Where did you learn to play poker, Sean?"

Sean, who used his new found acting skills to his best advantage, continually beat Jack by skillfully bluffing and by reading Jack's body language.

"Some of those days I was suspended from high school, I would wander down to the pool hall, and there was always a game going on in the back. I watched those guys and as long as I didn't say anything, I was allowed to stay. The game itself is simple but the art is in reading the eyes and how the body of your opponent sends out clear messages."

Jack thought back to the story of Molly Malone he had created for his own dear Molly, and how she had been able to read the eyes. (Seems like we share more than a sense of humor,) he reflected.

"What was I thinking about just then brother since you can read me like a book?"

"Not a book brother, a deck of cards, and I'm betting fifty cents that the message you were sending is going to make me a rich man." Sean tossed in the two coins. He laid down his cards and indeed, Jack the man had to defer to the pair of Jacks, staring him down.

On other nights, Jack would quiz Sean about the rule book he was asking Sean to digest. "Some of these rules are ridiculous, not even understandable to the rational mind," said Sean one evening.

"I agree Sean, but thank God there are men who really do understand every conceivable situation or exception and they are on the sidelines when we play. If anything seems out of the ordinary, just ask for a rules clarification and these guys can quote bible and verse."

"Good," said Sean, "if it's not in the fairway or on the green, don't look to me, brother."

"You just make sure my bag is loaded with anything and everything I might need; always make sure I have the right number of clubs. We will go over the yardage books and the

little notebook I keep for myself, the night before. Let's take a break and play cribbage," said Jack.

"You mean I passed the course!"

"Yes brother, it is indeed my pleasure to welcome you to the wonderful world of golf. Soon we will be walking the same fairways trudged by another Jack and an Arnold and a Tom. It's hard to believe that those afternoons spent with Dad on that course he was building would ever lead to this."

The first tournament they were together, a mini tour event, proved the chemistry was right and Jack felt the future was bright for the two brothers.

Sean was a free man between tournaments and made friends with the other caddies who were also hanging around. Sean

didn't drink at all any more so he created a social time for himself that would allow his personality to shine through without falling off the wagon. Sean invited his fellow caddies to the penthouse to play poker. These young men were lonely and away from home so Sean would prepare a big spaghetti meal. Dessert would be a game five card stud. Sean found these occasions would allow the actor in him to emerge and everybody had a good time. The camaraderie that grew from these games made Sean a popular guy with the other caddies. Sometimes these games took place in the evening but usually late afternoon. The stakes were small and nobody complained that Sean was a usual winner. Sean noticed that what he had told Jack about being able to read people, was keeping a little extra money in his pocket.

Jack was paying Sean but until Jack won some real money Sean knew money would be tight.

Jack had been placing well enough on the mini tour so that he was finally able to secure a sponsor's exemption and would get to play in his first PGA event on the West Coast in two weeks.

CHAPTER

Eighteen

With the tournament beginning the next day, the two brothers spent Wednesday evening going over the notes they had made during the practice sessions earlier in the week.

"I have everything in your bag and I counted your clubs for the third time," said Sean.

"The next two days are going to be a challenge Sean; we are going to see crowds like we have never seen before. Tiger Woods and David Duval are both in this tournament; it will be crazy. Try to think one step ahead of what I need to do next. I will have my hands full just trying to swing a club."

The next morning Jack walked around as if in a daze. He saw players whom he had watched on television using the practice range and putting before their tee time. The cameramen were interviewing the favorites as golf carts ran up and down the area carrying one dignitary after another.

By the time Jack got to the first tee and heard his name announced, he felt like the driver he was about to swing weighed ten pounds. He tried to create an image in his mind of what the ball flight would look like just before he swung. The final message, a mutter really, was as weak coming off his lips as the ball leaving the tee. "It will all be over soon, Dannyboy."

The one hundred and eighty yard drive barely managed to stay in bounds. Jack O'Shea had officially started his professional career on tour.

Jack, who prided himself on being totally prepared, was totally unprepared for the case of nerves he was experiencing. At the end of the first day Jack looked up and by the time he found his name on the large scoreboard his gaze had dropped nearly fifteen feet. The 76 Jack managed had him nine shots out of the lead. To make it to the final two rounds on the weekend, Jack would need to shoot at least 70 tomorrow.

He spent a sleepless night trying to imagine a scenario that could vault him ahead of the forty players standing on his name. The morning sun kissed the window of the van. Jack turned over, trying to stay out of the spotlight that in his dream had become an interview with one of the networks. He was being asked how it felt to miss the cut in his first tournament. In his dream, people were holding him back from attacking the commentator while the cameras rolled.

In reality it was Sean lightly shaking Jack, telling him it was time to make the doughnuts.

Jack shook his head, clearing away that last image.

The second round began on a higher note as Jack parred the first three holes. "I am feeling better about this today Sean, if we can stay steady as she goes and I can finish 2 under for the day, we should qualify for the weekend."

Jack would later say he should have just kept his mouth closed, and his driver's face open a bit. Two balls pulled out of bounds in the next five holes had Jack muttering again to Dannyboy and not speaking to Sean. Jack shot a 74 and missed the cut by the four strokes he had predicted.

Saturday morning found Jack and Sean at a small breakfast place. Jack suggested Sean walk the course behind the ropes with him for the next two days. Watching the leaders and absorbing the excitement that would not be theirs might be motivating. "I have some soul searching to do, Sean. I am not sure I belong here, not sure if I have the game for this level."

Sean tried to reassure Jack but didn't really have the knowledge of the game to be very convincing, but he knew his brother.

"All I know brother is that quitting isn't something you would be very good at. I can see you breaking the news to your journal there, after all the work that you two have put in, wouldn't be easy. Why don't we do just as you suggested and walk this tournament. Let's not follow the leaders though. Let's follow one of these guys who is grinding it out week after week trying to keep his card. I played poker a few times with a couple of them and their caddies; let's watch them get through the weekend," said Sean.

Jack looked at his brother and chuckled, "I thought I was supposed to be the insightful one, and you the fighter. Seems you're both, brother." Jack studied Sean for a moment and made a decision.

"I have some major thinking to do Sean, and much of it has nothing to do with golf. Order us up another cup of coffee. I have some things I need to tell you about your brother."

Just as Sean had bared his soul to Jack at night with the drinks flowing, the waitress was just setting out the lunch menu when Jack finished his own story.

"That's the story of an Irishman who's been lost at sea," quipped Jack.

Sean stretched, and reached over to touch Jack's shoulder. "I don't think walking this weekend is what you need, brother, I think you need to go to the beach with that beautiful woman you described. That is where your decision lies. You're right, what you're feeling isn't about golf."

Jack nodded, "I'll leave today. Can you get along without the van? I'll give you some money for a room," said a suddenly excited Jack.

"Don't worry about me. There are a lot of other guys sitting out the weekend so I ought to be able to scare up a poker game. Maybe look for a girl myself; so go brother, may the O'Shea magic light your way."

Jack knew now in his heart what he needed to do but he still turned to Dannyboy for some final advice. Jack spent two hours looking at various entries he had made over the years and was gaining no insight with Dannyboy offering no opinion whatsoever. All of a sudden Jack found his answer not in an entry but in something Sean had said. What you are feeling isn't about golf, he'd said. Here was an opinion Dannyboy hadn't offered. No small wonder, Jack had always used the opposite line when trying to make excuses for his thoughts, kidding himself. Now suddenly Jack had real live people in his life, who understood him well enough and cared enough to tell it straight. Dannyboy was no longer Jack's only means of communicating to himself; finally he could ask for help.

Shannon Erricson answered on the first ring somehow knowing it was Jack. "Jack, I just finished reading the sports section so I knew you would be calling this weekend. How are you?"

"I was disappointed at first but my brother straightened me out. That's why I am calling actually. I would like to drive up and see Molly, walk with Molly, just be with Molly."

"Of course, you're welcome anytime. Molly will be so glad to see you."

"It's her confidence I need right now. I'm beginning to think she does more for me than I do for her. How is she?"

"She has all her coordination back. You should see her scamper over the rocks, and she dances in her room, hugging you I presume."

"What do the doctors say?"

"They are amazed. She's off the charts as far as similar cases, so they tell me to keep on doing what we're doing, and to hope for the best."

"I will be there by tomorrow morning then. It's two pm now so mid-morning at the latest should find me begging a cup of coffee."

"Okay, drive carefully. I'll let you surprise Molly. I won't say a word."

When Jack hung up, he knew he was doing the right thing. He headed the van in a Northwest direction and found himself already humming his theme song.

∾∾

As Jack pulled into the driveway, he glanced up. Molly stood looking through the same window as if she had remained on vigil. There was no surprised expression, just a beaming smile that Jack wanted to wake up to every morning of his life.

After recounting his meltdown at the tournament using self-deprecating humor and wit, Jack and Molly found themselves alone on the porch.

"I have so much to tell you Molly. I wanted to wait until I was this successful golfer to tell you how I feel, but I realize you need to know who this story teller and dream weaver really is." Jack spent the next three days with Molly. They walked the beach; Jack telling Molly about his own family. There were no leprechauns, stories of Ireland, magic, or fairies, just the story of Jack O'Shea. Dannyboy no longer was the lone keeper of the keys, for Molly heard nearly everything there was to tell.

Jack shared his triumphs, and his tragedies, leaving out only the part about his relationship issues-those he still didn't fully understand himself. In the evening they held hands rocking in tandem; the only sound was the chairs, the ocean, and their own beating hearts. Having released his feelings from the rumpled pages seemed to lift Jack's spirits. While Molly obviously had not offered an opinion, Jack was sure she had accepted Jack, the man.

The three days proved a breakthrough for Jack and he saw in Molly's renewed confidence, a reaffirmation of his own. When he had said his goodbyes to the rest of the family, he found himself alone with Molly once again.

Molly reached for Jack and did the hugging. Her quiet strength was given freely, and it was clear she was able to give back some of what Jack had given her.

CHAPTER

Nineteen

When Jack arrived back at the apartment he shared with Sean, he walked up those thirty-six steps thinking that this is step one for me too. If I want to compete at this level of golf, I have to raise my mental game to a new level. Molly and her struggle to regain what she had lost would be the inspiration Jack would draw from as he prepared for his next tournament. Always a reader, Jack found a library and began researching the mental side of golf. I have to learn to trust my swing and to be able to keep self-doubt away, reasoned Jack. He pulled several books off the shelf and moved to a table in a corner. It was in a book by W. Timothy Gallway, called, <u>The Inner Game Of Golf</u>, that Jack found his answer. He began browsing through the book. When he came to the awareness mode the author was describing, Jack found himself being written about, or so it seemed. If athletes could allow this technique to take over their body while performing, they could keep any self-doubt at bay. Jack felt he had good concentration, but now he realized he could train his brain, just as he could any muscle in your body.

∾

A month later Jack entered his second PGA tournament. His preparation for this event had changed dramatically. Jack personalized what he read and created his own code for the exercise. He called it M&M. One obvious connection was Sean's love of chocolate candy, the code reminding Jack that Sean was firmly behind any decision he made. The other reminder the code triggered was the two M's in Jack's life. One, the imagined savior of Ireland would release the creative shot making, Jack might be called upon to make. The second "M" would remind Jack that as he stood watching himself strike that white ball in the arse, he would not be standing alone, and Molly Erricson was holding his hand. He found the technique was like watching himself from a distance. He watched himself set up for the shot, and he could even influence his stance and his swing thoughts.

"I feel like I am watching a movie a few frames ahead of the actors and directing the action," he told Sean.

Sean, who thought it pretty weird, kidded Jack.

"What am I doing during this movie, brother? If you see me picking my nose, please yell cut"

"I'll be sure to do that and by the way you should feel honored that your beloved candy is a part of my new approach." On the first tee Jack watched himself stand over the ball.-Nice setup, good balance, slow backswing, the briefest of pauses, and a down swing and full follow through. Gripping Molly's hand in his mind, Jack watched the ball soar down the left side, nearing the white out of bounds stakes that would blow this idea out of the water. Just as it hit, surely to turn left leaving Jack to tee it up again, the other M emerged. She must have Jack reasoned, as he found his ball just off the fairway. Spectators were pointing to what looked like a whitish rock that had changed the balls direction. Jack walked over and looked down, it was clear Molly Malone had been here, for there in the long grass just off the fairway lay a sea shell of some sort. Jack put it in his pocket and smiled.

Jack would go on to make his first cut and win a tidy sum of money when things wound down on Sunday afternoon. "I just know today's finish is only the beginning Sean, Your share isn't peanuts either, now don't spend it all in one place."

Sean, just as excited as Jack, assured his brother he would be investing his money.

"In what?" asked Jack.

"I'm intending to put my acting skills to work so I'll be investing in myself," said Sean mysteriously.

঩৺

Jack called the Houston family and told them he would be sending them their first return on their investment. Everyone was well, he was told. Carey Houston reminded Jack her daughter Whitney would be demanding that he visit her school when he got back there.

"I can't wait. Tell her I'll send her a clip of an interview I had with a writer out here, for her newsletter."

"She will love that Jack. By the way I won our club championship and I credit that lesson you gave me, a hundred years ago now it seems."

"Glad I was of some help. You gave me a valuable lesson too and it's making all the difference. I will stay in touch.

The two brothers went to dinner to celebrate, and afterwards made the long drive back to their apartment. When they were settled in, Jack went over the schedule they would be following in the weeks and months ahead. " We will be leaving here soon but now that I have a little money, I think I will extend the lease,so we have a place for our stuff and a place to come back to." Tired and satisfied, Jack should have slept well but instead,had a strange dream that had him tossing and turning. In the dream, Mr. O'Shea was holding Jack's hand while they stood on the golf course he had built. He was pointing to something in the distance just off the fairway. Jack strained to see what it was but he couldn't understand what his father was saying. The light was fading rapidly so father and son began running. Suddenly, it was not his father's hand gripping his. Molly was pulling him along while Sean held her other hand, and Mr. O'Shea dragging up the rear. Jack shouted to stop. He was a child in this dream while Molly, Sean, and Mr. O'Shea looked as they did now. Jack tried to break away but something was holding him back. "Let me go," he was shouting.

Sean startled, asked, "What's wrong Jack? Are you alright?" He nudged Jack and shook him gently.

Jack came awake, a ball of sweat; he got out of bed. "I… I guess it was a nightmare; sorry, Sean, go back to sleep. Jack toweled off and returned to his bed. He finally slept; the dream did not return.

In the morning, Jack remembered enough of the dream to tell Sean he thought he would call his father tonight.

"What was that all about last night, brother?"

"Overtired I guess; too much in my head. I think I'll just hang out today and maybe do some laundry. What are you going to do Sean?"

"I met some guys and I think maybe I can scare up a little poker game. You sure you don't want to come?"

"Take me out to a late breakfast and the van is yours. Laundry and vegging out is my exciting plan for the day," said Jack.

While Jack was doing laundry, and calling all his families and getting the well deserved verbal pats on the back, Sean was doing more than killing time.

Sean was kicking ass in a not so small stakes poker game. Sean had come to love the thrill of the game, the tension, and even the cigar smoke that sent a bluish cloud rising up into the glare of a shaded neon globe. Sean, the actor, was playing a role in an old gangster movie. He set his bag of M&M peanuts on his left side wanting the other players to see him reach across with his right hand. Letting the bag rustle lightly, he took just one. Sean would roll it between his thumb and forefinger, then let it click on his teeth before sucking away the sweetness. He would finally chew the peanut and begin the process again. The other players dubbed Sean, "The Candy Man", and that suited Sean perfectly. He used his candy to send subtle messages to his opponents' nervousness, a bluff, or confidence. Sean was no longer playing poker with a beer crowd; he was playing against men who took the game very seriously. These men, while not professional gamblers, were successful businessmen who played to win.

Whenever Jack left to work on his game and Sean wasn't needed, he would find his way to a game of his own. Sean was developing skills that were as finely honed as his brother's.

CHAPTER
Twenty

The brothers finished their first year together, both feeling like they had made a good decision. Jack won nearly $125,000, and Sean, with 10% of Jack's winnings and his own poker winnings, seemed pleased as well.

The two men sat in the penthouse apartment, preparing to take a break from one another and looking forward to the next year on tour. Jack spoke of a sophomore slump he hoped to avoid.

"I know you didn't get rich this year, Sean, but with a good start next year I should be able to get some major sponsorship.

That will get you a higher percentage of my winnings."

"I'm not complaining brother, I have money in the bank for the first time and I plan to do a little sightseeing before I go see Dad."

Jack gave Sean the van and watched him head down the drive knowing he would miss his brother over the next couple of months. He took out Dannyboy and reviewed the goals he had set at the start of the year. He nodded more than satisfied that he had met them. Jack found the letter he had read a dozen times in the last month and opened it once again. Molly was continuing to improve. The letter Jack held bore evidence. Molly had relearned how to put her thoughts down on paper. Her parents had thought a computer would be easier, but Molly surprised them by slowly and gracefully shaping her thoughts through the written word. Molly's writing showed she was thinking at a high level, but getting those thoughts down on paper was sheer hard work.

On his last visit home, shortly after receiving his first letter, Jack sat with Molly and tried to ease her frustrations. "Remember how long Molly Malone wandered those streets, trying to find her family. She never gave up. Right now your mind is wandering through streets of a different sort, trying to help you get all the way home. I remember your mother telling me how excited you became with a new smell or a different flower or bird. Enjoy the trip Molly, you are moving forward, and you are not alone like Molly Malone was. You have your family and you have me if you want me."

Jack didn't say I love you but he sensed she knew.

୬∽ଏ

Jack rented a car and with the penthouse secured, he began the trip he was becoming so familiar with. Jack loved the coastline and it was during the drive that he planned a last chapter he would relate to Molly. First however, he would try to teach Molly a little about the concentration technique that had helped him so much.

୬∽ଏ

"You see Molly, it is possible to create your own virtual reality." Jack and Molly were rocking back and forth holding hands as Jack explained how to close her eyes and practice visualizing the action of the story he was about to tell. During the past week together he had introduced the concept. Molly wrote on a notepad. She believed she was now ready to see this Molly Malone as well as to hear her voice.

Jack hoped to re-create those last few minutes underwater which had robbed Molly Erricson of oxygen. If she could stand outside her body and see herself become trapped, perhaps she could free herself from those lines and rise to the surface unharmed. Jack felt this last chapter of Molly Malone might be the final opportunity to bring this wonderful lady all the way back. "As I tell you this story Molly, close your eyes and pretend you are Molly Malone. You must watch her from a safe distance but see the story come alive."

"Did I tell you how Molly ran out of precious gems after a time?"

Molly shook her head.

"Well she did." Jack leaned back into the rocker.

"In that cave that she had discovered, all that remained were bits of wood. Molly surmised that other ships had gone aground during the fierce storms off the coast. Molly began a trip to the rugged coastline to look for signs of a wreck that had not completely broken up offshore. She knew she could best help by offering more than fish or mussels. The cries of hunger and disease filling her head followed her as she made her way towards the salty air. Alone, Molly was struck by the beauty that walked hand in hand with death and starvation. The meadows and woods were alive, a palette of pinks and purples, yellows and browns, greens and grays. Flowers and butterflies, birds and bees, small animals, were all going about their business untouched by the misery around them. As she neared the ocean, the rhythmic sound of waves filled another sense and her ears became her eyes. Molly heard the plaintive sound of the gulls and she knew she was close. Smells of salt and seaweed reached her nose and she smiled. She reached the last barrier to the world below - rough briars and brambles. It seemed God had planned for only the hearty to attempt to shake hands with the sea. Standing on the top of a field of boulders, Molly looked out over the expanse of blue and wondered aloud: 'How can a creator of all this, allow what I have been witnessing along those mean streets?' Molly climbed down, hands and feet seeking a grip. The surf crashing on the rocks below became louder and louder. Nearing the Ocean's edge, she began to move across the gigantic boulders looking for shards of wood. Just off shore, ships lay on the ocean floor, a watery grave that was constantly being shifted by the tides and coastal storms. Molly found a small cove where the tides had created a sandy beach and she fashioned a campsite. She found driftwood that had been thrown far up in the rocks and built a small fire. Molly threw out a line and hook and caught the most curious. Sitting on the rocks nibbling on her fresh catch, she watched the sun dive silently into the water to have a look around. Molly thought of how she would be doing the very same thing tomorrow. She threw the bones to the gulls and they caught them in the air. Molly finally had to throw stones at them to convince them supper was over and to leave her alone. After a good night's sleep, Molly found wood of all shapes and sizes during a morning search. She had soon built a small raft that she could cling to while trying to locate a wreck. By afternoon Molly was ready to do some diving. She attached a long rope, loaded a piece of canvas, and shoved off. A large stone attached to the rope would keep the float from drifting away, while Molly was under the surface. For three days, Molly pushed her float along, dropping anchor and diving to the Ocean floor. The sunlight above, created a greenish fog that allowed Molly to see only several yards ahead of her. Molly felt at home in this silent world. Holding her breath for minutes at a time seemed as natural as welcoming air back into her lungs. The schools of fish welcomed Molly as a visiting professor and were eager to learn all about her and show her their home. They swam through strands of Molly's hair that trailed her. They playfully brushed against her legs, rode on her shoulders, and looked her square in the eye. Molly struggled to keep from laughing. There was work to do however and Molly began her search. She found bits and pieces of glass and scraps of wood but no ship. Molly repeatedly dove, took a long look around, and surfaced to her float. She wrapped cooked fish in her canvas and put fresh water in a jar, staying out on the water as long as possible. Above, the gulls circled endlessly. Molly had to shoo them away from her wrapped fish every time she surfaced. On that third day, Molly traveled out just a bit further and down the coastline a half mile from her camp site. She pushed the rock attached to the rope overboard, and slipped below the surface using the line as a guide to the bottom. On this day the fish left her alone as if sensing there was no time left to play. Molly found herself going deeper than she had ever gone before. Molly remained relaxed, knowing panic was the silent enemy. There was no room for self-doubt. Not when the ocean bottom shows no remorse in claiming ownership, of anything or anyone foolish enough to slip beneath the surface. The ocean is good at keeping secrets and gives them up grudgingly. Molly knew this as she strained to find shadows on the bottom. Storms can move a mountain of sand and often does. Molly on this third day found what was buried below one such mountain. It was late afternoon on that third day. Molly prepared to dive for perhaps another hour at most. She had eaten a fish and quenched her thirst. After a short nap and experiencing a dream that left her smiling, Molly took a deep breath and dove. The momentum of diving from the platform gave her a few precious extra seconds of breath. She followed the line to the bottom and swam away, looking down. At first she didn't see the hulking wreck looming above her. When she did see it, startled, she nearly opened her mouth in surprise. The ship lay in about thirty-five feet of water, a skeleton with only its ribs visible. Molly quickly surfaced hand over hand, using the lifeline. She moved her platform directly over the spot. She said a silent prayer promising God if he would help her continue her work that she would not stop until she found her own family. She opened her eyes and looked out over the horizon, there was nothing above but fair weather clouds. (If only the waters below would promise as much,) she thought. Molly dropped the anchor and once again followed the stone to the bottom. The part of the ship visible, a ghostly skeleton, gave Molly a queasy feeling as she moved cautiously between the beams and began her search. She had removed the stone from the rope and with each dive; she tied the rope to an area of the ship last explored. When she got to the part of the ship lying on the bottom, she found much of it intact. If any cargo remained, it would be in this section, she reasoned. By now exhausted, Molly surfaced to plan for tomorrow. She left the platform in place and swam to shore. She walked back along the rocks and found her campsite. Molly built a fire, gathered mussels, and caught fish for supper. She wrapped them in seaweed and placed them on a stone she had set directly in the fire. Molly slept the sleep of the dead. It was the screeching of the birds waiting to be fed that let Molly know it was, - 'time to make the donuts'," Jack laughed.

Molly Erricson smiled.

"Let me say that another way Molly."

"The next morning, the seagulls wandered the campsite looking for any scraps of food not given them the night before.

They screeched at one another, threatening violence, and Molly finally was awakened. Shooing them away, she quickly swam to the float. Climbing aboard, she grabbed a small canvas bag she had fashioned and a knife. Slipping below the surface, she followed the rope to the wreck. Molly found dishes and pots and bits of wood that must have been a chest of drawers. She stuffed anything that would fit into her canvas bag. Each dive revealed a little more about the people who had been swept beneath the waves. Using her hands, Molly moved along finding what had once been the quarters of the crew. Tying off the rope to each section checked, Molly knew there was not much left to search. She rested on her platform, shielding her face from the afternoon sun. Molly quenched her thirst but ate nothing, trying to leave room for extra oxygen if that were possible.

She dove deep into the bowels of the ship, hauling herself along the line hand over hand, determined to find treasure. No light penetrated where Molly now explored. She tripped over something. Reaching out to keep her balance, a solid door stopped her fall. Recognizing what this might mean, suddenly Molly was excited. She tied off the rope and surfaced. Molly dove again and pried the rotted wood from the hinges with her knife. She tried to force the door; it wouldn't budge. Molly gave a mighty pull and it gave way.. She surfaced one more time and returned. Swimming through the entrance she found what must have been the captain's quarters. It was here she found the ship's safe. Once more Molly tied off the line and went up to get air. On her return, she moved immediately to the safe. She was leaning over it feeling for the handle when suddenly she was struck on the back by something heavy. The door Molly had freed from its iron shackles chose this moment to do a bit of exploring as well. Molly was driven forward and nearly lost her air. The heavy door now rested across Molly's back and shoulders. Molly immediately recognized the trouble she was in. She knew she had a minute at most to free herself and get to the surface. Molly lay draped over the safe, two feet from the ships floor. She pushed backward but the door wouldn't budge. She felt around with her feet and discovered a hole in the floor. If she could gain some leverage, and pull the safe into that hole; maybe she could follow behind letting the door cover the hole. Molly used her arms to try to pull the safe toward her. The metal band securing the safe had been eaten away; the safe moved slightly toward her. The pressure from the door was becoming unbearable, and Molly pulled with a desperation that gave her increased strength. The safe gave way without warning sliding into the hole, with Molly following, holding on for dear life.

Hoping to God that there was a way out, Molly now free looked for an escape route. She saw a lighter shade of darkness to her left. Molly swam to it, knowing she had very little time left, for specks of light were forming in her eyes. Molly rushed to the surface, her stomach beginning involuntary contractions. Locating and grasping the rope in her last few yards probably saved her life. Surfacing, she grabbed the float and screamed her lungs nearly exploding. Molly retched as her stomach began to spasm. She didn't move for nearly half an hour, simply holding on to the float, eyes closed, birds circling noisily above. Molly returned the next day and found the precious gems she had sought. She gave thanks to her God, and returned to the streets to continue her work while seeking her own family. Molly placed one gem in a mussel and hung it around her neck to remind her of how blessed she was to have the gifts God had provided. Molly had her faith restored, and would never question her Creator's intentions again.``

Jack looked at this wide eyed beauty sitting next to him and said, "So you see Molly if you try as hard as you can, you might be able to free yourself from beneath those waves." Molly Erricson laid her head on Jack's shoulder. Jack could only hope in the days ahead, that Molly would be able to verbalize the gesture.

These rocking chairs had become a special place for Jack. Walking into the kitchen, Jack looked back at those rockers holding vigil over the night; their silhouette seeming to promise, only good things are imagined out here. Jack felt secure. He would be able to get back to his career and not lose this woman who had become such a part of his life.

He walked Molly to her door where they embraced. Rocking side to side, the silence of the evening allowed them to create their own music. Jack could feel Molly's love in her heartbeat, and he returned that love thump for thump. If no words could ever be exchanged, to Jack that would be a small price to pay to have Molly in his life. He knew Molly would fight for all God would grant her and would be satisfied with that.

Goodnight was good-bye for a while. When Jack left the next morning, Molly ran to her room to once again send Jack on a safe journey holding a candle to her window to light his way.

CHAPTER
Twenty-One

Jack returned once more to the tour, determined that the sophomore jinx would not claim him as a victim. He rejoined Sean in the penthouse and they mapped out the year. Sean was a great help and the two brothers were popular at all the social occasions that surfaced. Jack found that when he was comfortable around a group of people, he could take any small occurrence and turn it into an Irish story that would always attract an audience. Sean, on the other hand, could dazzle a damsel, as Jack would say. The two had no shortage of people hanging around their apartment. On the road, Sean usually spent the evening either holding the hand of some lovely or holding a lovely hand of cards. In either case, he usually came out on top at evening's end. When their van headed to the next tour stop, usually a broken heart, or a guy dead broke, one or both would be clearly visible in the rear view mirror.

Jack had saved enough money that he could return the last two checks to the Houston's. He wrote thanking them but hoped he could make it on his own this year. Jack had saved $30,000 dollars from last year's earnings and Dannyboy documented all sales and purchases. This year Jack hoped to secure a sponsor who would help pay some of the costs of traveling and living on the road.

Sean told Jack that he should approach the Cadillac division of General Motors. Sean, riding to Poker games with some high rollers, said he loved the ride they produced.

"I don't plan on being too picky Sean. I haven't seen any new autos parked in the yard yet, or even a logoed hat for that matter," chuckled Jack.

"They will this year brother. I just know it," said Sean.

♋︎

Jack had spent some time with Khris during his stay with Molly's family. Khris was franchising their clinics this year throughout the three Western states. Reinvesting their earnings in the expansion left no profits but within a year they should be able to take a small salary. Mr. Erricson was guiding Khris and the two of them were inseparable these days. The thought of father and son brought Mr. O'Shea to mind.

"I believe I will check in on Mr. O'Shea; anything you want me to tell him for you, Sean."

"Tell him that your brother seems to have inherited his irresistible way with the ladies and I'd like to thank him for that." "I will tell him that for sure," said Jack as he dialed the number. When Mr. O'Shea picked up on the sixth ring, Jack was just about to hang up.

"I see you weren't sitting anxiously by the phone, waiting for your first born to call with an outrageous Irish tale to tell."

Mr. O'Shea chuckled, "To tell you the truth Jack, I was in a position where listening to a good story might have given me the inspiration I needed." He laughed. "I should have brought the portable into the toilet with me so I wouldn't be standing here with my trousers down so to speak."

It was Jack's turn to laugh and then both men were laughing. "Well if you aren't finished, grab that portable and hear me out." Jack's father did just that and Jack waited a moment before he continued.

"While you are sitting on your throne, King O'Shea, digest this. Could I interest the king in a bit of treasure I have accumulated this past year."

Mr. O'Shea answered without skipping a beat, "Why didn't you know I am a wealthy man with a kingdom that stretches at least across this room. Why would I have need of more.?"

The two men found common ground through their good natured kidding and when Jack finally hung up, Mr. O'Shea had agreed to accept a five thousand dollar gift.

"Tell Sean I will be trading in my old Oldsmobile and with a newer model I could still show him a thing or two when it comes to the ladies."

Jack hung up feeling good. Mr. O'Shea seemed to have his wit back and that meant one less fire that needed tending.

Jack called Molly every week. He would read aloud the letters she had written him. Her writing was becoming much more sophisticated in both shape and content. She told Jack of the improvements she could see in herself. The technique Jack had introduced did not free her speech but in all other ways Molly seemed back to her old self.

(Write me letters too, Jack. Since it seems the printed word is to be my language, I want us to become comfortable writing what we feel. You don't have to read my letters back to me any more; there is nothing wrong with my memory. Mom is doing a good job of adjusting to whom I am going to be and is so patient with me. Dad is just glad to have me alive. He just smiles and doesn't say much. So call; it's nice to hear your voice but write too. It's equally exciting to read your voice, Love Molly).

Sean loved this new life he was leading. This year, Jack had increased Sean's pay to 15% of his winnings and would pay all expenses. Sean continued to invest his earnings in the gaming industry, mostly poker. He used his acting ability to develop an approach to the game that was very successful. He was playing for larger and larger stakes. With an eye to his future, he began taking commuter flights to Las Vegas to learn all that he could about the whole gaming industry. The glitter of casinos and the almost carnival like atmosphere, where people pulled levers and dropped coins in machines, was to Sean, intoxicating. Sean, the alcoholic, found a new stimulant, and one he meant to control. Finding a high stakes poker game was as easy as finding a cheap breakfast. The candy man buoyed by his recent winnings walked along admiring the latest additions to the strip. (Do I want to go to New York or Paris, to Venice, or maybe take a magic carpet ride?) Sean asked himself, as he walked the strip. Sean watched the people filling these places daily and nightly.) He decided then and there, that he would become a part of this emotional intoxication. When he wasn't in Vegas, he was reading about it. He read every book he could find on the gambling industry. He realized it would take a good amount of money to get himself established. He wouldn't set up in Las Vegas though. A small casino or gambling boat was what Sean had in mind. He would take it slow like nursing a good drink. Sean could see how addicting this new stimulant could become and vowed to always be its master. While in Las Vegas, Sean studied the slots; machines of all description, each with its own language, crowded into small dark spaces. Flashing lights and eerie sounds from outer space invited the patron to tug on their arm. Acres of carpet allowed the crowd to move noiselessly from machine to machine as a smoky haze filled the permanent twilight. Sean watched in amazement as people holding a plastic cup in one hand, a cigarette dangling from their lips, fed quarters or tokens into these starving creatures. A quick tug of the arm or push of a button would send a series of revolving cylinders spinning to blur speed. With every pull a silent prayer wished for the stars to all line up. More often than not when the fruit stopped spinning, what would appear would make a good fruit salad. The three apples or lemons or cherries necessary to win or at least get your money back were oh so close,… ah well, perhaps next time. Some patrons would spend hours on one machine while others would wait till someone moved and immediately claim that space. Everybody seemed to be enjoying themselves and that was important to Sean. Studying books, watching people play, and trying different games himself Sean found that Video Poker seemed to offer the best chance of winning. These electronic poker games at least allowed the player to make decisions about which cards to hold. (You almost felt like you were interacting with the dealer,) thought Sean.

The typical player was here on vacation; usually husband and wife, celebrating an anniversary, or getting away from the cold back East. They had disposable income and Las Vegas would certainly show them a good time and provide the stimulus to loosen their wallet. Three days and nights on the strip would be comparable to a week anywhere else. Vegas never sleeps and can't tell time either. The city has its own unique time zone called a good-time zone. Vegas offered excitement that they couldn't begin to find in their life back home. Lavish shows, free food and drink, and twenty four hour service to fill their every need. Sean could picture himself standing behind the one way glass above the crowd, not here certainly, but involved in the industry nevertheless. Competition for the Vegas dollar was cropping up all over the country and Sean had a place in mind but that was a ways down the road. (All I need is a bankroll,) thought Sean. Armed with a bag of peanut M&M's and a club soda, Sean walked to a gaming table and bought in.

CHAPTER

Twenty-Two

Jack was playing good steady golf; he hoped his first top ten finish might occur in California. The season had begun in January in Hawaii, but Jack did not go. His plan carefully mapped out in Dannyboy's brain had him playing nearly every tournament once the tour hit the mainland. One top ten finish would secure the sponsor that would offer support financially in the months ahead. After leaving California, the tour moves to Arizona and then back to California. Early Spring would find the tour moving to Florida. Jack and Sean couldn't drive there. Expenses would mount up. Jack had determined he would wear a hat with the name of a golf ball, a club maker, or an automobile. It didn't matter if they would just show him the money.

Five tournaments later, Jack still didn't have a top ten finish and was not happy as he and Sean boarded the plane that would take them to Orlando; sunny Florida, home of Jack's hero, Arnold Palmer and his tournament at Bay Hill. Maybe that would be the proper setting playing well for his idol.

CHAPTER

Twenty-Three

While Jack struggled, Sean too was having winning problems. Commuter flights to Vegas had become routine. His first couple of weeks in Vegas had gone just as he planned with Sean reaching $150,000 in winnings. Then his luck changed and Sean watched his empire crumble. He got hot again and was sure his bad nights were behind him.

Sean was chewing on M&M's like there was no tomorrow as he raised one last time, in the final hand of the night. Two players called, and a pot of 60 thousand dollars lay there for the winner. Sean held three queens in a game of five card stud. He studied his cards once more and turned them face up. "Read 'em and weep," Sean said. The player to his left did just that when his two pairs were revealed. The gentleman directly across from Sean had no emotion showing on his face. He looked Sean in the eye and rolled three successive kings onto their backs. Without a word, Sean nodded and left the table. Sean continued to play poker night after night, and just this past week had taken out a very high interest loan. He won the following night and paid off the loan along with the two thousand dollar interest payment. Sean had no trouble securing the loan; his credit was excellent.

There was no need to tell Jack about his losing streak for that was Sean's personal business. Sean had found someone else to talk to who understood how things worked in the city that never sleeps.

In Vegas, the old bar saying of a girl looking better at closing time could be expanded to everything looking better. The caveat to that statement however, is that Vegas never closes. There is no examining what is real in the light of day. Sean got lucky though and it had nothing to do with cards.

Sean met Monique in a breakfast buffet line. Reaching for a piece of French toast, he got stabbed in the heart by a piece of French pastry. It was love at first bite.

Monique, a club singer at the Paris Hotel and Casino, used a sexy smoky voice garnished with an authentic French accent and liquid blue eyes, to create an audience of nightly regulars. Monique was tall and slightly built and wore very little makeup. From the moment he saw her, Sean knew his womanizing was over if Monique would date him.

Sean asked if he could join her at her table and when she said yes, the simple meal became a feast. Sean who prided himself on wearing a poker face found himself with his heart on his sleeve. Monique was not shy and by the end of their first meal together, she had heard most of Sean's life story. She asked Sean to come to one of her shows and they could go out after if he wished. Within a week of their meeting, Sean became one of those regulars. When Monique joined him after a performance he felt the envy of every man in the room. Late dinners and a little gaming led Sean to ask Monique if she would come watch him play poker.

Monique became Sean's good luck charm and not a single complaint was registered by the other players as she sat watching her man put on his own performance.

Monique attracted attention wherever she went. She had an Audrey Hepburn look, beauty and innocence, that turned heads. Monique radiated a sex appeal that was not contrived or accented with skimpy clothing; it was simply Monique being Monique. The reality that men found Monique irresistible was not lost on Sean, and he used the distraction to his advantage. The first month Monique was part of his life, Sean was a big winner at the poker table. After a successful evening of poker, Sean would take Monique to an early morning breakfast, and then they would spend the day in bed at Monique's apartment. Sean had big plans and now they included Monique. He realized playing poker for a living was not realistic but had managed to save a considerable sum of money. Sean, with someone else's future to consider, became conservative in his approach to the game and lady luck turned on him.

Sean also found himself being extravagant when it came to wining and dining Monique. That suddenly became the only

winning part of his days and nights. Monique never asked him to spend a penny on her, but Sean wanted to make sure she was happy. When Sean was away on tour, flowers would be sent, gifts would arrive, and money would be wired to Monique's bank.

Sean was in love, love, love.

He called nightly and if Monique was not home, he envisioned the worst. Sean was barely able to keep his feelings of jealousy hidden behind his poker face. He had no reason to doubt Monique's feelings for him but the very nature of her profession had men begging for her attention.

Jack knew Sean was seeing someone and it sounded serious. Sean would spend hours on the phone, and then reappear with that hang dog look that was unmistakable. Jack smiled to himself knowing he had his own special lady who no one else knew about. (Funny about love,) thought Jack, (it seems to strike in so many different emotional ways. Sean was an emotional wreck and he needed constant reassurance, while Molly lived and played in Jack's mind and heart. Perhaps, the courtship set the perimeters and the ground rules.)

This business of love was new to Jack too so he didn't feel qualified to give Sean any advice.

Sean tried to focus on being the caddie Jack needed but it was clear his heart wasn't in it. He intended to tell Jack he would need a new caddie when the tour moved to Florida.

Sean took a flight to Las Vegas on a whim and was waiting for Monique when she came in with shopping bags of clothing in her arms. Monique dropped the bags and rushed into his arms. "What a surprise you have given me! I did not expect you until the evening Sunday," gushed Monique as she buried her face in Sean's blond curls.

"Jack told me to get out of there. I was distracting him. Actually, he's just not playing that well right now and didn't make the cut so I am not needed till Tuesday morning."

After Monique modeled what she had purchased, the two lovers left for a late lunch. Arm in arm they walked the strip and Sean was sure they would be like this always. Sean at 6'1", tanned, well built with movie star good looks was a perfect compliment to this dark haired beauty. The two never argued accepting one another as equals with unique qualities.

Sean had experience with many women but was totally unprepared for the creative ways Monique found to please him. Monique was a performer and she brought her love of being on stage to the bedroom or the kitchen for that matter. Sean chuckled to himself as he recalled their first breakfast in Monique's apartment. That breakfast took several hours to serve and devour. Sean was still in bed when Monique entered with coffee clad in only an apron. She later returned with a pastry wearing a mask and a mink cape. Sean found himself laughing like he'd never laughed, looking forward to a lifetime of breakfasts.

Sean was relaxed while with Monique but back in California with only a voice on the line to console him, Sean feared the worst. When he was in Monique's apartment the constant arrival of flowers she received, didn't bother him. Away and wanting to be with her had Sean on an emotional roller coaster, wondering if she loved him as much as he loved her.

Sean couldn't think straight and his gambling was being affected. He decided to broach the subject of a more permanent relationship. This is Las Vegas, after all. When they were snuggled on the sofa sharing popcorn, Sean suddenly turned off the TV. Monique turned and was about to protest leaving a movie they had been watching.

Sean plopped a piece of popcorn in her open mouth and said, "Monique, I want you to be a permanent part of my life."

"I hope for that also Sean, someday."

"I love you and I'm crazy when I'm not with you"

"You are with me Sean when you are not with Jack." "I am afraid you will find someone else, Monique, someone a lot better."

"You Americans worry too much about such things, I love you Sean; you have to trust that."

"I do trust you Monique. It's all those guys who are always after you that I don't trust."

"Let's just enjoy the time we share. There are never guarantees. You have much to accomplish before you are ready to settle down. I love what I do and I don't know where it will lead, but I have to give it time."

Sean tried to say something else but Monique was not finished.

"Sean, when I sing it is for you only. Let them send flowers and drinks to my table. It is you who I spend my time with."

"Can I stay with you then?"

"You already do Sean whenever you are in town."

"I guess I mean I want to stay in town all the time."

"What about your brother the golfer? He needs you, yes?"

"I will just tell him I am done; he knows I didn't intend for it to be forever."

"What will you do here for work, Sean? Have you a plan?"

"I am trying to raise enough money to get involved as a partner in a small casino in the mountains, probably in another state. Would you come sing in my lounge?"

"I would like to record a song or an album maybe. I have dreams too. I can't promise you any more than right now, Sean." Sean took a deep breath, "I'm sorry Monique; you're right missing you is my problem. As long as you love me tonight and tomorrow, that's all I can hope for." Sean pulled Monique into his arms and she began to sing as he rocked her. Sean didn't recognize the words in French but it sounded like a lullaby a mother would sing to a child, promising all would be well.

To quote Dickens in his novel of the French revolution, "It was the best of times; it was the worst of times." Sean's decision to stay in Vegas left him with plenty of time to gamble. He was running hot and cold at the table, treading water really. The money that he was spending on Monique to have a good time, and enjoy the tonight and tomorrow, was draining his bank account. Sean would not suggest to Monique that they should slow down a little. Monique had grown fond of the slots, especially the twenty dollar ones. Setting in a special room, they were served finger food and any type of drink imaginable. Monique would pull violently on the arm of the space invader, trying to get three of the same creatures to rear their ugly heads on the same space ship. Sean could see the attraction as the new machines were more interactive than just pulling the arm. A little laser gun, mounted on the screen, allowed the player to bring each spinning cylinder to a stop by shooting a beam of light, thus, giving them more control of the outcome. Sean tried to explain that the odds had been set well before any aliens landed, but Monique didn't seem to care. She plunked three tokens at a time in the machine. Sean's head was spinning in tandem with the machine as he watched his money disappear. They would walk away and play other less expensive machines for a time, but then Monique would find her way back to these creatures who seemed intent on swallowing all of Sean's savings. Sean would leave Monique in her spaceship, armed with a plastic bucket of 20 dollar chips, while the people watched, worrying about his financial meltdown.

He refused to let Monique know but his game was taking a hit too. The candy man who had turned reading emotions while showing none of his own into an art form lost his focus. His ability to read body movement disappeared even as his own body betrayed his uncertainty. It became Sean who would fold his cards if he didn't have an immediate winner. The other players began kidding, Sean, asking him if he had changed candy. The candy man seemed to be eating candy with no nuts lately, they joked. Sean was being bluffed out of hand's he should have won. His savings melting like an ice cream cone on a Las Vegas street corner. Sean wanted to call his brother, tell Monique, do something but his stubborn Irish pride would not let him. "Oh, look Sean, I won 10,000 dollars! This is the best game, Sean; I love it."

"That should keep you in space for a while. Cash it in and I will take you to dinner."

"I am not in the least hungry; go ahead then come back."

"Let me help you settle up at least," said Sean as the attendant arrived. The attendant returned with $1000 dollars in tokens and a debit card that could be cashed out at any time. If Monique left with an amount over 700 dollars, she would have to pay taxes. By leaving the winnings on a card, she could play for as long as the money lasted without penalty.

Sean said, "Don't get captured by those aliens. I'll be back" and left to grab a bite to eat.

When he returned, Monique told Sean she was still winning and was up nearly $12,000 dollars. "I knew this was going to be my lucky day."

"What is so special about today, Monique?"

Monique motioned Sean close to her and whispered, "You don't play the game of hearts as well as you play poker Sean."

"What are you talking about?"

"If you counted the days like you do the cards, you would know this is our two month anniversary," said a sad faced Monique.

Sean looked directly into those liquid blue eyes, and knew there was but one way out of this mess. "You are so right Monique but let me make it up to you. I am going to take you to the nicest jewelry store on the strip and buy you a charm bracelet."

"What is this charm bracelet? Does it have stones?"

"This one will," said Sean, thinking on his feet. "It will have sapphires to match your eyes, rubies to match those lips that were pouting, and diamonds to match the way you make my life shine."

In the afternoon Sean signed a receipt for a $15,000 dollar bracelet being specially made for his beloved Monique. Tonight was Monique's night off so the two lovers walked hand in hand alone in the crowd. They stopped for an ice cream cone, and if only Sean had realized Monique didn't need diamonds from him, she just needed him. Sean and Monique were just big kids who loved and laughed but hadn't really gotten around to talking yet. They loved each other but really hadn't asked themselves why.

Sean took the night off from poker. On the way to Monique's apartment, he rationalized that even with the $15,000 dollars spent this afternoon, he probably saved money today. Lately it seemed, he had been losing $20,000 dollars a night so really he was $5,000 dollars to the good. (I certainly had more fun today than I would have had at a poker game,) chuckled Sean to himself. The problem was too many more of these profitable days, and he would be flat broke.

Laying in bed, and smelling the smell that was uniquely Monique, he tried to drift off. He shut his eyes, but sleep would not give him a reprieve from the worry he carried lately, twenty-four seven it seemed.

After a breakfast that Monique had ordered from a gourmet deli, Sean went in to shower. Alone with his thoughts Sean began singing. With his eyes closed he shampooed his hair still humming to himself.

Suddenly he was not alone. He hadn't heard or smelled Monique, but unless he had grown an extra pair of hands; wandering sensual hands, she had joined him. Sean rinsed his hair and was about to open his eyes when the same hands lightly touched his lips.

A soft, exquisite voice told him to, "just imagine." The water suddenly slowed to a trickle and Monique became the steam that was opening Sean's senses. She kissed his ears, his eyes, his neck, all the while her hands massaging Sean's body.

Sean felt himself responding.

Monique engulfed his manhood with her legs. Satisfied that Sean was ready, she jumped lightly into his arms, locking her legs around his waist.

Sean carried Monique to their bed and the two lovers tumble dried on satin sheets.

Sean went to watch Monique sing whenever he could, and she was indeed talented. Sean, like so many of the patrons, feasted on the natural beauty of Monique. She sang with passion in her voice. Tonight he really listened. Monique was indeed singing to him, and Sean was determined to do what was necessary to keep that song on her lips.

The next morning, Monique went to pick up a few things and Sean wandered into his bank. While he maintained a small checking account, Sean kept most of his money in a safe deposit box. Sean glanced at the small calendar on the stainless steel table where he was counting what money he had left. In the past two weeks he had lost a total of $240,000 dollars. Forty Five thousand remained, a small stack of $500 dollar bills. Sean had a big game going tonight and emptied the larder. As he walked out of the vault he noted the echo of his footsteps seemed louder than he remembered. (Think positive,) he told himself. There was barely a week left before the brothers were to fly to Florida. Sean didn't want to fly anywhere. He wanted to soar.

Las Vegas in late winter acts as a giant magnet drawing the pinched faces of a populace from the frozen North and East. The sunny skies and moderate weather allow the muscles to relax and the purse strings to loosen. Standing outside warming his face, Sean watched the sidewalks sprout colorful shirts, shorts, baseball caps and sunglasses. White legs seemed to be a requirement for passage to the glitter beyond the doors. Sean chuckled as he played word games in his head. (They should change the name from Las Vegas, to Lost Wages,) he mused. Circus, Circus, one of the long established casinos promised a good time under the big top. That had proven true for Sean, as it was in their famous breakfast buffet line, the beautiful Monique had entered his life. Sean was remembering the wonderful way this morning had started when suddenly his eyes were covered from behind.

"Give me all your money, don't look around; there is a pistol in your back."

Sean muttered, " I have no money."

"Then there is no reason for you to live. Wait; do you have at least some spare change?"

"That, I might be able to produce," chuckled Sean. He turned to greet his assailant. The two embraced. The love Sean felt for Monique removed the dark clouds circling within Sean's head. Sean attended Monique's show that evening. Her quiet strength and self assurance showed as she nailed one song after another. Between acts, Sean told Monique he would not be available after her show, he had a big game.

"Don't you want your good luck charm beside you tonight?"

"Not tonight honey, I have to have my mind well focused on the game of cards."

"I won't tell you then what will be awaiting your arrival home, Sean the gambler."

Sean smiled, "How am I supposed to keep my mind on poker when you say things like that."

"It is the mystery of Monique that promises nothing, imagine if you wish."

Sean gave Monique a kiss on the lips and walked out into the warmth and artificial light of the strip. Sean looked up. A full moon above was trying to compete for attention but drew only a small audience of sightseers.

๑ ๑

The game was straight five card stud. The seven men seated around the green felt covered table understood the simplicity and beauty of the game. There were no wild cards. There would be no surprises popping up that could ruin a pair of aces or three of a kind. The first card dealt face down started the hand. Bets and raises followed, then the first of three cards face up.

Each hand took on a life of its own, promising good things could begin with the turn of the next card. The beauty of the game is that an Ace, by itself, could be the high hand so folding your cards early was risky business. The fifth card joined the first, its face hidden from the curious, and it could change everything. It could turn a frown upside down, raise the blood pressure, or speed a heart beat. Keeping all those emotions under control was an art form that Sean had mastered, Sean vowed the candy man would show the doubters he was back.

Playing for Monique and the love she had brought him, Sean decided to let that love be his guide tonight. Ah love, it's a beautiful thing. It can do many things. It can turn a frown upside down, raise the blood pressure, speed a heart beat. It cannot change the cards you are dealt however and Sean found himself coming in second best in too many hands.

The outside world turned from inky black to predawn gray, as Sean watched his pile of chips dwindle. When he pushed himself away from the table, it was with mixed emotions. During what had proved to be a roller coaster ride, Sean lost all his money, took out a $10,000 dollar loan and then proceeded to win $25,000. He paid off his loan including the $2,000 in interest. Sean put the remaining $13,000. in his money belt thinking that maybe he should get into the loan business that seemed to be a guaranteed winner.

Sean entered the buffet line, his stomach empty, emotionally spent. The last two hours had seen his luck change for the good; he hoped it would continue. Patting his stomach, he added home fries to his plate and moved to the cashier. Reaching into his pocket for two dollars, he fingered two silver coins, body warmed. (Let's hope that the spare change line Monique delivered earlier wasn't prophetic,) Sean shivered.

When Sean entered Monique's apartment, he heard her singing in the shower. Mentally exhausted, Sean couldn't muster the energy to launch his own sneak attack. He slid into a bed still warm and full of the smell that had him under its spell. Lying there too tired to sleep, and planning a future for two, Sean worried, hoped, and silently prayed. Sean heard the water stop; the music became clear. Oddly Mr. O'Shea filled his mind. He suddenly realized how his father must have felt when his brother was snatched from him those years ago.

Monique entered the bedroom still singing softly; she saw Sean folded into the covers. She pulled the covers down, thinking he was teasing her. When she saw the tears on his face and heard his sobbing, she slipped in beside him and gently cradled him in her arms, humming softly.

Their relationship had not involved a lot of conversation. Born of passion; they knew little of one another's deepest hopes and fears. It was clear that they cared deeply, however. Who they were, and how they came to be, seeped out. Monique let Sean begin in his own good time and soon Monique was hearing of the boy Sean, and the world he came to inhabit. He revealed his addiction to alcohol and the relationship that was becoming stronger with both father and brother. Sean had never talked much about himself to anyone except Jack and that school counselor. Lying here with Monique, it had all come out and Sean felt good about it. If they were going to make it as a couple, there could be no secrets.

"I love you even more for the person you have become, Sean. You are strong and good and you always have spare change," added Monique, lightening the mood. "If you can stay awake, I will tell you about myself." She laid her head against Sean's shoulder.

"I have not always been a singer. My parents brought me here to America when I was four years old. My father came here to manage a winery and was gone most of the time. My parents felt I should go to public school and become part of this New World as they called it. I had trouble with your language. I became very quiet and withdrawn." She hugged Sean tightly. "Still there was a little person inside telling me I do not belong here. I was the only child in my class who spoke French. When I continued to struggle with the language, they brought a teacher from the high school. He had studied the language but he had no sense of how it should be used to communicate" She kissed Sean's hair.

"At home, I was lonely too. My father, who used to play with me, was busy with his new job. My mother, she would tell me stories of her childhood. I became addicted to your cartoons on television. I loved your, <u>Rocky The Flying Squirrel,</u> she laughed, "especially Boris and Natasha." Monique became serious again. "My mother too was lonesome and the day long she would play the records she had brought from France. I found myself listening to the words of love and loss, soon I was singing along. I came to know your language but the loneliness I felt as a child became part of Monique, the singer."

Waiting for her to continue, Sean squeezed her gently.

"Sean, I understand your pain, and please know you are not merely a song to me. You are not for just the good times. I am not ready to be married or to have children but if I were, it would be you I choose."

Sean held on for dear life as Monique told Sean one last thing. "I am not a nightclub singer who disappears when the spotlight is dark. I do not need your money, Sean; I need you. I am sorry I have been wasteful with your money. Please, cancel the order for the charm bracelet. You are my luck."

"I want you to have that bracelet more than ever. As long as you love me, nothing else matters. I will find my way through this mess."

୨ৎ

It was a different Sean who entered the game that evening. Buoyed by the last two hours of last night's game and the love of a good woman, Sean began the night with a smile on his face. Ah, but Lady Luck can be most fickle. Just as Mother Nature's storms, with feminine names attached continue to fool the experts, so too Lady luck can bob and weave. Surely the lady must have felt Sean being Irish was lucky enough; for the lady deserted him for the evening, not even teasing him a time two. Sean had to borrow $10,000 dollars but this time left the table owing that amount, plus the interest, due in a week. He flew back to California where Jack was to play in his final tournament before going East. Sean could only hope his brother would finish high enough this week that his share would cover the loan and interest.

DIDN'T HAPPEN!

The two days before flying East were hectic for Sean. He went to Vegas to say good-bye to Monique and to arrange for another loan to cover what he already owed. Sean realized he was on a slippery slope but didn't see an alternative. He borrowed a total of $42,000.00 and paid off the first loan. He fully intended to have all debts settled and to give up this life.

He planned to give caddying a chance and use the time to figure out a future with Monique.

Monique, while sorry to see Sean go, felt it was the best decision. "Call me every night after my show. I will save money too, and perhaps in a year we can think about the future." She hugged him tightly. "Being apart will be a good test for us, Sean, to see if we care enough to be alone."

Sean left Monique and headed for a showdown of sorts. (Life is like planning a meal,) thought Sean. You can set the menu, buy the ingredients, cook it, season it, and still find yourself eating alone, as circumstances change.) Just a few short weeks ago Sean's menu included buying into a small casino, marrying Monique, and living happily ever after. Now he needed to get things right just to leave town flat broke. Sean knew what he needed to do.

The first night, Sean stayed afloat, winning and losing small pots, no big waves. He left the game at four am, got himself a room, and slept restlessly. The entire next afternoon was spent examining his options. With one night left, Sean reasoned winning enough to pay off the loan was as optimistic as he could hope for. A year on the tour helping Jack get his first big win would be exciting. "Just need one little bit of luck," said Sean aloud as he left for his last night on the town.

Sean approached this last evening with a kind of giddiness, which somehow felt like the method of concentration Jack had explained but Sean couldn't follow until now.

The candy man watched himself from the corner of the room. He appeared relaxed, made proper bets, and his bluffs seemed to make sense. He drew good cards, hands that would normally win, but it seemed each player at the table took his turn at besting him. Sean observed no one player getting hot and when the game ended at six-thirty am, he had a total of three hundred dollars to his name. Sean took a shuttle flight back to California to pack his bags for the flight East. He told Jack nothing.

Twenty-Four

Orlando International Airport was busy. The arriving passengers seemed to know where they were headed and soon the 200 or so traveling companions had disappeared to continue their adventure. Walking past the well marked gates, Jack was amazed at how orderly everything moved along. As long as a little weather wasn't thrown in, airports seemed to have their acts together. Jack and Sean exited and found their rental car, filled out the paperwork and left the lot.

It was when they entered traffic that Orlando the city mirrored Disney World the destination. As they attempted to move forward creeping really, they hit a traffic light every quarter mile or so. Sean who was riding shotgun directed Jack to their motel, turning the map of Orlando in every direction Jack with his Irish wit at the ready refused to be intimidated by honking horns and shouts that were not, "welcome to the city. It makes no sense Sean. Surely there has to be a better and less expensive way to bring traffic to a dead stop every few yards. Did you notice the looks, straight in the eye, daring you to smile."

Jack laughed aloud, "And the unpleasantness they find necessary to share, and repeat, while a middle digit rises and falls. Did you notice, Sean, it's the red light that seems to cause it?" Jack pulled up to a red light.

"Now a reasoned mind would offer a simple solution. Leave the yellow caution light on all the time for everyone and let the people create their own sense of fair play. Call a penalty on themselves as we do in the game of golf."

Sean was busy reading the map and could only chuckle at the wit of his brother. The two brothers enjoying themselves had entered the Bee Line looking for Orange Blossom Trail. Jack had called ahead and located a motel outside the city. He had been cautioned by veteran players to stay away from International Drive.

After driving by once, they found the motel and were soon unpacking. Jack called one of the players he had met in California and was out the door when he pulled up outside their room. "I'll just hang out at the pool," said Sean. "I have a lot of thinking to do."

"Talk to you later then," said Jack. "We're going to hit balls.

I will bring back some sandwiches."

The week flew by, Jack did well enough to make the cut but he finished well back of the leaders.

Sean's share even at 15% was not going to make a dent in his debt load. He had a deadline to meet and no idea how to proceed. Sean called Monique every night, at least that part of his life seemed secure.

∾∾

Jack called Molly once a week and they wrote to each other regularly. While he waited for Molly to come to the phone, he idly flipped through a brochure placed in his room by the owner. Suddenly he had an idea to spring on Molly.

"Would you take me to DisneyLand when I get back home? I have never been so you will have to be my tour guide. I have a brochure in my room. I'm reading it as we speak. They call it Disney World here, but I assume it must be similar. He gave Molly the post office box address he had opened and said he would be in the area for at least three weeks. He told her how he was getting more and more comfortable with the mental side of his game and expected a breakthrough soon. So write me about any past experiences you've had in the Magic Kingdom while I will bore you with golf stories."

Jack called Mr. O'Shea next. The voice on the line sounded like the man Jack remembered as a boy. "I'm looking forward to seeing you later this summer when the tour moves North," said Jack.

"How are you doing son? You always seem to be taking care of someone else and worrying about someone else? How is the golf game?"

"I believe I am about ready for a major breakthrough, Dad. It feels weird to call you Dad instead of Mr. O'Shea. Anyway, as for how am I? I'll quote that famous Irishman, O'Shea," began Jack. "Here's to you as good as you are. Here's to me as bad as I am. As good as you are and as bad as I am, I'm as good as you are as bad as I am."

Mr. O'Shea laughed out loud. "I haven't heard that one in years Jack, not since you sat across from me at the kitchen table." "I remember many of the stories you told me and I'm learning to appreciate them more and more. The O'Shea magic has helped me on more than one occasion. I am proud to be your son." With tears welling in his eyes, Mr. O'Shea cleared his throat and changed the subject. "How is Sean doing? He doesn't call me as often as he did."

"Sean is in love, Dad. I haven't met her yet but she must be very special. Sean could have his pick of girls but he seems to believe this is the one. He's an O'Shea, Dad; he believes in magic."

"I am so glad you two are together. It makes up for a lot of things."

"I will call you soon Dad, hopefully with winning news. Goodbye-love you."

Sean was busy making calls too. He first called Monique, simply sharing small talk since they talked every night. Sean, having watched his brother write to his lady friend, at least he figured it must be a lady friend; decided he'd begin writing to Monique. He talked with her about the idea.

"It sounds romantic, Sean. I will rush to the mail each day waiting to hear from you."

"Will you write back?"

"Of course, I will share my hopes and dreams for us. It sounds so exciting; I have never had a letter from a man."

"Ok, expect a letter by the middle of the week but for now I will just say it out loud. I love you Monique. Talk to you soon."

Sean's next call was one of obligation and he did not expect it to be pleasant.

When Mr. Soledad finally came on the line, Sean was surprised the man seemed to know him. "Good to hear from you, Sean. I haven't seen you in town. Are you around?" "Actually, I am out of town at the moment but I wanted to touch base with someone about my loan."

"I would not normally be the guy you would talk to but go ahead."

"Have we met, Mr. Soledad?"

"Not officially, but I have seen you play cards. You are highly respected Sean."

"That's kind of why I called. I wanted to touch base and let someone know I was not forgetting my loan."

"I like your attitude Sean; up front, no funny business. You could go a long way out here. You ever need a job just look me up. I am serious."

"I don't have your money right now, sir, but I should have it soon. Is that something I can negotiate?"

"Not a problem Sean, I can extend it another week. Is that enough time? You can have two if you need it." "Two weeks would be great. Thank you Mr. Soledad"

"Let me sum up what we have agreed on Sean. You will receive a two week extension on a $50,000 loan which includes interest due. An extension of two weeks is going to cost you an additional $15,000. So call me when you have the $65,000 and I will tell you how to send it. Probably shouldn't trust the mail," he laughed. "I am dead serious about the job offer, Sean. I can always use a sharp guy on my team."

Sean hung up his heart racing. $65,000! Where in the world would he come up with that kind of money? Even if he asked Jack for help, there was no way the two of them could come up with that amount.

Sean spent the two weeks worrying, caddying, and praying Jack would win a tournament. He wrote his first letter to Monique and told her he was coming back to Vegas. He didn't explain himself. He would tell her all about it when he got there.

Sean broke the news to Jack when they had returned from the week's tournament. Jack had finished ahead of the expenses once again, but no big money was won. Jack gave Sean $1000 and was going to take him out to dinner.

"Jack, we have to talk. I need to go to Monique; she's sick."

"Not a problem brother, I won't need you for a couple of days anyway."

"Jack, I'm not sure I'll get back, that's the thing." "Is she that ill? Why didn't you tell me? I could have let you go earlier."

"Jack, it's real complicated and it's more than just Monique I can't explain. You have to trust me."

"Of course I trust you. Call me when you get there and don't worry about the caddying part. I think I know someone who can fill in."

Jack gave Sean a ride to the airport and told his brother that he loved him and not to worry about anything. "Just help Monique get well".

≈≈

Jack called Ron a college teammate who lived up the coast. Ron wasn't home but called back. Ron suggested a guy who had worked with him after college he thought was playing down there. He gave Jack his number.

"Why don't you come down and be my caddy, Ron? We'd have a great time."

"I would love to but I can't get away for four days. How about I join you for a day though, maybe we can have dinner and catch up?"

≈≈

The next day Ron made the two hour trip. He met Jack at the motel and the two former golf mates spent the first hour catching up on their lives, while downing a couple of beers. Jack explained his brother's predicament; then talk turned to this young guy Tim who had worked with Ron after college.

≈≈

"It's a small world Ron. I met Tim on the golf course and we started talking. All of a sudden your name came up." "He

241

worked in the same pro shop I did. I knew he had the game to make it. He won't win many tournaments but he'll make a living. He's found someone who can carry your bag?"

"A cousin I guess, playing golf in college here in Florida. I am meeting him tomorrow. Sorry Tim couldn't make it tonight, but he said to tell you he will try to get up to your course before he leaves Florida. I'd like to get up there too if I can."

"Hope it happens. Listen, here is my number at the course. You can reach me seven days a week. So you love this life, huh, Jack?"

"I was born for it, Ron. I don't think I could do a regular 9 to 5 job. My mind doesn't work that way."

Driving back to Palm Coast Ron felt good about taking the time to reconnect. He was proud of Jack and was sure he would be winning soon.

❧

Jack called the number of Tim's cousin and the young man seemed very excited about the opportunity to caddy at a PGA event. When he hung up Jack thought back to how he and Tim had met and how quickly the two had become friends. Jack had shot a good round that day in California and for once decided to celebrate. How he had ended up with Tim as a house guest was a mystery to this day. Sean hadn't met Monique back then so he was on the prowl and never did make it home.

Tim had three good looking women on his arm when Jack got bumped into by the group as he was leaving a bar. Tim started to apologize, but then recognized Jack from the practice range. "Hey you're the guy who writes to the golf gods aren't you? Just kidding, I have seen you on the range doing some strange things though."

Jack wasn't sure how to take this guy who had drunk at least as much as he had. Tim held out his hand, "I'm Tim Fischetto and you are Jack O'Shea."

"Well, that clears that up nicely. Who would this armful of beauties be and where would you be taking all of them?" The mood was set, with Jack just tagging along watching Two-finger Tim as he would come to call him. The quartet landed at Jack's apartment and before an Irishman could say 'one for the road,' Tim had passed out on the couch.

The ladies, in different stages of inebriation made themselves comfortable in the three beds. One landed with Tim on the couch, one took over Sean's bed, and Jack woke as the third crawled in with him. She snuggled up to Jack's back and they both fell fast asleep.

Tim woke first and found one of the young ladies in Jack's bed. On the spot he created his own version of Goldilocks and the three beds. As he told the story, "the first bed had Tim and a girl friend in it. The second bed had just a girlfriend friend. But the third bed had Jack in it and that was just right, so Goldilocks fell fast asleep." Tim would tell that story over and over, always bringing laughter. Tim would never believe Jack had not shared a little bedtime story of his own with Miss Goldilocks.

Tim became a good friend and the two got together whenever they played in the same tournament.

Tim's cousin carried Jack's bag for the four day tournament. Jack shot four sub par rounds. The young man had to be talked out of quitting college when Jack handed him a check for $2000. Jack had promised him $100 a day or 5% of his winnings. Jack won $40,000, his biggest payday yet. More importantly he had proved he could play at this level.

"I don't mean to pry Jack but what's up with Sean? Is he coming back?"

"He seems to have far greater concerns on his mind, Tim. I wouldn't bet he'll be on my bag any time soon. I understand; he's trying to find his own way. I'm just sorry he didn't get to see me play this week. We both knew caddying was a temporary job for him so no harm done."

Jack watched the way Tim held his beer mug using just two fingers and a thumb. "Can you explain why you leave those last two fingers floating in the air when you raise your glass? It looks a little otherworldly, to me Tim"

Tim laughed, "I hold a mug the same way I hold my putter, like the stem of a fine wine glass."

"Well that explains it then; here's to you," said Jack raising his own mug, "may you sink putts with the same regularity and skill you display on a bar stool." The two men clinked mugs. " While we're raising glasses Tim, would you care to travel together on the road and share expenses for the next couple of months?" Tim raised his own glass and proposed a toast. " To Sean, may he find what he is looking for." He continued, "May our travels be filled with adventures, and bedtime stories and may the golf gods treat us kindly."

☙❧

The two men hit it off well. They practiced together, with Tim taking special note of the journal Jack wrote in after each session. They partied together, with Jack taking special note of the number of girls Tim could balance on one arm, hand extended two fingers flying.

"I think it's that little finger thing you do Tim that attracts them," kidded Jack.

"I prefer to believe it's the delicate way I hold them that keeps them smiling," Tim responded.

Both men loved laughter and a good time. The profession allowed for many social occasions to appear spontaneously, almost nightly. Young men away from home with few ties to family found plenty of reasons to celebrate or to commiserate. Either way, the liquor flowed and the local girls would find their way to the party.

It was at one of the local night spots that Jack and Tim met a young lady who would later be described as a clinger and a clanker. It started off innocently enough. Ellen was with a group of girls who spent the evening laughing and flirting with two tables of men who had taken over a corner of the room. Dancing and drinking continued well past midnight. Somehow, the party landed at one of the players' apartment without spilling a drink. Jack noticed Ellen. She seemed content to watch the action from the sidelines, much the same approach he had mastered. Jack was a watcher, knowing his special girl was awaiting his return he kept his distance. He saw no harm in being an observer of mankind, however. He felt good. The personal growth he had achieved allowed his desire to watch others, to be an innocent pastime. When called upon, he would offer a witty story or opinion. This aloofness seemed to attract Ellen's attention.

Jack was daydreaming about his recent success and how excited he felt when telling Molly about making money. He was saving for the future, sharing expenses with a young guy he had met. Jack had bargained for a two room suite so he could have the privacy of his phone calls and his writing. He also was starting to negotiate for the long awaited sponsorship that would add logos to his shirt and money to his bank account. Life was good. Ellen interrupted his dream with a light tug on his sleeve. "I'm Ellen. I couldn't help noticing you sitting away from the action," she held out her hand in greeting.

Jack shook his head slightly, coming back to the present. "Hello Ellen, it's a fine evening. I would be Jack O'Shea; pleased I am to meet you."

"Do you always talk funny like that, Jack O'Shea?"

Jack, blessed with his father's ability to string words together, added to the moment. "When a man sees a flower blossom right before his eyes, wouldn't it be a pity to let the moment pass without stopping to enjoy the fragrance?"

Ellen didn't know what to say so the two simply watched the party continue.

It was Jack who broke the silence. "I noticed you earlier this evening. That was you in the corner booth quietly watching the goings on at the bar wasn't it? You seem to have adopted the same approach here since you arrived. Would you be gathering material for a book on the life and crimes of a golfer?"

The evening ended without Jack getting an answer to his question but Ellen continued to show up wherever a party landed. There were nights when the party goers slept on the rugs; someone confiscating keys, forcing the issue.

Ellen would be up making coffee and tidying up the place before anyone else stirred. Many times she would be gone. No one could figure her out.

Jack, ever the observer, was intrigued by her and they had long conversations that he deemed harmless. Mr. O'Shea had long ago shared an Irish proverb with Jack that best summed up Jack's feelings for Ellen. 'Time is a good story teller.' All Jack felt he was doing was killing time.

CHAPTER
Twenty-Five

Sean, on the other hand, was trying to buy time. When he landed in Las Vegas, he went immediately to Monique's apartment. After an emotional and stress releasing welcome, Sean told Monique everything.

"I know of these people. They are dangerous, Sean. Perhaps, I can ask some friends to help raise this money you owe."

"Thank you, Monique but this is my problem. I just needed to be honest with you. I wouldn't blame you if you told me to get lost."

"Good and bad times Sean, that is what will make us strong. There are no mistakes that can't be repaired." She hugged him fiercely.

"Thank you for that, I can do anything if you still believe in me."

"Do you have a plan for this man?"

"He seemed pleasant enough on the phone. Thanked me for being so up-front, and he even offered me a job. He said he was sure we could work something out."

"Be careful with this man, Sean. I have heard his name. I think he has even been to my club. He is a powerful man in this place. I do have people who could possibly help; big men with puffed out chests who come to the club. Always they say if I ever need anything, just ask."

"Let me meet the man. If he sounds dangerous or threatening, I will let you help, ok. Besides there's usually fine print to any help these high rollers of yours might offer."

❧❧

The next morning at nine-fifteen AM. Sean knocked on the door of suite 1501, the penthouse apartment and office of Phillipe Soledad. On the way up the elevator, he imagined what options or threats might be offered. The numbered floors sped by, moving in the opposite direction of the options he figured he would be given. Sean sighed, then rang the bell. He put on his poker face when he heard footsteps approaching from within.

Mr. Soledad opened the door with an outstretched hand and a smile of greeting. "Come in Sean. We have missed you in town. Can I fix you a drink? Oh that's right, you don't drink. How about a club soda?"

"Thank you, a club soda would be great, sir."

"Call me Phillipe." Moving to the bar to get Sean a club soda, he invited Sean to have a seat on the leather sofa facing a window.

"Look at that view, Sean. I can see nearly all the casinos in this part of the city. I actually have an interest in several of them. But look beyond those casinos, there to the West, the mountains. Beautiful aren't they to look up into. I am always amazed that most people look beyond the possibilities that exist right in front of their nose. They prefer to live a life that only sees the horizons." He paused for effect. "This city was built on a scraggly, barren, lifeless, piece of ground nobody wanted. A few doers saw the possibility of enticing people over those mountains. The mountains on this side, anyway, are worthless." He handed Sean his club soda. Sean nodded his thanks.

"We have grown buildings on this barren desert. Now this whole state has become a magnet for young and old alike. Those mountains are for dreamers, Sean. People gaze into them, get all starry eyed. They come into the casinos to make those dreams come true. Gambling is all about trying to bring change to their lives."

Mr. Soledad pulled the curtains closed and joined Sean on the couch. He was a powerful looking man in his early sixties. Sean looked him straight in the eye wondering when the ax would fall. Mr. Soledad didn't seem to be in a hurry to get down to business. He walked across the room and turned on a sound system. The room filled with instrumental music that Sean didn't recognize. "I like music, Sean; don't you? Well, of course, you do, that lady of yours, Monique isn't it, now she can sing. I respect you, Sean. I really do. It couldn't have been easy but you kept me involved in what you were going through. It must have been tough leaving your brother like that.

Sean realized he was receiving a message, subtle conversation, but a message nevertheless. Obviously, Mr. Soledad did his homework. Sean had never mentioned Monique or his brother to this man.

As if hearing the unspoken, Mr. Soledad responded. "Yes I know everything there is to know about you Sean. I even know the candy you use as a prop when you gamble. It's my business; don't take offense."

"I would rather my brother not know my business situation sir; it doesn't concern him."

"Looks like he might be one of the few to make it in the golfing business. I'd bet on him if I was a gambling man, which I'm not. Does that surprise you, Sean? Here I am part owner in several casinos, I have plenty of money, yet I don't gamble. I don't even buy scratch tickets." Mr. Soledad laughed. "Excuse me Sean. I'm not laughing at you but rather at the dreamer you are."

"What do you mean? I guess I don't understand."

"Ok, I will cut to the chase. I don't gamble. You want money. I lend it to you, then extend the deadline at your request. Still with me? I don't gamble so I must have a fall back position in case you don't pay up. That position in this case has to be your brother." Mr. Soledad moved to the window and drew the curtains back once again.

"Those mountains are still there, always will be and anyone can look at them, no charge. They don't pay the rent though. People have to pay the rent. Now, I know we can work out a solution. There should be no reason your brother will ever need to know. I agree with you Sean, that it's your business. Let's get down to it. "What is your plan for paying back the money you borrowed, with interest of course?"

"Honestly, I don't know. All I can offer is my word that I will pay you back, given some time."

"I thought as much, Sean. You gazed into those mountains and dreamed what a little nest egg might allow you to do with your life. Don't be ashamed; it happens to people everyday. The only flaw in your dream is you don't have a fall back position. As I said, I make it my business to know all about the people who borrow money from me, so let me offer a possible solution." He sat down across from Sean.

"Let me tell you a little about you. You have a good way with people. You hide your feelings and emotions well. You're honest, and straight forward. All skills I could use in certain situations. What I don't know is, are you loyal and trustworthy? Those are the two key words in my organization." He clasped his hands together for emphasis.

"Mr. Soledad, I don't mean to be rude but would you please just tell me what's on your mind. I know I owe you money. You know I can't pay you immediately. So unless you intend to hurt me physically which, I hope, is not the case, please tell me what's on your mind."

Mr. Soledad laughed again, "Young people are always in such a rush, instant this instant that. I'm not going to hurt you, Sean. In fact I was planning just the opposite." He leaned back into his chair.

"This is what I propose, but I do need to tell you if you find my proposal unacceptable, I will have to contact your brother to arrange payment. I have checked and he would be squeezed, but could cover your debt within a month. I realize you don't want that to happen so please listen with an open mind" Sean knew he was trapped, he listened to the words Mr. Soledad spoke, but his thoughts were of his brother Jack. (The family O'Shea had been put back together by Jack, the pieces just recently healed. Sean could not, would not, get his brother involved in this mess.)

Mr. Soledad moved to the bar, checked his watch, shrugged his shoulders and poured himself a diet Pepsi. "Alright Sean, here it is. I am a businessman as I said earlier. My company offers services to people who frequent our little town. My business works on a cash only system. People who use our services do not want a paper trail so everything depends on communication and trust. Trust is critical to both sides of this unwritten agreement. Here's an example Sean." Mr. Soledad rubbed his mustache and began a series of small stretching exercises as he continued. "Let's say a business man comes to town. He wants a discreet place to stay. He needs a little companionship, food, transportation - all strictly legal - but done on a cash basis with no receipts. Say this business man needs some extra cash while he's here. We provide that too. Sean nearly 60% of my business is simply providing a few extra dollars to a client."

Sean closed his eyes. (Where do I fit in to all this,) he thought.

As if psychic, Mr. Soledad answered. "Sean, I want you to run the day to day part of my business. With your good looks and personality you will be my public face. You will decide who we lend money to. I have three employees who spend their day doing background checks so a potential client who makes it to your door will have been screened carefully. I want you to meet and greet people. Smile and make sure they are having a good time. Any client wanting to borrow money will have to get the heads up from you. My associates also act as drivers and they understand discreet." He continued to stretch and bend. "You will report to me directly once a week. We look at cash flow, possible new trends that we might act on, all with an eye on how we might expand our business."

Sean just had to ask, "What's in it for me?"

"Instant instant," chuckled Mr. Soledad. "For starters Sean, we cancel your debt. We will discuss a fair salary; what it would take to have you work for me."

"What's the downside here? What am I missing?" "Good question, Sean? You should know the good and the bad, the Ying and the Yang as they say. I trust you, Sean. I think I already said that, but it can't be said often enough. I don't usually sit talking face to face about my business. When you needed money a while back, you asked around and I contacted you. I don't usually do that either." Mr. Soledad did deep knee bends as he continued to explain

"You see Sean, this business doesn't exist. I'm not really in business at all. I just do favors for people. If you work for me, you would be paid for loyalty. Trust and loyalty are priceless.

For everything else there's MasterCard," Mr. Soledad laughed out loud.

Suddenly Mr. Soledad came back to the sofa, sat down and looked Sean directly in the eyes. "This job offer comes out of loyalty. The man who did what I am asking you to do is sitting in a jail cell somewhere. He refuses to involve me in his current problems. I am taking financial care of his family. He is being loyal, Sean. There are people who would like to destroy my business, and put me away. The only way that could ever happen is a breach of loyalty. I pay well for loyalty"

"I'm listening sir," said Sean.

"I need a sharp guy like yourself with good instincts about people. You would do well, Sean. Roy made a mistake and didn't do his homework in a particular situation. Sloppy doesn't cut it and he's paying the price. It will probably cost him five years of his life, but when he gets out there will be a place for him. I pay for loyalty, as I said."

Mr. Soledad moved once more to the window. "Those mountains, Sean, contain many secrets. I'm like those mountains; I have many secrets. I seldom revealed them to anyone. I have taken you into those mountains with me this morning, and laid bare my soul. You asked about the downside. Here it is. My business, that is not a business, is not geared to paying taxes." Once more he pulled the curtain. "I would gladly pay them Sean, but Uncle Sam won't let me. They won't just accept the money, they have to poke around and try to tell me how to run my life. It's a shame really. What I do has been done since God's garden got dug up. What I do - millions of Americans do every day. I work under the table, a cash economy, the old barter system."

"How long a commitment are you asking for?"

Mr. Soledad laughed out loud. "You sure don't make small talk, Sean, maybe that's a good thing; loose lips and all that.

How about a one year contract which can be renewed by mutual consent. The loyalty has to last forever though. You must agree to never speak of me to anyone. Let them guess all they wish. To Family, friends, it does not matter, my name does not leave your lips. The only reason you know my name, is because I chose to ask you to replace another loyal soul." "I guess I don't have a choice," said Sean.

"Of course you do. You can call your brother right now. You know he will help. If you feel trapped, Sean, it's a trap of your own making. I have been completely open with you."

"I know," said Sean sighing, "when do I begin?"

Twenty-Six

Sean called Jack with the news later that day. "I won't be coming back brother, Monique needs me here. I'm sorry to let you down." "I could read the signs, Sean. Don't worry about it. Do you need some money? When do I get to meet this lady, anyway?"

"She is starting to feel better, a lingering flu thing, I guess it's really just an excuse for me anyway. I may have a job that I will tell you about if it works out. Maybe Monique and I can get to a tournament. If not, when you get back out here, we'll see you for sure."

"Sounds good, Sean. Make sure you call Mr. O'Shea regularly; he misses his two boys. I am hoping to stop in, later this spring or summer. My game is starting to jell; I have Tim rooming with me. He is a crazy man but we get along well. You sure you don't need some money?"

"I'm fine, save it for a rainy day or for the lucky gal who captures the heart of Jack O'Shea. Have you met any of those Southern girls who want to hear an Irish folk tale?

"She would have to be Southern Irish for Mr. O'Shea to approve. He didn't have much luck bringing the Bible belt to the snow belt as we both witnessed," chuckled Jack.

"I sure hope he doesn't mind me traveling through France to get to Ireland," said Sean.

"It's that serious is it? I hope I get to meet her before she throws a garter in my lap."

"I don't think that's how it goes brother," chuckled Sean. "We are serious, but there are a hundred little issues that need to settle first. So no immediate plans, except to be together. I will stay in touch brother. I love you, and thanks for all you did for me."

❧☙

That evening after Monique returned from her show, she found Sean sitting in the darkened apartment. "Why do you sit in the gloom, Sean?"

"It was light when I sat down. I guess I must have dozed off. When I woke up, I was too lazy to get up and turn on the light. Anyway sitting here in the dark helped me see things more clearly. How was your show tonight?

"Everything was fine; the usual crowd but what of the day you had. This man, was he a monster? Tell me, what did he propose?"

Sean told Monique about the man, the offer, and the acceptance.

"What are the risks, Sean? Could you go to jail working for this man?"

"All it is," explained Sean, downplaying the dark side of the business, "is providing services to a cash paying clientele. Hell, half of this country operates partly under the table. They trade services to avoid paying taxes. The big corporations find loopholes in the tax laws or do offshore accounting and banking to reap the same benefits. The little guy is the one who carries this country. Look at the waste created by the government with the money they do raise." Sean went on and on about Pentagon waste, no bid contracts, politicians, and lobbyists, all the time creating a justification for his new job.

"You know Monique, this job I'm taking is more honest than what's going on throughout this country. Business being conducted with a wink and a nod and a legal stamp of approval." Monique listened watching Sean, who kept his emotions hidden from all but her, get red faced and loud; angry even. "I love you, Sean. Do what you must; just please be careful. I worry only that a job that brings such strong feelings is not one you truly believe in."

Sean had no answer for Monique. She could obviously read him like a book.

⤙∽⤚

The new job was just as Mr. Soledad had described. Sean began meeting people, mostly men, who were in town for an escape from the world they inhabited the other fifty–one weeks of the year. Sean had learned that a week in this town was like two or three weeks anywhere else. The men Sean met were still on the learning curve of that reality. A day or two into the experience of 24 hour gambling, drinking, and carousing left them wanting more without the money on hand to finish off the week. These loans were the easy ones and a quick payback was a certainty.

Many of these men had arranged their entire trip through one of Mr. Soledad's associates so no lengthy check was necessary. The challenge for Sean were men who lived their life on the edge. His own gambling debt was a perfect example of the desperate situation good men could find themselves in.

Mr. Soledad sat atop his mountain, like those mountains he was always pointing to, and let money like little streams of water dribble down the sides. These streams of money offered renewed life to whatever activity these men were engaged in. It was only when examined closely that you could see the vast cracks and crevices that would prevent a smooth trip to the summit for the dreamer.

Sean looking out his office window was reminded of what Mr. Soledad had said about the mountains not paying the rent. Sean wasn't so sure. It seemed this mountain of debt formed by addiction, greed, and avoidance paid Mr. Soledad's rent very nicely, thank you very much.

That first week Sean listened to a myriad of excuses - valid reasons according to the gentlemen needing a loan extension. This was where his real job lay. Making the decision of whether to grant the extra time or demanding payment. Sean quickly realized what desperate acts he was setting in motion when he studied the eyes of these men. Normally confident men, successful men, well-dressed men were pleading with him for a little extra time. Some would finally confess their problems to their loved ones, combine resources, and pay off the loan. Others actually had a stash of disposable income they could access when necessary. These men were not the norm. Sean found that in general his clients were as desperate as he himself had become.

An empty feeling in the pit of the stomach, all your senses heightened to the point of overload, even the eyes ached. A feeling that everyone on the street knows of your quiet desperation. The people closest to you have been hurt, and still you approach the one person who can provide a fix. Sean saw himself in these men and he came to realize that those meetings that he and Mr. O'Shea had attended were in the cards for many of these men. Alcohol, drugs, gambling, sex; these men had become prostitutes, selling their lives for one more go round. Sean listened day after day, lied to himself, and tried to rationalize that someone would be doing this job if he wasn't. Within the first month however, Sean realized he could not continue working for Mr. Soledad. He toyed with the idea of calling Jack, asking his brother for help one last time.

Monique advised him to do just that. "You have made mistakes but you are a wonderful person. Don't throw your life away. This man will throw you in the trash heap when he is finished with you."

"I know you're right Monique. I just have to figure out a way. I don't want to put you in danger; there's no telling what he's capable of. Conjuring up images of all the monsters out there in the night, Sean held Monique tightly pulling the covers over their head.

Sean continued to play poker, not live poker, however. He now played video poker that allowed him to show all kinds of emotion. These machines didn't care if he was the candy man or the handyman. Sean found comfort sitting before the screen, letting his mind wander, taking as much time as he wanted between hands. He pondered his future as he pushed buttons determining which cards to hold and which to discard. *If only I could discard the past two months as easily as these, cards,* thought Sean, *not Monique though she mustn't disappear*. She was keeping Sean from acting out his fantasy of using violence to solve his financial woes. Sean was so absorbed in his thoughts, pushing buttons and reaching for coins to feed the machine, that he didn't notice the lady who sat down beside him.

"Are you having any luck?"

"In the total scheme of things, I would have to answer no," said Sean, still reflecting on his predicament.

"Luck is a funny thing, you never know when she's going to touch down or get up and leave for that matter. Luck offers no scheduled flights like an airline."

"Guess you're right about that," Sean muttered as he put 5 more coins in the machine. He pushed the button and two black aces appeared side by side. A 6, 3, and a 9 completed the hand. Sean discarded the three small cards then turned to the lady. "What are my chances of getting a third ace, or God forbid, a fourth. A full boat would be good."

"I guess, this just might be your lucky day," she smiled. Sean pushed the button and a pair of 10's and a 6 appeared to go with the aces. Sean shook his head.

"Well, you got your money back and a little more, nothing wrong with that."

"You said this might be my lucky day. I was hoping for a little more."

"Oh, luck doesn't limit itself to cards as you well know Sean." Sean spun in his seat really looking at the lady for the first time. "How do you know my name? Have we met?"

"Not really, Sean, but I have a strong suspicion that we are going to get to know each other well."

Sean looked quizzically at this lady wearing sunglasses in the half light of the casino. She had short hair and was wearing a business suit. Sean didn't even know what to ask so he sat there waiting for the next line to be delivered.

"I am Rachel Watson," hand extended she reached across to Sean. She seemed confident Sean would take that hand.

Sean felt the strength of someone who obviously worked out. He didn't say a word so Rachel continued.

"As I said, you never know what form luck is going to take. This morning, for instance, your luck might just have arrived disguised as a 35 year old woman." Rachel rose, and moved behind Sean's seat. "No, Sean, I am not talking about jumping your bones, not that there would be anything wrong with that, as Jerry Seinfeld would say," she chuckled. Before Sean could say anything, Rachel continued.

"Luck can be fleeting, Sean; something you also know well. I suggest you play a couple more hands and if lady luck doesn't do video, meet me at the hotel across from here in - say in - twenty minutes. Take the elevator to the fourth floor, and then take a right turn to room 426. I will explain just how lucky you are to have met me this morning. By the way, it wasn't luck."

Rachel just walked away, putting dollar tokens in every third machine, turning to look at Sean when luck did not slow her exit. Sean began imagining the worst. (Was Mr. Soledad unhappy with his work?) Could this be the cops, had he been sloppy, could he be joining Mr. Soledad's former employee in jail? Sean placed five one dollar tokens in the machine, but the spinning in his own mind kept him from paying attention to the three pairs of eyes that now watched him walk away.

Twenty minutes later, as luck would have it, a man working his way along the bank of machines noticed the deal that had not been completed. He discarded the two cards that didn't sequence and pulled the lever. When the nine and ten of clubs appeared, a straight flush rewarded him to the tune of $2,500. "Well, this is certainly my lucky day," he muttered as the bells and whistles attracted a small crowd of onlookers.

Sean found a phone, called Monique and told her to stay put till he could get there. "I will explain as soon as I know what is going on," he told her.

Room 426 was at the end of the corridor, the longest corridor Sean had ever walked it seemed. Do not disturb signs on some doors and food trays setting on the carpet assured Sean he was not alone. A laundry cart stood outside an open door. Inside two ladies were laughing as they changed the linens.

Sean finally reached the door. He knocked and the door opened almost immediately. Rachel once more extended her hand and the smile that accompanied it seemed genuine. Sean relaxed just a little.

Pointing to a small couch, Rachel led the way and sat down first. A man emerged from the bathroom and sat on the edge of a bed that had not been slept in. Rachel introduced the man as Gary Small. The man grunted but made no attempt to offer his hand.

"Would you like some coffee or juice, some danish? " "No, I'm okay," said Sean looking around the room.

"I can see why you had some success as a poker player, Sean. You don't give away much; do you? I'll begin then. Maybe I can answer your questions without you asking. I am Rachel Watson and I work for the Federal Government. The Internal Revenue Service to be exact. Gary is my partner. The man you are working for, a Mr. Phillipe Soledad, has been under investigation for tax evasion for a long time. He might have told you all this, he is a pretty clever individual." She took a sip of coffee.

"He also might have shared with you that a former employee is in prison and he is taking care of the man's family. Mr. Soledad has managed to stay out of prison himself by creating a loyal group of employees who, through fear and Mr. Soledad's warped version of loyalty, believe he will always be there for them." Agent Watson stood up.

"I am here to tell you, Sean, that he will not be there for you because I intend to put this man away for a long time. We will nail this guy with or without your help. The Internal Revenue is not the only agency looking at Mr. Soledad. He's breaking or causing laws of all kinds to be broken. This man has a strong connection to drugs, armed robberies, burglary, possibly even a murder or two." Rachel was up and moving around the room. Anger entered her voice as she continued.

"We haven't been able to cut off the head of this monster, but we intend to remove the limbs that allow movement. You are his arms and legs Sean and its up to you to decide where your loyalty lies. I think you are an honest man who has been forced by circumstance to work for Mr. Soledad. He's never been more vulnerable and I'll tell you why." Her voice softened.

Gary Small tried to interrupt but Rachel stared him down. "I believe in you Sean. I know you better than you think. It wasn't lady luck that put me in the casino this morning. It was the result of an investigation of you. One of those three men who answer to you, actually works for us. He's gathered a good deal of information, but without you to tie it to Mr. Soledad, there's not enough. Our man is vulnerable though, and we can't keep him there much longer. We need your help Sean. Phillipe Soledad is a kingpin in an organization that runs coast to coast. We caught a break a while back with a small timer on the East Coast giving some names that led out here. Phillipe Soledad has managed to dodge the bullet up to now, but he is no longer bullet proof. With the information we can give you, you can help us bring down a nationwide crime organization.

Sean continued to remain silent but had already made up his mind. Monique was right; Sean was not a criminal. Brother Jack doesn't deserve this either. Sean nodded to himself. (One last gamble in a game with the highest stakes I've ever played for. I have to be a better poker player than Mr. Soledad, who doesn't gamble but hasn't lost a single hand up to now,) he said to himself.

Sean voiced his decision. "I'll help. I hate this man too. I need some guarantees first though. Protection for my fiancée and my family."

"Done! Your lady will have someone looking over her shoulder every time she leaves your apartment. We figure you will need about a month to gather all the information we need. Mr. Soledad won't even know the information is coming from you. You shouldn't even need to testify. Here is what we want you to do."

CHAPTER

Twenty-Seven

"Jack, this is Sean. Please listen and don't ask any questions till I'm finished, ok?" Sean told Jack about his gambling and how it had gotten out of control. He didn't have to lend drama to his explanation, for the facts spoke for themselves. Even as he related the darkest moments, a sense of relief and lightness filled his mind.

"I am so sorry to have involved you in this, but I need your help to get out of this mess. I need you to send $10,000 a week to this, Mr. Soledad, for the next month. The plan is to keep him from getting suspicious of what I'm doing for the Feds. By the end of the month Mr. Soledad should be in jail and you will get your money back. This whole thing hinges on everything appearing above board on my part."

Jack sat stunned. For the past half hour he had listened to a story that sounded like a B Movie. The creative mind of an O'Shea would have had difficulty conjuring up such a predicament. "I can't get back brother or I would have told you all this sitting on a bar stool where I've emptied my soul to you before. The only good I have taken away from all this Jack, is even with all the stress, I don't hanker a drink. Weird huh."

Sean turned deadly serious. "These Government people seem to have their act together so don't worry. If anything should go wrong, I will call you immediately. So brother, any questions for this sorry assed individual?"

"I will send the money, Sean. If I can do anything else just let me know. I won't blister you with a rant about not coming to me in the first place. I know how stubborn the O'Sheas can be. You're doing the right thing now and that's all that matters. Help nail this bastard, Sean. There's an Old Irish saying that goes like this: 'There's many a dry eye at a money lenders funeral.'

Sean contacted Mr. Soledad and asked to meet. Once more Sean knocked on the door to Mr. Soledad's penthouse. This time, however, he felt like his future was very much in his own hands. Mr. Soledad invited him to sit down. The ritual being acted out by Mr. Soledad was repeated as if following a script. When Mr. Soledad opened the curtain, Sean decided to take the stage. "I can't work for you Mr. Soledad. I've tried but I can't do it. My brother knows everything about my loan and he will pay it back in weekly installments of $10,000 till it's paid off."

Mr. Soledad didn't even turn from the window; he continued to gaze into those damned mountains.

"I know we have an agreement for a year, but its not working for me and I need to be right up front with you, sir."

Mr. Soledad spent a few more seconds studying the terrain as if looking for a path he should follow in his response to this young man.

"I am disappointed, Sean. All reports of your work have been excellent and your co-workers indicate their satisfaction as well. What if I sweeten the salary part we discussed, would that help?"

"No sir, it's not the money. You have been more than fair."

"I would be lying to you Sean if I said I am happy with this decision, but I am a man of my word." He wandered back and forth with his finger drumming his bottom lip. " Here is what I am willing to do. You give me two months to replace you, your brother pays that $10,000 a week for those two months, and you walk away, free and clear."

Sean rose and started to leave. Mr. Soledad took Sean's hand, held it firmly and looked Sean in the eye. "Remember the loyalty piece Sean, that part never ends. I have your word."

"You have my word. I won't ever tell any secrets," Sean responded and he meant it. When he left the room, he could almost hear Rachel, the writer and director of this little play, yelling cut and print.

Over the next two weeks Sean continued to arrange loans and repayments. He tried to figure out which of the three men, whom he dealt with on a daily basis, was the undercover agent. He couldn't figure it out, but was quietly pleased that the Feds had people who were truly gifted. (I wouldn't want to play poker against the guy,) thought Sean.

Sean and Monique discussed the situation on a nightly basis and the ongoing drama seemed to draw them even closer. Sean felt so fortunate to have Monique in his life; she was a pillar of strength.

Sean called Agent Watson at the beginning of the second week. "What should I be doing?"

"You're doing just fine Sean, not to worry, our Mr. Soledad is on a collision course with reality and it should happen within the week."

"What if he asks me for help when things happen?" "You do everything he asks. There's no reason to put yourself in jeopardy. We will protect you from any prosecution." "I sure hope your plan works. He's a smart man, not much gets past him from what I have observed.

❧❧

Just like clockwork, three days later Sean was summoned to Mr. Soledad's suite. Mr. Soledad shouted for Sean to come in. He was already at his window, with the curtain open. The script had obviously changed. When he turned, his face was grave and he offered no greeting.

"Sean, one of the men working directly below you has been arrested."

"Who?" asked Sean, not faking his surprise.

"Fred Ortiz," said Mr. Soledad, offering no more information.

"Arrested for what?" probed Sean.

"I am not really sure; the Feds have him and a lawyer we keep on retainer has not been allowed to see him."

"Do we have something to worry about?"

"I'm not sure. Fred knows a lot. Things could get uncomfortable but he's not a smoking gun. He couldn't, by himself, bring down the house. What is worrying me are the Feds. They may be inept but they aren't stupid. They wouldn't be making a play like this unless there's something else going on. Why arrest Fred? I'm going over all this in my mind; what is playing out here?"

"Fred took his orders from me. Should I go over all the accounts he's privy to, possibly I can spot something?" offered Sean.

"That's what is troubling. Fred's work is pretty transparent. Investigate a potential client and report back. He's been at it for two years. Why the sudden interest?"

"When did this happen?"

"I spoke with Fred on Wednesday, and he asked if I would like to attend a college baseball game to watch his son play. The kid has a future. I have gone to a game or two. This one was a short drive away so Fred asked me if I wanted to go. I had a meeting." The puzzled look remained.

"Another odd thing, they went right into the stands and hauled him away in cuffs like they were sending a message. Sean I am concerned that this arrest isn't about Fred. They are laughing at me like they know the punch line to a joke I haven't been told." Mr. Soledad was clearly upset and that was exactly what Rachel Watson was hoping for.

"Are we vulnerable on any front Mr. Soledad? I haven't been with the company long enough to have any idea what they might be after."

"I will level with you, Sean. The only way they can get me is if they located where I keep my money. They can bully and intimidate all they want but without those account numbers, all they have is speculation."

Sean, who was as confused as Mr. Soledad about the actions taken by Agent Watson, didn't know what else to say.

Mr. Soledad paced the floor, stopped to look into the mountains for an answer, and then resumed pacing all the while muttering under his breath. Suddenly, he stopped, and stood directly in front of Sean.

"Sean, this is what I want you to do. I'm sure I will be followed and my phones may even be tapped. I will write down some phone numbers. Go to a public place well away from here, and using a public phone, call these numbers. When someone answers, just say the phrase, 'on any given day'. You will hear a message, write it down word for word, and number for number in the order they are given, and bring them to me."

"Anything else?"

"Yeah, bring me a Starbucks expresso," chuckled Mr. Soledad.

(That's the first time that man has cracked a smile this morning,) thought Sean as the elevator headed toward the lobby. This man is no fool. I sure as hell hope the Federal agents know who they are dealing with. The first call Sean made was to Agent Watson.

"You make a copy of those messages, and we will do a check on those numbers. I think our little show and tell with Fred lit a fire."

"What if this is just a test of my loyalty?"

"We will be discreet; he won't know we even have the messages or any numbers. We won't spring the trap till you are out of harm's way."

"I am trusting you people. I'll call back with the messages," said Sean, not thoroughly convinced.

❧

Sean made the calls. Each time he was given a series of words and numbers. He reported them to agent Watson, and took them to Mr. Soledad as instructed.

Mr. Soledad, sipping on his expresso, studied the words and numbers after creating a pattern for himself by placing them in some sequence. He looked Sean in the eyes.

"You did well, Sean. All appears to be secure. Go on about your business. I will call you if I need you. Our lawyer should be interviewing Fred within a few hours. Hopefully this arrest is a house of cards. Who knows, maybe Fred had something else going on in his life and it's not about me after all."

With a wave of dismissal from Mr. Soledad Sean left the suite. (This place and this man are becoming way too familiar to suit me,) he thought.

੭ঞ

Sean told Monique he felt like a ping pong ball being served back and forth across the net. "I'm being cuffed gently from both sides as they look for a weakness in one another. Then slam!" The ping pong game lasted another week. Jack had been sending his cash with a courier who picked it up at an arranged site and somehow got it to Mr. Soledad.

੭ঞ

Mr. Fred Ortiz, it seemed had been arrested for a hit and run accident that involved some visiting foreign dignitary. Later when his son volunteered that he was the driver, Fred was released. Nevertheless, Fred was removed from the team. With his name reaching the headlines, he was of no further use to Mr. Soledad. He was given a generous severance and relocation package. He was urged to leave the state. Mr. Soledad prided himself on taking care of his associates.

Sean contacted agent Watson to fill her in on Fred Ortiz, but she didn't seem too surprised. "Poor Fred might have to find employment with a federal agency or something, you think." Sean's look of shock drew a big smile. "We had to figure out a way to get Fred out from his undercover assignment that would draw Mr. Soledad's attention and suspicion. Then we let Fred off the hook, and made it all sound like a big mix up, complete with a public apology. Just the kind of publicity Mr. Soledad discourages in his employees. There really was a fender bender, but the visiting foreign dignitary, unnamed of course, was really an agent. Fred's boy gets a slap on the wrist and a full scholarship at a larger school where Fred will be reassigned. Mr. Soledad got a little paranoid. It really should be over by the weekend Sean, I promise."

Sean could not believe how intricate this web was being woven. "I will believe it when he is behind bars, not till then. He scares me."

Agent Watson was right. The weekend brought the game to an end but the slam came from the wrong team.

Saturday morning dawned brightly. Sean and Monique sat at a small table overlooking the courtyard below. Sean was pouring a second cup of coffee when the phone rang. Agent Watson was on the line.

⋙⋘

"Sean, there has been an accident. Fred Ortiz was hit by a car last night. A hit and run, he's dead! My partner Gary is missing; no one can locate him. I think Phillipe Soledad directed both those actions." The anger Rachel Watson had shown when he first met her, sounded more like fear as she finished.

"What the hell are you telling me?" shouted Sean. Monique looked up from the paper, alarmed.

"I am saying maybe my partner Gary had two bosses, not one. I don't know this for certain, but to be safe you should pack and leave immediately. Call your brother too; this man has a long reach. I will be in touch. Take down this number, it's my personal cell, I always have it with me.

When Sean finished repeating the number, he heard a weak click. The sound a ping pong paddle makes in a feeble attempt to return an overpowering slam. (Game over,) he said to himself. While Monique packed, Sean called Jack. "I won't call again unless there has been a new development. I am afraid for Monique so we will disappear for now. Brother, this guy is dangerous so please be careful yourself. Maybe you should lay low till this blows over. They will get him, I'm sure, but till then."

Jack, always trying to relieve the worry, made light of the situation. "Sean, dear brother, it appears that your recent development, as sticky as it is, will save me money. I'll just open a long term CD I believe."

Sean chuckled in spite of his fear. "Jack, I know you don't scare easily, but trust me please. He may try to get to me through you."

"I will be careful, Sean. You just worry about Monique and yourself. If you need anything, call me. I love you brother." Jack went immediately to his journal, writing down the date and the barest of details. The entries for the $10,000 payments stared up at him from the page. He could imagine the worst if he chose to but was not ready to jump to conclusions like Ellen had. He chuckled, thinking back to the night Ellen had questioned his gender preference. It would have been funny if it had been an accident but Ellen was no accident.

CHAPTER

Twenty-Eight

Ellen had continued to hang around being helpful or so Jack thought. She had managed to get into the apartment when neither Jack nor Tim was there. She apologized when confronted, saying she just wanted to surprise them with a home cooked meal. It did turn out to be a tasty meal even though it was fresh from the deli and all was forgiven. After that she would always leave a little note, saying she had stopped in to straighten up or to drop off groceries, always some excuse to be in the apartment. In the end, the true Ellen emerged. Towards the end of a long party night that ended up at Jack's place, three people remained. Jack, more than a little intoxicated, went to his room and stumbled out of his clothing at the same time singing an Irish ballad. Under the covers, he fell fast asleep. Molly Erricson entered his head and was holding him in her arms as somehow she had found her way to the East Coast. Jack was trying to think how she could have gotten here. Soon it didn't matter, as Molly began caressing his body, gently planting kisses on his lips. Jack stopped trying to think about his body responding to her touch. He began moaning softly, thinking he was finally going to make love to his beloved, Molly. He became hard and he ached to take Molly to a depth of feeling no undersea adventure could match. A warm breath on his neck caused him to groan.

Ellen, who had slipped into Jack's bed, was certain Jack cared for her. They had talked for hours and Jack was always respectful, complimenting Ellen on her looks and dress. Ellen took Jack's moaning as a sign she should continue. As she slid beneath him she whispered, "I love you Jack."

For just a moment, Jack thought, (oh, my god, she's found her voice.) Suddenly though, even in his stupor, he realized Molly would never be able to voice her love in words. He became stone cold sober.

Ellen had taken possession of his penis and was guiding it to her own secret place, still whispering, "I love you, Jack."

Jack rolled quickly to the side, threw back the covers, and leaped out of bed like a man on fire. He snapped on the light. A bewildered look on his face and a wild look in his unfocused eyes. Ellen, more than a little confused, asked, "What's wrong, Jack. I thought you loved me."

"Please, just get dressed and leave."

"What's wrong? I thought you'd like a little company."

"Well you were wrong. Please get dressed and leave immediately!"

"But I thought you cared for me. You always spent time talking to me at the parties."

"I do like you Ellen, but not in that way. Now please just go." Ellen's face suddenly darkened, "Oh, I get it. You'd rather pay for it I guess."

"What are you talking about? Please, just leave. No harm has been done. Ok."

"What's the big secret? Maybe your she is a he huh, Jack?" Jack was baffled. Still under the influence, he shook his head to clear the picture. "Ellen, please just leave. I'm going back to sleep."

"Don't kid me," said Ellen, getting her own clothes back together. "I know all about you paying Dannyboy for services. Does that ring a bell? You certainly pay him well; he must be special."

Jack couldn't believe what he was hearing. "You have been going through my personal business? Needed a dusting, did it?" "Yes, I found out who you really are! I should have known, never responding to all the invitations you got from the girls at the parties."

Jack refused to give Ellen an explanation. "Would you shut the light when you're finished with your rant, Ellen and don't let the door hit your backside."

"I'll tell everyone that the famous Mr. Jack O'Shea is gay. Hey that rhymes. Jack O'Shea is gay! Jack O'Shea is gay! Ellen began laughing hysterically. Then she began crying.

Jack heard the door close, and then Ellen shouting loudly to Tim. He heard Tim's voice muffled, trying to calm her down. All went quiet. Molly refused to re-enter Jack's head and he slept restlessly.

In the morning Ellen was gone. Tim asked what the hell had happened and Jack simply said, "I misjudged the girl. She's a sneak and I don't want to be around her ever again."

"She accused you of being gay Jack, and said she had proof. She was really angry. I told her I'd talk with her later today. I'll get her to keep her mouth shut."

"Tim, I will say it one time and only to you, I am not gay, but my personal business is not open to discussion. Thank you for trying to help. That girl is trouble. I'm going to take a room by myself for now. I don't want to be around her. The rent is paid through next week when we would be heading North, anyway." Tim was thoroughly confused but was not going to let Ellen ruin Jack's reputation on tour. Hell, this kind of thing could even hit the media. "I believe you, Jack. I'll let her hang around and calm her down. We don't need ugly rumors in the locker room."

"Thanks Tim, but watch out. She is a sneak. Don't let her get her hooks into you."

❧

Jack left that morning and when he was settled in a new room, called Sean to let him know he had moved. Sean said he was not sure where he and Monique should go. He would like to join Jack, but didn't think it would be safe.

"I am a little nervous; this guy is smart. He's dodged every bullet thrown at him in the past but I have to trust the system I guess."

"I have some great friends, the Erricson's up on the Monterey peninsula. Write this number down they will be glad to help." "What about you? This guy has a long reach, Jack."

"If something goes wrong, call my cell phone. I'm about to head North to the Carolinas. I'll be ok. I just got rid of one shark; I'll tell you about her when I see you. Love you, brother. Take care."

❧

Jack rented a car and drove East on route 4 toward Daytona and Interstate 95. The radio this early morning gave traffic conditions, and from what he was observing, Jack was glad he was headed East not back toward Orlando. Cars were backed up for at least a mile as police cleaned up an accident. The construction itself slowed everything to a crawl. The sun stared him straight in the eyes and by the time he entered a fast food drive through and picked up a breakfast sandwich, he was ready to stretch.

Standing in a parking lot doing stretches and deep knee bends probably struck others as odd but Jack didn't care. He polished off his sandwich between push-ups, again drawing stares. Finally headed North on 95 the sun no longer assaulted his eyes, but rode shotgun, a travel companion joining Dannyboy who lay on the passenger seat. Jack had thought he might stop in Palm Coast and see his friend Ron but the mind is a funny thing. Lost in thought, he missed the two exits that announced the arrival of a city on the move. Jack was thinking of his recent success on the golf course, and was looking forward to the next tournament. Interwoven in all his thinking was Molly. Sean too jumped into his head and by the time his friend Ron joined this mental party, Jack was hitting construction in St. Augustine. Jack was directed to a single lane. Slowing down, it dawned on him that he had missed Ron's exit. (Damn.)

Jack drove toward Jacksonville. He passed the sign for the World Golf Village up ahead. Many of his heroes had created permanent memories here that he would love to visit. There wasn't time however. Besides, he wanted to come here with Molly. This would be his own Disney World. The greatest legends in golf. He pulled over and made a note to write to Molly about the many stories and legends here.

Jack entered Georgia. He chuckled at how immortal the words to that tune had become. He had no room in his mind for Georgia; his brothers call had his head spinning. Sean had called as Jack was on the outskirts of Jacksonville about to enter Georgia. He and Monique had grabbed a few clothes and were headed toward Carmel and the safety of the Erricson family. Jack spent the evening after Sean's call talking to the Ericsson's. Mr. Erricson told Jack he would offer Sean a place in the mountains that he and Shannon used as a little hideaway. "No one knows where this cabin is except Shannon and myself.

We never even shared it with the kids growing up. Your brother and his fiancee will be safe there Jack."

"I will fly back after this week's tournament. Thank you so much, Paul. Could I speak to Molly?" When Molly tapped the phone with her pencil, Jack had something he needed to tell her. "I love you, Molly!" There was nothing else to be said. It was the first time he had voiced his own feelings in words.

Molly asked her mother to read what she had hastily written. Hastily written, but thought about for many months! {I love you too, Jack. I have met your brother Sean and Monique. He has told me everything. Please be careful. We have many beaches to walk.}

Tears entered Jack's eyes, "And Golf legends to meet. I will explain when I see you right after this tournament."

Jack found a room in a small motel. After putting things away he drove to the course to practice. Jack had a hard time focusing. So many things happening to the people he loved. It would be wonderful to get back to Molly, but the reasons for heading back right now were weighing on his mind.

Jack didn't notice the large man watching him hit club after club. He was swinging pretty well and was focused on something he had heard in a restaurant in Jacksonville. He had been sitting behind two guys who had stopped at the World Golf village. They were discussing some of the old wooden shafted clubs, and asking how in the world did those early players hit them. The two guys were in their fifties. When talk turned to more recent players, Jack heard one mention Tom Watson. What sparked Jack's attention was when one guy said, 'Tom hummed a tune when he swung his club.' (How come I've never heard that before,) thought Jack.

'Yeah, he hums the word, Edelweiss, an old German tune on his back swing. drags it out, Keeps his tempo,' Jack hadn't really remembered the conversation till just this morning when he began swinging his own clubs. He didn't know the tune but found lyrics that worked for him. All morning he hummed the words, cockles and mussels, to himself and developed a perfect tempo. (It seems Molly Malone might just take up the game of golf, as if she has nothing better to do,) Jack chuckled to himself.

⁓◅

When Jack arrived back at his motel, his door was open. Not one to panic, he went to his car and grabbed a 5 iron. He began humming cockles and mussels, ready to try out his new swing if necessary. No one was there but his room had been ransacked and Dannyboy was missing. Jack called the front desk but no one had seen anything. (This isn't random,) thought Jack. A quick call from his cell to the Ericsson's, alerted them that he was safe, but heading back to Orlando to gather his other Journals from storage.

"There are no locations mentioned in my writing and all of my letters from Molly are safely tucked away. I am going to remove all the numbers from my cell phone, just in case. I think the break-in was a scare tactic, letting me know they know how to find me. I will be in touch but, I think, I'll just disappear for now."

Jack headed South with one eye on the road and one in the rearview mirror. He left Interstate 95 and found route 17. Small towns greeted him as he became a tourist.

He found a floppy hat at a flea market, even bought some aviator sunglasses with yellow lenses. When he got back into Florida, he stopped to eat. Checking the yellow pages, he located a rental car dealership and swapped vehicles.

(Jack O'Shea, man on the run.) It might be kind of exciting if people he loved weren't at risk. These thoughts and a million more passed through his head as he took the scenic route-A1A-down the Florida coastline. Jack stopped for the night in an upscale Bed and Breakfast. He slept fitfully and was on the beach for a run before the moon left the sky. He showered but decided not to shave. Add to the new look. Three couples were having breakfast in a small dining room when Jack entered. The room faced the ocean. When Jack saw the expanse of blue, Molly came immediately to mind.

The couples each living in their own world weren't including unshaven strangers in their conversation.

Jack was fine with that. Gazing out over the water, he couldn't wait to be on the other Coast. Thank goodness, he had been a little unfaithful in sharing all the details of his life lately. Dannyboy, his trusted confidant, would not reveal where Sean was hiding or put Molly in danger. The owner interrupted his thoughts when she wandered over to inquire how he'd slept.

"I hope you slept better than you are eating, young man." Jack looked into a pair of merry blue eyes that showed a life well lived. The Irishman Jack O'Shea found his voice.

"A fine morning such as this is all the nourishment a man needs. And, of course, the pleasure of meeting a lady such as yourself." "May I sit?"

Jack rose and pulled out a chair, "I would be honored to share a second cup of your excellent coffee." He filled both cups from the percolator and sat down.

"You seem to have a lot on your mind. I just wanted to offer a little company before you continued on your journey."

"That is very kind of you, Mrs. Howard. Your sign out front is what prompted me to stay here last night. 'Mrs. Howard's Home', it surely is that."

"Thank you, I'll just sip my coffee and not bother you. You seem to have a lot on your plate besides those uneaten eggs and toast."

Jack took her at her word and the two finished their coffee in silence. (I can see Molly and I sitting like this, gazing out over the water just enjoying each other's company, no words to break the spell,) thought Jack.

When Jack left, he penned a little thank you and placed it on his night stand. Mrs. Howard had provided him with more than a place to stay.

The ocean on his left side provided him with glimpses of blue from time to time as he moved south. The morning sun on his left promised to complete the tan he'd started on his trip North just days ago. Jack drove right through Flagler Beach, probably right by Ron's home. This time he didn't stop on purpose, determined to distance any of his friends from possible danger.

In Daytona Beach he left the ocean behind and headed West toward Route 4. He passed the Daytona Speedway and thought how he seemed to be moving in one big circle himself. The parking lot was full; large tents had been erected on the grounds advertising some trade show going on.

Jack made it back to Orlando and parked his car. He wandered the street going in and out of several small shops. Finally, he went into the bank and checked on his beloved journals. All was well and he patted his original Dannyboy lightly and said aloud, "It will all soon be over, Dannyboy."

☎♲

It was just a day later that he heard Michael Grason was looking for him. (Why didn't I think to call him. He's a friend and a cop to boot. Maybe he can help me figure out what to do next.) Jack dialed the number Michael had left and when Michael didn't answer, Jack left a brief message.

PART THREE

CHAPTER

Twenty-Nine

"It's good to see you too Michael, my boy. Is this the line they taught you at the academy when you have your suspect subdued?"

Michael looked at this tall lanky man stretched out on the bed. Jack O' Shea, unshaven sitting in the dark. His sunglasses perched on his nose, a smile on his face, Michael just shook his head.

"All I am missing is my hot light. Do I need to read you your rights, you big lug?"

"I guess I have given up my right to be silent by calling you, Michael, so here's my story."

Jack told a story as few others could. He had Michael moving between laughter and tears as he related the tale that Dannyboy had faithfully recorded - Finding his father and his brother after years apart, their ups and downs as they regrouped as a family, and Sean's joining him as a caddy. When the stage had been set, Jack added a little suspense by taking a break to use the toilet. Michael sat there, waiting to hear the installment that had summoned his help.

"Sean became an accomplished gambler, Michael," said Jack as he landed back on the bed. "He did quite well; he tells me. He's met a wonderful girl who means the world to him; he tells me. His luck changed, and he lost all his money. He had to borrow money, to win his money back; this he didn't tell me." Both men chuckled.

"He was hired by a money lender of some sort, to run his business. The man said his debt would be forgiven as part of his salary. Sean found the situation intolerable. Then Federal Agents got involved. They convinced Sean to help them bring this man to justice."

Michael sat straight up and started taking notes.

"Sean gets me to send money, to use as a cover for his leaving the man's business. My brother tells me this man is dangerous and has influence on both coasts. Anyway, the plan fails miserably and this Mr. Soledad is his name, he finds out Sean was leaking information."

Michael stood up.

"Sean is in hiding, my room has been ransacked, and to be perfectly honest Michael, I am at a loss as to what to do next. Sean tells me there has been at least one murder already. So after the ransacking of my room I am taking all this quite seriously." Jack stretched and yawned.

Michael began pacing and yawned in tandem with Jack.

"Who knows where you are right now besides me?"

"No one as far as I know. I've used my cell phone so there is no way anyone could know unless I've been followed. I changed cars, and have slipped around from place to place at night. I think I have been careful. It's been like a TV. movie"

"Who is this guy? You say his name is Mr. Soledad. Do you know his first name.?"

"No idea. I just know he supposedly operates here in the East as well as in Vegas."

Michael made notes in a small notebook and continued to ask questions. "Do you know how Sean met this man? There is usually a middleman involved."

"All I know is supposedly this guy took a shine to Sean, and when Sean got into debt, asked him to work for him."

"Let me see if I have this straight," said Michael looking at his notes. "Sean didn't tell you about his loan, couldn't pay it back, went to work for this man, decided he couldn't work for him, then became part of a Federal investigation. You start making loan payments to make it look like Sean is going to repay the loan after all. Now a Federal agent is dead and you two guys are scrambling for your lives."

"Dannyboy couldn't have reported it with more accuracy," kidded Jack, feeling a sense of relief that his friend was here. "I believe it's every man for himself just now with the Feds scrambling to cover their own arses. I didn't know who to trust, but after that little burglary, your call was like divine intervention." "I'm glad you called back. I need some time to sort out all that's happened. I have to think about all this, but for now anyway we'll leave the Feds out of this. They have a tendency to clean up a mess by leveling the building and convincing you there was always a hole in the ground on that spot."

"I'll trust your judgment on this Michael. The whole situation is harder to read than a 40 foot downhill putt."

"Are you sure Sean and his girlfriend are safely hidden? It would make it easier if it's just you that we're needing to protect." "I would say yes; in fact, I need to be where they are for a different reason but I don't want to put them in danger."

Michael sat quietly, looking down at his notes. "If Sean calls, tell him not to have any contact with the Federal agent he was working with." Michael rose and began walking the room, studying himself in the mirror over the dresser.

Jack turned on the light, grabbed his putter and a sleeve of balls. He placed a water glass on its side at one end of the room and proceeded to fill it. All three putts found their target. Michael smiled as he heard the last of the balls clink, "Let's hope our way out of this runs as true as your putts Jack."

◈

The men's eyes locked; Michael laid out the first step of the journey.

"You stay here tonight. I'm going back to Ron's and pretend this meeting didn't take place. Tomorrow we will return your car here if we can. If not, you'll follow Meg and I to Daytona. There will definitely be a dealer there. Then we all go to Orlando together." Jack suddenly was smiling. "Meg is it? Surely you speak of a pet of some kind. The Michael who I remember had little use for two legged creatures."

"Actually she is a two legged creature and Irish to boot. She's anxious to meet you." Meg's a good Irish name. Tell me she's just off the boat and I'll know we're all saved."

"She has been here in the States for about a year now, but she is special Jack. I can't believe how lucky I was to meet her."

"How about you, Jack, still the storyteller who leaves them after they are fast asleep, dreaming a fairy tale?"

"Truth is Michael, I am living a fairy tale. It's a story of a real live princess, who's been put under a spell. She lives beneath the sea. It's only recently she has learned to navigate in this world. The sooner Sean and I are rid of this nightmare, the better. I am ready to turn my fairy tale into the proper ending, 'They lived happily ever after.'"

"It sounds like we both have a reason to go to battle. You stay inside; I will see you tomorrow morning." Michael left and Jack resumed putting.

Standing over the ball, Jack's mind unearthed a memory of a story Mr. O'Shea had told him years ago. An Englishman stood over a three foot putt that would save his country and himself from disgrace. Jack was now asking Michael to save his world by sinking a much longer putt with life and death consequences. (Maybe being Irish is not lucky enough after all.) He suddenly shuddered, his putt running three feet by.

∽∾

Michael picked up the groceries he needed and returned to Ron's house.

"Where have you been for the last three hours? I was about to send for the police, and then I realized you are the police," kidded Ron.

"Well, I kinda got lost," answered Michael. "First, I was lost in thought - thinking of Jack and what could be going on with him. Then I got physically lost. I passed the turnoff to Route 100, where you said I would find a supermarket. So I kept going South on A1A thinking there must be another way to double back without turning around. I got all the way into Ormond Beach before I turned around and headed back. When the pier came into view, I pulled over and walked the beach for awhile, trying to make some sense of Jack's secrecy."

By now everyone was gathered, listening to Michael. "Sorry if I worried all of you, but if the ladies will do some slicing and dicing, I will whip up my version of a fast food Fajita, with a twist of lime."

Meg had watched Michael as he spun his tale but made no comment. (I will be getting the real story out of him later,) she thought to herself.

Their eyes met just as she completed her thought. Michael knew she knew, and she knew Michael knew that she knew. They both just smiled.

Small talk dominated the evening. No one wanted to even speculate what was happening with Jack. Michael turned in early as he spun another small white lie. "I have been called back to Orlando by my lieutenant. One of my cases has taken a sudden twist and I need to be there. We'll have to leave early in the morning."

Michael was in bed first and when Meg joined him, they both lay quiet. Slowly the furniture emerged as their eyes adjusted to the darkness. It appeared no creatures would be stirring tonight unless Michael voiced an explanation. Michael could hear his own heart beating and turned to Meg to bring the two hearts into rhythm.

He told Meg everything - The calls, Jack popping up out of the bunker, the visit to his motel, and the sudden urgency to get back to Orlando. He told of Sean's gambling debt, the federal investigation, and its failure. Michael finished with, "So you will be meeting Jack in the morning."

Meg had taken Michael's hand as the story unfolded. When the story ended, she was tucked securely in his arms. The two hearts were beating as one when Meg spoke for the first time since the banter during dinner. "It would seem we've work to do, Michael, to save these good Irishmen. Do you have a plan that goes beyond running them ragged, and me jumping up and down on them?"

Michael laughed aloud in the darkness. "Maybe that's not such a bad idea. We may have to be a little unconventional with this man. Mr. Soledad appears, from what Jack told me, to be a clever fellow. So some of our running and bouncing may just be called for."

"So that's it then, baffle him with bouncing, ruin him with running, and he won't stand a chance," giggled Meg.

"First, we need to get back to Orlando, that's my turf. I need to talk with my lieutenant and have him do some research on this guy. Jack said he operates in the East, so maybe we have something on him. We will get Jack a place to stay and start from there. Michael and Meg turned away from each other; both lost in thought.

Michael had nearly thought himself to sleep when Meg was suddenly sitting on his lower stomach. She began to move up and down, gently.

"Would you care to explain your actions, young lady. I was nearly asleep?"

"I thought it best to practice my bouncing technique. Since we didn't pack my ball, you will have to do."

"Oh I believe you are right, Meg. Bouncing will be part of any plan we finally end up with. We should practice at every opportunity. When we're through bouncing, we can practice running them ragged." The two laughed. The bouncing soon turned into something else entirely.

The morning sun stretched, yawned, and appeared, looking refreshed after a good night's rest. Michael turned to Meg and whispered in her ear. "I smell coffee brewing, and the sun's promising a good day so awake sleeping beauty."

Beth had made Almond French Toast. After a third cup of coffee, Michael finally rose to leave. I wish we could stay a while longer but we really need to get to Orlando. The two ladies hugged and Michael shook Ron's hand.

"Thanks Beth, for everything. Ron, we will keep in touch, I promise. If we hear from Jack, we'll make him call to explain himself."

Michael drove into the parking lot at the Topaz Motel. Meg walked with him as they crossed the lot to Jack's room. No one answered the knock. Michael tried the door handle. It turned and the door opened. (That's odd these rooms don't usually open without a key,) thought Michael. A lamp on the dresser was off, and there was no sign of Jack or his belongings. When Michael returned from checking the bath room Meg was seated on the bed. She pointed to the door where a piece of tape had been placed over the lock. They closed the door. The two didn't speak, but it was clear the same thoughts were running through their minds. No sign of a struggle, to Michael that was a good sign. The room appeared undisturbed; the bed looked as if Jack had slept there. Suddenly someone else was at the door. Michael motioned Meg to the bathroom and he slipped behind the door just as it opened. The morning sun followed the man into the room and Michael was instantly blinded as he moved to face the intruder. The intruder's eyes had not adjusted to the darkened room. Both startled, they leaped at one other landing in a heap on the bed. Meg ran from the bathroom and jumped on the man's back, attempting to bounce Michael out of harm's way. The two men wrestled, with Meg holding on for all she was worth.

Suddenly, the bed collapsed and they fell away from each other. Michael was about to slug this guy when things became clear. Both men's jaws dropped open.

"Would this be part of the plan for saving me, Michael?" managed a now smiling Jack O'Shea.

Meg struggled to her feet disoriented; she saw the two men grinning. Laughter followed, and the three were once more on the mattress rolling around clutching their sides. Every time it quieted for a moment, one of the three would begin laughing again, prompting another fit. Finally exhausted, they continued to lay strewn about like three life sized dolls. To a passerby, it would have appeared a mass murder might have taken place. They repaired the room as best they could, while Jack explained he had merely crossed the road and found Snack Jack's Restaurant overlooking the water.

"I needed to clear my head. I took my suitcase with me just in case. I taped the door so you could get in. I never thought that would lead you to think something had happened to me." Jack began chuckling again, "By the way, I think I would have kicked your arse, if your partner hadn't jumped me."

This brought more laughter, and the trio was in great spirits as they began the first leg of their shared journey. They found a dealer in Palm Coast who would take Jack's rental car. Michael drove while Jack and Meg talked of Ireland. Jack asked so many questions that Meg had to finally say she needed a nap. The remainder of the trip was spent listening to CDs from Michael's collection. By the time they reached Meg's apartment, it was decided that Jack should stay here for a while.

"Are you sure I won't be in the way. This is not a very big place."

"It should be fine. Michael and I are training for a marathon, so he says, so I'll be at his place most of the time - working out, don't you know."

Michael could hardly keep from laughing. Meg was the wittiest girl he'd ever met. He couldn't keep from laughing though, when Jack asked to join in.

"I really need to get in shape, Michael. If you guys could include me in some of your workouts, I've been so busy hiding I..."

Meg and Michael both broke up at this and Jack was stopped in mid sentence.

Meg tried to contain her laughter as she continued the joke, "You'll have to be running alone. Michael insists our training take place in the dead of night, with an Irish mouse acting as coach." Michael was roaring.

"I give up," said an exasperated Jack. " I won't even ask. Listen, please let me know what you come up with for a plan. I will stay put for now, but I hate this hiding business."

"I am going to call the lieutenant right now so hang in there, Jack. As you have said time after time, it will soon be over Dannyboy."

Michael called his lieutenant who agreed to meet him that evening.

Meg packed more clothes and tidied up the apartment for Jack. When they left, Jack was studying the picture of Meg's soccer team.

Jack heard the door close and the stairs creaking as they descended and was suddenly very aware that he was no longer in control of his life. Jack the son, the brother, the family fixer was no longer in charge.

Meg stopped downstairs to tell the landlord that her cousin would be staying with her for a while, so if they saw a man with a scraggly beard hanging around, not to worry. Meg had never been to Michael's apartment.

Knowing they would be sharing the place for a while, Michael decided to clear the air regarding sleeping arrangements.

"I am willing to sleep on the couch, Meg, if you like." "There's two ways to approach this, Michael. We can creep forward one step at a time, pretending, or we can make the leap and hope for a soft landing.

"Which approach are you more comfortable with, Meg? I will follow your lead."

"I've never agreed with me mum's approach in forming a relationship, but walking your stairs seems as natural as climbing me own."

Michael reached across and took Meg's hand.

"I feel the same way, Meg. You have brought something into my life that, with all that's been going on, I haven't really processed. I just know there is a lightness of spirit that wasn't there before."

Meg had no comeback; there was no need.

When they arrived, Michael's landlord George was mowing the lawn. A ball of sweat, he moved with a purpose. He wore sound protecting head gear, a pair of shorts, hat on backwards, and a big smile. When he saw Michael and Meg, he turned off the mower and greeted them in his usual kidding way.

"I show you a beautiful flower last time I saw you Michael, and you bring one home even more lovely."

"I'd have to agree, George. This is a rare Irish rose, named Meg."

George tried to find some way to wipe the sweat from his hands but it wasn't possible.

"I'll save a handshake for next time; pleased to meet you Meg. I am so busy with all the yard work that I can't keep up." "It's beautiful here, George. You have done a wonderful job of landscaping," said Meg.

"Meg will be staying here for a while George, so if that changes anything in my rent let me know."

"Not a problem Michael, and thanks for the compliment, Meg. If you are interested in a little part time yard work, I could use the help. I am working extra hours trying to get caught up."

"I think I would like that George; just tell me when."

"Good," said George, "we start at eight AM., I don't like to disturb my tenant's sleep. I'll meet you right here. We work four hours a day, before it gets too hot. You get eight dollars an hour, cash money, paid at the end of every day."

"I will be standing at attention on this spot at eight AM," laughed Meg as she saluted George.

George returned to his work. Michael and Meg climbed the stairs to what Michael suddenly felt was a home.

CHAPTER

Thirty

Lieutenant Aubrey approached Michael's table with a quizzical look on his face. Michael stood and introduced Meg as a friend who would be helping in this situation.

The lieutenant took Meg's hand. "It's nice to meet you, Meg. I have no problem with Meg helping, as long as we don't get officially involved."

The lieutenant sat down. "So tell me what's going on, and I'll fill you in with what I found out about one, Phillipe Soledad." The waitress brought water and menus. Michael told his story in much the same fashion - first, a general description of what was going on with Jack and Sean, served as an appetizer. As they finished their meal and waved off dessert, Michael was finishing up all that he knew of Jack's situation.

When the bill arrived, the lieutenant insisted on paying. "You have great instincts, Michael. Your Mr. Soledad is really our Mr. Soledad. You have been working while on vacation without even knowing it, and that's why I insist on picking up the tab. Believe it or not, Phillipe Soledad has ties to that ABC loan operation you busted. He's at the top of the criminal food chain." The lieutenant belched and excused himself. "We have managed to keep our hands in the investigation with the Feds claiming jurisdiction and fighting us the whole way. We convinced the police commissioner to use what contacts he has to track these guys up and down the East Coast."

Michael sat, simply astonished at the coincidence.

"These people reach from Maine to Miami. This is the first we knew he was on the West Coast too but it makes sense. The Feds knew but they don't share well. They have been laughing at us all along, bumbling along with our investigation while they sit there knowing things that could help."

"I think sir, the laughter might have stopped when one of their own was killed. It was no accident and they know it. They also have a traitor in their camp, that might stop the laughter don't you think. Whatever we do, we need to keep them out of this."

"So do you have a plan, Michael?"

Michael looked at Meg who had not said a word throughout the meal. They smiled at their private plan of bouncing and running, thinking, (probably shouldn't share that part of the plan.)

"I need one more piece of information; then I think I do have a plan, yes. Can you tell me who's the second biggest fish in this operation on the East Coast?"

The lieutenant smiled, "Do you want the tuna with the great taste or the one that tastes great?"

"Give me the one in the tuxedo. We'll see how he likes the prospects of ending up in a can," kidded Michael.

"Remember you can't officially involve the department in this. If it all falls apart, I haven't seen you since you left for vacation." "I understand lieutenant; thanks for your help. I will discreetly stay in touch."

After the lieutenant left, Meg and Michael continued to sit at the table.

"Do you have a plan Michael?"

"Why of course, I do. I just need to put the pieces together and with what the lieutenant gave me, I just need to think it through. By the way, I do some of my best thinking when I am exercising."

"Well then, let's get to that little room of yours. There's more than one way to use that rubber ball you know."

Morning would be soon enough to call Jack, Michael rationalized, as hand in hand, they entered what used to be called a torture chamber.

♋♋

The call to Jack the next morning revealed the plan Michael had dreamed up overnight. "Meg and I talked well into the night; we believe we need to be on the offensive with this man." Meg was meeting George outside planning their work day. Michael could hear them joking as he laid out the plan for removing the weed from Jack's garden.

Thirty-One

Sean was fishing in a mountain stream when his cell phone rang. "Sean. This is your brother Jack. Have I caught you at a good time?"

"You caught me with my fly down and my pants wet, but just give me a second to get to dry ground."

Jack was laughing at the other end. "That sounds like a personal problem brother, and one even I can't fix, nor care to." Sean explained, "The fishing is incredible. Monique and I have been living on trout since we got here. If I have to hide, I couldn't think of a better place."

"Your hiding days are over. I have sent a money order to Mr. Erricson's bank. You are coming back to caddy for me. Bring Monique with you. We aren't running any more."

"I like that idea. I assume we have a plan to end this nightmare."

"With Michael's help, and his department connections, we are going to conduct a little sting operation of our own."

"Good, you know staying up in these mountains has been incredible. Mr. Soledad tried to make me believe that the mountains were useless, just a barrier to reality. These mountains are alive Jack, and they made me aware of what it took to create them. Monique and I have taken walks and watched the sun paint landscapes that man could never hope to duplicate. This mess needs to end. Mr. Soledad can't be left in charge of deciding what mountain streams Monique and I fish."

"Conjure up a little O'Shea magic and bring it with you brother. We have friends who will help us get to spend some time in that stream together. Call me with your travel plans, someone will pick you two up at the airport"

With Sean and Monique snuggled in the back seat, Meg drove to Michael's apartment. By the time they arrived, they were chatting like old friends. Jack sat waiting on the steps. Sean laughed out loud when he saw his brother. "We look like the Smith brothers on those boxes of cough drops we used to take." Both men now sported a full face of hair and could have passed for woodsmen.

Meg and Monique walked the yard with Meg explaining her new job. The brothers found a football and tossed it back and forth, waiting for Michael to arrive. "Fill me in on this plan; what's the mystery?"

"Michael will fill all of us in when he gets here. It's a work in progress and he's still gathering information."

Michael ordered pizza, and the 'gang of five', as Jack dubbed them, chatted away. After much catching up and small talk, Michael became all business and asked Sean to tell him about Phillipe Soledad.

"Tell me all you know about this man, Sean; his habits, what angers him or anything else that might give us an edge."

"He definitely needs to be in control. His office is like a command center. He has three phones. Even the location

overlooking the casinos on the strip seems to give him a sense of power and control. He looks directly into the mountains and uses them as a point of reference for his lectures on how to rule his world. He never asks a question he doesn't know the answer to. He does his homework Michael, that's for sure."

"What are his weaknesses, Sean? What do you see as the best way to get him to come to the East Coast?"

"I would say his need for control and his need to punish disloyalty. So challenge his authority! I have already supplied the disloyalty part."

Michael nodded his head, "Then we have a plan, people." Jack needed some clarification. "What does getting him to come here do for Sean and me? What have you found out?"

"This man is a kind of Medusa; he has a head in many places. With what we have been able to find out from a recent associate we arrested, Mr. Soledad has business interests up and down the East Coast as well as out West. If we can play on his weaknesses of control and loyalty you mentioned we can bring him to our playing field."

"I still don't know what good bringing him here does us, Michael," said Jack.

"Mr. Soledad is first a business man. With the recent killing of an agent out West, the Feds are applying pressure to his people here in the East. He runs loan operations, escort services, and pawn shops. They are all being compromised as we speak. Mr. Soledad who likes control would have a reason to come East, discreetly of course, to try to stop the bleeding."

Meg had silently watched her guy take charge. She asked the question that would answer Jack's. "Will that do it then, Michael, or do I hear the sound of another shoe dropping in your voice?" Michael smiled at Meg. She could read him like a book.

"You're right! Sean, we need to create in Mr. Soledad's mind an opportunity to kill two birds with one stone. I guess that I am asking you to be one of those birds."

Monique jumped up. "You must not do this, Sean! You could be killed! Is it not so?"

"Monique, listen. We can't hide forever. This man is running our lives. I got us into this situation, I want to be part of bringing him down. I would rather die fighting than running away."

Michael cleared his throat, "Hopefully there won't be any fighting; the plan is to out smart him. I am sorry Monique I used a poor choice of words in asking Sean to be part of the plan. What we will do is use his weaknesses against him." Michael spent the next thirty minutes outlining what each of the 'gang of five' must do.

In the end it was Jack who settled matters. "It seems you are playing number one position on this team, Michael. I for one will follow you into battle."

Thirty-Two

Mr. Phillipe Soledad got the call he'd been waiting for-finally some good news. The past weeks had been very unsettling. He had been forced to expose his 'mole in a hole', agent Small, to stop a planned Federal raid here in Las Vegas. He had used violence to silence a disloyal employee. He smiled at that one. Using a supposed traffic accident after the Feds had faked one earlier, to remove the double crosser Fred Ortiz from his grasp, was pure genius. (I bet they are still fuming,) smiled Phillipe to himself. Now the East Coast was falling down around his ears. (Do I have to do everything myself? Why do I pay money for mediocrity?) He silently lamented. No one had been able to locate Sean. The ringing of his private line had just changed all that. So his brother is playing in a golf tournament, wearing a beard. "Have you actually seen Sean?" A moment later, "He too is wearing a beard. That is too comical. Sounds like Sean though. He has a flair for acting. Apparently, he thinks I forgive and forget. I told him different, but I guess I should scold him in person."

The voice on the line gave more information, and then Mr. Soledad finished the conversation by saying, "Make travel plans for me. Arrange a car and have my top associate in Raleigh, North Carolina give me a call."

Mr. Soledad went to his window and looked West. The mountains offered no opinion on what Mr. Soledad had planned. "Just rocks, Sean; I tried to tell you; there's no escape for a dreamer," he said to the window that seemed to mirror his view of life.

CHAPTER

Thirty-Three

Sean had altered the name 'gang of five' slightly. With Jack in the tournament and Sean caddying, those left he dubbed 'The M&M's Gang -' Michael, Meg, and Monique.

The three sat discussing the next four days; in a motel room in Cary, North Carolina. Jack and Sean were at the course for a practice round. There was a policeman in street clothes watching from a distance. Michael was sure they would be safe until Mr. Soledad arrived.

"The lieutenant made sure Mr. Soledad received information on Sean's location. The same source made Mr. Soledad's flight connections, lodging, and a rental vehicle. If the plan worked quickly enough, Mr. Soledad would never know who blind sided him."

Monique looked worried, "Still, Sean is at risk. What else can we M&M's do to help?"

"I believe Mr. Soledad will personally try to end this with Sean. He will then straighten out his business interests and fly back, a very smug individual."

"But what of us, what can we do?"

"I will tell you exactly what we do, Monique. Now listen carefully."

306

Thursday morning was day one of the 'Breath of Life' Golf Tournament being held in the famed triangle between Raleigh and Durham. Ironically, one of the major sponsors was a tobacco company. The irony was lost on no one, and the jokes were opening many an early morning radio show.

In truth, tobacco companies still reeling from the tobacco settlement with the states were trying to project a kinder, gentler, death sentence. They were providing millions of dollars for respiratory research and what better way to get the word out than a Golf Tournament. The purse being offered had attracted the best players on tour and a national audience on network television.

The weather promised warm spring days and cloudless skies. The kind of days a person wants to open a window and take a deep breath, if able.

Jack and Sean arrived at seven AM, showed their credentials, and went to the locker room. Jack put on his golf shoes while Sean checked Jack's bag for the fifth time.

"Everything is a go, brother."

"Everything's in place brother except a guarantee of victory. We'll have to add that little bit of drama. It seems strange but even with all that's going on, I feel like I am going to play well, Sean."

The two brothers walked to the club house for a light breakfast.

"Where have you been, Jack? I hope you don't get disqualified for that beard," they kidded. Some of the other players gathered round to hear from Jack. Rumors had been running rampant. "I promised myself I'd wear a beard till I win on tour. I made Sean promise too. If you want that clean cut image to survive, you better let me win this week," kidded Jack right back. "We heard some strange stories about your disappearance. One rumor even had you dating guys. That one we didn't believe, anyway welcome back." That sentiment was shared by half a dozen guys who knew Jack.

Jack and Sean went through the breakfast line and moved to a table in the corner. "Standing in this line, I was thinking about how Monique and I met. I love that girl. I hope Michael knows what he's doing. Sorry, brother, to be thinking like this, but the last time a cop tried to fix things, was the last time I shaved." "I'm worried too Sean, but we both have girls to protect and I'll be damned if this guy is going to keep me from her."

Sean brightened, "Molly is amazing Jack. She has more courage than anyone I've ever met. You're right; we owe them a future." The two brothers grasped hands. "Do you have your two way radio with you?"

"Yup right here, Jack. When I see Mr. Soledad, I just push the button as a signal for Michael and the girls."

"You really think he will show himself to you, Sean, right out in the open?"

"I really think so. If he is going to be the one who takes care of business with me, he will want me to see it coming."

Jack returned to the locker room to kill a little time. He still had thirty five minutes to tee time. He took his nervous pee and then walked to the practice tee where Sean was waiting with his clubs.

Sean had heard from Michael via the two way radio. A simple message; the M&M's had arrived.

❧❦

Michael called his lieutenant and all was in place. The law enforcement fraternity provided brother policemen with assistance, wherever they might be. The lieutenant had made them aware Michael was tracking a dangerous individual in their neck of the woods. It was all unofficial, of course, and that added to the fun. No damn reports to write, file, and justify. There would be men in the crowd, and Michael was given a number to call if he needed their assistance.

◈

For the past two days Michael had scouted the course. He saw several locations that would be isolated enough for an attack on Sean. Those same spots would be an ideal place to capture Mr. Soledad, if it came to that.

Overall, the golf course was lined and shaded with tall Oaks. Small ponds strategically placed challenged a player's approach to the green. Water was more prevalent than sand traps. The sand that was there, came in to play on only four holes. It was these four holes that would provide the best opportunity for Mr. Soledad to harm Sean. The sand traps were all on the right side of the fairway and were designed to keep a ball from going out of bounds. These sand bunkers were built into a high bank that dropped off dramatically. The sand would stop a ball immediately and save a player a two stroke penalty. There would be no spectators standing on the right hand side on these holes, for there was no room. A person with a weapon would have the cover of the bank and an escape route through the woods to a nearby road.

Meg had been given the assignment of keeping Mr. Soledad in view once Sean pointed him out. No one had been able to provide a picture of the man. Sean had described him as best he could, but a sighting was hoped for. Monique would follow Jack and Sean from hole to hole. It was not known if Mr. Soledad had ever seen Monique, but her presence added innocence to any suspicions he might have.

Their plan included their best guess of when Mr. Soledad might strike. Jack had spoken up first.

"I would think Thursday or Friday, Michael. If he knows anything about golf at all, he will know those two days are his only guarantee. If I don't play well and don't make the cut, the weekend is gone."

"He will have done his homework. You can be sure of that," added Sean.

"I'm betting on Friday. He will do some looking around on Thursday, to see if the course offers a reasonable place to take action. He'll decide if he is being set up and if he is going to reveal himself to you, Sean. That should happen on Thursday too. Let you know that he's here and going to settle matters." Michael rose as he finished and spoke directly to Monique.

"Stay close to these guys but don't draw attention to yourself. Let him discover you if he does recognize you. Meg you are just part of the crowd. Once Sean describes him, find him, and keep him in sight."

"I will cover him like a full back," said Meg putting on her game face.

Michael looked at each face and saw that he indeed had a team. "Look at us, ready to do battle with a man the Federal Government hasn't been able to bring down."

The group was silent and then Monique squeezed Sean's hand and tied everything together.

With the insight of a true romantic she said. "Perhaps your government has used the wrong approach with this man. They go after him in anger. We will show him something he has not before seen."

"What would that be?" asked Sean.

"Why - the power of love of course, you big dummy!" WHO COULD ARGUE WITH THAT!

CHAPTER
Thirty-Four

Just as Jack hit his drive on hole number two, Mr. Phillipe Soledad was completing his own drive.

He pulled into parking Lot B in his Maroon Lincoln Navigator and noted he was in Row 14. It was Thursday and the crowd was just beginning to arrive. He walked the 100 yards to a lady selling day passes. Decked out in a straw hat with a banner on the crown, she worked feverishly to keep up. Mr. Soledad approached with a smile.

"You look like you could use some extra help here." He handed her a crisp, new fifty dollar bill.

"If you can believe my hat, I don't need anything else," chuckled the lady.

Mr. Soledad read the slogan aloud, "All I need is the air that I breathe." He laughed. "Amen to that." Counting his change, he moved to join the people meandering along the golf course. He had never been to a golf tournament and was surprised at the support necessary to make the week run smoothly. He wandered along, noting the tents lining the entrance. Vendors were selling everything from food to memorabilia.

He put his ticket around his neck as instructed by a man dressed in khaki shorts and dark blue collar shirt. The man had a badge of bright yellow cloth, identifying him as security. Volunteers were everywhere, carrying maps of the entire layout. Mr. Soledad took one from a small table and moved to a shade tree to study it. With one eye on the map and the other studying the crowd, he noted the local police department had a few men in uniform wandering among the spectators. They had their own tent, and several of them stood drinking coffee just outside. The crowd continued to pour in; Mr. Soledad was pleased. The more people the more confusion. He watched a player strike the ball. He played golf himself maybe a dozen rounds a year, and would be considered a duffer at best. He had never broken a hundred, but enjoyed the peacefulness of the sport; quiet, not like today. Phillipe Soledad treated the sport as an extension of his business. He played with powerful people, he was willing to lose a few bucks to feed their ego. Usually he came away with something more important to him - influence.

(Golf is like my mountains; it offers a scenic view that should be capitalized on,) mused Mr. Soledad. Look at that hospitality tent with a cigarette logo on the front, if that doesn't say it all. That lady out front should be wearing her slogan around her neck, real tight. Maybe then she would see the irony of what she was selling.)

Smart people, these tobacco guys. Recently they had learned a valuable lesson - a costly one - but a necessary one. They no longer did business in the dark of night. Since settling lawsuits with the States, they were practicing a new philosophy. If you can't lick them, join them, and were now part of local school budgets. Throughout the country, they now planted their product in rows of school children. Telling kids not to start smoking was the most creative advertising gimmick they had ever come up with. (My business gets the full treatment from every law enforcement agency imaginable, and the tobacco companies come across as concerned corporate citizens. Gotta love America,) thought Mr. Soledad.

Coming back to the task at hand, Mr. Soledad concluded he had entered the course at the ninth hole. He saw players striding up the fairway. This looks like a good spot to begin. They will have to pass through here. He looked at the map he had been given and circled several areas he would need to check out this afternoon.

∿∿

Jack was playing well. He was two under through seven holes. The crowd continued to grow. Monique, who was following the action by walking along the ropes that kept the crowd back, had to struggle to keep up.

Meg blended into the crowd, staying one hole behind Jack and Sean. This was her first Golf tournament and she was amazed at the serenity of it all. Soccer, her beloved sport, involved a team effort, combining long passes, quick bursts of speed, and position, position, position. This game of Golf seemed to require concentration above all else. Speed was a requirement for success in soccer. This sport demanded that you slow down, and let all the parts work in unison. She noted how respectful most of the fans seemed to be. When a player stood over his ball ready to hit it, a number of hands would go up asking for quiet and the crowd responded.

Meg continued to look around for Mr. Soledad. Sean's description and rough sketch had not proved useful. The crowd seemed filled with men 5' 11" tall, gray hair, mustaches, and all appeared deeply tanned.

Several men had tried to strike up a conversation as Meg wandered the course. Meg just smiled and moved on, focusing on her assignment. Meg had not seen Michael since they arrived, but knew he was nearby. (Probably watching me this minute through his field glasses,) thought Meg and she smiled for the camera.

∽∾

What a couple of weeks it had been! From the first moment she met Michael, her heart beat had been raised a level. First, the excitement of meeting someone she actually wanted to get to know better. And then quitting a dead end job, to joining Michael on a road trip with the barest of details. Now she was playing detective. Meg continued to wander and ponder. Her radio suddenly crackled.

"Where are you Meg?"

"You've let me out of your sight then, Michael, I could be in mortal danger you know," kidded Meg.

"I'll make it up to you if you let me buy lunch at the finest restaurant on the course."

"If I survive till then, you have a date. I am on the 8th hole approaching that little circle of green grass where the players have to acknowledge that they aren't playing alone. What a crazy sport this is Michael."

Michael laughed. "I can see tents just up ahead, is there a circus in town?"

"You are the only clown I have in view, a pretty clown at that. If you walk straight ahead another 60 yards or so, we will eat under the big top," answered Michael. "I'll be the guy wearing the biggest smile."

"Well don't let that smile cover your eyes, you're on a dangerous assignment."

314

"Roger that."

"Roger who?"

"Never mind," laughed Michael. "I'll tell you all about Roger at lunch."

❧

Mr. Soledad saw the eight men approaching the green. He had been waiting, wondering if his information had been accurate. He had been given Jack's starting time of 8:52 am. It was now 11:09 am. The time was about right. Four of the men were obviously players and the men on their bags, caddies. Mr. Soledad studied the caddies. Sean's new beard would have fooled him if he hadn't been told of the new look he was sporting these days. When his brother sunk a 15 foot putt, Sean revealed himself through his smile. There was no mistaking that smile. Mr. Soledad had observed that smile when Sean was first winning big in Vegas. He now scanned the crowd to see if anything seemed out of place. The men walked toward the ropes heading for the next hole. A beautiful young lady handed them a sandwich and they moved to a set of tables under a canopy ringed with rope. (That is Monique the singer, perhaps later, first things first,) mused Phillipe not clear in his own head what he was thinking.

The sandwiches looked good, and suddenly his stomach growled. "Golf always makes me hungry," he said aloud, and chuckled.

Mr. Soledad took one long last look at Sean, to remind himself why he was away from his office. Whether he meant Sean to see him would be pure speculation, but it would seem his ego demanded it.

Sean, wearing sunglasses and his best poker face, munched his sandwich with a purpose. Sipping iced tea, he scanned the crowd without seeming to look up from his meal. Like two lasers, his eyes probed the sea of humanity that moved in waves in front of their table.

Suddenly he was there, looking directly at Sean, as if he were gazing into his precious mountains. In one innocent action Sean spilled his tea, moved away from his table, and got all the description he would need - dark green golf shirt, tan slacks, and aviator sunglasses, all shaded with a Greg Norman straw hat. Sean took his time cleaning up and waited for Mr. Soledad to turn away. Sean made his way to a player's potty and called Michael.

Michael and Meg were in a long line in a tent that Michael had assured Meg was the best restaurant on the course. "Since you were a waitress in a former life, suppose I sit down and you bring my lunch to me with a juice," kidded Michael. Meg's eyes lit up and she was about to respond when they heard the beep.

Michael joined the dozen or so other people who had a phone stuck in their ear and turned away from what would have been Meg's biting wit. He walked toward the exit as he listened to Sean's description. Michael nearly dropped his radio when Mr. Soledad walked by him barely six feet away.

"He just entered the waiting line for lunch; we will handle it from here. Tell Jack to keep those birdies coming. This may be a week to remember for a lot of reasons. Sean, don't call me. I will contact you; just work the plan."

Mr. Soledad looked around the tent. (There must be fifty people in line but it seems to be moving along,) he thought. He took his place at the end of the line and looked around. Everyone seemed to be having a good time. Nobody was rushing to be someplace else. He watched as a man joined a beautiful lady, just as she reached the makeshift counter. The two moved along with a tray picking up two beverages. The man whispered something in her ear, and she laughed out loud. (Must be a couple, too bad, she is top shelf,) thought Phillipe. They got their food and moved to a table, leaving his sight and his mind.

Soon Mr. Soledad found himself at the counter. He had been too busy studying faces to study the menu on the banner above his head.

"I'll have a Tuna on Rye and a Diet Pepsi," said Phillipe innocently.

"Sorry sir, there is no Rye bread, and we don't serve Pepsi. Will a Coke do? They are one of our sponsors," she smiled. Mr. Soledad, a little miffed, gestured with his hands, "Okay let's start again. What's on the menu?"

"It's right above your head sir and would you mind stepping back while you decide. We're really busy." She smiled sweetly. Mr. Soledad became agitated; he was not a man who was usually dismissed. He was reluctant to leave the line. The laughter and good-natured banter behind him, turned to murmurs of impatience. His ears turned red.

Suddenly he had to get out of here, the color moving from his ears to his face. He stumbled toward the exit, nearly mowing down a mother with a three year old in tow. People began to notice him. Michael and Meg watched him leave like an actor fumbling his lines.

"Now there is a side Sean must not have seen," said Michael. "He does appear to have little patience with the world we live in; doesn't he?" observed Meg.

"I don't think this man has had to wait in line before. Usually he has someone fetching for him. It looks like he is planning to solve this little problem with Sean himself though, that's interesting."

"Perhaps, being out here on his own will prove his undoing Michael," said Meg with a funny look on her face.

Michael didn't notice the look and perhaps it was just as well. The two finished their lunch quickly and soon Meg had Mr. Soledad in view.

Phillipe Soledad seemed to have calmed down. He wandered the back nine, stopping, and studying the sand bunkers Michael had discovered.

Meg beeped Michael. She continued to keep Mr. Soledad in sight. She would meet Michael in the stands at the last hole.

"Don't contact me again. I want to get a little closer." Before Michael could respond, Meg had shut off her radio.

✄✄

Mr. Soledad walked onto the small bridge that separated the 16th green from the 17th tee. There, standing at the railing, was the beautiful lady he had seen earlier in the tent. This time she appeared to be alone. (I will just say hello, no harm in that, just being friendly,) voiced Phillipe to himself.

"What a beautiful setting," he began as he joined Meg at the railing. When Meg did not respond he continued, "Do you have a favorite player you are following this week."

Meg turned her head and gave him a dazzling smile, "I'm sorry, sir. Were you speaking to me? What was the question you were asking?"

Mr. Soledad was taken aback by both the accent and the mouth that gave life to her words.

Meg's green eyes challenged his sunglasses and he quickly took them off.

Phillipe repeated his lines; those he could remember anyway. Meg spoke then. "Oh it's you, from the tent. You were treated horribly sir. I saw that. I don't blame you for being upset. The wait was long enough without being dismissed like a school boy." Mr. Soledad beamed. "I'm glad someone understands the incompetence of service today. I thought that the crowd in line was going to attack me if I didn't leave."

Meg smiled, (Now that's a novel interpretation of what I witnessed,) "Did you get anything to eat at all?"

"Not really, but I managed to find a bottle of water, so I'll survive."

"My name is Mary Margaret Casey and who would you be?" she offered her hand.

"Mr. Phillipe Soledad at your service." He took Meg's hand in both of his and bowed slightly.

The two chatted lightly about food, golf, and the weather.

"Are you here with friends, family, or both?"

"I am visiting relatives in the area. My cousin, Michael, brought me here today. He loves golf and is probably following one of his heroes at this very minute."

Mr. Soledad smiled to himself, (Perhaps I can mix a little pleasure with the unpleasant task at hand.)

༶

Michael wondered what Meg's message was all about. He did, in fact, get to watch one of his heroes complete a hole from tee to green. Michael understood not communicating unless necessary but why turn the phone off? He couldn't see her anywhere so he would just work the plan.

The crowd was growing by the minute. The grandstand at the 18th was filling up quickly. Jack had been one of the earlier groups to start the day so a seat at 18 would give a good view of nearly all the players as they completed their round.

Sitting in the stands, Michael thought back to college when the only people attending a golf match might be a parent or two and the inevitable stray mutt. He had loved that part of his life and now a good friend, his former teammate, was competing on this giant stage. Life certainly seemed to operate in circles, bringing the people we care about back into focus over and over again. The circumstances and twists of fate might not always bring good news, but true friendship would grow from the challenge. Instead of being here to simply bask in the success Jack was having, Michael was being asked to play a major role in a real life drama. He would remain backstage, watching from the wings, making sure Jack and Sean got to complete their lines. Michael was still wrestling with the best way to stop this man. He had convinced the gang he had control, but self-doubt entered his mind, much the same way a golfer doubts his swing from time to time.

Jack and Sean came into view. Jack's drive had come to rest 140 yards from the flagstick. A glance at the leader board showed a red minus 3 following Jack's name. A birdie on this hole would put Jack in third place, two strokes back of the leader, one of Michael's heroes. Jack did his little waggle and you could see him talking to himself. Jack's 9 iron arced through the air and the ball lifted as if on angels wings, settling 8 feet from the hole.

The crowd cheered appreciatively. Michael stood and cheered wildly, proud of his good friend. As Jack approached the green, Michael tried to locate the other M&M's. Monique came into view, walking toward the stands to watch Jack putt. Where was Meg? He knew her outfit, but the crowd was huge and he couldn't see her anywhere. He had just resigned himself to finding her after Jack finished, when she came into view. His heart popped into his mouth.

Meg was walking with Mr. Soledad, a smile on her face and words leaving her mouth. (I can't believe she's doing this! What could she be thinking!) Michael was beside himself. He wanted to shout, but his good sense kept him quiet, watching.

Jack made his putt, but Michael never saw it, for he was too intent on watching the show on the other channel. Jack shook hands with his fellow players just as Meg was shaking Mr. Soledad's hand. She turned to leave.

Michael watched Mr. Soledad stare after her as she disappeared into a forest of colorful limbs. Michael sat in the stands stunned.

Ten minutes and two finishing groups later, Meg climbed the stairs to join him. The reality of trudging up stairs seemed a continuing part of Meg's story. Once again the irony was not lost on Michael. He waved weakly, still in shock. The crowd alternated between dead silence and loud applause as groups finished putting out.

Meg sat down beside Michael, took a long sip of bottled water, and gazed out over the 18th fairway at the crowd beyond. "You've a wonderful view of the world from up here. Have you been here long?"

"Long enough to see you talking to our Mr. Soledad. Care to explain the change in plans?"

"Let's get away from here and I'll tell you what I did and why. If you don't agree with me, then there's little harm I've done. I think you'll see we may just have him right where we want him." Michael reached to take her hand.

"Don't do anything that makes it look like we are a couple, Michael. I'll explain soon enough why you have become, my American cousin."

Michael, following Meg down the bleachers, started to ask a question.

"Just trust me, Michael. Remember what Monique said recently, about fighting this man differently. Fight him with love she said," she paused, "or pretend to."

The two walked quietly to their car; Michael lagging slightly behind.

Michael drove away from the course and Meg fiddled with the radio. Michael finally broke the silence. He turned off the radio and made eye contact. "OK, cousin; I'm listening."

Meg began explaining what would become Plan B.

"As I was walking along the course, I was thinking about things. I thought about us, and our new friends. Then I thought about Ireland and soccer, and my Mum, and why I left there. Your plan to be on the offense makes perfect sense, but it doesn't put anyone directly in front of the goal, if you know what I mean. In Ireland, I played a sweeper position. If the other team was going to score, they had to go through me. Anyway with all that I was thinking, I realized we have to keep this man from ruining this new life I have found with you."

"I still don't understand Meg. What are you planning?"

"There's an old saying that me mum practiced to an art form. 'Many a man's head has been broken with his tongue'." She waited for the quote to register with Michael. "I know I am looking from a different angle than you, Michael but it's because I am a woman. I know men and what makes them tick. The more we can find out about this man the better chance he'll break his head with his tongue. Don't you see."

Michael started to protest.

"Remember what happened in the lunch line? Sean hadn't seen that side of him. If we get close to him, maybe we can find some other weaknesses."

"So what did you find out, detective. I mean cousin," said Michael sighing.

"Well for openers, he wants me to have dinner with him tonight."

"What! No way! You have to be kidding me, right?" "Michael, hear me out." Meg spent the remainder of the trip back to their motel convincing Michael she could handle Mr. Soledad. By the time the door closed to Room 23, Michael had grudgingly accepted the idea.

"Where are you going on this date? You won't be alone with him. I can guarantee you that."

"I accepted his dinner proposal only if he would take me to an Irish pub. He agreed. I told him I was missing the Old Country and needed a fix. He is checking out the location of one in Raleigh and will call me on my cell."

"How will you handle him if he tries something? You know what I mean."

"A fair number of those stepfathers I mentioned looked to me for a little sympathy. Had their own ideas, they did, about what form that sympathy should take. Mr. Soledad will have a good number of stairs to climb before he'll be let in my door, Michael."

Michael studied Meg. "It looks like you are leading this charge now, and I will follow your lead, but you have to tell me everything you plan to do before you do it. No more surprises, ok?" "That's wonderful, but Michael, you are still in charge of the offense. I'm just a girl who happens to know men - the good and the bad."

Michael took Meg in his arms and could feel her strength. (I'm glad she's on my team,) he said to himself as they clung to each other.

Jack called their room. Meg answered and handed the phone to Michael.

"Did you get to see any of my swings, Michael, or were you occupied with your official duties?"

"I saw that putt at the last hole, he lied. Keep that up we'll have much to celebrate Sunday night."

Speaking of celebrating, how's the plan working?"

"Well, I'm sure Sean told you, Mr. Soledad showed up and made sure Sean saw him. Keep your head down and keep making those putts. We have everything under control on this end. There's not much else to report at this point. Really the less you know right now the better. How is Sean doing?"

"He wants to punch this guy's lights out. He figures it's his problem. He's a team player though, so he'll keep his poker face on."

"Tell him maybe he'll get that shot in if we end this the way I hope."

"When do you think that might be?"

"Hopefully, tomorrow night. I can't give you details but by the time the sun rises Saturday morning, Mr. Soledad should be out of our hair."

"Sounds good buddy. I'll tell Sean when he gets back."

"He's not there?"

"No, he left with Monique to get sandwiches and a movie. We are staying put tonight."

"I hope he's careful; this guy seems to anticipate things well. He hasn't survived this long without being a sharp character."
"Sean is staying in the car. Monique is picking up the food and the video. It's just down the street."

❧❧

Just as Michael hung up the phone, Meg's cell phone rang. It was Phillipe Soledad. Meg answered on the third ring. Mr. Soledad, with a hint of laughter in his voice, asked to speak to the Irish Princess being held captive in a foreign land.

"Obviously a lack of eating has affected your mind. No Princess inhabits this castle," she kidded right back.

"Perhaps you're right. A good dinner will clear my head and I'll take another look."

"From the sound of your voice you enjoyed the day. Let's hope the evening keeps you smiling as well."

"Ah, Meg, is it all right to call you Meg? Mary Margaret seems too formal for dining at an Irish Pub. Please call me Phillipe." "How did you know Meg is what I prefer to be called? Only after I've met someone and have agreed to have dinner with them of course. So you found us an Irish Pub."

"Yes, I let my fingers do the walking and found what sounds like a unique little place. The ad read, visit 'O'HARA BROTHERS, IRISH @Y@S' and you'll leave feeling like family. I called an associate of mine who happens to be Irish. I invited him along but he had other business to attend to. He said it was a good choice. Apparently, a brief history of Ireland and the impact it's had on the rest of the world is written on a wooden tablet of some sort inside the door. Perhaps you could read it to me, and tell me how it compares with your own memories. I would love to hear your lovely voice again."

"You sound like a bit of a sweet talker, sir. Do I need to worry about your intentions?"

"I promise you that I am a gentleman. I'll treat you like a lady. We'll just enjoy the moment. Are you sure you don't want me to pick you up?"

"No thanks, I'm sure my cousin knows of this place. I'll meet you there."

"I will be waiting for you to share your own Irish history. 8 pm, it is then, good bye Meg."

As Meg began telling Michael where she was going, the phone on the bed stand shrieked.

"It seems the whole world needs our attention, Meg."

"Michael, we have a problem! Monique is missing!"

"What! Is Sean there? Put him on the phone."

When Sean came on the line, Michael asked him to go over what had happened since the time they left their room.

"We drove straight to a sandwich shop. Monique picked up the order and brought it to the car. There is a supermarket in the same little plaza, so Monique went in to pick up some chips, soft drinks, and a movie. She never came out. I went in to find her after twenty minutes or so. I looked around, couldn't find her, so I had her paged. Nothing! I went back to the car and she wasn't there, but my headlight and fender on the driver's side was smashed. Michael, I was parked in the last space to the left. No other vehicle did this damage. It was done with a tire iron or something. What can we do?"

Michael's mind was racing. Obviously, Mr. Soledad had a different plan in mind. (I wonder if he changed his mind after seeing Monique or felt the Golf course was too risky. This man could think on his feet. He was going to make Sean come to him on his terms.)

"Sean, don't do anything yet. I am sure he won't hurt Monique; he is using her to get to you. That little fender bender was a subtle reminder of what he did to that guy in Vegas. He's playing with you. He'll contact you when he's ready, probably soon. Trust me. We have an Ace up our sleeve too. Sean, I promise you will get the opportunity to smack this guy - have no doubt. Put Jack back on, will you?"

"Keep Sean from doing anything rash. He might jeopardize Monique and our plan. Call me if you are contacted. I'll let you know if we get any information on this end."

Meg had heard only one end of the conversation, but it was clear that the good humor Mr. Soledad seemed infected with had little to do with her or a lack of food.

There was little left to be said as Meg watched the cab pull up. "Please, be careful! There will be a detective in that pub tonight. Don't let your guard down, Meg."

Meg recited a little homily she had learned as a girl, perhaps as a defense against one of those step-fathers. "Learn to look beyond the pale, for it's the least expected that wets the sail." Michael looked at Meg quizzically.

"Mr. Soledad will never see the storm I'm building, that I promise, you Michael." With that statement she left and scanned the sky before entering the cab. (Looks like a clear night out there but you can never be sure of the weather,) she smiled to herself.

Michael called his lieutenant and reported the latest turn of events.

"I will make some calls and there will be a detective in that pub I promise you, Michael. We finally have pictures of this guy, so we know who we are looking for."

"Can you get up here yourself, sir? I'd feel better if you were here in case anything else goes wrong." Michael had just explained the plan to his boss.

"I have some time coming to me. I think I could take a few days and explore that area. I'll bring a couple of my hunting buddies with me. They just happen to be cops. I'll be there sometime tomorrow. Don't do anything to scare this guy, Michael. It sounds like your girl has a good plan."

❧❧

Michael called Jack; they needed to talk. "We shouldn't meet at your motel. Who knows, you and Sean may still be being watched. They obviously followed you. Why don't you take a run; there's just time before dark. I'll meet you in the men's room at the city park; twenty minutes, okay?"

Jack put on a light windbreaker and shorts. He tied his sneakers in a double knot and left his room. The two friends had discovered the park and the jogging trails that wove through and around it on Tuesday afternoon that suddenly seemed like a long time ago.

Standing at the urinal, Michael didn't say anything. He left when Jack entered and waited for him along the trail.

The sun was taking one last gasp before calling it a day. The horizon retained a healthy glow for a time before a tinge of deep gray gave way to blackness.

Jack spoke to what appeared as more shadow than substance. "As long as the day is, evening comes. Who can believe any harm can come to Monique when the Creator allows us to witness such a finish to a day."

"How do you manage to stay so calm, Jack? The world could be falling down around our shoulders, and you comment on the beauty of a sunset."

"Actually, it's only fairly recent that I've begun to see the world in a different light. I had to go to the bottom of the ocean to do it. I have found a wonderful girl, Michael. Her name is Molly. She does for me what Meg, and Monique, do for you and Sean. For a long, long time I wallowed in self pity. I kept my thoughts to myself; my journal was my only voice. I didn't realize what losing my family had done to me until I rediscovered my father and brother." Jack couldn't see Michael but knew he was listening. "We all seem to be healing now and I've been able to move on. It took a family that I met doing golf clinics, to appreciate the work that goes into keeping relationships alive. I stayed with another family in California, Khris Ericsson's family. Remember him from the team? Molly is Khris's sister and when this is over, I'll tell you all about her."

Michael waited; Jack had not finished.

"So now I see sunrises and sunsets for what they are. They are God's promise that no matter how hopeless a situation might seem, twice a day - first in the East and then in the West - there's an opportunity for a different beginning or ending."

"I am really happy for you, Jack. I only wish I had your optimism. Here is what we are facing." Michael went through the events that had taken place today; Meg meeting and going to dinner with Mr. Soledad, his discussion and plea for help from his boss, and his own feeling of helplessness.

Jack listened and waited for Michael to finish. "Michael, you must have faith. I have recently seen miraculous things happen to people close to me. Shannon Erricson, Khris's Mom, believes if you are Irish, you are lucky enough. Meg's Irish Michael, we are in good hands."

CHAPTER

Thirty-Five

Meg was waiting inside the door. A small lobby with its walls covered in memorabilia blunted the noise inside the bar. A man, probably a bouncer judging the size of him, stood collecting the cover charge for the live music playing tonight.

The O'Hara brothers seemed to offer a unique approach, for even their cover charge was cause for a smile. When you handed over your five dollars you were given a coupon declaring you part owner in the pub. Now If you attended the pub nightly for the next 50 years and saved your coupons, you could claim 10% ownership in the business. The other alternative was to exchange the coupon at the bar for a mug of ale. Meg laughed again. She knew when she first exited the cab that this was going to be a fun place.

The Sign over the pub was painted with eyeballs replacing the e's in 'Eyes'. It was lit in a way to produce a blurred effect to the sober eye. Meg quickly realized the intent. When a patron exited O'Haras all liquored up, a body looking up at that sign could easily convince themselves they were seeing as well as when they entered. Surely their conscience should be as clear. Meg glanced at her watch; it was eight-fourteen.

She began reading the wooden tablet that covered one entire wall in the lobby. She suddenly felt a hand on her shoulder. "Have you been waiting long? I apologize for being late; something came up."

Meg turned, "No harm, I was just becoming acquainted with the O'Hara Brothers. There's no doubt they are Irish." "Would you care to introduce me to them? Perhaps, read me their story?"

"I was just beginning to read it myself. Sure I'd be glad to." She began with the heading.

'O'Hara Brothers, Irish @y@s.'

"Hundreds of years ago, believe it or not, Ireland was the center of the universe. We Irish were chosen by our Creator to set the rest of the world on the proper path. We were to be sent to all manner of places. Just as we Irish have a sense of humor, so too did our Creator. Seeing as how we had become a little too comfortable there in our little towns, he decided to prod us to be moving along. Wars, disease, the English, and finally famine were the bits of humor that he threw at us. Spread out as we became, our only traveling companions were our wit and sense of humor. At the end of the day we used that wit and ability to raise a laugh, and to find us a warm fire and a glass of cheer. The history books would have you believe otherwise, but really it was but part of God's design to enlighten the masses that took us to far flung shores.

You've only to spend an evening with us to see the truth of the matter. When the music begins, and the sound of glass clinking reaches your ears, a toast to what matters most, you will find yourself under our spell. No matter the burden you carry; your voice will lighten and your toes will start tapping.

For when, "Irish @y@s are smiling, the whole world smiles with you."

Meg turned and saw the smile on Phillipe's face. "You see, the magic is working on you already."

"Yes, indeed Meg. I have a great deal to be smiling about this evening."

Phillipe paid the cover charge and they entered an environment that was totally foreign to him. Men at the bar winked, and raised their glasses and toasted his good fortune to have such beauty on his arm.

When they reached a table toward the back, a waitress dressed in a simple peasant smock approached.

"Meg, what would you suggest? I am not a beer drinker."

"Do you like Whiskey sir, sorry, Phillipe? I would suggest a Jameson. It's honest, non pretentious, straight forward."

"That could be you who you're describing, Meg."

"Thank you, but it's a little early in the evening to be voicing that observation. So, how would you like to meet Mr. Jameson? Naked, chilled, or wearing a sweater."

Phillipe laughed, "More information, please."

"Naked is simply poured in a glass; warm to the tongue. Chilled, is over ice. Add a jigger of Irish cream poured over Mr. Jameson and he is sporting a sweater guaranteed to warm your soul."

Phillipe was intrigued. "You decide. Does this old soul need warming?"

Meg ordered Phillipe a Jameson with Irish cream and a black and tan for herself.

The music started and any small talk about warmed souls was lost in the strains of a fiddle and a penny whistle. A trio of voices joined in, and soon everyone in the room was witness to a lad lost at sea. After half a dozen songs, the band paused to wet their own whistles.

Meg explained the seriousness with which the Irish imbibed. Phillipe sat mesmerized by her voice and the emotion it carried, as the world she knew through books and her own life growing up in Ireland joined them at the table.

The evening wound its way through the music, drink, and a simple meal of Guinness Irish stew served in a bread bowl.

When they rose to leave, Phillipe was bidding good night to Jameson and four brothers who had joined them during the evening. (He'll be needing to have his vision checked and declared sober as a judge by those @y@s,) thought Meg to herself.

Meg seized the moment and asked Phillipe if he'd care for another go round tomorrow night. She glanced at her watch and corrected herself.

"I mean tonight. It seems we danced the night away. I had a good time, Phillipe. You're a fair dancer. Another lesson might just get you an honorary O' in front of your name," she kidded. Phillipe readily agreed but wasn't ready for this evening to end. He invited Meg back to his hotel for a night cap.

"You're sounding like an Irishman not wanting to give up his glass. If it's simply a drink we'll be sharing, the answer is yes." "I promise to be a gentleman. I wouldn't jeopardize the opportunity to spend another evening doing an Irish Jig."

Just as he promised, Phillipe toasted the fun evening they had shared. They chatted about nothing for half an hour, and then Meg had the desk call her a cab. As they said good night, Phillipe suddenly took her hand and brought her into his arms. Meg allowed a moment's contact, moved away, and looked directly into his eyes.

"Are you married, Phillipe?"

Phillipe hesitated only a moment before answering, "Yes." "Thank you for your honesty Phillipe. Tomorrow night I might reward that honesty but I have to leave now. Are you attending the tournament tomorrow, I mean, today?"

"No, I came here on business which is about to be concluded. So I need to wrap things up today. What about you?"

"My cousin hasn't shared plans yet, but he's quite a golf nut so, probably."

"May I pick you up this evening? Where are you staying?" "Let's begin the evening the same way as tonight. Only this time you read the history of Ireland to me. I'd like that. Perhaps I'll have an Irish bedtime story to share with you when the music stops."

Phillipe chuckled, "You certainly have a way with words. I can hardly wait." He reached for Meg but she stepped outside his reach and pointed a finger, as if scolding a child.

"It's a whole day to wait but wait you must," she finished. With a light peck on his cheek, she turned and closed the door behind her.

❧

Michael had returned hours ago from his conversation with Jack. Sitting in the dark, he prayed Jack was right about the Irish being lucky enough. When the lights of the cab announced Meg's return, Michael moved to the door.

He opened the door just as Meg reached to put her key in the lock. The key clattered on the pavement. They knelt in unison, heads bumping, then arms reaching. The key would lay there for some time as they found the carpet just inside the doorway. A single light at the end of the parking lot framed a scene that to the casual observer might signal a crime of passion. Michael finally managed to kick the door closed. There would be no vertical movement. The two lovers wrestled out of their clothes and into a place that seemed to offer their only security. Later, they lay in one another's arms, light from the bathroom lending shape but no color to their conversation.

"So we now know where he's staying. Sean hasn't heard from him yet though?"

"Not that I have been told," said Michael. "I keep thinking I can predict this guy, then he throws a curveball."

"Well I know where he's going to be this evening," offered Meg. "And I know what is going to be on his mind."

"That is our Ace in the hole," acknowledged Michael, "but I'm not sure what good that does us with Monique still missing." "We saw his impatience in that tent. What if we change his timetable, delay his departure? He plans to leave tomorrow morning."

"What are you thinking, Meg?"

"It's times such as these that me Mum comes to mind. She is a clever woman Michael, misguided perhaps, but clever nonetheless."

"So what would your Mother do to disrupt Mr. Soledad, Meg, and don't suggest spending the night."

Meg laughed, "Those uncles thought they was being rewarded, Michael, but they had it backward."

"How so?"

"Don't you see Michael? Those stairs creaked both coming and going. It was only after wringing something she wanted out of 'em that she might delay the going. Sometimes that trip was delayed a week or even a month. But I promise you, the comings and goings always tallied the same."

Michael couldn't help but laugh. "Meg you have more insight into the human condition than anyone I've ever met. So tell me how we get Mr. Soledad up those stairs and get what we want without rewarding him."

"Let me just say this, tonight I plan to loosen his tie a little. Last night he matched me drink for drink; a man thing, I suppose. Tonight I'll get the Jameson clan to bring Mr. Soledad to his knees. I read an Irish proverb once, on one of my own pub crawls back in the Old Country. It was posted on the back of a toilet tank. She laughed, remembering.

"It read: 'Thirst is the end of drinking and sorrow the end of drunkenness.' My plan is for Mr. Soledad to be carried up those stairs, wring out of him what we need to rescue Monique, and leave him in no condition to reap a reward." She sat up. "Just be sure your lieutenant is around to carry him down those stairs." Michael lay there needing to pee, but the warmth of Meg in his arms and the security of her voice, put him sound asleep.

In Sean's dream he and Monique were sharing one of their private breakfasts. Monique had just served coffee and was back in the kitchen preparing her version of French toast. Sean was chuckling in his sleep, envisioning Monique re-appearing, covered with syrup and confectioner's sugar. The ringing of the phone, at first, merely delayed Monique's entrance. When Jack's voice entered his head, Sean's eyes snapped open and Monique dissolved. "Who is this!" Jack was demanding.

"Hey, don't shoot the messenger. Is Sean there or not?" Jack handed the phone to Sean but stayed close trying to pick up both ends of the conversation.

"This is Sean. What's the deal? Is Monique safe? I'll kill the bastard who harms her!"

"Let's stay calm. Your girl is fine. You haven't called the cops, right?"

"No, this is between Mr. Soledad and me so let's get to it." "I was told you shoot from the hip. Here's how it's gonna work and I wasn't lying when I said your girl is fine."

Sean began to speak.

"I talk. You listen. Follow instructions and Monique will be released safe and sound. By the way, tell your brother he is playing well. We wish him luck. Anyway, after today's round, walk out the exit at the ninth hole. You will be contacted and given final instructions. No one will pick you up. You follow directions and before you know it, you can explain your actions to your old boss."

"What about Monique?" Sean managed.

"At the same time you make your appearance, your lady friend will be set free; that much your old boss guarantees. He's a man who keeps his word, I am to remind you." The phone clicked and Sean filled in the gaps for his brother.

Sean called Michael's cell phone and repeated the conversation.

Michael told Sean to do exactly as he had been told. "I know this is hard Sean but we do have a plan. We have had to bob and weave with this guy and you have to trust me."

"I don't see that I have a choice and if it comes down to going to meet him and face the consequences, I'm willing as long as Monique is safe."

Michael and Meg, both exhausted from the stress of the last few days, slept in. When the phone rang, Michael rolled to answer but it was Meg's cell. He caught himself and passed it to her.

"Good morning Miss Irish Tour Guide, I just had to tell you what a pleasant evening you provided. I also wanted to confirm tonight's engagement, while my head's not spinning."

Meg stifled a yawn. "I'm glad the morning light finds you in the same good spirits as evening last. I was afraid those Jameson boys might have revisited you during the night. Yes, we'll have another go at that dance floor."

"Let's say eight pm. again, you can tell me a little more about yourself and I may have a proposition for you."

"That sounds mysterious, Phillipe, and I'd like to know more but wait I will. Enjoy your day."

❦

Michael listened and watched Meg during the conversation. When she reached across to put her cell down on the stand, he quickly rolled her onto her stomach. Straddling her back, he playfully demanded to know if that had been her secret lover on the phone. "You can smother me with bed clothes or apply that hot light of yours, detective; I'll admit nothing."

"What if I apply that power of love technique Monique speaks of would that work?"

"I can't be providing you with the words to the music, Michael. Follow the tune in your head."

"Do you ever speak American, Meg, plain old boring vanilla." "Why, whatever do you mean? I speak plain as day."

Michael stopped talking and started humming. He followed the tune in his heart, not his head and slowly turned Meg so their eyes met. The urgency of last night became a slow waltz with sunlight peeking around the curtains. It was obvious they were hearing the same song.

❦

Jack and Sean followed the same routine as yesterday. Even Jack's tee time remained the same. If he played well and survived the cut, the pairings and tee times would likely change for the weekend.

A hearty breakfast greeted them and they moved slowly through the buffet line. Various meats, breads, fruit, and cereals offered a colorful accent to the main event; eggs. Dish them up scrambled, poached, in a sauce, lying on their back, or staring straight up at you. If you preferred, an omelet could be created right before your eyes. Jack chose a Spanish Omelet and Sean chose scrambled. They moved to a table laid out with cups and silverware and Jack chuckled. "If I can play as smoothly as they serve breakfast. Making the cut should be a cinch."

☙

Players stopped by to congratulate Jack on his round. Sean sat in silence. Sean was so proud of his brother and angry with himself. How could he have put Jack and Monique in this position? Jack finally noticed his brother not eating and asked what was wrong.

"Oh, just thinking brother. I am so sorry for dragging you into this mess."

Jack put his hand on his brother's shoulder. "Sean, you haven't known Michael for long. He wasn't the best golfer on our team - far from it. What he was though, was prepared. He got the most out of his talent and gutted out the rest. Michael prepares for battle better than anyone I have ever played with. He has great insight. If this problem can be resolved, he's the guy to trust."

"I've never been part of a team so trusting anyone but myself isn't easy, but I do trust you Jack and if you believe in Michael, I'll have to go along. Go ahead and get ready, brother. I'll follow you into battle."

Sean was true to his word. Joking and kidding around, he kept Jack relaxed as he prepared to tee off. Sean had his radio well hidden and had been instructed not to signal Michael.

"I will be in sight of you at all times. After you are contacted, call me and someone will follow the messenger," Michael had told him.

Jack played steady golf and remained -3 after nine holes. Michael made eye contact with Jack at the turn and moved ahead to get a good view of the tenth green.

It was a gorgeous day in North Carolina. The humidity was kept at bay by a breeze that did not influence the flight of the golf ball, yet kept the crowd crisp and dry. Blue skies and an unblinking sun assured all in attendance that surely God himself had blessed this event in spite of the sponsor. For surely, we could all breathe a little easier on a day such as this.

The back nine found Jack struggling. After he had managed par on 10,11 and 12, Jack hooked a drive on 13 that ended with a two putt double bogey. On fourteen Jack's problems continued. His drive was fine, but he left his approach shot well short of the green. He needed to chip close and one putt for a par. Didn't happen!

With four holes to play, Jack was back to even par. The two men talked, checked the leader board, and reasoned Jack would need to get back to -4 to make the cut. The crowd thinned around Jack, sensing they were watching a man self-destruct.

(Time to conjure up a bit of O'Shea magic, if you wouldn't mind,) Jack said to himself as he entered the porta potty. Standing at the urinal, Jack heard a voice he at first assumed was coming from outside.

Suddenly he realized the voice was in his head; a voice he had never heard before. (Looks like you're in a tight spot Jack, and I don't mean the toilet.) Jack chuckled in spite of himself.

(You know who this is Jack; just relax and hear the message.) It all became clear as the words hit Jack like a ton of bricks.

(Molly Malone faced a much tougher situation than you're facing, Jack O'Shea and she didn't need magic either. So take a deep breath Jack. Well, you might want to wait on that breath. Get back to what you are best at, taking care of those depending on you. I'll be waiting.)

When Jack emerged from that plastic capsule, it was as if he had landed on a different planet. With a deep breath, over the next four holes he caused the crowd to collectively hold theirs. He conducted a golf clinic of shots that left them shaking their heads in disbelief. He one putted each of the greens and was whistling a brand new tune. No longer was it <u>Oh Danny Boy</u> that left his lips but the tune of the fishmonger, <u>Molly Malone</u>.

Jack finished at -5 and was fairly mobbed by a crowd who knew they had truly witnessed something special. The two brothers hugged and Jack was left to tend to the crowd while Sean left to face his own music. Jack told Sean he would meet him at the car when he could break free. He had to get his score posted. Sean left the course as instructed and began what felt like a death march. Somewhere among the hundreds of people walking to and from the parking lot was a messenger who would deliver Sean's fate. "Hey there wait up," said a young lady about Sean's age. Sean, not realizing who she was shouting to, continued walking.

"Sean O'Shea, please wait up. I have a message for you." Turning around Sean saw a well tanned, athletic looking young woman approaching.

"You are Sean O'Shea, right," she said, trying to catch her breath.

"That would be me. What's up?"

"As I said, I have a message to deliver."

Before Sean could ask anything further, the girl's cell phone rang. The girl held her finger up signaling she would get right back to him and walked away.

With the crowd continuing to stream in to watch the players who started later in the day, Sean nearly lost sight of her. She put her phone away, and found Sean. Together they moved to a grove of trees that lined the exit.

"Okay, what is going on? What's the message?"

"I had a message for you, but that call changed everything." The girl appeared nervous so Sean kept his poker face on.

"Please, deliver the messages in the order you received them, Miss, uh."

"Smith, of course, okay here goes. Write them down if you want. She took out a small piece of paper and delivered message one. Drive back to that shopping center, and park as close as you can to where you parked yesterday. Monique will be a passenger in a limo that will pull up beside you. Get out of your car and get into the passenger seat of the limo beside the driver. As you get in, your friend will be allowed to take your vehicle and drive away."

Sean began to speak.

"Hold it! Let me give you message two before I forget it. Let's see? Congratulate your brother for making the weekend. He may need your help over the next two days so we'll just delay our meeting until Sunday evening. Enjoy the weekend. I plan to."

Sean let the messages sink in. His emotions suddenly took over and he grabbed Miss Smith by the arm. "What do you know about all this, Miss Smith?"

"You're hurting my arm! Please, let go!"

As suddenly as Sean had reacted, he regained control. "I'm sorry, this situation is upsetting me. Will you tell me how you became the messenger?"

"My father asked me to come to the tournament, locate you on the course, and to deliver the message when you came out. I was told where you would be exiting. I just didn't know when."

"Who is your father? How would he know about me?" "He's a lawyer here in Raleigh. One of his clients asked him to contact you, I guess, I don't know. I was to deliver the message. I get $200."

Sean turned to leave, there was nothing else to learn from Miss Smith.

Miss Smith started to say something but Sean kept walking. Jack freed himself from the crowd and had just reached the car when Sean approached. "You don't look like it was good news, brother."

"They're going to keep Monique and wait till Sunday night to deal with me. They will contact me when they are ready." Sean explained about Miss Smith and the two messages.

Jack's face became a chunk of granite. His success today was being added into the mix. The stones and gravel flying from the wheels were the only emotion expressed. Both men lost in their own thoughts.

ৡৡ

Meg answered Michael's cell phone and recognizing Jack's voice, began to congratulate him.

"Thanks Meg, but there's trouble riding on the coattails of angels so there's little pleasure I'm taking in my round. Is Michael there?"

Michael's face hardened as he heard the same message Sean had given Jack.

"He's putting Sean through hell - the bastard. Sean is as mad as I have ever seen him. Can't we do something? He's still wearing a poker face, but he knows he's not holding a winning hand."

"Jack, my lieutenant should be here any minute. He called a short time ago. Right now, I have to figure out how Meg is going to handle this little plot twist."

"I will try to keep Sean occupied. If you guys figure something out, or find Monique…" Jacks voice trailed off.

Meg heard Michael's end of the conversation. "I guess it was wise for me to stay here and rest today, Michael. It could be a long night. Me Mum never had a rascal such as this climbing her stairs."

"That's what I was thinking. So any ideas?"

"I need to think about this recent development Michael. Why don't you go for a run? When you get back, we'll compare ideas. We need to gain control of this timetable of his. Think about how we might cause him to stumble on those stairs."

"When the lieutenant shows up, fill him in. I'll be back in half an hour."

Michael usually tried to find a quiet less traveled route to run, where he could let his mind wander. Today he traveled a different path. The busiest section of the city had him sprinting across traffic and running in place while looking for an opening to change direction. Sudden stops and starts seemed to be the pace Phillipe Soledad was setting. Michael reasoned his thinking needed to take some sharp turns if he was to keep up. He returned dripping wet, heart racing, and not cooling down before finishing his run. The lieutenant was sitting in the one chair in the room; Meg sat on the edge of the bed.

Meg rose and excused herself. "I am going for a walk, Michael. I have an idea but you talk with the lieutenant. I have told him what I know."

When Meg returned, Michael was just getting out of the shower and the lieutenant was watching a cartoon show on TV. Michael took a seat on the bed and Meg joined him.

The lieutenant spoke. "As I see it, we have two choices. We can arrest him now and charge him with kidnapping which we may not be able to prove. Doing so raises the risk of Monique's being hurt or possibly killed."

"What's the second choice? I don't like the first one at all," inserted Meg.

"The second one comes with a large warning label attached," said Michael. "We let Mr. Soledad think he is in charge for a while longer and grab him when he finally contacts Sean."

"What is this warning label, Michael?"

"You remain in danger. We both know how he expects this evening to end."

Meg shook her head. "I've an idea of how we might keep him off those stairs for tonight at least."

"What are these stairs you're talking about?" asked the lieutenant.

"Private joke, sir. Meg means she intends to take the offensive."

Meg continued, "He's meaning to make a weekend of it. I have an excuse for Saturday night all planned. A family reunion I can't get out of." She shared her plan for tonight and when she finished, they nodded their head in approval. "I know just the guy," said Michael.

☙❧

Meg entered the pub and noted two things that would aid her plan; live music again tonight, and a weekend crowd gathering. (The more the merrier,) she thought to herself. She returned to the wooden tablet telling of her ancestor's journey and wondered about her own journey tonight. She hoped her plan for the evening was in sync with the message on the wall.

Phillipe startled her. "I'm sorry, Meg. You had your eyes closed. I didn't tire you out last evening, did I?"

"No, I was just daydreaming, wondering what a man such as yourself could want with a simple Irish girl."

"What I want, since you've asked, is to spend the entire weekend with you."

"Well, you're an honest man, one who doesn't beat around the rushes. Tis an admirable quality and a rare one. I'm afraid my relatives have plans for tomorrow evening, but perhaps Sunday we could watch the moon rise and fall."

Phillipe took Meg's hand, paid the cover charge, and left the reading to another time. They were ushered to a table; the music and drinks soon followed.

With the larger crowd intent on enjoying the weekend, Meg had to shout to be heard. "What would you like to drink tonight Phillipe to get your toes tapping?"

"A good whiskey, but let's let him dance naked tonight."

"You have a touch of mischief in your voice, sir. I fear you're becoming an Irishman, and you'll be wanting to teach me a dance step or two." Meg ordered Phillipe a Jameson whiskey and a mug of ale for herself.

Conversation was impossible, but after two drinks they found themselves on the dance floor. Phillipe was really getting into the music, trying to follow Meg's flying feet. The music slowed, and Phillipe knew these steps by heart. He brought her into his arms and they floated along the floor. Phillipe was beaming. His heart raced as he imagined how he would like the evening to end. Suddenly, it was eleven PM and the band took a break. Conversation kept the noise level on screech. Squeals of laughter, good natured bantering, and an occasional argument told a story as accurate as any song.

❧

The pub was packed. Meg excused herself to the ladies room. As she passed the bar, her eyes locked with a man who would change Phillipe's happy ending.

Phillipe Soledad sat quietly folding and unfolding his drink napkin. His eyes glazed, partly from liquor, but also with self satisfaction and anticipation.

The man approached his table from behind and tapped Phillipe on the shoulder. Phillipe turned out of instinct, raising his head slightly to the right. His gaze upward was met by a fist that meant to do damage. His cheekbone collapsed, and his nose spouted blood instantly. Phillipe's head struck the table, and bounced once. The cocktail napkin turned into a crimson pillow.

When Meg left the ladies room, a young man was being escorted bodily out of the pub. Seeing Phillipe unconscious, she moved quickly. With the lieutenant and two of his hunting buddies shooing everyone away, Meg acted quickly.

She copied the numbers from Phillipe's cell phone directory. Shielded from view, she took his credit cards from his wallet and noted numbers. She found several more phone numbers in his wallet. She replaced everything as she had found it. The sound of an ambulance pulling up outside competed for the crowd's attention. She dumped a glass of ice water on Phillipe.

The paramedics reached the table just as Phillipe regained consciousness. He tried to raise his head but could not, his eyes opening and closing, unfocused. Blood matted his hair and face. He looked like he had been in a severe accident.

They took his pulse and listened to his breathing, talking to one another like Phillipe wasn't there. Phillipe finally managed, "Meg are you there?

The Paramedics finally allowed him to sit up straight. They cleaned his face looking for more injuries.

"I was in the ladies room, and when I came out, the bouncers were giving a man a free ride out of here on their boots. I came back to find you sound asleep on the table."

Phillipe tried to get up but groaned in pain.

"You will need to go to the hospital for x-rays, it looks like your cheek might be broken and you have a pretty good knot on your head, probably from the table." The paramedic in charge didn't leave room for negotiation; they helped Phillipe onto the stretcher dolly.

Phillipe tried to protest being strapped in, but Meg spoke up. "I'll go to the hospital with you, Phillipe. It seems we're to spend the night together after all. I'm terribly sorry for what's happened here, but if they put you in one of those funny little coverings, I might not be able to keep a giggle or two from surfacing." Phillipe looked up and tried to smile, but it hurt too much, and he groaned.

Sean, on the other hand, felt the best he had in weeks. When Michael called earlier with the plan, Sean had jumped at the chance to finally be involved. Meg knew what was coming, but she had no idea it was going to be Sean delivering the message. When Sean told Jack how things went, he lamented that he'd only been able to hit him once.

Jack quoted an Old Irish proverb. "It's good enough for who it's for, Sean."

Sean felt for the first time like the gang had wrested some control back. If he had learned anything at all about Mr. Soledad, it was this. He would be trying to regain his balance as quickly as possible. Sean could only hope that any information gathered tonight would be available in time.

⁂

Saturday morning found Jack and Sean preparing for day three-hopeful on all fronts. They ate their breakfast with a sense that today would be a good day and toasted recent events with orange juice.

The early morning Sun followed Meg home from the hospital. She had remained in Phillipe's room for hours, looking out the window. Phillipe remained under heavy sedation but in the last hour had come to. She assured him he was going to be alright but would need an operation to repair his cheekbone. Two of Mr. Soledad's associates stood outside his door. Phillipe showed no recognition of his attacker, and the police had no information to offer.

Meg returned from the hospital so exhausted she climbed into bed immediately, a note from Michael telling her he was at the golf tournament went unread.

Michael returned to his room in the early afternoon. He saw that Meg was fast asleep so he quickly removed his clothes and joined her. He lay with his arm resting lightly on her hip. His chest and legs fit to her like a joined piece of puzzle. His breathing found Meg's rhythmic pattern and soon he joined her in a shared dream. When they awoke, neither spoke; they simply shifted their bodies slightly. That tiny movement made all the difference. The final piece of the puzzle was solved; they became one.

While others slept, Jack had been putting together a solid round of golf. He was not visited by voices or talked to in toilets. He simply did what he was capable of doing. When he made his putt for par on 18, he looked up at the leaderboard for the first time today. He was listed in the top four - 4 strokes off the lead. When Jack left the green, he was asked to shake hands, sign hats, booklets, and bodies. (I could get used to this attention,) thought Jack.

The same sun that had followed Meg home this morning made the return trip to Phillipe's hospital room. After getting past the bodyguards, Meg entered to find Phillipe sitting up in his bed sucking ice chips. The TV. was on. Phillipe was watching Jack O'Shea putt out on 18.

"He's going to be a good one," said Phillipe huskily.

"Who is that you're speaking of?"

"Why the Irishman Jack O'Shea; you should be cheering for him."

Not sure if she was being played like last night's fiddle, Meg responded, "Never heard of the man, though he looks like he's a capable lad. Do you know him?"

"I've only met the brother. There - see him. He has a beard too."

Meg decided to change the subject. "How are you feeling this warm spring afternoon?"

"I'm a mess," he groaned.

"You sound like an Irishman talking into his glass at evening's end," laughed Meg.

Phillipe shook his head, "And how do I look?"

"To be honest, you look a bit like that same Irishman who ordered twice but had only money for a single."

Phillipe laughed out loud, and then groaned. He studied Meg for what seemed a full minute, but said nothing.

"The nurse at the desk say's you'll be released tomorrow morning. You are going to wait to get back home for your operation?"

"If I can move the timetable on a last piece of business, I'm on a private plane tomorrow morning. Would you see me off?"

"Of course I will. Just rest now. We'll let this tournament put you to sleep. I'll be right here, watching over you."

"You have been wonderful, Meg. How will I ever forget you?"

"You're not supposed to forget. It's said that once you let a true Irishman enter your life, you're changed forever. That tablet in the bar tells the gospel truth or so we believe."

Meg sat and watched Phillipe sleep. This man had chosen a path in life that could not have a happy ending. Meg had little sympathy, she had met men like Phillipe all her life-men who tried to prey on the weaknesses of others. (Mum learned that lesson so well,)thought Meg, so well she had become just like them. Phillipe awoke after an hour. Meg left, promising him she would be there early in the morning.

When Meg reached the motel room, Michael and the lieutenant were deep in conversation. The golf tournament was just winding down for the day. Meg noted that Jack was still four shots out of the lead. She couldn't wait for this crisis to pass so she and Michael might get to spend some time with him. She loved listening to Jack's Irish brogue but had not really had the opportunity to come to know him. Michael asked what she had learned.

Meg clicked off the TV. "We have to move quickly. Phillipe is planning to finish this business with Sean tonight. He will have a plane waiting to take him back home tomorrow morning." "The information you gathered will convict him of some serious crimes, Meg."

"That's good to hear. Do we have any idea where Monique is being held?"

"Not yet; but we can monitor his cell phone now that we have his number. We can't hear what he's saying but we can trace the location of his calls."

The lieutenant spoke up. "If Sean is called, we will have a tail on him. If a swap takes place, we'll nab this Mr. Soledad as soon as Monique is set free."

"I have a theory," said Meg. "Would you care to hear it?" Both men nodded. "I believe when Mr. Soledad flies West in the morning, Sean and Monique are going to be on that plane." Both men raised their eyebrows. "Why do you think that Meg?" asked Michael.

"Look at how this whole thing has played out from the beginning. He could simply have had Sean injured or killed without involving himself personally. He chose a path, Michael. I was thinking about this man while he slept. He can't change who he is. He needs to finish what he started, and that means letting Sean wait till he's fit to finish it. He has lost control here and has been hurt in the process. At home he would never have been without security, like he allowed in that pub."

"She makes good sense, Michael," offered the lieutenant. "By the way Meg if you would like a career in police work, I'd hire you in a minute."

"I'll leave the detective work to Michael. I just know men. You all want to control your comfort level."

Michael started to speak but Meg interrupted; she wasn't through.

"Don't get me wrong. I'm not damning men at all. For the most part it's a comfort for a lady to know the question before it's asked. Gives us time to prepare a proper answer. So bear with me a minute. I will give you the question Mr. Soledad is going to ask me before the night is over."

The two men looked at one another. They both threw open their hands in a gesture that signaled surrender. Please continue. "If we had the time, I'd play twenty questions but simply put, Mr. Soledad will be asking me to join him on that plane." Michael's mouth dropped open once again.

"You're killing me, Jerry." he said, referring to a line used often on the Seinfeld Show. When Meg looked at him strangely, Michael tried to explain. Meg grew more confused.

Finally, Michael realized he could not explain the humor of the show adequately so he just shut up and listened.

"I'm going back to see him this evening. He isn't expecting that. I'm worried about him; don't you know. Part of his unfinished business concerns me. I can see it in his eyes."

"So you will join him on that plane and fly back to Las Vegas? Meg this is crazy."

The lieutenant interrupted. "Wait a minute, Michael. Maybe this is just the break we're looking for. You did say Meg, that it's to be a chartered plane."

Meg nodded her head.

"If we are going to end this little drama with us applauding we have to keep that plane from leaving. There should be some calls taking place to secure a plane and crew. Now I have a plan." Meg chuckled, " Now you're talking like an Irishman lieutenant." She got up and headed for the bathroom.

"I think the less I know the better. I will keep Mr. Soledad off his heels and cloud his thinking while you two gentlemen clip his wings. Wouldn't me Mum be proud."

When the Lieutenant left to make some arrangements, Michael called Jack.

Sean answered the phone. "Jack's out for an evening jog. He should be back in twenty minutes or so. What's going on? By the way, thanks for giving me a shot at that creep. Did I hurt him bad?"

"He will recover. You did make him change plans again, Sean, and I think it's finally to our advantage." Michael explained that Mr. Soledad intended to leave the next morning and Sean would probably be joining him on the plane.

"I believe Monique will also be a passenger. When you get called, do as they say. Call me immediately with any information they give you. We have a plan."

"I'll tell Jack to arrange for a caddie for tomorrow. I really hate to screw up his last round. Jesus, I'm mad at myself for all this mess."

"Keep your chin up! We're going to end this, Sean, and soon. Wish Jack luck for me. Ask him to tell you about that eternal time clock he wears around his heart - the one that runs on pure faith. Tell him Michael is beginning to think he's right."

Meg rapped lightly on the door. When Phillipe told her to come in, she smiled sweetly to the stone faced bodyguard and brushed past him.

Mr. Soledad was laying on his left side facing the window. Darkness had fallen some time ago. A small night light provided the only illumination.

"Would you be wishing on a star, sir, uh Phillipe?"

Phillipe slowly turned onto his back. "I guess it must have been a falling star one that landed in my room." He groaned with the effort. "I wasn't expecting you. A reunion of some sort - wasn't it?"

Meg sat on the side of his bed and took his hand. He looked old and defeated.

"They are indeed meeting at this very hour. I've managed to see most of them individually. Actually, they are like a good prescription medicine - easier to take in small doses."

Phillipe chuckled and groaned again.

Meg threw caution to the wind. "Why do you suppose you were attacked? You aren't from here."

Phillipe shrugged, "Who knows. Maybe it was because of you. An old man out having fun with a beautiful girl. I have people asking around, but we haven't a clue." He closed his eyes briefly. "I feel worse tonight than when it happened."

"Do you need a dose of that medicine I was talking about earlier?"

"I would love some but I have to keep my mind clear. Making plans to leave, I need to be involved."

"So you are still planning on leaving in the morning?"

"Yes, which leads me to what I was really thinking about when you came in. I wasn't wishing on stars. I was imagining you up in that sky with me." Phillipe paused.

"I'm not sure I understand."

"Fly back to Vegas with me. Come to work for me."

Meg pretended surprise and confusion. "I…, I couldn't do that."

"Why not? You seem independent enough. You said yourself, that you don't have an active career you're involved with presently."

"That's all true but I have never been West. I don't even know you, really"

"Tell you what. Come out for a week. I'll get you a beautiful suite, and let you look around. Give you some money to go shopping - gamble if you'd like." He groaned with the effort this invitation was taking. "A week in Vegas is like a month anywhere else. No obligations - I will remain a gentleman. Hell, I'll probably be in the hospital for most of the week, anyway."

Meg appeared to waver slightly.

"If you like it out there, I have a job for you just being you. Say the word and I'll get you a ticket back this way. Sound fair?" "I don't know. You've got my head spinning. No obligations on my part?"

"I love my wife Meg. I'm not asking you to be, or do anything you aren't comfortable with. If, over time we end up enjoying one another, it will be on your terms."

"That sounds like an Irishman promising a fish he won't gobble him up if he'll just spend a little time in his boat. But if you're telling me certain that I have the pole in my hand, then yes, I will join you in the morning." Then Meg smiled, "Spontaneous combustion is what I call it."

Phillipe was too thrilled to ask Meg what she meant by that, so Meg completed her thought.

"Over the years, my best decisions have been the ones that ignite in the moment; spontaneous combustion. Now that I've set myself aflame, I'll need some particulars to be ready for this plane ride."

ᔜᔪ

While Meg was receiving particulars, Sean was getting his marching orders. After hanging up, Sean immediately called Michael. "All I was given was orders. I'm supposed to go back to that shopping center at five am tomorrow morning. The man wouldn't even discuss Monique. The whole conversation was abrupt."

"Do as they say, Sean. We should know their plan soon. We'll get Monique back, Meg has been incredible."

"I must admit I was pretty shocked to see her in the pub that night."

"I couldn't risk telling anyone anything at that point. I knew with your famous poker face you'd handle it. Get some sleep if you can, Sean and believe in that Irish luck Jack keeps telling me about."

ᔜᔪ

When Meg arrived back at the motel, she had the time, the place, and even a password.

"A password; what's that all about?"

"Phillipe doesn't know any of the men involved so he's created a password to be given to his top man. He has to clear anyone getting close to the air strip."

Armed with Meg's information, Michael and the lieutenant put their plan into action. After Michael hung up, he asked Meg about her own plans.

"I am to be at the hospital at six-thirty am to help Phillipe prepare himself. He is to be discharged at seven am and driven directly to the plane. Right now, my plan is to take a long hot shower.

Michael lay on the bed with his eyes closed. From the bathroom he could hear soft humming. He put his hands behind his head and listened. Meg turned on the shower. When he heard her enter the water, he turned to watch her behind the opaque glass. (What a couple of weeks it has been,) thought Michael. (First, Jack appears outside the restaurant glass. Meeting Meg in a restaurant. Watching the hold-up take place through the glass. Going undercover to help Jack and Sean. Finding out there was a connection between Mr. Soledad, the loan sharking company, and Jack's problem. Now having the best thing that ever happened to him, Meg, just beyond the glass. Well, my life isn't silent and empty anymore that's for sure, he mused.)

He emerged from his reverie when Meg dropped her soap, and changed her tune. Michael quickly stripped and without a word entered the shower.

Meg felt his arms reach around her from the back as he moved to embrace her.

"Would you be here to keep me from slipping and sliding and dropping my soap, Michael? Or is it your plan to take advantage of a defenseless girl with soap in her eyes?"

"That was another part of our academy training, Meg; one I haven't practiced enough so if you'd help me out here." Later as they lay cuddled in the darkness trying to sleep, Meg confessed her nervousness of what the morning would bring. "With what you have brought us, we could probably finish up without you, Meg."

"I think that you are probably right. I just worry that any sudden switch in plans on my part might change his thinking." "That's true you have him off balance; his mind is on other things. If you want out, that's more than ok with me."

"No, I want to be there. I can always Mace him if I have to." "I thought bouncing up and down was the preferred method; that's what we have been practicing."

"Only if I could coax him into a shower. I thought you were going to drown earlier."

They both laughed, which broke the tension and sleep subdued them.

♾

Sean dressed quietly in the dark. He gently shook his brother to say good-bye. "Brother, I'll see you at the end of the day." Jack was immediately awake. "Kick their arses for me, Sean. Jack took his brother's hand. "Are you sure you don't want my help?"

"There's nothing you can do except kick arses out on the course."

"May the O'Shea magic be working overtime today, Sean. We'll all celebrate tonight."

Sean walked out into the predawn darkness. His fate in the hands of others.

He was picked up by limousine at five twenty-six. The driver opened a rear door and a voice beckoned Sean to get in. Sean could smell coffee and something sweet and spicy. His senses were on high alert. Every sound and movement seemed exaggerated. The man sitting opposite him in a lounge type chair offered him coffee and a Danish. Sean declined but asked where Monique was.

"She is in a vehicle similar to this one and hopefully she's eating. That danish will be your last opportunity to eat for a while."

"Where are we going?" asked Sean.

"All in due time, my boy. Be patient and thankful. I would have ended this foolishness before now if it was up to me." "Well then, let's hope you never climb the management ladder where decisions rest with you."

"Don't be a wise ass with me. I'll knock you around some. The boss wouldn't mind too much."

Sean closed his mouth. His poker face returned. He said maybe he would have a little coffee and something sweet if it was still being offered.

The limousine drove around without a destination, making sure they weren't being tailed. Nearly an hour later they pulled up outside a warehouse. A large overhead door opened and they entered. A limousine with its headlights on stared directly at them. They stopped and waited. A minute passed. The passenger door opened and Sean saw Monique slowly emerge.

Sean moved to join her.

The man put his hand on Sean's arm. "You can go see her but don't try anything stupid."

Sean waited till he removed his hand, and opened the car door. Two sets of headlights witnessed their tearful embrace.

The men in the cars got out, and met in a little group off to the side.

The conversation was heated. They took turns showing anger and disgust about the foolishness they were being asked to be involved in.

꧁꧂

Sean and Monique continued to hug and talk quietly. "No, Sean, they did not mistreat me. They have been very business-like. They must have been under strict orders not to harm me. What is going to happen now? Have you been told?"

"Not by them. Don't react if you see someone you have met before. Just follow my lead."

Monique started to ask Sean to explain but he put his finger to his lips. "To quote my brother, 'it will all be over soon Dannyboy.' Trust the plan Monique."

Sean and Monique were told to enter one of the limousines. As they headed onto the highway, Sean asked where they were headed.

"West young man, West," was the reply.

Sean took Monique's hand, and the conversation stopped.

꧁꧂

Meg arrived at Phillipe Soledad's hospital room carrying an overnight bag. The bodyguard had obviously been told she was welcome, for he even opened the door for her. Meg turned and gave him a big smile.

Phillipe was dressed, and sitting in a wheelchair. He was holding a cell phone to the uninjured side of his face, trying to make himself understood.

"Everything's all set - you're sure? You have them both - good. We'll be there in thirty minutes." Phillipe waved Meg to sit down, and continued. "No, I want them already aboard when I arrive. They are not to see me like this."

Phillipe hung up the phone and rose slowly to greet Meg. " That little bag looks like a day at the beach. No matter, we will find some wonderful things in Las Vegas."

"I don't require a lot of clothes, Phillipe, but a shopping trip would be a grand way to begin."

"I'm so glad you have agreed to come with me. You have removed a lot of the unpleasantness of the past couple of days." Phillipe reached for Meg and she let him embrace her.

"What can I do to help?" Meg slowly pulled away.

"They insist that I ride in this damn chair to the exit. Would you push me, please?"

Meg helped Phillipe into the chair and stepped behind him.

"Why are you doing this Meg?"

Meg suddenly uneasy, managed, "What do you mean, Phillipe?"

"Look at me for God's sake. I am an old man in a wheelchair. Why are you willing to spend time with me?"

Relieved, Meg answered, "I don't know, perhaps a piece of me needs a father figure. My own was a drunk I never knew. You have been kind and honest with me. Maybe, I am even a little attracted to you. You are a good looking man, Phillipe Soledad, when you aren't brawling in a bar room."

They both chuckled. Phillipe reached back behind his shoulder to touch Meg's hand. "Thank you, Meg, let's make this a trip to remember.

After the formalities of signing out, the glass doors opened to early morning sunshine and to the smell of flowers in full bloom. Meg saw the crepe myrtles lining the walkway and was reminded of how George, Michael's landlord, had described God's work and man's work. She wondered which she was doing this morning.

There was little time to reflect, for a long black Lincoln sat at the end of the curved walkway, with its rear door open. Meg helped Phillipe out of the wheelchair and into the car. Meg joined Phillipe in the rear seat. The solid sound of the door closing removed all noise and most of the light. The smell of leather replaced the flowers and Meg sensed this morning was all about man's work.

A corporate jet equipped to carry 10 passengers, with a small meeting room and a back bedroom, was idling on the edge of the runway.

Meg helped Phillipe aboard where he settled into one of the two large seats at the front of the plane. He spoke briefly with one of his associates, who pointed to the back bedroom. A small smile crossed Phillipe's face; he felt himself regaining control. The associate left the plane, and one more door was closed in this ongoing drama.

Phillipe ordered a coffee from the flight attendant. "As soon as we are in the air, sir. You don't want to risk a spill and a possible burn."

Phillipe settled back and closed his eyes.

Meg would later say Monique was right; about the power of love. How else could you explain the simplicity with which the drama ended. No shots were fired, and no voices were raised. The plane taxied half a mile and simply stopped. The co-pilot entered the passenger compartment and introduced himself. Phillipe was read his rights and placed under arrest for kidnapping. Other crimes Phillipe Soledad was guilty of would have to wait their turn. Phillipe simply sat there with his eyes closed.

Phillipe had no idea the role Meg played in his quick descent from the summit. When he did speak, it was to apologize to her. "Meg, they will release you in a very short time. Please forgive me."

Meg acted confused. " I don't understand any of this Phillipe but it's clear you have been deceiving me. I won't offer my tears, but simply put, we won't be reading any more Irish history together."

Meg was led away in handcuffs.

Next came Sean and Monique; they walked past Mr. Soledad without a word. Sean looked down at his former boss and could almost feel pity. It looked like Mr. Soledad had melted into his chair, for his clothes held no shape, his face offered no color, his eyes remained closed; to keep the mountains from falling on him.

⊱⊰

Michael received the call he'd been pacing the floor over.

"Everyone is safe Michael. Meg has been taken to headquarters to make it appear that she must prove she was just an innocent bystander. Sean and Monique are writing statements as we speak."

"Thank you, lieutenant. Will you see that Meg is brought here?"

"Sure thing. Sean and Monique should be done and back by noon time.

"Do you think Sean could caddy for Jack this afternoon? Is it safe?"

"Oh, I think so. A number of Mr. Soledad's associates were picked up this morning throughout the country. I think they have more to worry about than Sean."

"What happened out there lieutenant - any violence at all?"
"No, no violence. It was strange actually. I can only speculate Michael, but in my view, Meg had him emotionally arrested

before we ever put the cuffs on him. What else would cause a man like him to let down his guard. This guy has lived on instinct and no one has ever been able to touch him. The only change in the mix is Meg. You have yourself one hell of a lady there Michael. Don't let her go."

Michael didn't know what to say. He was always without words it seemed when it came to Meg.

"Why don't you get out to the course and tell Jack the good news. Maybe it will be the boost he needs. I will see that all three of them get out there as soon as possible."

"Thanks again, lieutenant. I know what you did for us." "It was your instincts that allowed us to stop this man, I just wish you could take the credit. The important thing here is, the next time you are sitting out in the dark watching some evil taking place, at least you'll know Mr. Soledad is sitting in a pretty evil place himself."

Michael found Jack on the second hole. He flashed his badge and entered the ropes. Jack hit his second shot, and then shook his head with satisfaction as the ball landed at the edge of the green, rolling toward the pin. Michael yelled to him. Jack ambled across the fairway.

A smile on Michael's face assured Jack that things had gone well.

"It's not a golf lesson you've come to give me this morning is it? I hope for better than that," Jack chuckled.

"Everything turned out fine, Jack. Sean and Monique are both safe."

Jack embraced Michael. His demeanor cracked, finally the emotional roller coaster he had ridden finally came to rest. The crowd had no idea what was going on. It didn't matter. Two friends hugging. That was more emotion than they were used to seeing on a golf course. They clapped loudly.

Jack wiped his eyes and took Michael's hand. "Thank you, Michael. I owe you so much."

"Just kick their arses out here today, Jack. By the way your brother just may be here to walk the final nine holes with you." Michael moved back beyond the ropes to watch his friend approach the green with a new bounce in his step.

Michael walked along, fingering the rope, thinking of how the boundaries in his own life had expanded over the last month. He thought back briefly to the silent image of Jack on a street in Orlando. That moment had certainly taken on a life of its own. Meg had added noise to his life - good noise, laughter and love. Ron and Beth had reintroduced him to the good that can come from a loving relationship. Sean and Monique were sure to become his close friends for life. He was smiling to himself when his cell phone rang. The smile turned to a grin when Meg's voice came on the line. "Michael, is that you?"

"Yes, Meg, it's your long lost cousin wandering alone among the pines, wishing his cousin were here. Jack is doing super; he's on the sixth hole in third place. Are you ok?"

They have been putting me under that hot light of theirs for the past two hours. You didn't put them up to that did you?" Michael laughed. "No honestly, I already know who you are and I'm so proud of you I could bust out crying." Michael could hear a stifled sob on the other end.

"Did they find out about your relationship with Mickey Mouse," kidded Michael trying to lighten the conversation.

"Would you come and get me Michael? They have offered me a ride but I need you, right now. All these men in blue keep peeking in at me and talking among themselves. I need you, Michael. I love you."

Michael was too stunned to speak immediately. "I love…" he managed, but the lieutenant's voice responded.

"Don't finish that line Michael or we won't be allowed to work a stakeout together," he laughed.

"Don't be a wise guy, I'm coming to pick up Meg. She all right sir?"

She's been through a pretty traumatic morning. She's a tough cookie, but right now would be a good time to just let her melt in your arms."

Michael asked for directions and was soon weaving through traffic, practicing his own declaration of love.

࿇

Sean and Monique were dropped off at the parking lot where Sean had started his day. They would be given protection for the remainder of the time they were in North Carolina. They drove directly to the golf course.

"Are you sure you don't want to stay at the motel? You could watch the round on TV? The police will have someone nearby." "I wish to see you and your brother walking together again. I can rest later when I have you there with me." Monique had described her ordeal to Sean in detail. She had written down pretty much the same thing for the police.

She had been approached in the supermarket by a man who had said if she did not go with him, Sean would be killed in his car outside. Two men had ushered her out a service entrance. In the car she was blindfolded and driven around for what seemed like hours; but was probably a half hour at most. When they stopped, Monique climbed a set of steps leading to what seemed like an older house. She smelled mold and mildew when she was placed in the room. The door was locked immediately by one of her captors. Country music played constantly, probably CDs, not a radio. She was kept tied on a bed and blindfolded for the entire time she was captive. Three times a day she was fed takeout food - pizza, soft drinks, and fried chicken. She was escorted to the bathroom just outside the room and twice allowed to shower. In the bathroom when she showered she was untied, the blindfold removed. One of her captors would put his own mask in place before she was allowed to see anything.

"I had only the sense of smell to keep me going, Sean. I didn't tell the police this, but it was you I smelled when we bathed together, and your smell as a man when we made love. It was you who kept me safe and I don't want to be away from you." Sean squeezed her hand. "You are safe now. Let's go help my brother win this thing. I love you Monique. You're right, Jack would want us both there."

"We can't go back to Las Vegas, Sean. You know that - don't you. That man may still have enough power to ruin our lives." "I wasn't planning on going back there anyway. I was hoping we could start fresh - someplace brand new." Sean pulled the car to the side out of traffic and the couple hugged for a minute. Eyes still wet they reentered traffic.

On the course Jack was still slugging it out. He reached the ninth hole still three shots back of the leader. He tapped in for a par. He walked toward the tenth tee knowing he would need to summon some O'Shea magic to catch the leaders. He looked around for Sean, but he had not arrived yet.

Michael, on arriving to pick up Meg, felt like he was back home. The police headquarters were laid out similarly. When he showed his badge to a Desk sergeant, he was quickly ushered along a hallway to the Captain's office. His lieutenant was standing at the window sipping coffee. When he turned, Michael could see a trace of sugar on his face. A box of Krispy Krème donuts had been violated, and the lieutenant hadn't cleaned up the crime scene. The lieutenant introduced Michael to the captain, then offered him a cup of coffee.

"Meg will be joining us shortly."

"Thanks, lieutenant. I will have a cup, maybe even one of those fat pills if you don't plan to finish the box."

"No, I saved you a raspberry filled one. I know you won't eat the donut, but the filling won't hurt you," the lieutenant laughed, and then grew serious. "This Mr. Soledad won't be leaving town any time soon. They take kidnapping real seriously and bond won't be allowed. Mr. Soledad was not thinking very clearly when he planned to take Sean and Monique with him. I believe we can thank Sean's punch and Meg for that mental breakdown. Anyway with all the information we gathered, we have shut down a major crime family."

⤺⤻

Meg entered the room and immediately melted in Michael's arms. She began to cry. The lieutenant and captain made a quick exit. The emotion of the week bubbled up, spilling on Michael's shirt. Michael rocked her gently back and forth, letting the strength of his embrace do his talking for now.

Meg with her eyes closed continued to sob as her mind left the shore, with Michael rowing her to a quiet and peaceful place. The waves of emotion were slowly replaced by the soothing warmth and security of her lover. Meg regained her composure, and Michael knew she was safely back on land when she spoke. "That was a good deal more comforting than sitting on my kitchen floor, hugging my knees," she managed.

"Glad I could help. In fact, I offer to be your personal hugging post for as long as you'd like."

"I bet you say that to all the girls from Ireland."

Michael laughed, "If they are all like you, I just might quit my day job, maybe rent myself out."

"I've got to fix my eyes, Michael. Do you think you could find me a mirror that wouldn't have anyone staring back at me but myself."

Michael laughed again. "It's good to have you back, Meg. I'll wait to discuss that last phone conversation we had. Hopefully it wasn't a crank call."

❧❧

Michael and Meg reached the golf course where they found Monique behind the ropes of the sixteenth tee. They all hugged and then dried their eyes ready to watch Jack tee off. Sean stood off to the side, with a big grin on his face. Michael looked up at the leaderboard. Jack was now in second place at -7. The new leader was 9 under and playing in the group ahead of Jack. What the players faced on the sixteenth was being described over the air waves. Usually a par five is a reprieve of sorts for the really good players - a certain par and often a birdie hole. The par five at the sixteenth was none of the above.

This 578 yard dog leg left, had a bunker along the entire right side. Michael mentally played the hole as Jack took a practice swing. The smart tee shot would carry just 250 yards, probably a three wood, staying just right of center. If hit correctly, this shot would cut nearly 100 yards off the dog leg, allowing the chance to be on the green in two. A drive left of center would force a second shot that had to bend around the dog leg, which was much more difficult to execute.

Down two strokes, Michael knew what Jack intended. Jack looked across the tee and caught Michael's eye. He patted his driver as if to say, it will all be over soon Dannyboy. Throwing caution to the wind, Jack swung with a controlled fury. The ball flew as if it were a caged bird suddenly given freedom. Riding out over the man made desert, it looked at first as if that was where it would nest. Suddenly, a different pair of wings carried the ball to the left where it came to rest a mere yard outside the bunker - 315 yards from where its flight began. Jack's ball had flown the dog leg and Jack was whistling as he walked to strike that little ball in the arse.

Michael following closely along the ropes remembered that Jack always whistled when he putted. What was this new music in the air? Michael dragged Meg and Monique behind him, all holding hands. He flashed his badge when necessary to get through a knot of people.

Sean struggled to keep up with Jack, partly because of the weight of the bag, but mostly because he could not keep from checking on the safety of Monique every few seconds. Jack's second shot was just picture perfect. Not content to leave himself a short chip for his third shot, Jack hit his three wood 250 yards straight at the flag. He ran his first putt by but sunk his birdie. He was only one back with two to play.

The 17th was a par 3, 212 yard shot with little trouble, until a player reached the green. The green was huge and lulled a player into thinking it was an easy birdie hole. Jack hit the center of the green, but he still had 45 feet to the pin which was tucked in the right corner. The green had subtle breaks with undulations that defied a good read.

Jack's putt was on line for forty of the forty-five feet then took a left. He tapped in for his par. His opponent a hole ahead had parred also. One hole left to play. Jack needed at least a birdie to tie.

The final hole was intended to let a leader play conservative and to walk away with at least a par. It was the easiest hole on the course according to the scorecard. Tell that to the leader.

Jack had no way of knowing that up ahead, the leader was finishing up his round with a rare bogey. Before Jack ever swung

his club on the final hole he was tied for the lead. His drive landed dead center in the fairway. He didn't hear the applause up ahead.

He went into a kind of trance and didn't see Michael trying to get his attention. Sean was too busy trying to catch up to Jack to have any information. The crowd began clapping wildly as he approached his drive -180 yards from the green.

Jack heard none of it. He was sharing the moment with Molly, who had a final message for him.

(Remember Molly Malone never asked for anything for herself to be reunited with family was enough. You have made all our lives richer Jack, so there is no need for O'Shea magic here. Just be yourself and get back here to your new family.)

The analyst in the tower described Jack's second shot as a bit conservative. "Perhaps, he knows he's tied for the lead and would be content with a playoff."

"You may be right, but he has never been this close to winning a tournament on tour. A sudden death playoff possibly looks good from there." Their banter continued as Jack walked to the edge of the putting surface.

He had left himself with a long putt of 60 feet. Jack and brother Sean studied the putt briefly.

"This is a feel putt, Sean. Studying it will only confuse me. Jack stood over the putt and to the spectators it appeared he was reading the break.

Jack was once again remembering that putt his father had invented to defeat the English oppressors centuries ago. A single putt - imagine it - could raise the level of respect an entire nation felt for itself. Molly was right. Jack was at peace now and whether he made this putt or not, he was a whole person. His family had come to terms with who they were. Their heritage was intact. So much had happened since Jack had missed his final putt in that motel room. Jack took a last look, and let his own magic take over. No angels interfered. Jack didn't even whistle to calm himself. The putt simply covered the centuries as if time had stopped and dropped into the hole with a deafening silence. Jack looked up and smiled.

He didn't jump or click his heels ready to head to a pub to celebrate, he simply turned and embraced his brother.

The smile had little to do with sinking the putt or winning the tournament. It was in a sudden flood of images entering his head that Jack saw his personal struggle end. He had finally become a whole person. In that moment he realized he no longer had to use a notebook to voice his emotions.

Sitting in his hotel room he could not recall what he said to the listening audience. He had to laugh when he heard that victory speech on tape, Sean and the M&M gang hanging on every word. He had reverted to his Irish brogue which had become so a part of him.

When asked what he attributed his success here this week, his first victory on the PGA, Jack answered. "It may sound silly, but this week had little to do with the game of golf. I swung the clubs and putted the ball, but it was a group of dear people, who gave the week a soft landing." Jack refused to elaborate on his comments and had simply walked away from the interview.

A knock on the door brought Mr. O'Shea to the celebration. Sunday night was turning into more than Jack could have hoped for. Mr. O'Shea embraced his son. They hugged, saying nothing but understanding everything. When the emotion of the moment passed, Jack asked his father when he had arrived.

"I got a call on Saturday and caught a shuttle flight early this morning. I arrived in time to watch your final nine holes.

It would seem those lessons I gave you years ago have finally paid off," he laughed.

"More than you know, Mr. O'Shea, more than you know." Before Jack could ask who had called his father, the phone rang.

Carey Houston began by congratulating Jack.

"I wish both you and your husband had been able to be here." "Actually we were - I mean we are. We're three doors down and one flight up. We have a suite all set up with food and drink. Come on up and we'll explain.

The suite filled up rapidly, and after introductions the group broke into little pockets of conversation. Jack walked Mrs. Houston and her husband to the balcony.

"Thank you for believing in me, and for bringing my dad with you. It means the world to have him here."

Wallace Houston spoke up. "You have been good for business. Those autographed hats and balls you sent gave Whitney the idea of starting a website and a fan club. She posted your picture. All her friends see you as a kind of hunk. So it's currently fashionable to be doing business with the Houston family."

Jack laughed.

Michael and Meg watched the suite fill with Jack's fellow competitors and friends. Soon the two rooms were humming with noise. When Ron and Beth arrived, Michael and Meg quickly joined them.

"Where is Jack? What the hell was going on anyway?" Ron had been left in the dark since that night in Flagler Beach. "It's a long story, Ron, but if you still have a room for Meg and me at the beach, we'll tell you all about it."

Ron wasn't ready to give up his questioning. When Michael went to greet his lieutenant who had just appeared, he questioned Meg.

"How about the Reader's Digest version of what happened with Jack?"

"I'm still sorting it all out myself, Ron. I don't know this Readers Digest you mention, but what happened here would make a fantastic book or movie. All I know is, Michael is a true friend to you golf mates, if you ever need him he'll be there." Sean and Monique joined Meg. She introduced them to Ron and Beth. The conversation covered small talk at first but when Monique agreed to sing a song, the room quieted.

Monique sang a song in French that summed up the week. The words were foreign, yet each person listening felt she spoke directly to them. When she finished, eyes were wet throughout the room.

Beth immediately offered Monique a job as manager and performer at the private club where she and Ron worked.

Jack listened to Monique's song but his mind was already on a plane heading west. Fortunately, his body stayed in North Carolina.

Michael was just coming out of the bathroom when he heard the knock. When he opened the door, Molly Erricson looked him straight in the eye and handed him a note card.

Michael read the card: 'Please ask Jack O'Shea to invite me in'.

"I would be glad to take you to him Miss, uh."

Molly waved the idea away and again pointed to the message on the card.

Michael wasn't positive but suddenly he thought he understood. He went to find Jack.

Jack was listening to Mr. O'Shea captivate a dozen guests with one of his Irish tales. Lost in thought with his father's story and his own tales of Molly Malone competing for air time, Jack ignored Michael's voice. Michael took his arm and Jack returned to the present.

"What are you doing, Michael, kidnapping me? You know yourself, there's little profit in that." He was chuckling, planning his next line when he came face to face with Molly Erricson standing at the door.

Suddenly his eyes filled with tears, he swept Molly into his arms and rather than entering the room, he danced with her along the empty corridor.

"Molly,… Molly,… Molly,… what a perfect ending to a wonderful day. I have so much to tell you."

Molly gently pushed Jack away, quickly jotting down her response. 'We have so much to tell one another'.

"Did you know you were with me during the week, Molly?" 'I was thinking of you everyday, but I didn't know if I got through,' she wrote.

"You helped me find my way home, you and Molly Malone." Jack took Molly by the hand. He introduced her to each person in the room. It was clear to the people closest to him that Jack O'Shea was head over heels in love.

There was an abundance of love in that room. When Mr. O'Shea quieted them to tell one last story everyone gathered around.

∾∞∾

"Meg, you were born and raised in Ireland so you will recognize the truth in what I am about to say." He winked at Meg, and began. "Did you know celebrations such as this originated with the Irish? My grandfather was born in Ireland, and I was fortunate to live with him and my grandmother for 17 years. He would often sit by the stove in the evenings, telling me of his native land." Everyone in the room was thinking maybe they had a little Irish somewhere in their background as Mr. O'Shea continued. "My grandfather told of the little towns that dotted the coastline and the farms throughout the countryside. The people in these small communities loved family above all else."

Hands were joining.

"The birth of a child was cause for an entire town to celebrate. Even small things, that today might go unnoticed, were celebrated. A warm day with the smell of new hay in the barn would cause glasses to be raised. Yet smaller things still, a yapping dog suddenly gone quiet, could give a man pause to reflect."

Everyone in the room seemed lost in their own memories. "Indeed, the very institutions that prompt reflection arose from the need to celebrate. You see no man wishes to celebrate alone. It was only logical to create a common place to celebrate small triumphs. Men found themselves at day's end raising their glasses in a public gathering place called a pub."

Mr. O'Shea raised the glass of beer he had held the entire evening. He studied the amber liquid for a moment and continued. "Of course, the women, not to be outdone, gathered also. Since in most cases it was men, women wished to discuss, they needed their own place to meet." Everyone laughed.

"Let me clarify this idea of talking about men. I should have said, pray for."

Everyone in the room roared.

"So as the pubs grew in number so did the churches. It might seem that the two institutions would be at odds, but that's not true at all. They have both been good for business." Again his audience chuckled at a master storyteller. He smiled, winked again at Meg, raised his glass once again and proposed a toast.

"To celebrations and small triumphs - may you find one or the other at the end of each day."

Michael looked at Meg and realized he needed to speak. He cleared his throat and tapped his glass. "It's no coincidence that we're all sitting here tonight celebrating those small triumphs Mr. O'Shea just spoke of. Everyone here tonight has at least one connection. I'm not a religious man, but the powers that brought this group together are not easily explained. Each and every one of us will leave with a different memory of what went on here this week. For me, it has been about trusting in friends, believing in myself, and something else we all feel, but can't easily explain." Michael walked over to Jack O'Shea and clasped his hand.

"A long time ago, a man I played golf with and lived with, stood in a sand bunker with a near impossible shot to make. I questioned him about his club selection. Before he squared his shoulders, and took a mighty swing, he looked me dead in the eye and said, "You have to play it, 'AS IT LIES'."

THE END

About the Author

What does a rural Maine boy growing up with seven brothers and seven sisters do to find his own way in the world? He reads and watches. "Teaching and administering school for 32 years provided me with many opportunities to continue reading and watching. I am now writing about what I've read and observed over the years." R. Wesley Clement now resides in Florida with his wife Carey.

www.ingramcontent.com/pod-product-compliance
Lightning Source LLC
Chambersburg PA
CBHW070205310726
48976CB00001B/216